★ ★ ★ ★ ★

Praise for
Murder at the Universe

Craig has kicked off his series with a bang, a big bang of a book... wonderfully clever and well executed. —CRIMESPREE MAGAZINE

Lambert's wry turn as an accidental house detective puts Craig's erudite whodunit solidly on the map. —PUBLISHERS WEEKLY

An entertaining insider's look at the hotel business by a first timer. —LIBRARY JOURNAL

Craig takes readers on a raucous, quick-paced murder mystery through the glamorous halls of the fictional Universe Hotel in New York. —LOS ANGELES CONFIDENTIAL

More than just a crime novel, *Murder at the Universe* is an entertaining satire of the modern hospitality industry. — CALGARY SUN

Hit List. [This] is kind of like an episode of *Survivor* in five-star accommodations. —WISH MAGAZINE

Best in the West this Month! —WESTERN LIVING MAGAZINE

The compellingly readable story weaves together ideas about family, love, alcohol, and the real cost of a job....Reading about it is entertaining, from the meet-and-greet right up to the guest departure experience. —VANCOUVER SUN

Editors' Choice: A mysterious tale of intrigue. —ENROUTE MAGAZINE

★ ★ ★ ★ ★

Praise for
Murder at Hotel Cinema

Even more fun than *Murder at the Universe* . . . Daniel Craig is a five-star read [that] should be on everyone's list.—CRIMESPREE MAGAZINE

This fast-paced puzzler shines with droll wit and hotel-savvy details.—PUBLISHERS WEEKLY

An amusing romp.—BOOKLIST

Hotel Cinema, the sequel to Craig's Murder at the Universe, manages to poke fun at our fascination with fame while at the same time revealing Lambert's coming to terms with his own life and love.—LOS ANGELES CONFIDENTIAL

The dialogue is snappy, the plot twists dizzying. And by drawing effectively on his background in the hospitality industry, Craig has earned a reservation on your cottage-season reading list.
—MOVIE ENTERTAINMENT MAGAZINE

Murder at Hotel Cinema brings together a cast of hilarious Tinseltown caricatures . . . Take it with you on vacation for a rainy day, and you may not even notice when it rains.
—MYSTERY SCENE

Craig uses his detailed and intimate knowledge of the hotel world and the magnetic pull it generates to weave a mystery that makes for fine summer reading.—THE HAMILTON SPECTATOR

★ ★ ★ ★ ★

A FIVE-STAR MYSTERY

DANIEL EDWARD
CRAIG

A FIVE-STAR MYSTERY

MURDER

—— AT ——

GRAVERLY MANOR

MIDNIGHT INK
WOODBURY, MINNESOTA

FIRST EDITION
First Printing, 2009

Cover design by Ellen L. Dahl
Cover photo © . Denkou Images/TIPS Images

"The Lost Lagoon" was originally published in E. Pauline Johnson's book *Legends of Vancouver* (Vancouver & Victoria, B.C.: David Spencer, Limited, 1911)

Midnight Ink, an imprint of Llewellyn Publications

Cover model(s) used for illustrative purposes only
and may not endorse or represent the book's subject

Library of Congress Cataloging-in-Publication Data
Craig, Daniel Edward, 1966-
   Murder at Graverly Manor / Daniel Edward Craig.
      p. cm.—(A five-star mystery; no. 3)
   ISBN 978-0-7387-1473-8
   I. Title.
   PS3603.R353M84 2009
   813'.6—dc22

                                                                2009006343

Midnight Ink
2143 Wooddale Drive, Dept. 978-0-7387-1473-8
Woodbury, MN 55125-2989

www.midnightinkbooks.com

Printed in the United States of America

The Lost Lagoon

It is dusk on the Lost Lagoon,
And we two dreaming the dusk away,
Beneath the drift of a twilight grey–
Beneath the drowse of an ending day
And the curve of a golden moon.

It is dark in the Lost Lagoon,
And gone are the depths of haunting blue,
The grouping gulls, and the old canoe,
The singing firs, and the dusk and–you,
And gone is the golden moon.

O! lure of the Lost Lagoon–
I dream to-night that my paddle blurs
The purple shade where the seaweed stirs–
I hear the call of the singing firs
In the hush of the golden moon.

—E. Pauline Johnson (Tekahionwake)

Skeletons in the Closet

The metal door shrieked in protest as I turned the key in the lock. Lifting the latch, I gently pulled the trap door open. A draft of putrid air escaped. Covering my nose, I turned to Shanna.

"Are you coming or going?"

She was standing behind me in the walk-in closet, hands squeezing her throat. "I have a better idea," she said, her British-Pakistani accent growing more pronounced. "Why don't we close this door, go back to my hotel, order some champagne, and pretend we never heard about this creepy old house?"

"I can't, Shanna. I've got a house full of guests. Besides, I'm not going anywhere until I find out what's down there."

She crouched beside me and set the candelabra on the floor. "Do you really think someone is down there?" she whispered.

"I don't know," I said, peering into the dark abyss.

"Who would it be, the chambermaid?" She placed a hand on my shoulder and pulled me toward her, searching my eyes. "Lord Graverly, then? Surely not the butler?" Her long nails pressed into my skin. "My god—all of them?"

"There's only one way to find out." Reaching for the candelabra, I began to climb inside.

"Wait!" Shanna cried, pulling me back. "Darling, I give you full points for being all manly and brave, but can't we just call the police?"

"If we find something, we'll call the police, okay? I don't want our guests disturbed unless there's a good reason. If you're too afraid—"

"I'm not afraid," she retorted, too quickly to be convincing. "I'm simply being practical. What if someone is down there, waiting to ambush us?"

"Judging by that smell, whoever it is isn't a threat anymore. Can you see if you can find a flashlight? And something to prop this door open."

"With pleasure," she said, hurrying off.

As I waited, I jammed my knee against the door to keep it from closing and turned to survey the contents of the closet, my eyes moving over the rows of large, well-worn ladies' shoes, the shelves crowded with feather hats, handbags, furs, and synthetic corsages, the racks crammed with old-fashioned, theatrical clothing. To my right hung a costume of a different sort: a faded British army uniform draped in yellowed plastic, a bronze cross pinned over the left pocket. Clarissa's words echoed in my ears. *Oh, it's haunted all right—haunted by a pathetic old lady in a red wig who's still pining for her husband, as though he's going to walk through that door after fifty years.*

The door was pressing against my knee, as though possessing a will of its own.

"Shanna?" I called out, beginning to lose my nerve. "Are you coming?"

There was no reply. Outside, the storm was gaining in force. The manor's foundation groaned as the wind whipped the exterior of the house and swirled through the chimney, making it wail like a grieving old woman. For over an hour now, the power had been out.

Shanna reappeared at last, brandishing a large book and a tall red candle.

"*The Consummate Host*?" I said, taking the book from her. "Isn't that a little blasphemous, considering the rules of etiquette we're breaking?"

"I thought it quite fitting, considering its title. I couldn't find a flashlight. The seniors' brigade must have taken all of them."

"Ladies first," I offered.

"After you, I insist."

Taking a last breath of fresh air, I climbed down the steps to a landing. I found myself in a small chamber, tall enough to stand in, well over six feet high at the apex of its arched ceiling. At my feet, a stone staircase descended into darkness.

Shanna joined me on the landing. "It stinks to high heaven in here."

"More like the depths of hell." I started down the staircase, using the cool stone wall to guide me. Something sticky on the steps gripped my shoes, impeding my progress. "Keep to the right," I cautioned Shanna. "There doesn't seem to be a wall on the left." My voice echoed loudly, suggesting a large, empty room below. After a dozen more steps, I stopped and turned.

"Are you coming?"

Shanna lingered at the top of the stairs, looking like a ghostly apparition in her white pantsuit, the flickering candlelight exaggerating her prominent cheekbones and aquiline nose. "Darling, I didn't dress for trudging through catacombs. My pantsuit—it's Alexander McQueen."

"I'll pay for the dry cleaning, Maharani."

With a slight groan, she took a step down. "Ew, sticky." She teetered on her feet and let out a cry. Something clattered down the stairs, striking my heel.

Our candles flickered out.

"What the hell was that?" I shouted.

"Sorry, I kicked something. It was leaning against the wall."

I reached down and felt a sharp metal blade. "So this is where the axe has been hiding."

"Axe?" Shanna said, her voice shrill. "What on earth is an axe doing here?"

"Maybe Lincoln kept spare firewood down here," I said, handing it back to her. "Here, put it on the landing. Careful, it's sharp."

With a growing sense of dread, I continued down the staircase, wiping residue from the blade on my pant legs. When I reached the bottom, I peered around but could see nothing but blackness. The stench was horrific down here. Forgetting the power was out, I set the candelabra down and felt along the wall for a light switch.

"Do you have a match?" I called up to Shanna.

There was no response.

"Shanna, are you there?"

Peering upward, I saw that the staircase was empty.

Telling myself she had gone to find matches, I folded my arms and waited, unwilling to venture any farther on my own. The jugular vein was throbbing in my neck. My mind raced over the bizarre sequence of events that had taken place since I moved into the manor. *I forgive you for what you did to Agnes,* Lady Graverly had written in her letter. What did she think I had done to Agnes? I shivered and rubbed my hands together, trying to rid them of the residue.

At the top of the stairs, a figure appeared.

"Is that you, Shanna?" I called out.

A beam of light struck my face. "Of course it is, silly," she said. The light bounced on the walls and ceiling as she made her way daintily down the stairs. "I remembered where I saw a flashlight," she added.

She stopped and let out a shriek.

"What is it?" I called out.

"Why, you wicked little feline! You scared the life out of me!"

I felt Sir Fester's lithe body begin to perform figure eights around my ankles. The cat was purring loudly, a tactic I now knew was intended to lull victims into a false sense of security. Gently, I nudged him aside with my foot, bracing myself for the stab of claws. I felt his body stiffen. He hissed and emitted a terrifying yowl, then scampered up the stairs, disappearing through the doorway.

"Bad kitty," Shanna called after him. As she joined me at the bottom of the stairs, her perfume engulfed me. It was a welcome break from the fetid odor.

Taking the flashlight, I guided the light along the wall, exploring the room. "It looks vacant," I said hopefully. My heart leapt as something skittered over my feet. Lowering the flashlight, I caught sight of a rat's tail slithering along the floor. The rat reached the corner and turned to regard us, its eyes gleaming red.

"Well, hello there, little mister," Shanna called out.

"You're not afraid of rats?"

"That's a rat? I thought it was a small hyena. When I was a girl, rats used to come up from the sewers during the rains and take refuge in our hut. My brother and I would trap them and keep them as pets."

"And eat them?"

"Please. We weren't that destitute."

I had always found it difficult to reconcile Shanna's stories of an impoverished childhood with her regal manners and lavish tastes, which suggested a privileged upbringing. She insisted she had cultivated them over her years of working in luxury hotels.

The rat disappeared behind a shallow rectangular box set against the wall.

"My god," Shanna said, gripping my arm. "Is that a coffin?"

"No," I said, trying to steady the tremor in my voice. "It looks like an old icebox." I inspected the box with the flashlight. It appeared to be made of oak, with rusted metal trim and an old padlock securing the lid. Next to the box sat a stained wooden table. "The house's original owner was a hunter. That must have been his butcher block."

"I just remembered I forgot to dry the dishes," Shanna said, turning to flee.

"Not so fast," I said, reaching out to pull her back. "Let's check this box out first, then we can get the hell out of here."

We moved a few steps closer.

Shanna's nails dug into my arm. "Is that …?"

I shone the flashlight closer, illuminating what looked like a tuft of human hair poking from the lid. My hand trembled. "Christ, I think it is."

"Let's get out of here," Shanna cried, yanking at my arm.

I resisted, and she dropped my arm, hurrying off.

Reaching out, I tugged at the tuft of hair, expecting it to come loose, but it resisted. As I let it go, I heard something strike the bottom of the box.

"Trevor, I hear footsteps!" Shanna hissed. "Let's go!"

Deciding I had seen enough, I headed back toward the staircase. On the way, I stepped on something and lost my balance, stumbling forward and falling. The flashlight flew out of my hand, striking the floor and flickering out.

"Trevor?" Shanna called out. "Are you okay?"

I was lying facedown. Something was pinned beneath my chest. The stench was so powerful, I almost retched. I reached out and searched the floor with my hands, touching something soft. Clothing? My fingers found a hard, pliant material like rubber. Tracing its curve, I came to two small bumps, like—

"Hurry, Trevor! Someone's coming!"

—lips. I scrambled to my feet and dashed toward the stairs. In the darkness, I grappled for Shanna's hand and pulled her up the steps. Halfway up, a loud thud made us halt.

At the top of the staircase, a dark figure peered into the opening. The door slammed shut, and we heard the clang of the metal latch.

2

The Inn at Lost Lagoon

They say the hotel business gets into your blood.

Most people are attracted to the hotels because they seem like a glamorous place to work, because the pay and perks sound generous, because they consider themselves "people people." They soon discover that hotels are a glamorous place to stay as a guest; the work is more about mundane tasks and plumbing problems during graveyard shifts than hobnobbing with celebrities. They learn that the pay isn't quite so lucrative when all the hours are taken into account. And they discover that being a people person requires more than a winning smile and a knack for remembering names; it demands an unflinching ability to handle all types of people in all kinds of situations. These are the employees who quit within a year or two. The rest of us are lifers—or, in industry terms, hoteliers.

Moving up in the ranks is a numbers game. The employee willing to work more hours than any other employee will eventually become a manager. The manager willing to work more hours than any other manager will eventually become a department head. And the department head willing to work the most hours of all gets to be the general manager. Good communication skills are important too, as are a sharp eye for detail, an aptitude for multitasking, and the ability to maintain an expression of empathy and concern while being publicly flagellated by an irrational guest. But most important is simply being present. A socially inept manager might get by if he works a lot of hours, but a charismatic manager won't have a successful hotel if he's rarely on-property.

Hotels are a twenty-four-hour business. People come to sleep, to work, to play, to relax, to recover, and sometimes to die—and they don't limit these activities to a nine-to-five workweek. When my mother, a head nurse in the pediatrics ward at Surrey Memorial Hospital, thinks I'm starting to sound too self-important, she likes to point out that a hotel manager is not a doctor. But, like a doctor, a hotel manager receives emergency calls in the middle of the night and has no choice but to drop everything and go into work. Rarely is a life at stake, but a flood, a late-night party, or a raging guest can wreak a lot of damage.

Like nomads, hoteliers travel from hotel to hotel, city to city, and, particularly if working for a chain, must be prepared to relocate at a moment's notice, whether to an exotic locale, a crowded, polluted city, or a war-torn region. Our career is dedicated to the comfort and well-being of strangers, and this can come at the expense of our own comfort and well-being. Raising a family, being a good friend, and committing to social occasions can interfere with our work. Colleagues and guests become quasi friends and family. Our need for socializing is satisfied on the job, and when the day is over, we often just want to be alone. Yet home life can seem dull and uninspiring compared to the dynamic environment of a hotel.

My career in hotels started haphazardly, or so it seemed at the time, while I was in high school, when I landed a position as bellman at the Westin Bayshore Hotel in Vancouver, British Columbia. I discovered a natural affinity for the formality of hotels, and of luxury hotels in particular, and for the spirited optimism of hospitality employees. Eager to please, hardworking, and agreeable, I had the qualities required of a hotelier, qualities I later discovered could be liabilities in one's personal life. I moved through the ranks quickly, transferring to the front desk at the Bayshore, a breeding ground for management, and then moving to the Park Harbour Hotel, where I worked my way up to director of rooms. At the Park Harbour, called the Pearl Harbour by staff for being a frequent target for Japanese tour groups, I encountered some trouble with a young business-center employee whose affections I misinterpreted, and I resigned under a cloud of shame. The cheerfulness of hotel employees suddenly rang false to me; disillusioned, I explored other career options. After two years of struggle in university, a disastrous stint in film production, and a bone-chilling winter in residential construction, I finally accepted that resistance was futile. Hotels were in my blood; I was a lifer.

I moved to New York to accept a position as director of rooms at the futuristic Universe Hotel. There I met Nancy Swinton, the beguiling duty manager with the dark, lustrous hair who disarmed irate guests like a trained assassin with her sweet disposition. Two years later, the hotel's owner was killed in a controversial hit-and-run, prompting a riot that destroyed the hotel's lobby, and again I found myself out of work. At my mother's urging, I moved back to Vancouver with Nancy, and we experienced a period of utter bliss. And then Nancy died, suddenly and unexpectedly, and I was devastated. I wallowed for months, but that's a story for another place, another time.

Shanna Virani, a former colleague from the Universe, convinced me to take a position as general manager of the soon-to-open Hotel Cinema in Hollywood. The star-studded opening party started well but ended tragically when the world-famous starlet Chelsea Fricks was murdered. A few days later, the hotel burned to the ground, and I returned to Vancouver to lick my wounds.

I resolved to stay in Vancouver for a short time only. Despite its unparalleled natural beauty and healthy lifestyle, the city was a graveyard for my failures. It was my hometown, but it didn't feel like home. Living in the same city as my mother and sisters had its challenges; life was too complex, the expectations too high. In New York and Los Angeles, my relationships had been blessedly superficial and fleeting, little more demanding than a hotel guest's expectations of a front desk agent. Resigned to feeling a constant sense of displacement, to being a restless traveler, the host who never feels at home himself, I resolved to continue my travels.

And then I came upon Graverly Manor, and everything changed.

It was a bright, unseasonably cold day in late October when Mom's silver Audi lurched to a stop in front of my condo building in Yaletown. The front wheel rolled onto the curb, the bumper halting inches from my knee. At fifty-nine, Mom drove like she conducted her life: reckless and easily distracted, full of passion and enthusiasm, sometimes lost but always aware of her final destination.

As we sped off, she leaned over to peck me on the cheek. "I thought we'd go down to Lost Lagoon for a change. It's so beautiful this time of year."

It was a change in our usual plans and vaguely unsettling. We had always gone for our walks along English Bay, and, unlike Mom, I am not the spontaneous type. As we charged up Smithe Street and passed a Do Not Enter sign, I scrambled to fasten my seatbelt and slid my hands into the deep impressions on the leather armrests made by previous passengers. Blurs of fall colors flashed as we careened through the West End. Mom steered with one palm, sipping from a paper cup of Tim Horton's coffee with the other hand. I only half-listened to her caffeine-fueled chatter; the sound of her voice was comforting enough. My thoughts were absorbed by the growing anxiety I was feeling over my job search. Three months of unemployment had begun to take its toll.

"…spends hours in that tree fort all by himself," she was saying. "He pretends it's a hotel and he's the manager—just like Uncle Trevor. Isn't that adorable? Except he never lets anyone check in. He's a bit of a loner, that one. He reminds me of you as a boy with those pillow forts. Remember?"

"Not really. Who are we talking about again?"

"Quinn!"

"Quinn…"

"Your nephew."

"Right." Having lived away for most of the past six years, I was not yet able to distinguish one nephew or niece from another. There were a lot of them, six, possibly seven, all under the age of ten, a collective mass of chaos and demands. Mom was dismissive toward all children except for her grandchildren, in whose lives she was intricately involved.

"Are we in a hurry, Mom?"

"I want to get there while it's still light out," she said, skidding to a stop halfway through an intersection. "The lagoon gets kind of eerie when night falls."

We reached the foot of Nelson Street and drove around in search of a parking spot. Mom settled on a tiny space on Barclay Street that required her to nudge the cars in front and behind to make room.

"There!" she said. "Shall we?"

After a short walk, we reached the meandering path that led to the lagoon. Set on the southern tip of Stanley Park, Lost Lagoon was part of Coal Harbour, an inlet from the Pacific Ocean, until 1916, when a new causeway opened that cut through the park and over Lions Gate Bridge, creating a separate body of water. Mom chatted as we made our way down to the water. Her prattle sounded random and scattered, but like a seasoned tour guide she always had an eye on her agenda, mentally checking off each item before moving on to the next. Something on today's agenda was making her nervous, I realized, detecting a note of anxiousness in her tone.

"Did Derrick get hold of you?" she asked.

"He left me a message."

"He didn't even know you moved out. I thought you two were best pals."

"I haven't seen him in over a year, Mom."

Derrick was an old high-school friend, now living with a bipolar wife, twin girls from his wife's first marriage, and a chain-smoking mother-in-law who had been on disability for years for no apparent reason. He often invited me to his place for dinner, but I always found an excuse. While I was here, I wanted to keep life uncomplicated so that when the next job came along, I could pack up and leave without feeling like I was abandoning anyone. That's what I told myself, anyway, but frankly, Derrick's family depressed me.

"Have you called him back?" Mom asked.

"No. I've been busy."

"Busy?" she said, laughing. "Doing what, may I ask?"

I bristled but let it roll off. "Settling into my condo. Looking for work. Running the meth lab."

"Trevor, you really need to make time for your friends. I don't know what I would do without Thomas."

"Thomas is your brother."

"And my best friend."

I had moved back into my Yaletown condo a month prior, after living with Mom for two months in the house where I was raised. There Mom and I experienced a little too much alone time together, and when the day finally arrived that my tenants were due to move out, they found me waiting outside the door with a sleeping bag in hand. But I quickly discovered that the condo wasn't the refuge I needed. Nancy and I had purchased it together, and although she had never lived there with me, I felt her presence—a ghost, leaning on the doorframe with arms loosely folded, observing me with a sad, disappointed expression. I couldn't live there, and I didn't want to stay in Vancouver, so I resolved to step up my out-of-town job search. A mammoth hotel in Vegas. A luxury fishing resort up the coast. A nudist retreat for Brazilian supermodels. The options seemed unlimited.

We reached the edge of the lagoon, and Mom stopped, looking left and right, as though torn over which way to go, even though it didn't matter; the path cut a circle around the lagoon and could be traversed in under an hour. To the right, the path ran parallel to the causeway for a stretch, where the red lights of rush-hour traffic inched toward Lions Gate Bridge. To the left, it passed a cluster of weeping willows and entered the forest. Mom opted to go clockwise, and I followed, watching the faux-fur trim of her suede coat sweep leaves along the path. Her high heels were better suited to a runway than a forest path, but she maintained a graceful gait even as the pavement turned to dirt. Her white-blond hair fluttered in the breeze, thin and fashionably cut, its original luster and density still lacking a year after the chemo treatments had ended.

"When I was a little girl, my parents used to take Thomas and me down here," she said, stopping to contemplate the drooping branches of a willow tree. "My mother liked to recite a poem about the lagoon. I wish I could remember it now, it was so beautiful." She turned to the water, where the fountain had been turned off in anticipation of winter weather, her eyes half-closing in remembrance. "My father once told us a story about an Englishman who brought his young lover here for a moonlight canoe ride. When they reached the middle, he tied an anchor to her foot and pushed her overboard. The anchor caught his jaw like a hook to a fish and pulled him in too. The bodies were never found. They say the lagoon is bottomless."

I shivered, and my eyes scanned the water's calm surface. "Your father sounds a bit macabre."

"Not at all. He had a great sense of fun. It's such a shame that you and the girls never knew him." She resumed walking, burying her hands in her pockets.

The path darkened as we entered a shroud of trees. I could hear ducks and geese quacking in the reeds, the rustle of raccoons, squirrels, and other rodents, but could see none of them. A trio of female joggers trotted by, quietly chatting, trailed by a long-haired boy hunched over a mountain bike.

"I think about my father every day," Mom said. "Do you think of Charles often?"

The next item on her agenda—and likely the one making her nervous. It was still jarring to hear her say this name that had been banned from our household for so many years. We referred to him as Charles now, like a character in a TV show. As a teenager, I had replayed memories of my father so many times that they had lost their clarity, like a collection of scratchy old LPs. After his death, Mom had slipped into a sort of walking coma, a semi-catatonic state in which she went through the motions of life but was never fully present. My memories of adolescence are dominated by an image of her swaddled in blankets on the sofa, endlessly clicking the remote control in search of a TV program she never found. My sisters were younger than me, and therefore were less affected by my father's death, but they suffered equally from my mother's despondence. Wendy, a skittish and sniveling child, always seemed to have a cold. Janet was brusque and scrappy, and was sent home on numerous occasions for beating up boys at school. I felt increasingly estranged from all three, and about three seconds after graduation, I moved out.

Then, miraculously, about five years ago, Mom awakened from her walking coma and transformed into one of those maniacally happy women in infomercials who swear life doesn't start until the fifties. I was in New York at the time, and when she came to visit I was so astonished by the changes, I worried she was on medication—and not the over-the-counter kind. She credited the change to a book called *Refurbish Your Life!* written by a cancer survivor who was a former host of a home improvement program. She bought me a copy, and it was only when I forced myself to start reading it that I realized what had prompted her reawakening: a cancer diagnosis. By then, she had had the lump in her breast removed. But the cancer came back, and early last year she underwent a mastectomy.

"Cancer saved my life," she liked to declare, knowing it provoked the questions she loved to answer. "I cashed in a boob for a new lease on life." Determined to make up for lost time, she launched a campaign to become an integral part of the lives of her children and grandchildren. She lost the excess weight and started spending more liberally on clothes, her hair and nails, a new Audi A4. In her professional life, she earned a promotion to head nurse in the pediatrics ward at Surrey Memorial Hospital; in her personal life, she became an avid practitioner of pop psychology. She read self-help books voraciously, credited them for various breakthroughs in her life, and considered it her duty to spread the gospel. I was her favorite subject. Over the years, she had diagnosed afflictions in me that I'd never heard of, prescribing treatment programs that invariably involved psychotherapy sessions conducted by her. After a time, she would either pronounce me cured and herself a genius or would grow quiet on the subject and quickly move on to the next revolutionary new trend. From time to time, I looked back on her former despondence with teary-eyed longing.

"No, not really," I said now in answer to her question about Charles.

"Your father was not the man you think he was, Trevor."

"Haven't we charted this territory?"

"This is new territory."

"Can we cover it another time? I can't find a job, Mom. It's all I can think about. I'm going to leave Vancouver."

She caught her breath. She was silent for a moment, reluctant to abandon the subject of my father without having thoroughly covered it but eager to address this new, unexpected item that required her urgent attention. When she spoke, her words were measured.

"Trevor, this is your home."

"It doesn't feel like home, Mom. It never has, really."

"You've only been back three months! How can you give up so soon? What about the Four Seasons—did they call back?"

"I met with the general manager, Frank Parsons, a few days ago. He's got nothing for me, and he's not going anywhere."

"What about a lower-level position, something to get your foot in the door? It's such a fabulous company. You're perfectly suited for them."

Mom considered the hotel business—catering to the whims of the wealthy and spoiled—frivolous and indulgent compared to her noble profession of healing the sick and comforting the dying. Yet, in one of her many contradictions, she was completely enamored with the Four Seasons.

"Mom, I don't want to work for a chain. They'll transfer me to somewhere like Taipei, I just know it."

"Why not enjoy your time off, then? The right job will come along. In the meantime, you could be spending quality time with family and friends rather than holing up in that condo like Howard Hughes. How are your sisters, anyway?"

"I don't know. I haven't spoken to them since moving day."

"An entire month?" She would have known this; she talked to them daily. "Now that you're settled, why don't you start coming out for Sunday dinners again?"

"We'll see."

We emerged from the trees on the other side of the lagoon. "Wendy says you never call," she said.

"We don't have much in common anymore."

She stopped walking. I felt a stab of guilt, but I was speaking the truth. I loved my sisters, but we had taken separate paths in life. They were married and obsessed with their children; I was unmarried and ambivalent about children. They had jobs; I had a career. They got lost and afraid in the city; I got lost and afraid in the suburbs. Shaped by the hotel business, I took special care with my appearance and conduct, whereas they dressed and acted like they had just stumbled from a three-day country-and-western camping jamboree. Janet carried a chip on her shoulder that grew heavier with each extra pound she put on. Wendy was nicer, but sensitive and single-minded. Both considered my single, work-centric lifestyle hollow and pointless. Mom, equally at home in the city and the suburbs, conducted her life with more levity than the three of us combined. She refused to acknowledge our differences and wanted us to be best friends like Thomas and her.

"Trevor, they're your sisters," she said, turning to me with a pained expression. "You need to try harder." She gave a shake of her head and resumed walking, picking up her pace.

We reached our starting point, and, instead of embarking on another lap, she began to climb toward the street. Her shoes skidded on the damp leaves that were strewn on the path. I hurried after her and took her by the arm.

"I'll come over for dinner on Sunday," I said.

She forced a smile. "That would be nice."

At the top of the hill, she turned toward Haro Street.

"The car's over here," I said, pointing in the opposite direction.

"I thought we could walk around the block."

I nodded and followed, perplexed but knowing better than to question.

A few minutes later, we passed a stately Victorian-style mansion, and Mom stopped to admire it. "I remember this house from when I was a little girl. It must be a hundred years old now."

I hadn't noticed the house before, but now I was captivated by it. My eyes moved over its fairytale-like façade, the ornate gables and gingerbread trim, the four-story tower, its pitched roof slightly bent at the top like a witch's hat. An enormous oak tree rose to the left of the house, reaching as high as the tower, its gnarled branches clutching the rose-colored exterior.

"I love how it stands defiant among all these apartment buildings and condos," I said. "It must be one of the last remaining houses in the West End."

"It's been an inn for as long as I can remember," Mom said, reaching for my arm. Just inside the front gate, a weathered sign suspended from a wrought-iron post quivered in the breeze. The words "Graverly Manor," painted in a once-ostentatious script, were now faded and peeling. "I visited it once, before you were born, and met its eccentric proprietor. They call her the Grande Dame of Graverly Manor. She's still around to this day."

"Look, it's for sale," I said, pointing to a poster spiked into the lawn next to the sign. A middle-aged, coiffed realtor flashed a predatory smile above the caption, "Your search is over! Call Lynne Crocker at Remax today and move into your dream home tomorrow!" My eyes moved back to the sign. Graverly Manor. Why did the name sound so familiar?

A conversation with Shanna Virani came back to me. It was early August, and Hotel Cinema's brassy director of sales and marketing was camped out in my office, her favorite haunt. It was a few days after the hotel's opening, which had been disastrous. Fearing our days were numbered, she was searching for jobs online. "Trevor, darling," she had said, "there's a quaint-looking inn for sale in Vancouver. Haven't you always wanted to open a bed-and-breakfast?"

It was a dream I shared with many in the hotel business. I loved the idea of leaving behind the frenetic, impersonal environment of hotels in favor of an intimate guesthouse, where I would deal with only a handful of guests and could personally control every aspect of their stay.

"Yes, but I always envisioned a B&B as the final stop in my career," I said to Shanna. "With a hardworking, buxom wife to share the responsibilities."

"Personally, I can't imagine anything more unappealing," Shanna said. "Making beds, serving breakfast, caring about the petty concerns of guests—I couldn't possibly do that again."

"Have you ever done those things?"

"I'll have you know my first hotel job was chambermaid in a squalid half-star roach-house in Karachi. I also worked the front desk and as concierge at other hotels. I think you should call this realtor."

"I'm not moving back to Vancouver."

"What have you got against Vancouver? It's positively charming, with all those healthy sorts running around in shorts in the dead of winter." Her manicured nails tapped at the keyboard. "This price can't be right."

"Real estate in that city is pricey."

"I mean it's a steal."

"Then it must be a dive."

"It looks lovely in this picture. The name is ghastly, though. Graverly Manor—it sounds like a cemetery. You'll have to change it to the Sunshine Inn or something. I'm printing this."

Now, as I stood next to my mother and regarded the manor's enchanting exterior, the new name came to me: the Inn at Lost Lagoon.

"I can't believe it's still on the market," I said.

Mom turned to me in surprise. "You know about this house?"

"Shanna told me about it a few months ago. I've always wanted to open a bed-and-breakfast. Maybe it's time."

"What? You're joking, aren't you?"

"Not in the least."

She gave a shrill laugh. "You, running a fussy old inn? I can't picture it. Besides, you could never afford it."

"I've saved a few bucks over the years. I could put a sizable deposit down. A bank might be willing to loan me the rest."

"Trevor, this is crazy. Let's go. I'm freezing." When I didn't move, she abandoned me and hurried up the street.

My mind raced with possibilities.

"Trevor, come on!" Mom shouted from the corner. "It's starting to rain."

Tearing my eyes away, I walked up the street to join her. She was right, I could never afford a house like that. Nevertheless, I pulled out my cell phone and punched in the realtor's number, storing it just in case I reconsidered.

On the drive back, an uncomfortable silence ensued. I had expected Mom to return to the agenda item she hadn't fully covered, but she kept quiet, keeping her eyes fixed on the road ahead as she lurched and stalled her way back to my place. I was grateful for the reprieve but knew it was only temporary.

In front of my building, as I climbed out of the car, she leaned over the passenger's seat. "Don't forget about dinner Sunday. I'm going to tell the girls to sit this one out. Just the two of us. Won't that be nice?"

"Sounds great, Mom."

I watched the Audi screech off. Whatever agenda item she hadn't covered this afternoon would be added to Sunday night's itinerary, a time when she would have a solitary, captive audience.

Something told me it was going to hurt.

3

The Grande Dame of Graverly Manor

The weather shifted from unseasonably cold to unseasonably warm. On an early November evening a few days later, I was standing under a street lamp outside Graverly Manor waiting for realtor Lynne Crocker. Haro Street was busy with residents returning from work, walking dogs, hurrying out to night classes or the gym, whizzing past on bicycles and motorized wheelchairs. Bordered by sprawling Stanley Park and the beaches of English Bay, and bisected by the resort-town vibe of Denman Street, the West End is one the most desirable and densely populated neighborhoods in Vancouver. In the eighties, it was the neighborhood of choice for the young and urbane, but since then the sparkling glass towers of Yaletown and Gastown had lured away many of them. Now the aging apartment buildings are occupied predominantly by foreign students, middle-aged gay men, and senior citizens.

Since first setting eyes on the manor, I had returned three times to gaze at its façade like a love-struck teenager. Lurking in the shadows of the evergreen tree in the front yard, I began to envision a dramatically different future. Did I really want to resume the restless life of a perennially displaced hotelier? What if I were to purchase the manor, move in, and embark on a civilized new life as an innkeeper? Graverly

Manor could be reborn as the Inn at Lost Lagoon, a thriving guest-house popular with world travelers, wealthy eccentrics, artists, musicians, and Playboy centerfolds. Guests would be drawn by the house's history and the vibrant neighborhood, and I could entertain them with anecdotes from my frenetic former life in hotels. Admired and respected by guests and neighbors alike, I would tend to the gardens, restore antique furniture, pay visits to the local senior center, and jog in the park.

My plans hinged on the minor issue of affordability. I had called Lynne Crocker to inquire about the asking price, and when she disclosed the number I was rendered speechless. Shanna Virani's definition of "a steal" differed substantially from mine.

"Financing going to be a problem?" Lynne asked, sensing my shock. Her words were garbled by whatever she was eating—an apple, I guessed.

"Money will not be a problem," I said firmly.

"What exactly are your intentions? You planning to flip it? Subdivide? Resell to a developer?"

"I'm planning to operate it as a bed-and-breakfast."

She launched into an aggressive sales pitch. "It's an absolute bargain when you consider the prime location, the size—*enormous* by downtown standards—and the superb condition. The front and back yards are ideal for wedding receptions, corporate events, bar mitzvahs—you name it. The potential is simply unlimited. It's been on the market a few months now, not for lack of interest but because the seller keeps rejecting interested parties. But she's highly motivated to sell now. I really don't expect it to be on the market much longer."

"I'd like to see it," I said, feeling a rush of adrenaline.

Lynne agreed to forward the request to her client. "Be forewarned," she said, "the seller insists on meeting all prescreened buyers, and let's just say she's a little ... discriminating."

In the hotel business, I had dealt with all types, from the wealthy and famous to the down and out, and I wasn't daunted by an old lady who fashioned herself as a grande dame. All the same, when Lynne called back to confirm, I decided to dress up for the occasion. Then I began to scheme to acquire the money—a brilliant business plan that would provoke a bidding war among banks; a silent partner; a wealthy benefactress; a bank heist. If the house was rundown inside, the issue would resolve itself; if not, then I would figure out financing later.

Now, as I waited outside the manor, a pointy-faced woman in jean shorts with a high elastic waistband approached me. "Waitin' for Lynne?"

I nodded. Lynne hadn't said anything about other suitors. "You are too?"

"Yep. We got a B&B on Pender Island, lookin' to expand, maybe have a small chain someday. I'm Pam Hurle, and this is my husband, Jack." She gestured to a man behind her, his belly spilling out of a purple golf shirt.

I shook their hands. "Beautiful house, isn't it?"

"Seen better." Eyeing my pinstriped suit and shiny black shoes, Mrs. Hurle flashed a disingenuous smile, revealing more gums than teeth, and then moved away, dismissing me as no threat to a pair of seasoned innkeepers.

A slight woman wearing rectangular glasses with thick black frames joined us, trailed by a heavyset woman in a University of British Columbia sweatshirt. They stopped to observe the manor, murmuring to one another and sneaking furtive glances at the Hurles and me. A young man trotted toward us with a rottweiler on a leash, and the dog suddenly turned on the two women, snarling and gnashing its teeth. The owner struggled to pull the dog back. The heavyset woman cowered back, terrified. Her companion stepped forward and shook her fist at the rottweiler. "Fuck. *Off*!" she commanded. The dog ceased barking, let out a whimper, and scampered off, dragging its master along with him. I grinned, impressed, but my smile faded as it occurred to me I might be vying for the manor with this fearless woman.

Lynne was late. A third couple joined us, a fiftyish woman with blond hair braided down her back and a tall, broad-shouldered young man with a crew cut. I nodded to them amicably, concealing my growing agitation. What I had assumed was a private viewing had become a group competition. No one spoke as we waited, as though by chance we all happened to be loitering in front of the same house.

At seven twenty, a screech of tires drew our attention to a yellow Mercedes convertible as it pulled in front of a No Parking sign across the street. The door opened, unleashing Whitney Houston belting out, "It's not right, but it's okay," and out climbed an older, less-kempt version of the coiffed female on the realtor sign. She was wearing leopard-print shoes and a short red skirt.

"Hi, hi, everyone!" she called out, fluttering her fingers. She turned and bent down to retrieve a file from the seat, mooning us, then slammed the car door and clipped toward us. "Come along now," she sang out. "Her Highness doesn't take kindly to tardiness."

As we made our way up the paved path, a tall, handsome woman in a black cocktail dress and pearls hurried to join us. I turned and flashed a friendly smile, but her eyes were firmly fixed on the manor.

As we gathered on the verandah, we avoided eye contact, as though something shameful and nefarious was about to take place. Lynne pressed the doorbell and then lifted the brass knocker, letting it fall three times. Stepping aside, she withdrew a cigarette from her purse, lit it, and smoked furiously.

"It takes forever for him to answer," she muttered.

I wandered off to survey the barren verandah, envisioning hot summer nights sipping iced tea with guests and neighbors on country-club-like furniture. A mangy Siamese cat sat perched on the railing, paws tucked in, purring loudly. I reached out to pet him, and he lifted his head, blinking in gratitude, revealing one blue eye and one yellow eye. Behind me, the front door opened, and as I turned I felt a stab of claws. The cat leapt off the railing, disappearing into the underbrush. Blood seeped from four parallel trenches on the back of my hand. Indignant, I tucked my hands behind my back and rejoined the others.

The rottweiler tamer was smirking.

An elderly, distinguished-looking black man in a classic tuxedo and tails was standing at the door, looking perplexed to see us, and for a moment I feared he was going to slam the door in our faces. I was reminded of a childhood game, when I used to pretend I was a rich British duke, and Janet and Wendy played peasants who had come to my castle to beg. I would invite them in for tea and crumpets—orange Kool-Aid served in Dixie cups and Dare cookies on Royal Chinet plates—and then call for the guards to seize them. They would beg for mercy, Wendy claiming to be a princess from a faraway land, Janet professing to have magical powers to grant me eternal happiness. Sometimes I took pity on them and let them go, but usually I ordered them beheaded or drowned in the moat. It was a game I never tired of playing, although Wendy and Janet grew weary of playing victims, and sometimes they rebelled. When Janet got so big that she could almost overpower me, we stopped playing.

"Hiya, Lincoln!" Lynne said, flicking her cigarette over the railing. "We're here for the showing."

"Why, yes, of course," Lincoln replied in a dignified British accent, his voice thin and raspy. "Her ladyship is expecting you. Please do come in." He bowed, revealing short-cropped grey hair like steel wool, and gestured for us to enter.

As we filed in I nodded to him, but he looked right through me. His eyes were pink and cloudy with age, and I wondered if he was going blind.

"A real live butler," Pam Hurle whispered to her husband. "Wouldn't that be nice."

There were murmurs of excitement as we assembled in the cavernous foyer. The mahogany walls were lined with gild-framed portraits of nineteenth-century noblemen, their proud expressions obscured in the dim lighting of the room. A small tulip lamp on the antique reception desk provided the only light; the massive crystal chandelier above us was unlit. Next to the lamp sat an old computer monitor, a brass bell, and an old-fashioned black-lacquered telephone. In the background, somber baroque music was playing softly.

Lincoln excused himself and made his way laboriously up a sweeping staircase opposite the front door, leaning heavily on the banister.

While we waited, Lynne Crocker made successive calls on her cell phone, her jaw cracking with gum. "What? If that little cow backs out, I'll kill her!" she cried between curses and huffs of indignation. "I've worked my butt off to unload that little hovel … Fine, just forget it, okay? … I'll be over as soon as I can. I'm at …"—she turned her back to us and lowered her voice—"you-know-where … Yes, *again* … God, you said it, totally … Anyway, I gotta go. She's about to make her appearance. Ciao!"

Lincoln appeared on the stairs again, descending one agonizingly slow step at a time. All eyes followed him as he crossed the foyer and disappeared into a parlor to the right of the main entrance. Above us, the chandelier flared to life, flooding the room with light, and with a scratch of a record needle the music changed to an exalted choral piece. Lincoln reappeared and climbed to the first landing of the staircase, turning to address us.

"Ladies and gentlemen," he rasped, "it is my distinct pleasure to introduce Lady Andrew Graverly, the Marchioness of Middlesex."

Lynne began clapping enthusiastically, encouraging the rest of us to follow suit. Lincoln hobbled down the stairs and stood at attention next to the parlor door.

At the top of the stairs, a small, ancient woman in a pale-green ball gown and elaborate jewel necklace appeared, stroking ringlets of red hair that cascaded over her shoulders. She looked like she had stepped out of one of the paintings around us. She floated down the stairs and stopped on the landing, clasping her hands together in a rapturous expression.

"Welcome, welcome! How simply lovely to see you all!" she sang out in a throaty, commanding voice. Her accent was British and regal, and her face was heavily powdered, with smears of rouge and crimson lipstick. "Thank you ever so much for coming to my humble little home." She flashed a sly smile as though to suggest that such humility was preposterous. Her eyes darted around the room, scrutinizing each guest, and came to a rest on me. I looked at her squarely, mesmerized by her green eyes, and a strange sensation of warmth and well-being flooded through me. Unnerved, I looked away.

We quickly lined up to pay our respects. Pam Hurle stepped forward first. "Nice to meet you, Your Highness," she said, giving an awkward curtsy.

"My official title is Lady Andrew Graverly, after my husband, Lord Andrew Graverly, but you may call me Lady Elinor Graverly, or simply Lady Graverly, as people are wont to do."

"This is my husband, Jack," Pam said, nudging him forward. "We run the Smoky Bear Inn on Pender Island. Been in the biz for twenty-five years."

"How wonderful!" exclaimed Lady Graverly, glancing down at Mrs. Hurle's elastic waistband.

The rottweiler tamer stepped forward next. "I'm Denise, and this is my life partner, Joanne," she said, reaching up to give Lady Graverly a firm handshake. "We've been renting out rooms at our duplex on Commercial Drive for years, and now we want to open a guesthouse for womyn only—as in W-O-M-Y-N."

"What a charming idea," Lady Graverly said coolly. "Women have always adored Graverly Manor."

Next, the braided woman introduced herself as Jeanette Bradford Baird, an antiques dealer from Toronto; her companion was named Brian.

She was followed by the handsome woman in pearls, who looked to be in her early sixties and extremely well-preserved. "How do you do, I'm Mrs. Gertrude Fishburne from Boston, Massachusetts," she said in a New England accent that suggested a lifetime of wealth and privilege. "I've heard so much about Graverly Manor and its enigmatic proprietress, I just had to visit while I was in town."

Lady Graverly's gaze rested on the woman for a moment, her expression hardening slightly. With a sniff, she looked away and turned her attention to me. "And who might this dashing young fellow be?"

I took both her hands in mine. "Lady Graverly, it's such a pleasure to meet you. I'm Trevor Lambert." I could practically hear the others gagging as I kissed her hand, but I was certain that chivalry was the way to this woman's heart.

"Lambert, did you say?" she squawked, peering more closely. "And what brings you to Graverly Manor?"

I felt all eyes on me. "I've managed luxury hotels for years. It's my dream to open a bed-and-breakfast in a beautiful old house like this."

She snatched her hand away. "Young man, Graverly Manor is not a 'bed-and-breakfast,' nor is it a guesthouse, an inn, or a pension. I will not have my home debased by such vulgar monikers. Graverly Manor is a manor in the tradition of Britain's finest estates, providing the exquisite accommodations and impeccable service one might expect of a five-star hotel but with far greater intimacy and discretion."

"I apologize," I said, feeling my face burn. "I didn't mean to offend."

"Of course you didn't." She patted my face and dismissed me with a wave of her hand. "Very well, then! I shall provide a brief introduction, after which I shall retire to my private quarters and allow Miss Crocker to conduct a brief tour."

She waited until she had our undivided attention and then began, making theatrical gesticulations as she spoke, her mannerisms both mannish and dainty at the same time. "Graverly Manor has a most illustrious history, having been erected almost a century ago, in 1904. I see that some of you are trying to divine which is older, the manor or me, and I assure you I was born almost two decades after the manor was built." She gave a mischievous smile, eliciting titters from the group. "The first occupant, David Orwell Denby, had made a fortune in brick-making. A widower and avid hunter, he lived here with his three daughters, Emily, Edna, and Edith, until his premature death from tuberculosis in 1906. After his death, his daughters enjoyed a spirited life, hosting numerous social affairs and welcoming dignitaries, artisans, and performers from around the world, including such distinguished guests as the famed poet Pauline Johnson. In 1955, the eldest and only surviving daughter, Edith, passed on, and the house was put up for sale. It remained empty for two years, until my husband, Lord Andrew Graverly, the second son of the seventh Marquess of Middlesex, purchased it. Having grown disillusioned with the excesses of his aristocratic family in Great Britain, Lord Graverly had renounced all ties to his family and moved to Canada to begin anew. I was to accompany him, but shortly before we were to set sail, my mother fell ill, and I was obliged to remain in London to nurse her. While in London I learned I was with child, and my son was born a few days after my mother's death. I set sail for Canada shortly thereafter, and I have lived in this house ever since, almost fifty years."

"Is your husband still alive?" inquired Mrs. Fishburne.

"Sadly, no. Upon reaching Canada, I discovered that Lord Graverly had passed on."

There was a collective sigh of sympathy.

"What happened?" the rottweiler tamer blurted out.

Lady Graverly's eyelids fluttered. We watched her expectantly, embarrassed by the blunt question but curious nonetheless. At last she said, "They say he drowned." She gave a wistful smile, and then her expression brightened. "What was a girl to do? I found myself alone in this large house with a newborn infant, and I knew not a soul in this city. But I was a resourceful young woman, and—"

"Did you ever remarry?" someone interrupted.

Looking annoyed, Lady Graverly searched the crowd and locked eyes with Gertrude Fishburne. "Remarry? Certainly not. My heart will always belong to Lord Andrew."

"How romantic," the antiques dealer uttered under her breath, goosing her young companion's behind.

Lady Graverly continued. "Had not dear Lincoln come from England to assist me, I might have died of loneliness. Shortly after he arrived, I began renting out rooms, mostly to doctors and other professionals visiting from England. I had a new wing added to the house for my residence, with a separate entrance at the back so that I could maintain a private life. Soon I grew bored with the long-term residents and began to rent out rooms nightly; this was far more lucrative and ensured a steady stream of entertaining personalities. Thus I established the flourishing business you see today." She swept her arms out and broke into a grand smile. "Have you any questions?"

I raised my hand. "May I ask what kind of occupancy rate you're running?"

"The manor is always fully occupied, naturally," Lady Graverly replied, then added, "at present, all of my guests are out for dinner."

The antiques dealer raised her hand. "I read somewhere that this place is supposed to be haunted. Is that true? Any ghosts we should be keeping an eye out for on the tour?"

There were nervous giggles.

A bemused smile crept over Lady Graverly's face. "Ghosts? Why, none that I've seen. Though Lincoln does have a habit of vanishing for long periods of time and miraculously materializing the moment the housework is completed." She flashed a look of comic disapproval at Lincoln, eliciting more laughter.

Lincoln remained perfectly rigid.

"And your son? What happened to him?"

Lady Graverly let out a gasp and swooned slightly, reaching out to clutch the banister. I hurried forward to steady her, but she brushed me off. "Who said that?" she said sharply, her eyes searching the crowd.

"I did." Gertrude Fishburne raised her hand.

The group froze, our eyes darting from Mrs. Fishburne to Lady Graverly and back again.

"My darling Alexander," Lady Graverly said ruefully, her eyes growing distant. "There was a terrible mishap at birth. The doctors said the poor boy would live for no more than a few months. He…" Her words trailed off, and an uncomfortable silence ensued.

Mrs. Fishburne arched her eyebrows.

Lady Graverly jerked back to life and clapped her hands together. "Enough! If there are no further questions, I shall bid you adieu." She descended the stairs from the landing, pulled a set of keys from her pocket, and unlocked an arched, Gothic-style door to the left of the main entrance, disappearing behind it with the click of a lock.

I stared at the door, admiring the crisscross of wrought-iron bars over its faux window, and hoped she would reappear.

"Gather 'round, everyone!" Lynne shouted.

My spirits sank as I turned my attention to the realtor, who now seemed unbearably crass and unrefined in comparison to the lady of the manor. Lynne distributed information sheets and stepped onto the landing. "The manor comes fully furnished with all the fine artwork and priceless antiques you see today. It features eight rentable guestrooms—four on the second floor and four on the third—and an additional two rooms on the fourth floor, currently occupied by the resident chambermaid and the butler. On the main level are the parlor, dining room, kitchen, pantry, and a separate wing that Elinor uses as her private apartment. Please keep close during the tour, don't dawdle, and don't touch anything. Elinor wants us out before her guests return. Come along!"

We followed her into a parlor cluttered with antique furniture, trinkets, and oil paintings of pastoral landscapes. Farther on, in a dining room, an oval rosewood table was set with crystal goblets and gleaming silverware on a lace tablecloth, in marked contrast to the kitchen, accessed through a swinging door, and its meager and dated equipment: two old refrigerators, no microwave or dishwasher, and a stove that appeared to be as old as the house itself. My eyes were drawn to the window, where the silhouette of a majestic oak tree similar to the tree out front could be seen through a small, lattice-framed window.

Lynne hustled us down a hallway back to the foyer and up the stairs to the second floor. Along the way, I noted surface scratches, tears in carpeting, and peeling wallpaper, but the house's structure seemed solid, and details like arched ceilings, wainscoting, and crown molding gave it a comfortable opulence. Having worked predominantly in contemporary hotels and having been raised in a home where furniture looked antique but was just old, I had no appreciation or eye for antiques; to me, the house looked fussy and old-fashioned. It would require a dramatic uncluttering and a significant investment to bring it into the twenty-first century, yet it had unmistakable charm and character—much like its proprietress.

On the second floor, Lynne pointed out the brass plaques affixed to each door. "Elinor named the guestrooms after her favorite royals," she explained. "On this floor, you'll find the Elizabeth I suite, the Mary I room, the Henry VIII suite, and the Edward I room." All the doors were closed, and she didn't offer to open them. We climbed the narrow staircase to the third floor, where the plaques were inscribed with the names Victoria, Jane Grey, Elizabeth II, and Edward VI. Lynne opened the doors to three of these rooms to allow us a quick peek inside. In the first room I saw a canopy bed draped in red silk, in the second a claw-foot bathtub, and in the third a gold-trimmed vanity.

"Come along, people!" Lynne called out, herding us like kindergarten children. "No loitering!"

"Can't we see the fourth floor?" the antiques dealer asked.

"Sorry, out of time!" Lynne replied. "You'll have to wait for the next viewing—if Elinor allows any of you back."

In the foyer, Lincoln was waiting with the door open.

"Can we have a quick look at her private quarters?" I asked Lynne, gesturing to the Gothic door.

"Uh-uh. She never lets anyone in there."

"Is there a basement?" the antiques dealer asked, closing her eyes and breathing in, as though she had picked up a scent she wished to follow. "A cellar? Anything beneath us?"

Lynne frowned at her. "Nope. Not that I've seen, anyway."

As we spilled onto the verandah, dazed by the whirlwind tour, the antiques dealer lingered in the foyer, her head turning this way and that. When she stepped out, her eyes were alert, her nose twitching.

Lincoln bid us good night and started to close the door, but Mrs. Fishburne placed her foot in the opening. "Lincoln," I overheard her say in a low voice, "you must have known Lord Andrew Graverly. Tell me, did he—?"

"I'm terribly sorry," he interrupted, "but you'll have to address all questions to her ladyship." He pushed on the door until Gertrude Fishburne gave a yelp and yanked her foot out.

"People, please!" Lynne called from the path, a cigarette hanging from her lips. "Let's not overstay our welcome!"

We made our way down the steps and lingered on the path, stopping to admire the house.

"I'm going to call her first thing to put in an offer," Pam Hurle said to her husband.

"We should too," Denise whispered to her girlfriend. "It'll need some work, but can you imagine how gorgeous it will be? The girls will be clamoring to stay."

I felt my back go up, a primordial impulse, as though a clan of spear-wielding tribesmen had surrounded my cave. My competition was worthy: a pair of seasoned innkeepers, a rich antiques dealer, two aggressive businesswomen, and a member of New England's elite. None of them seemed to be lacking in money; I could hardly compete in a bidding war. And yet, as I wished them a pleasant evening and took one last look at the manor's façade, it struck me that Graverly Manor already felt like home.

I simply had to find a way to buy it.

4

Queen of the Universe

The following day, I called Lynne Crocker to request a second viewing. "A private viewing this time," I said.

"You've got financing in place, then?" she asked, sounding skeptical.

"Pretty much."

"What's that supposed to mean?"

"I—I have an appointment with the bank ... to finalize everything ... tomorrow." That would be my next call.

"Tell you what," she said. "Call me back *after* your loan is approved."

"Why? If I decide to move forward, I can always make an offer subject to financing, can't I?"

She sighed. "I'm going to be straight with you, Trevor. It's how I roll. The seller is an extremely busy and important woman—a relative of the Queen of England, in fact. She's simply not interested in having her time wasted. The manor attracts all sorts of gawkers and, you know, weirdos, and she's super guarded about her privacy. It's up to me to screen out the undesirables. Like that antiques dealer—I knew she was up to no good."

"What do you mean, weirdos?"

She hesitated. "Let's just say Graverly Manor has a bit of a reputation."

My heart sank. I should have known it was too good to be true. "What kind of reputation, Lynne?"

"Over the years, there have been rumors about what happened to her husband."

"What kind of rumors?"

"Oh, you know. Silly things like she hacked him to pieces with an axe and buried him in the cellar."

I coughed. "Didn't she say he drowned?"

"No one really knows what happened. He just vanished one day."

I felt a crick in my neck. "So that antiques dealer wasn't kidding when she said the manor was haunted?"

"That woman is no antiques dealer. I got an inkling last night and looked her up. She's a local clairvoyant. She was probably snooping around for ghosts. I'm suspicious about that uppity woman from Boston too, although she looks like she carries enough money around in her purse to pay for the manor in cash. Elinor was enraged by all those personal questions, I could tell. She takes her privacy extremely seriously."

"A haunted inn," I said wryly. "That should be good for business."

"You could position it that way—host murder mystery nights and stuff."

"That's not quite the kind of inn I had in mind, Lynne. Are there any grounds to the rumors? Have you ever seen anything strange in the house?"

Silence, accompanied by chewing.

"Lynne?"

"Um … no, not really. I've heard the occasional strange noise, but it's an old house. She's a bit of an oddball, no question about that, but

I can't imagine her, you know, *murdering* anyone. She doesn't socialize with neighbors at all, which adds to her mysterious persona. If she wasn't such an impossible bitch, I might even feel sorry for her. She acts like her husband went out for milk and is expected back any minute. I tell you, Trevor, with its prime location and well-below-market price, I'd buy it myself if my funds weren't tied up in two leaky condos in Kitsilano."

"Well, I don't believe in ghosts. I'd like to see the house again."

"Let me see if she'll agree to a private viewing. In the meantime, get to work on that financing. That couple who own that B&B on Pender Island already called me twice this morning. They're interested in putting in an offer. And I expect to hear from those lesbians too. I don't foresee it being on the market for more than a few more days."

"Surely no one would purchase the house without a proper inspection and appraisal? I've had more thorough tours of hotel rooms I rented for one night."

"The market's red-hot right now, Trevor. You snooze, you lose. Besides, there's no point in going through all this trouble if you can't afford the place, is there?"

How the hell did she know I couldn't afford it? "I assure you, Lynne, money will not be a problem. I simply need time to get my finances in order."

More chewing. It was like listening to the sound of her brain working. "You got a place you need to sell?" she asked.

I hadn't even thought that far. "I guess I'll need to sell my condo."

Her interest perked up. "Maybe I can help. Where do you live? What did you pay? How many square feet? Major features and benefits?"

I relayed the details to her. I wasn't keen on giving her the listing, but if it gave me more of a competitive edge, I was game. She was familiar with the building and gave me a quick estimate of the listing price.

"That much?" I said, shocked.

"I told you, the market's sizzling, especially Yaletown. I might even have a buyer for you. Let me make a few calls. I'll swing by this afternoon to have a look, and I'll bring some papers for you to sign."

"Not so fast, Lynne. I'm only interested in selling if I purchase the manor."

"Absolutely. I understand completely."

After I hung up, I wandered through my condo, admiring its contemporary design, the floor-to-ceiling windows that flooded the rooms with light. Was I prepared to abandon this place for the dark, aging environs of Graverly Manor? Suddenly Nancy was with me, perched on the kitchen countertop, arms folded, a bemused, slightly frustrated glint in her eye.

For god's sake, Trevor, I heard her say. *Just buy it.*

Graverly Manor wasn't the only place that was haunted. I picked up the phone and made an appointment with my bank.

"It's fate," I said to Shanna over the phone the next night.

"Are you sure, darling?"

"I can't explain it. It just feels right. You know how displaced I've always felt, no matter where I've been? In that house I felt right at home."

"Hmm ... Have you had it inspected?"

"Not yet, but don't worry, I'll do my due diligence. I met with the bank today, and the account manager was optimistic, but they want to see a five-year business plan. I'm hoping you can help me out."

"I'd be happy to. As long as it's what you really want."

I was sprawled on my bed, fully dressed, in full view of residents in the condo towers around me. The room felt like a fishbowl at night, but having the blinds open gave me a sense of connection to the city, a feeling of community with no obligation to interact. Upon returning from the bank, I had mulled over the pros and cons of the manor. I knew I would never be happy in this condo, not without Nancy. But it was paid off, and the prospect of taking on a staggering amount of debt was terrifying. As a hotel manager, I had made decisions involving tens of thousands of dollars, affecting hundreds of employees. Yet I agonized over minor decisions in my personal life: which laundry detergent to buy, where to eat dinner, whether to turn left or right at an intersection. Now, as the manor came closer within reach, my conservative nature reared its head, roaring with indignation. I told myself I should have confidence in my intuition and experience; in my career, I had been responsible for hundreds of hotel rooms, for restaurants, lounges, spas, and function space. I had encountered every conceivable scenario: fire, flood, recession, riot, strike, hostile takeover—even murder. How hard could it be make an eight-room inn successful? It was time to be spontaneous and entrepreneurial.

The doubt in Shanna's voice was worrying. She had worked in luxury hotels on five continents—Ritz Carlton Hotels, Mandarin Oriental, Four Seasons, and the St. Regis, among others—and her business instincts were almost always spot-on.

"What kind of average rate and occupancy is she getting?" Shanna asked.

"It sounds like a busy place, but I still need to get the stats from the realtor."

"If the asking price is so low, why hasn't the house sold?"

"The realtor says Elinor Graverly is highly particular."

"Why does she care who buys the place? I loathed the consortium that bought the Universe, but they came in with the highest bid, so they won."

I could hear Shanna sipping. I envisioned her drinking red wine, her beverage of choice—Italian, full-bodied, expensive—her legs curled up on the divan on her balcony, seagulls crying over the distant drone of the ocean. We had first met in New York, during the preopening days of the Universe, where she was director of sales and marketing and I was director of rooms. We hadn't been friends back then. She had considered me naïve, and I had found her insufferable. Although a brilliant marketer and a multitalented sales director, she had a reputation for being difficult. A clandestine relationship with the hotel's owner, Willard Godfrey, had only heightened her self-importance. She earned a reputation for being a bit of a Leona Helmsley, and staff started calling her Queen of the Fucking Universe behind her back. Then Mr. Godfrey was killed in a hit-and-run. She was devastated but refused to show it. He left her the Universe, but it was bleeding money, and she sold it soon after, relocating to Los Angeles to be closer to her estranged son and daughter. A few months later, I moved to Los Angeles too, and the ordeal of opening Hotel Cinema, perhaps the most difficult birth of a hotel in history, had forged a strong bond between us.

"I hope you're prepared to work your butt off," Shanna said. "And you won't have a cast of thousands to help you. Are there any staff?"

"A butler and a chambermaid, but I assume she'll let them go when the manor is sold. I like the idea of doing everything myself. If I can't handle things on my own, I'll hire someone locally and convert the staff quarters into rentable rooms. If Lady Graverly can run that place at her age, it should be a breeze for me."

Through the doorway I spotted my cat, a corpulent, rust-colored tabby I had picked up from a local animal shelter. Janet's three-year-old daughter had named him Nuggle, and, despite my resolve to find a more grown-up name, it had stuck. He was stalking the hallway in search of prey. Coming upon a house spider, he scampered off in fright.

"Lady Graverly," Shanna said in a mocking British accent. "Does she really insist people address her that way?"

"All this attitude from the Queen of the Fucking Universe?"

"I was horrified when I found out about that name. I've mellowed since then, haven't I, darling?"

"Yes, Shanna, you have."

"How old is the manor, anyway?"

"About a hundred years old."

"My god, we're practically the same age. I hope it's been better maintained. And its soul? What's its soul like?"

"What do you mean by soul?"

"Houses are like people, Trevor. They have an old soul or a young soul, a good soul or a bad soul."

I pondered the question. "I'd say it has an old soul, but a good one." Nuggle hopped onto the bed, purring and kneading the honeycomb throw. I pulled him toward me, and he complied willingly, rolling onto his back so I could massage his fat belly. I remembered my encounter with the rakish cat at Graverly Manor. The wound it had inflicted was refusing to heal; I reached for a tissue and spotted it dry. "Why don't you come up for a visit?" I said to Shanna. "I'd love your opinion. I can inquire about a room."

"Sorry, darling, but I'm far too busy. Besides, I refuse to stay in a bed-and-breakfast. They attract lonely, desperate travelers who lurk around, waiting to ambush fellow residents with incessant chatter.

The walls are so thin you can't have a pee without the entire household knowing, and everyone monitors your comings and goings. I find the concept of paying to stay in a stranger's home bizarre. It's too intimate and awkward. I far prefer the anonymity of a hotel."

"Well, misanthropists won't be my target market," I said, feeling defensive.

"Oh, I don't mind being around people. I'll often take a book to the hotel lobby or lounge to feel part of the activity. I just don't want people talking to me unless I address them first."

"Speaking of royalty."

"You're a bit antisocial too, darling. How will you cope with the sanctity of your own home being violated by strangers?"

"There's a private apartment for the innkeeper," I said, a niggling uncertainty creeping over me. "Why are you being so negative? I was counting on your support."

Nuggle bolted upright and hopped off the bed.

"I'm simply playing devil's advocate. Couples often open restaurants because the husband's a great cook and the wife's a charming host, and it almost invariably results in disaster. People make the same mistake with B&Bs. A couple enjoys hosting out-of-town friends and reasons that a B&B will be as simple as a few more settings at the breakfast table. But paying guests are far more demanding than friends. Frankly, darling, I'm disappointed that you're prepared to walk away from the hotel business. I was counting on you becoming a bitter old hotel has-been like me."

"I'm not retiring, I'm taking my career in a new direction."

"What about that number two position at the Pan Pacific you applied for?"

"I didn't get it."

"What? Why?"

"The HR director said my reference checks came back a bit spotty."

"Darling, your credentials are impeccable."

"Tony Cavalli told her I burned down Hotel Cinema."

"That's insane. You were trying to save a woman's life!"

"And someone told her I incited a riot at the Universe. I'm blacklisted."

"You can't be held accountable for those incidents. Trevor, you're one of the most hardworking, diligent hoteliers I know. You tell that woman to call me. I'll set her straight."

"I'm done with hotels. I only have eyes for the manor now."

"Be careful not to romanticize the notion. Sometimes we think we want something, and when we get it we realize it's not what we need."

Rolling over, I spotted an elderly woman in the adjacent tower gawking at me with a pair of binoculars. I got up and closed the blinds. "Are we talking about me or you, Shanna?"

"Were we ever talking about you?" She sighed. "Ever since I moved to LA, I've wanted to own one of these smart-looking condos overlooking Santa Monica beach. Now that I have one, I loathe it."

"Why?"

"It turns out that being forced to watch beautiful young people compels me to drink vodka and smoke cigarettes. They're all so smug, so oblivious, I'm tempted to stand up and scream that they'll be old and fat like me someday, and much sooner than they think. I can't stand seeing them exercise and socialize and participate in life while I sit here like a brain-damaged senior in a wheelchair. I'd enjoy the view better if my home overlooked a concrete wall."

"You could try joining them."

She took another sip of what I now feared was vodka. "Too much effort. I'm exhausted after work. This is all I can muster the energy for."

"I thought you were getting help for your youth obsession."

"Your mother has missed our last few phone sessions. I think she's come to realize I'm right, there is no upside to aging."

I got up, pacing the room. "My mother is a nurse, not a psychiatrist."

"She's a brilliant woman, a role model for aging with dignity. Though she seemed a bit off when we last spoke. Have you seen her lately? How is she?"

"I was supposed to have dinner with her Sunday, but I couldn't make it." It occurred to me that Mom had been badgering me less lately because she had found a new patient in Shanna Virani. I was grateful for the reprieve but also concerned that Shanna sounded so down. "How's the new job?" I asked, wanting to lighten the conversation. Two months earlier, Shanna had taken a job as director of sales and marketing at the Chateau Beverly Hills.

"Fabulous," she replied, a little too quickly. "The ratio of staff to guests is so high I feel like I'm in Singapore again. I have several hundred highly competent staff to ensure I never have to deal with guests."

"And the new GM, what's he like?"

"Mr. Neville? He came to us from that 'seven star' hotel in Dubai, the Burj Al Arab. He's a Brit, schooled in Switzerland, a stickler for details and highly fastidious. We're getting along famously, just famously."

"Uh-huh." Now I was dubious.

"Okay, so he's a pompous windbag. He parades around the hotel like Louis XIV, expecting staff to genuflect when he enters the room. I'll never understand what possesses hotel managers to behave like royalty. To manage a hotel requires humility, respect, self-sacrifice. I swear some people choose this business so they can lord over their domain in modern-day feudal systems. I just hope I can hold out until he gets the axe."

"Are you smoking, Shanna?"

"Just a little puff."

"Should I be worried about you?"

"No."

"How are Eliza and Bantu?"

Another drag, followed by a gulp. "We're having a ball. Did I tell you they're moving? Their father has taken a job in New York, and they've decided to transfer to Princeton. Isn't that marvelous?"

"But didn't you move to LA to be closer to them?" Years ago, Shanna's husband, Ramin, had left her for "an adolescent Iranian trollop" and had since filled her kids' ears with propaganda about what a bad mother she had been. She had moved to LA to rebuild her relationships with them.

"I have to run," Shanna said. "Mr. Neville is on the other line. Darling, please don't jump into something you'll regret. You never know what kind of unpleasant surprises might be lurking in that old house. For all you know, she's been poisoning her guests and burying them in the basement. God knows she'd be fulfilling the fantasy of many a hotelier."

5

Mystery Shopper

Graverly Manor became an obsession. In the following days, I scrambled to put together a business plan. I found a wealth of information on bed-and-breakfasts in the library and online, but data on Graverly Manor was scarce. Eventually I culled together enough information to create a bare-bones plan, but I needed facts and figures. I picked up the phone and called Lynne Crocker to request the manor's rates and occupancy statistics from the past several years. She hemmed and hawed, then finally agreed to ask Lady Graverly.

A few hours later, she called back. "Sorry, hon. Not gonna happen."

"Not even some aggregate figures?"

"Elinor finds talk about money distasteful. She's very British that way."

"How can someone run a business without discussing money? Surely you don't expect me to buy this house without this information. Any financial institution will demand it."

She spoke softly, as if to a child. "Trevor, please understand that the manor is priced as a single-family residence. If it was priced as a business, you'd be paying much, much more. The fact that it has a license to rent out rooms is a bonus. Even if you opt not to, it's still a great investment. You can get some stats on B&Bs from Tourism Vancouver and Tourism BC. And try HVS Global Hospitality Services. I'm afraid that'll have to suffice."

"Fine. Then can I spend a night at the manor to get a feel for the operation?"

"Nope. I already inquired on behalf of that lady from Boston, Gertrude Fishburne, and Elinor said the manor is way too busy. You having trouble getting that loan or something?"

"No! I just need—"

"Gotta run—that's Pam Hurle on the other line. She's putting in an offer today. Want me to cancel your request for a second viewing? Elinor's still mulling it over."

"No! I'll figure things out."

I hung up, fuming. Was Lynne truly fielding multiple offers or just employing pressure tactics? Whatever she was up to, it was working. Now that I knew the manor was priced like a normal residence, I was even more determined. Under proper management, the place could be a goldmine. Resuming my online research, I searched Expedia, Orbitz, and several other accommodation websites, but the manor wasn't listed on any of them. To my surprise, buried several pages into Google, I came upon a link to the manor's very own website. The site looked like it had been slapped together by a teenager in an introductory web design course, with a shoddy design and little useful content. In place of a booking engine was a note to "contact the maner for rats and reservations." Lady Graverly would be horrified, to be sure; likely she had never seen the website. I clicked it closed.

I was being shut out. How could I write a business plan without a solid understanding of room rates, market demand, and operational costs? It occurred to me I didn't have to go through Lynne. Hotels often hired "mystery shoppers" to stay anonymously and evaluate services. I couldn't check into the manor without Lady Graverly recognizing me, of course—unless I wore a disguise, but that would be risky. I could ask my sisters to stay, but what did they know about a luxury inn? Janet worked behind the counter at a donut shop, and Wendy worked in the kitchen at Langley Hospital. When they stayed at the Universe, they had acted like hillbillies. Janet had eaten half the contents of the mini-bar amenity tray, thinking they came with the room, whereas Wendy had been afraid to touch the wine and truffles I had left her, fearing she would be charged. Mom was a better option; she was more worldly and discerning, although far from an expert in hospitality, having once complained that my staff at the Universe smiled too much. But if I got her involved in the manor, I might never be able to extract her. Deciding an anonymous call would be harmless, I picked up the phone and dialed the manor.

After fifteen rings, I was about to hang up, thinking I must have misdialed, when the line opened. There was a long pause, then Lincoln's raspy voice pronounced joylessly, "Good afternoon, this is Graverly Manor." I might have been calling a funeral home.

"Well, hullo there!" I said. "I'm callin' from Dallas. Y'all got a room available next Tuesday for three nights?"

"I'm sorry, sir, the manor is fully reserved."

"Shucks. How 'bout Sunday, then? Sunday for two nights?"

"I'm afraid the manor is fully occupied then as well."

"Darn it all, anyway. Just so's I know for my next trip, what are your rates?"

There was a long pause. I heard Lady Graverly's chastising voice in the background, and a moment later she was on the phone.

"This is Lady Andrew Graverly. To whom am I speaking?"

There was no danger of call display given the relic of a phone I had seen on the front desk, but I feared she might recognize my voice or detect deceit in my atrocious Texan accent, so I dropped the accent and deepened my voice.

"This is Shawn Virani. I'm inquiring about a room on Sunday, December 3." Hotels were typically quiet on Sundays, particularly in December.

"Virani, did you say? And where are you calling from?"

"I'm in Vancouver now, but I'm from … Chicago."

"How lovely! Will you be traveling with children?"

"Children? Uh, yes … my little boy and girl. And my wife."

"I'm terribly sorry. I have nothing available."

"For future reference, may I ask the rate for a standard room?"

She chortled. "My good sir, there are no standard rooms at Graverly Manor. All of our rooms are of the finest quality. The most economical is the Jane Grey room, located on the third floor of the tower. I dare say it is a tad small, but rather symbolic of its namesake's short-lived reign. They called her the Nine Days Queen. She might have been one of England's greatest queens had she not been beheaded at the Tower of London in 1553 at the age of sixteen, by order of Queen Mary I. Rest assured, none of our guests have met the same fate. At least not yet." She chortled again.

"And the rate on that room?"

"The Jane Grey room is priced at $575 per night. Thank you ever so much for calling Graverly Manor." The line went dead.

I stared at the receiver. Lady Graverly's sales skills were abominable, the room was outrageously overpriced, and she had broken every rule in the reservations handbook. But that she could command such a high rate, coupled with the lack of availability, was extremely encouraging. With renewed optimism, I began to put together a revenue forecast and an expenditure budget. Hours later, however, I was still unable to show a profit. I picked up the phone to consult Shanna.

"Just fudge the numbers," she said.

"Fudge them?"

"Budgets are about guestimation, sandbagging, and setting benchmarks you'll probably never achieve. Use market forecasts for B&Bs in the city, add a few points, set aside 20 percent of revenues for sales and marketing, add a 4 percent capital reserve, and tweak until you reach the minimal performance you think the bank will accept. Everyone does it that way. At the Ritz Carlton, the annual budget took me about three hours, although I spent weeks storming around, fretting and cursing, to keep up appearances. Just make sure you leave a little padding. Ownership always wants more."

"But I'm the owner. I would only be deceiving myself."

"If you're confident the business will be successful, then give the bank the numbers they need to approve the loan, otherwise you have no business. Add a lot of statistics to bore and confuse them."

"What if I don't make the numbers? They could foreclose on me!"

"Darling, relax. A bank won't foreclose unless the business is an utter disaster—and I know you will never let that happen. It's a long-term investment for the bank *and* for you."

Shanna had a way of making things sound deceptively simple. Thanking her, I hung up and adjusted the numbers until I reached an average rate not much lower than that quoted by Lady Graverly. With minor refurbishments, smart marketing, and a tight fist on expenses, I was confident I could achieve these numbers. If I managed to exceed them, I could invest the difference into further upgrades.

Now it was time to write an overview. I went back online and clicked on TripAdvisor to read recent traveler reviews, and found entries with titles ranging from SUPERB to APPALLING!!! The latter assailed the manor as overpriced, the proprietor as "cheap as day-old bread!!", and the house as "crammed with fake antiques!" The

SUPERB reviewer described the manor as "beautifully charming" and Lady Graverly as "attentive and gracious." There were three favorable reviews in succession, all raving about the manor and its proprietress. The next review was entitled GRAVE MANOR—HAUNTED? "Great location," it said, "but I was awakened in the night by an eerie moaning sound. I was so freaked out, I checked out the next day." Online reviews, the bane of hoteliers, turned amateur travelers into authorities. In a just world, there would be a review site for managers to evaluate hotel guests. Choosing to disregard the negative reviews, I transcribed the positive reviews into the business plan.

Next, I found a website called The History of Metropolitan Vancouver, which carried an article entitled VANCOUVER'S MOST FAMOUS—AND INFAMOUS—RESIDENCES. Under the subheading GRAVERLY MANOR was a reference to "Lord Andrew Graverly's mysterious disappearance" in 1958. "A young Scottish woman named Sarah Kilpatrick who had been working as a housekeeper in the manor for almost a year vanished around the same time," the article related. "Police were alerted to the disappearances by Lord Graverly's wife, Lady Elinor, who filed a police report shortly after arriving from England with her newborn son. A final notation in the Vancouver Police Department archives concludes that Lord Graverly and Miss Kilpatrick ran off together.

"Popular folklore tells a different story, however. At the time, neighbors speculated that, upon learning of his wife's impending arrival, Lord Graverly had taken his lover to the lagoon and drowned her, inadvertently drowning himself at the same time. It is believed that their ghosts wander the hallways of Graverly Manor in search of one another, but on alternating nights, so they have yet to reunite."

I shivered, disturbed by the tragic story. It was the very tale my mother had told me at Lost Lagoon. Did she know there was a connection to Graverly Manor? Closing my eyes, I envisioned a younger Elinor Graverly making the long journey to Vancouver with her sickly newborn son, only to find an empty house. Was her proud, imperious persona a front for the pain she had suffered? At least I now knew how the haunting rumors had begun. People's love of ghost stories, of scandal and intrigue, had kept this urban myth alive all these years. If I were to purchase the manor, I would immediately squelch such rumors. Not only were they bad for business, but they were hurtful to Lady Graverly. Closing the window, I powered down the computer. Whatever may or may not have happened fifty years ago was of no consequence to me, and it certainly had no place in my business plan.

Some things were better left in the past.

The following Monday afternoon, I arrived at the bank in my best suit, clutching a briefcase full of service awards, training certificates, and letters from former hotel guests. An assistant led me into a glass-enclosed office and told me that Raphael Ortega, my account manager, would be with me shortly. She pulled the door closed.

I sat down to wait and drummed my fingers on the table. Should I display my awards on the table for Raphael and I to admire together? I doubted it would be necessary. I was confident that the business plan I had submitted three days prior was sufficient. Sitting back, I observed the activity around me through the windows. What a pleasant place, with so many smartly dressed, purposeful-looking employees. In the office next door, a woman in a pale grey suit and pink scarf was reviewing a document with an attractive young couple. The husband, looking uncomfortable in his ill-fitting suit and short tie, scratched the patch of hair under his lip and frowned as he watched the manager's manicured fingernail move down the form. His wife turned away suddenly, and her forlorn eyes met mine. The word "foreclosure" popped into my head. Embarrassed, I broke eye contact and turned away, directing my attention to a video monitor mounted on the faux granite pillar outside the door. An ecstatic couple, who might easily have been the couple next door in a "before" scenario, was shaking hands with a winsome male employee. Preferring this happy scene, I watched it for some time, mesmerized, until the screen flickered and went blank.

The door opened and in walked Raphael. The eager, solicitous expression of our first meeting was gone, replaced by a slight grimace. He shook my hand briskly and sat down. Earlier, I had anticipated the amusing comments he would make as we waded through the pile of loan documents: "Sign your life away!" "Only twenty-three more forms to go!" But his hands were empty, his fists clenched.

"Trevor, we're not able to approve your loan application. I'm sorry."

"What? Why?"

"Your debt ratio would be too high to carry a mortgage of this size," he said, absently stroking his gold watch. "We feel your numbers are a bit optimistic."

"But I was being conservative."

"I'm sorry. There's nothing I can do."

I stood up. "I'd like to speak to your manager."

"She'll only tell you the same thing."

"I said I'd like to speak to your manager."

Shooting me a wary look, Raphael excused himself and slipped out the door. Blood coursed through my veins as I prepared for a confrontation with his manager. Indignation, outrage, pleading, tears, threats, a hostage-taking—whatever it took to get this loan, I was willing to try. Marching to the window, I glowered at the smug employees around me. They were all so young; did any of them know what it was like to dream of starting a new business, of owning one's own home? The foreclosure specialist next door was leading the couple out of her office, her face pinched in an expression similar to Raphael's. The husband's eyes looked shell-shocked, yet he held his head high and walked with dignity. Behind him, his wife, the color drained from her face, stumbled slightly and clutched the doorframe, her eyes again catching mine. With a shudder, I turned away.

Raphael returned with a big-hipped black woman with silver ear-rings shaped like scythes. Introducing herself as Mrs. Mavis Banfield, she gestured for me to be seated and sat down at Raphael's desk. Raphael remained by the door, arms crossed like a security guard.

"You wanted to see me?" she said, blinking.

"Yes." I took a deep breath and leaned toward her, folding my hands on the desk to steady their trembling. "I've worked in hotels since I was a teenager. I've been a manager since I was twenty-two. I want to purchase a house that is listed well below market value and has enormous revenue potential. Yet Raphael tells me a loan would be too risky. There's no risk here."

Mrs. Banfield proceeded to repeat Raphael's words, except in a firmer, calmer tone. I retorted, employing the various tactics I had devised, and she dug in her heels. After ten minutes of tense debate, I realized that even a hostage-taking wasn't going to change her mind.

"So that's it?" I said. "No negotiation? There are other banks, you know."

"Mr. Lambert, if any bank is going to give you this loan, it's us. We sincerely wish we could help, but we can't. Not without a significantly larger deposit over and above your available funds and the market value of your condominium."

My eyes moved to the briefcase at my feet. Should I show her my service awards? No, I would only humiliate myself further.

"Have you considered a business partner?" Mrs. Banfield said. "A bed-and-breakfast can be a lot of work. Do you know anyone with substantial assets who might be willing to cosign the loan?"

Shanna Virani popped into my head. She claimed to have no interest in the bed-and-breakfast business, but perhaps she would be interested in being a silent partner. But no, she was deep in debt due to her lavish spending habits. My sisters could barely make ends meet as it was, and I wasn't about to make this a family affair—which ruled out my mother too. There was no one else. No generous friends who had struck it rich in the stock market, no girlfriend with loaded parents, no lonely aunt desperate for my affections. In my career, I had met thousands of wealthy people, had suffered their abuse without a peep of protest and had gone to great lengths to make them comfortable, yet in my time of need I could turn to no one.

"Mr. Lambert?" Mavis Banfield said, glancing at her watch.

My thoughts returned to my mother. That big house in Surrey had been paid off years ago. Should I ask her to be my silent partner? Was she capable of silence? A vision came to me of returning to the manor after a day of running errands only to find the house repainted in pastels and Mom conducting a group therapy session with guests in the parlor. If not a partnership, then what about a simple cosigning arrangement—with an accompanying restraining order? No. Even under court order, Mom wouldn't be able to refrain from meddling.

I shook my head. "There's no one."

"Then there's nothing we can do, I'm afraid. I'm terribly sorry."

I bent down to pick up my briefcase. As I walked out, I saw Mrs. Banfield exchange a meaningful look with Raphael, and I couldn't help but feel that I was being rejected because they too believed that Graverly Manor was haunted.

A few minutes later, I was cursing my way up Burrard Street when my cell phone rang. Expecting Lynne Crocker, I hesitated. I dreaded the prospect of admitting that I couldn't afford the manor. But the display window read "Private Name," so I took and chance and answered.

"Trevor?" said a young male voice. "It's Mr. Chagani from the Vancouver Harbourside Hotel, Resort, Conference Centre & Spa. We received your résumé, and I'd like to set up a screening interview."

"Mr. Chagani, nice to hear from you!" I said, my spirits lifting. I turned in the direction of the hotel, which was perched on the outer fringe of downtown next to the Pearl Harbour Hotel, and my spirits deflated. Its aging edifice was a blight among the modern buildings around it. From where I stood, it appeared to be tilting precariously toward Coal Harbour. I had sent in my résumé on a whim after coming across an advertisement in the *Vancouver Sun* for a general manager of a "four-star hotel with five-star aspirations." Even to call it three-star was a stretch. It had looked shabby when I last ventured inside ten years ago, and according to Frank Parsons at the Four Seasons, not a dollar had been invested since. My impulse was to tell Mr. Chagani I was no longer interested, but maybe it was time to accept that I wasn't going to find my dream job, not as an innkeeper and not as the general manager of a luxury hotel. I needed to work to maintain my sanity if not yet out of financial necessity. If the Vancouver Harbourside Hotel, Resort, Conference Centre & Spa aspired to go five-star, it could be a challenge worth pursuing—if only to convince ownership to shorten the name. "I'd love to come in!" I said with all the enthusiasm I could muster.

"Sweet. I have an opening at two tomorrow. Otherwise I can't get you in for two or three weeks. We're inundated with candidates."

Unlike his schedule, my schedule was wide open, but I didn't want to sound too available. "Hmm...let me see," I said, consulting an imaginary schedule. "Yes, I think I can make that work."

He said sweet again and gave me his coordinates. "Ask for Mr. Chagani," he said and hung up. His office was located on Hastings Street, adjacent to the hotel; he probably worked for the ownership, an impression reinforced by his youthful voice and overconfident tone. A son of one of the owners, I guessed.

I crossed Pender Street and cast another wary look in the direction of the hotel. The tilt looked even more exaggerated from this perspective, as though the tower might topple into the harbor at any moment. An optical illusion, I assured myself—not an omen.

As I climbed into my car, my cell phone rang again.

"Trevor, is that you? Hold on a sec."

Lynne Crocker. In the background, I could hear the sound of traffic. She was driving, talking on her cell phone, and probably unwrapping a chocolate bar—a menace on the roads. I heard a crunch. "How's it going?"

"Not great, Lynne. I—"

"Listen, I gotta be quick. I'm late for a showing in Gastown, huge deal. I've got great news! Elinor wants to meet with you."

"She does? Why?"

"She's looking for a specific type to take possession, you know, someone who will"—she broke into a bad British accent—"'honor the illustrious history and cherished traditions of my exquisite manor.' She doesn't want the house to get into the wrong hands. She's afraid it'll be torn down and replaced with condos, a Walmart, or—god forbid—social housing. Know what I mean?" Crunch, crunch—a carrot or popcorn.

"That's nice to hear, Lynne, but—"

"She was quite taken with you. She said you remind her of an aristocrat."

"She said that?"

A horn blared in the background. "Watch where you're going, asshole!" Lynne hollered. "Sorry, hon, traffic's a total nightmare today. How'd everything go at the bank?"

A flicker of hope had flared to life, and I felt reluctant to extinguish it. "As well as could be expected, I guess."

"Great! She wants you to come by at nine tomorrow night. I have another showing at your place, so I'll need you out anyway. This guy needs a place for December 1, and I know he's going to love your place. If all goes well, in a matter of days you'll have sold your condo and bought the manor. Isn't that exciting?"

"Yeah, about the financing..."

Furious honking. "Screw you, jerk!" Lynne cried. Then an ambulance siren.

"Lynne, is everything okay?"

"Of course. Treat it like a job interview, Trevor. Don't blow it."

"I won't. I promise."

There was a screech of tires, followed by another curse from Lynne, and the line went dead.

6

Noble Blood

I was sitting at a faux cherrywood desk across from the junior executive who called himself Mr. Chagani. "I'm sorry?" I said, thinking I had misheard.

"If you were a vegetable, what kind of vegetable would you be?"

"A very unhappy vegetable, I would think."

"I don't mean a retard, I mean something you eat."

"That's not what I meant," I said, bristling at the unseemly reference. I shifted in my seat. The question might be appropriate if I were applying for a gardener position, but otherwise it was ridiculous, an attempt to sound clever that had the opposite effect and would elicit no relevant information about me. Reminding myself I needed a job, I replied with alacrity.

"I guess I would be a tomato. Reliable, prolific, popular. I've always strived to be as—"

He squeezed his eyes shut. "A tomato is a fruit."

"It's not a vegetable?"

"It's a *fruit*." He scribbled something in the margin of my résumé and placed the pencil down. Leaning back in his chair, he folded his hands behind his head, revealing yellow stains in his armpits. "Allow me to be frank, Taylor."

"Trevor."

"The Vancouver Harbourside Hotel, Resort, Conference Centre & Spa is not like other hotels. Here we think outside the box." He drew a box in the air and gave me an expectant look, as though introducing a revolutionary concept.

"You were looking for a different answer."

"Frankly, I expect more from someone at your level. A carrot, for example—a sharp eye for detail. Spinach—healthy and strong. A baked yam—warm and sweet. But a fruit? Come on."

A Brussels sprout—nauseating. "Would you like me to try again?" I asked.

"The Vancouver Harbourside Hotel, Resort, Conference Centre & Spa is a home away from home for our guests. Our employees are like family. We work hard, but fun is one of our *fun*damental values. Above all, our service sets us apart. Our employees are dedicated to providing the highest level of service possible in a nonbranded, value-priced hotel. Every employee from the bottom up is committed to going that extra mile, to anticipating guests' needs, to committing random acts of service excellence ..."

Mr. Chagani's voice faded off as he spouted more clichés, quoting from a Hotel 101 textbook written decades ago. Every hotel from Best Western to Ritz Carlton claimed that service distinguished them, but few hotels mastered it. Prior to the interview, I had toured the hotel lobby, and it was even more depressing than I remembered. At the front desk, the agent ignored me for a full minute before lifting her head from her Facebook account. Now I was forced to endure an interview for the hotel's most senior position with this adolescent smartass in a Van Heusen tie. Did I want to work here? No. But I needed a job. Suddenly I wanted this job more than anything, for the sole purpose of making him suffer. *What vegetable would you be?* I'd turn him into compost.

"…going to ask you a scenario question," Mr. Chagani was saying. Squinting to alert me to the fact that he was about to say something profound, he said, "So you're delivering luggage to a room. A guy answers the door and asks you to get him a hooker. What do you do?"

I raised an eyebrow. "I assume by a guy you mean a guest? Does this happen regularly here?"

"It happens everywhere." He sat back, looking smug. "So?"

"As general manager, I'll be delivering luggage?"

"Got a problem with that?"

"Of course not. At my last hotel, I delivered room service, parked cars, and babysat the owner's daughter. It's just an unusual question. If I've made it this far in my career, I should know how to deal with—"

He squeezed his eyes shut again. "You gonna answer?"

I scratched my chin, pretending to be thinking hard, and fought the impulse to make a run for the door. If I pleaded my case to Elinor Graverly, would she take pity on me and come up with a more palatable financial arrangement? Lynne Crocker had said she thought I was "aristocratic." The word had a pleasant ring. I glanced in the mirror on the wall to my left. I did have quite a prominent, noble-looking chin. What was a hundred thousand dollars between aristocrats? I hadn't canceled my appointment yet. If I showed up and charmed her—

"Taylor?"

I snapped to attention. "I would politely tell the guest that I'm unable to assist with such a request, and then I would ask if there is anything else I could help him with."

He looked disappointed, as though he had hoped I would tell him I would rub my thumb and forefinger together and tell the guest I could make a few calls if he made it worth my while. Scribbling another note, he said, "I'm gonna be honest. I'm not convinced you're ready for a job of this magnitude. But I'm going to give you the benefit of the doubt and set you up for a personality test. If you ace it, I'll book you an interview with Mr. Gupta." He stood up and offered his hand.

I realized with some trepidation that I had passed the interview. Shaking his sweaty hand, I made a beeline for the door, then stopped and turned to him. "I should inform you that I've put in an offer on a local bed-and-breakfast—inn … manor. If the deal goes through, I'll have to withdraw my candidacy."

"Oh yeah? Which B&B?"

"Graverly Manor."

He coughed, eyes bulging.

"You're familiar with it?" I asked, holding my smile.

"My father looked into buying it, but the old lady wanted too much. He didn't want it, anyway. He's superstitious. He was afraid the house was sick."

"What do you mean, sick?"

"You know, like something's wrong with it, and no matter what you do it won't get better." His thick black eyebrows furrowed. "They say she murdered her husband when she found out he was cheating, then buried him under the house, and his rotting corpse has poisoned the foundation."

I felt that crick in my neck again, but gave a laugh. "You believe that?"

"I don't know. I went over there with my dad once. It was nice and everything, but it kinda creeped me out. That old broad is nuts."

"She's not nuts," I said, feeling defensive. "She's just a bit eccentric."

He held up his hands. "I'm just telling you, the place is cursed."

"Well, I appreciate your candor," I lied.

"We'll be in touch. Oh, hey, I'll need some references from previous employers."

"References?" I said.

Somewhere down the hall, I heard a door slam shut.

"I'm sorry, Trevor, I can't."

I was completely taken aback. I had never asked my mother for anything, in part because I prided myself on my independence, but also because I feared she would leverage any indebtedness to further impose upon my life. I had been so torn over whether I wanted to bring her in as a silent partner, it hadn't even occurred to me she might decline. I got up and wandered to the kitchen window, where the yellow curtains gave an illusion of perpetual sunshine. A couple neighborhood kids, two miniature Shanna Viranis in pink saris, were perched on the hood of my BMW pulling at imaginary steering wheels.

"I'm not asking you to give me the money," I said. "I just need you to cosign the loan."

"That would require a lien on this house. What if things go sour? I could lose my home. I've lived here since Charles and I got married."

"They're not going to go sour, Mom. And you won't have to be involved in the operation of the manor in any way whatsoever." I emphasized this point to make sure she understood the arrangement I was proposing.

The kettle began sputtering and screeching on the stove. Mom got up to unplug it and poured steaming water into two ceramic mugs. "I don't get why you're so set on owning a bed-and-breakfast. It'd be a life sentence to hard labor."

"Sure, at the outset it'll be a lot of work, but once things are up and running I expect to have more time on my hands than ever. And more flexibility."

"What about your condo?"

"I'm selling it."

"What? Why on earth would you give up your home?"

"Graverly Manor will be my new home."

She pressed her fingers against her temple and closed her eyes, as though I were inflicting physical pain. "How will you separate your personal life from your work? You've never been good at that."

"It's the perfect scenario. I'll never have to leave home to go to work. No commute."

"Or leave work to go home." She set down a mug of vile-looking green liquid before me and patted my head, as though delivering a cup of hot chocolate.

I stared into the mug. "What's this, stewed compost?"

"It's green tea enriched with special organic herbs. I got the recipe from a fabulous new book I found, *Our Food Is Killing Us*. I bought copies for you and the girls."

So this was her latest fad: organic foods. Not a bad thing, considering the processed food she had raised us on.

"What about the Four Seasons?" she asked. "Did you check back?"

"*I* don't want to work at the Four Seasons, Mom, *you* want me to. Don't you understand that buying this manor is my dream?"

"Trevor, before we happened upon that house, I had never heard you say a word about wanting to operate a bed-and-breakfast, so forgive me if I'm having a hard time accepting it's your lifelong dream. I know you, sometimes better than you know yourself. This isn't the right move for you. You need the structure of a hotel, the order, the team environment. Have you got a contingency plan if this scheme doesn't work out?"

"Maybe."

She stared at me for a moment. "You're planning to move away, aren't you?"

"We'll see."

She set down her mug on the table and lowered herself into a chair, letting out a soft moan.

"Are you okay?" I asked.

"I'm fine, my back is just a little sore. I don't understand why you would move to another city to do something you can do here. There are plenty of hotels in Vancouver. You're not trying hard enough."

"If I buy the manor, it will keep me here."

"We'll never see you. We barely see you as it is, and you're unemployed. You missed dinner on Sunday, and you didn't even call."

"I completely forgot. I'm sorry. Next Sunday for sure." I got up to look out the window again. The girls were standing on my hood now, pulling at imaginary gears and making speeding sounds as they flew down an imaginary highway. I looked back at Mom. "Shouldn't you be at work?"

"I'm taking a few days off."

I studied her face and was reminded of the vacant expression I had grown up with. Since her awakening, her diehard optimism had often annoyed me, but now she was being a downer—and at a time when I had been counting on her support.

"Drink your tea," she said, taking a sip of her own.

"Is there actual tea in this, or are you trying to poison me?"

"It'll cure what ails you." She got up and left the room, returning with a book. "Here, read this," she said, handing me a copy of *Our Food Is Killing Us*. "You'll never use the microwave again."

I took the book and set it on the table. Across the hall, I could see a tin box on my old bed, its contents strewn across the checkered blanket. "You've been going through old photos?"

She craned her neck to follow my gaze. "Oh yes, I guess I was."

"Charles would have given me the money."

Her jaw hardened. "What did you say?"

"After he died, you turned this house into a funeral home. Now you have an opportunity to use it to generate some happiness."

"Trevor, that's not fair. Can't we put this discussion on the back burner for a couple of weeks?"

"I don't have a couple weeks. The house will be sold."

"Then I guess it wasn't meant to be."

"You think it's haunted too, don't you?"

She was quiet for a moment. "In a way, yes, I do."

I dumped the tea down the sink, grabbed the book, and went out to chase the girls off my car.

That evening, at nine o'clock precisely, I mounted the steps to Graverly Manor, a small bouquet of lilacs in my hand. Lifting the brass knocker, I hesitated, once again filled with doubt. To present myself as a viable purchaser, particularly after Lynne had warned me not to waste her client's time, was false and deceitful. Yet each time I had picked up the phone to cancel, I had set it down again. Now, propelled by the faint hope that if I disclosed my predicament Lady Graverly might be open to a special financial arrangement, I was here. All I could do was ask. I had nothing else to lose. Letting the knocker fall, I stepped back and waited.

Five minutes later, Lincoln answered. Without a word, he bowed and took my coat, setting the flowers on top of a copper urn next to the door. My attempts at polite conversation were met with silence, as though he were deaf as well as half-blind. He led me into the parlor and left, pulling the door closed.

While I waited, I hummed along to the classical music playing on the old-fashioned gramophone and discreetly explored the room. The dying embers in the fireplace and a three-pronged candelabra on the mantel provided the only light in the room. A floral-patterned chesterfield sat against the windows, which were shrouded in thick draperies. Next to an upright piano was a rosewood bookcase containing a single book on its top shelf, its lower shelves consigned to ceramic figurines. Two ornately carved throne chairs, upholstered in royal blue velvet, faced the fireplace.

I listened to the ticktock of a grandfather clock. Ten minutes passed. Feeling restless, I ran my finger along the top of one of the picture frames, and it came back caked with dust. *Shame, Lincoln.* Another fifteen minutes passed. I was beginning to lose my nerve. The old woman's crafty eyes would see through my scheme, and she would banish me from the property. I wandered to the piano and lifted the cover, nervously testing some of the yellowed keys. The notes were shrill and out of tune.

A voice startled me from behind. "Do you play?"

Lady Elinor Graverly had swept in without a sound. She was extravagantly dressed in a floor-length gown buttoned to her chin.

I shook my head. "I'm not musically inclined."

"Pity. Nor am I. Lincoln plays, but his timing is off." She broke into a smile and came to me, arms outstretched, turning each cheek for a kiss. "How lovely to see you again, Mr. Lambert."

"And you, Lady Graverly," I said, feeling an inexplicable rush of joy.

"Please do sit down," she said, gesturing to one of the throne chairs. She settled in across from me, her cobbled feet, stuffed into red patent-leather high heels, dangling in the air.

The door opened, and Lincoln padded across the room to the bar.

"I understand you wish to purchase my home," Lady Graverly said, arranging the folds of her gown.

I cleared my throat. "That's my hope. I'm still negotiating with the bank."

"Banks," she said, making a spitting sound.

I grinned and waited for her to elaborate, but she said nothing more. She observed me with a bemused smile, fingering her ringlets of hair in a disarmingly coquettish manner. Sensing that she knew why I was there and was waiting for me to plead my case, I searched for the right words. But Lynne's remark about Lady Graverly's aversion to discussing money echoed in my mind, and I found I was too proud to admit to being anything but very wealthy.

Lincoln brought over two martinis on a silver tray.

"To your future home," Lady Graverly said, lifting her glass in a toast.

"To my future home," I mumbled. Taking a sip, I suppressed a gasp. Straight gin, room temperature, garnished with a tiny, shriveled olive. It tasted like lighter fluid.

Lady Graverly swallowed half the contents of her glass and set it down. "How lovely! That will be all, Lincoln."

"Yes, my lady."

"All sorts of people wish to buy this house," she said after Lincoln had left, her face scrunching into an expression of distaste. "Developers, opportunists, charlatans, philistines. You, dear boy, are different. I can tell just by looking at you. Such presence you have, such gracious manners and noble features. You belong in a different century. You are a descendant of aristocracy, to be sure."

I laughed. "I wish. My roots are decidedly common. I grew up in Surrey with my mom and two sisters." I took another sip and gazed about the room, basking in the warmth of her remarks. What a comfortable house, with its beguiling hostess and a butler to attend to our whims.

"Tell me about your father," she said, leaning toward me, her eyes bright.

"My father?" I crossed my legs and uncrossed them. "There's not much to tell. I didn't know him that well. I'm told he was a bit of a cynic, down-to-earth, a homebody—everything I'm not. He died when I was twelve."

"Good heavens. What happened?"

"His car was rear-ended. It was totaled, but he walked away without a scratch—or so he thought. The impact had caused a tiny rupture in his aorta. For two weeks following the accident, he complained about chest pain but attributed it to stress. He had lost his job in the factory at Scott Paper a few months prior. Meanwhile, his aorta was bubbling out like a balloon. One morning, shortly after my sisters and I left for school, it burst."

"Dear boy, how you must have suffered!"

"Me? A little, I guess."

"Twelve years old—not quite a man." She reached for my hand and clutched it with surprising strength. "You must have been a pillar of strength, an immense comfort, to your mother and sisters. Your family must think so extraordinarily highly of you."

I nodded slowly and tried to smile, but a lump took hold in my throat, a little ball of shame. I tried to imagine how my sisters would respond to such a remark—with smirks, sarcasm, contempt. After my father died, I hadn't been a source of comfort, I had withdrawn completely.

"As the eldest son, you were the heir?" asked Lady Graverly.

I chuckled softly. "There was nothing to inherit."

"Your father was an Englishman."

"No, he was French, born in Montreal, but his parents came from the south of France. It's my mother who's British—or at least her grandparents were."

She withdrew her hand and sat back in the chair. "Lord Andrew fought in the Second World War. He never forgave the French for cooperating with the Nazis."

By the sour look on her face she hadn't forgiven them either. I reached for my glass. The liquid burned in my chest—a not entirely unpleasant sensation. Her questions were unusual, almost inappropriate. What did my family history have to do with Graverly Manor? Had this been a job interview, as Lynne had suggested, Lady Graverly would be breaking a lot of rules. Yet her questions were far preferable to those of the smart aleck at the Harbourside Hotel.

Lady Graverly reached for the brass bell on the table and rang it loudly. "Lincoln will refresh your drink, Mr. Lambert."

"Oh, no. I've had enough."

"I insist."

I shifted in my seat. "May I ask why you're selling the manor?"

She folded her hands, twisted and misshapen by arthritis. "I am to inherit a large fortune. My husband had but one sibling, an elder brother named Lord Wakefield Graverly, who became the eighth Marquess of Middlesex upon their father's death in 1981. A few months ago, Lord Wakefield passed on."

"I'm sorry."

"Don't be. I've been anxiously awaiting the old fool's death for decades. I met him only once, forty years ago, when he came to this house accompanied by a young woman half his age and tried to make amends for his family's deplorable treatment of my husband. I slammed the door in his face. Lord Wakefield lived a privileged life but suffered a loveless, childless marriage. When he died, he left a small sum to a son no one had known existed, and the rest to the only being that ever loved him: his dog. He might have left the family estate to the dog too, but that decision was not his to make. Are you familiar with England's rules of peerage?"

"Not at all, I'm afraid."

"Peerage is a system of nobility created by William of Normandy, also known as William the Bastard for his illegitimate birth. After conquering England in 1066 in the Battle of Hastings, William introduced the continental feudal system to England and divided the nation into manors, rewarding men with land and titles in return for their loyalty. The system remains in place today. There are five classes—baron, viscount, earl, marquess, and duke. A title is either for life, in which case it is bestowed upon the recipient alone and expires when the holder dies, or hereditary, in which case it is passed on to the eldest living son through generations. If there are no living male descendants, the title becomes extinct and reverts to the crown. Rules were painstakingly recorded in the Letters Patent to ensure titles went only to legitimate heirs—for it is a great British noble tradition to have all sorts of lovers and illegitimate children." She stopped to swallow the rest of her drink, a mischievous smile spreading across her lips.

Lincoln entered the room and proceeded to the bar. I lifted my hand to decline, but he either did not see me or chose to ignore me.

Lady Graverly continued, "The Marquessate of Middlesex is a hereditary title created in 1789 for Thomas Ludlow Graverly, of Uxbridge, in the County of Middlesex, now part of Greater London. The title is a rarity today in that it comes with entailed property. The right to the Graverly title and estate are presently being contested in the British courts. A ruling is expected in a matter of days."

"If Lord Wakefield had a son, wouldn't he be entitled to everything?"

She opened her mouth, looking mortally offended. "Lord Wakefield's son is entitled to nothing! He is a bastard." Her eyes fluttered, and she composed herself. "Special remainders in the Graverly peerage stipulate that if the holder does not produce a legitimate son, the title shall be passed on to his younger brother and, in turn, to that brother's eldest male issue. This would mean that my husband is the rightful heir, and in turn our son. Since neither is in a position to claim the estate, it falls to me to do so on their behalf."

"Well! I guess congratulations are in order, then."

Her expression remained grave. "Titles and riches mean nothing to me, Mr. Lambert. I am only concerned that tradition is honored. I expect to move to London and into Graverly Castle posthaste." She observed me in silence for a moment. "Tell me, Mr. Lambert, are you a loyal man?"

"Loyal? Yes, very."

"Do you value privacy and discretion?"

"It's a requirement of my profession."

She nodded, pleased. A scratching sound drew my attention to the dining room door. It opened slightly, and a mangy cat skulked in and hopped onto Lady Graverly's lap. She let out a cry of delight, lifting him to her face and smothering him with kisses. "Have you met Sir Fester?" she asked, lifting a paw toward me.

"We've had the pleasure," I said, displaying my scratches, which had finally begun to heal.

She laughed heartily. "Sir Fester can be quite territorial. Can't you, my little precious?"

Staring aghast at the cat's matted black fur, I wondered if he had been thrown into a bathtub with a plugged-in toaster. "Sir Fester—what an unusual name."

"Isn't it? Lincoln named him, and I added Sir for greater dignity. The little devil showed up on our doorstep during a storm and demanded we take him in."

I turned to smile conspiratorially at Lincoln, thinking that by the name he must share my disdain for the feline, but his eyes remained fixed ahead as he moved toward us carrying a tray.

"You're not joining me?" I asked Lady Graverly, accepting the martini out of politeness. I was feeling fuzzy-headed as it was and wanted to stay alert.

"Oh, no. I have one martini each evening, and only one. Alcohol turns me into a shameless coquette."

I gave a nervous laugh and silently agreed it was for the best.

Lincoln let himself out, and Lady Graverly resumed her questioning. "Are you forgiving, Mr. Lambert?"

I hesitated, observing Sir Fester, who was arching his back to meet her vigorous strokes and clawing the arm of the chair. He winked, as though taunting me. I was certain I would never forgive him for attacking me. I would probably never forgive my mother for my miserable youth. I would never forgive Janet for wearing acid-wash jeans two decades after they went out of style. And would I ever forgive Nancy for abandoning me? Probably not.

"Oh, very," I said, sipping. "But why all these questions, may I ask?"

"Such qualities are essential to an innkeeper, naturally. Loyalty to the house, respect for the privacy of your guests, forgiveness for the mistakes your servants will make. Graverly Manor has quite a colorful history, as you may have heard. Only an individual who cherishes such virtues is worthy of becoming its proprietor."

In the front hall, the telephone began to ring. Sir Fester leapt off her lap, as though running to answer it.

"I could demand double the price from a developer," Lady Graverly continued. "But there are too many memories within these walls to allow them to be torn down. Whoever buys the manor must preserve its present state."

"I assure you that is my intention."

"Excellent. I'm so glad we're in agreement. Tomorrow I shall inform Miss Crocker to proceed with the sale." She lifted herself from the chair.

"Wait," I said. "There's something I need to tell you." In the front hall, the phone continued to ring, heightening my anxiety. "I'm a bit short with the deposit the bank requires. I was hoping we could discuss a special arrangement, a payment plan, perhaps, to make the purchase possible."

She stared at me, not responding, her eyes burning into me. The only sound was the ticking of the clock.

Lincoln appeared in the doorway. "My lady, a telephone call for you."

"Tell whoever it is that I've retired," she said without moving her eyes.

"It's London, my lady. Your lawyer. He says it's urgent."

"Very well, then. I shall take it in my private quarters." With a heavy sigh, she unlocked her gaze and started toward the door. "Lincoln will see you out, Mr. Lambert."

"But…" I followed her across the hall, toward her private quarters.

Lincoln stepped in front of me. "Kindly follow me, sir."

I watched Lady Graverly enter her apartment, slamming the door behind her. The lilacs toppled off the urn and hit the floor, the petals scattering.

Lincoln opened the door. "Have a pleasant evening, sir."

As I passed him, I detected a faint glimmer of satisfaction in his pink eyes, as though he were happy to see me leave a place where I didn't belong.

★ ★ ★ ★ ★

The next morning, Mom called early and woke me up.

"I'll give you the money," she said.

I sat up in bed, groggy. "What money?"

"For the manor. I didn't want to rush into this, but I understand we don't have the luxury of time. I'll arrange a transfer today."

By her resigned tone, it was obvious the gesture was incited by guilt. "I appreciate the offer, Mom, but I don't want you to loan me the money unless you want to."

"I'm not loaning it to you, Trevor. I'm giving it to you."

"That's crazy. All I need is a cosigner."

"I don't want a lien on my house. It wouldn't be fair to your sisters. I'll give you enough money to make the deposit, and the bank can loan you the rest."

I felt a rush of gratitude. "I'd prefer to borrow the money, Mom. I won't feel right if I don't pay you back."

"Fine. I won't argue."

When I hung up, I remembered the abrupt conclusion to my meeting with Lady Graverly. I quickly dialed Lynne Crocker's number.

"Trevor, I was just going to call you," she said. "I've got great news: I sold your condo! The buyer came in just over the asking price, if you can believe it. The only condition is he needs to close the sale right away. I'm on my way over with the papers now."

"Whoa, Lynne, I told you—the sale hinges on the manor. I think I blew it last night."

"Don't tell me your financing fell through?"

"My financing looks better than ever. It was my meeting with Elinor Graverly that didn't go so well. I think I offended her."

"Are you kidding? She loves you. She called me first thing this morning and gave me the green light. Why, you devil you, what did you do to convince her to lower the price? From now on, I'm bringing you when I need to negotiate a sale."

"She lowered the price?"

"By fifty grand! We'd better move quickly before the old bat comes to her senses. I can give you the names of a good inspector and a real estate lawyer. Elinor has agreed to allow you in for a full inspection tomorrow night. Am I the best realtor in the world or what?"

"Absolutely the best, Lynne. I think I love you."

In Vancouver, the rain comes not in brief, explosive tantrums followed by brilliant sunshine like in eastern Canada; it falls gently over long periods, elongating the suffering over days and weeks. Yet when I arrived at Graverly Manor to meet Lynne and the housing inspector the next night, the skies had erupted in a torrent of anger, and the wind was driving the rain over the city in sheets. I was early, so I waited out front, taking refuge under the evergreen tree.

My appointment at the bank earlier that day had fulfilled the fantasy that had been so cruelly crushed at the last meeting. Raphael wisecracked predictably as we reviewed the loan documents, adding hackneyed little comments reserved for successful loan applicants, but I laughed merrily nonetheless. Between signatures, I gazed out the windows that separated the offices, curious about the fate of other hopefuls, and watched the ecstatic "before" couple on the video monitor, feeling their joy. The first time I had purchased a home had been with Nancy, and I could feel her presence beside me, soothing my worries by stoically encouraging me.

Lynne was late. Across the lawn, the house was dark, the curtains drawn. Globules of rain fell from the branches above and burst open on my head, sending streams of icy water down my neck and back. I made a run for the verandah, arriving just as the front door burst open.

Lynne Crocker stormed out, slamming the door behind her.

"Lynne, hi!"

She opened her purse, rummaging inside. "Hi, Trevor."

"Has the inspector arrived yet?" I asked.

"Arrived and departed."

"He left? Why?"

She pulled out a cigarette and struck a match, sheltering it in the wind. Taking a deep drag, she exhaled the words, "Deal's off."

"What do you mean? We're signing the papers tonight."

She rested her elbow on her arm and stared into the rain. "Well, sweetie, I guess that ain't gonna happen now, is it?"

I watched the wind sweep the smoke away. "She can't cancel this late in the game. Can she?"

"Lady Elinor Graverly does whatever the fuck she wants."

"It's me, isn't it? She didn't like me begging like a peasant. She went with another buyer."

She turned to me, a trace of pity softening her harsh features. "No, Trevor, it's not you." Closing her eyes, she sucked on the cigarette as though it were much-needed oxygen. "The house is off the market. She's not moving back to England anymore."

"Why?"

"Who knows? I can't get a straight answer out of the old hag. Something about a lawsuit and the family estate—I think she lost it. You know what? I don't care. I just want my commission. I worked my butt off for three months, and not a cent."

"Maybe I should try to talk to her," I said, turning to contemplate the door.

"Don't bother. She's on a rampage. I had to get out before she hurt me."

There was a angry shriek inside the house, followed by a crash. Alarmed, I backed away from the door. "Maybe we should go," I said, descending the steps. Lynne remained on the verandah, smoking furiously.

I remembered my condo. "I'll have to cancel the sale of my condo."

She laughed. "It's a little late for that. The subjects were removed today. The new owners move in on December 1."

"What? The sale was subject to my buying the manor."

"No, Trevor, the purchase of the manor was subject to the sale of your condo. There's no backing out now. Want me to look into other houses for you?"

"No, Lynne," I said curtly. "I don't."

She dropped the cigarette on the verandah steps, and I watched it sizzle on the damp wood. Opening her umbrella, she descended the steps, crushing the cigarette with her heel, and hurried down the path and out the gate.

7

Noblesse Oblige

I thought Lady Graverly would call to offer an explanation or apology, perhaps even to tell me it was all a big mistake and the manor would be mine after all, but days passed and the call didn't come. With each day I grew more depressed. I felt betrayed, seduced into falling for the manor and then callously rejected. I phoned Lynne Crocker several times to see if Lady Graverly had reconsidered, to ask if she had heard from her at all, but she didn't return my calls. One night, feeling especially distraught, I drove to the manor and stood under the evergreen tree, hoping to catch a glimpse of the Grande Dame of Graverly Manor. But the curtains remained tightly shut, the front door resolutely closed. I saw no sign of guests and wondered if she had closed the manor. I had no choice but to accept that it was not meant to be. It was time to move on.

Not only did I not have a job, I was soon to be homeless too. I asked my mother if I could move back in with her until I got back on my feet. She complied willingly, feigning great sympathy for my disappointment. I suspected she was secretly pleased to have me back in her clutches.

As moving day approached, I stepped up plans for my escape, applying for general manager positions at four- and five-star hotels in cities across North America. My inquiries were met by a resounding silence. Only the Harbourside Hotel demonstrated any interest. I went through the motions half-heartedly, agreeing to take the personality assessment, which I must have passed, however unintentionally, because I was summoned to meet with Mr. Gupta, Mr. Chagani's uncle, a reptilian man in a silvery suit with protruding eyes and slicked-back hair. He didn't ask me what kind of vegetable I would be, but he did inquire about salary expectations and responded to my modest reply with a full minute of grave silence. Next, I was interviewed by his daughter, a self-styled Ismaili Ivanka Trump fresh out of Cornell, whose questions about yield management theory and guest loyalty metrics seemed more intended to show off her knowledge, rudimentary at best, than to test mine. I made it to the next round, an interview with a perspiring, thuggish fellow named Mr. Salani, whose connection to the business was nebulous.

Then… nothing.

I began to fear my career had peaked, that my prime had come and gone without my knowing it had arrived. I was destined to work in middle management at a third-rate hotel, to die a bachelor in my mother's home. Above all, I loathed my indolence, which sucked every last watt of energy from me, turning me into a sloth and playing nasty tricks on my self-esteem. I resolved to take the first job offered to me, even if I had to don a visor and serve donuts and coffee side by side with Janet at Tim Horton's. But Tim Horton's wasn't hiring.

The day before I was scheduled to vacate my condo, I received a couriered offer from the Harbourside. My expectations took another blow when I saw the wage: a lowball offer, well below the number I had given Mr. Gupta. The start date was four days away. It was a job, I told myself, an opportunity for a fresh start. I went into the kitchen to grab a pen and tried to ignore Nancy's presence there, seated on the countertop, observing me with a pained expression. I signed the contract and placed it in an envelope by the door, intending to drop it off in person the next day, then resumed packing.

A few hours later, the intercom buzzed.

"It's Mom! I thought I'd help you pack."

"No worries," I said, surveying the chaos around me. "I've got everything under control."

"Then I'll just pop up for a quick visit. I brought you something."

"Um …" Beginning tomorrow, she would have unfettered access to me. Why did she have to see me tonight, on my last night of peace?

"Buzz me in, for god's sake. It's freezing out here!"

I pulled on some jeans, ran a comb through my hair, and went to answer the door. Mom gave me a peck on the cheek and waltzed in, handing me a plastic grocery bag. "An early Christmas present. Good lord, what a disaster! I thought you said you had everything under control?"

"I do. It just doesn't look that way." I pulled boxes, stacks of news-papers, and dying plants out of the way to clear a path to the sofa.

"Where are the cushions?" she asked.

"In my car."

With a sigh, she sat on the hard surface of the sofa and patted the place next to her. "I thought we could have a little visit, then I'll give you a hand."

Visiting was the last thing I wanted to do. Mom was in one of her semi-manic states, fluttering her arms and twitching her head like a skittish bird.

"Open the gift!" she cried, clapping her hands.

"The wrapping is beautiful," I said, reaching into the plastic bag with trepidation and pulling out an encyclopedic book. Another self-help book for hopeless losers? "*The Consummate Host*?" I said, shooting her a quizzical look. "Is that like Miss Manners?"

"No, it's written especially for hoteliers and innkeepers. You've never heard of it? It was penned by a British aristocrat who handled travel accommodations for the Queen for three decades and then converted his family's castle into a luxury inn."

"Have you been there or something?" I asked, opening the book. It was a curious choice for my mother, who was more likely to buy me books like *What Color Is Your Parachute?* to encourage me to explore other vocations.

"I wish. It sounds gorgeous. But he died recently, and the inn has since been closed. I thought you might benefit from some of his trade secrets. I browsed through it when it first came out. I've been looking for it in bookstores, but it's gone out of print. I'm giving you my only copy."

She slid closer to me as I flipped through pages filled with glossy photos of grand salons decorated with tapestries and bearskin rugs, a drawbridge and moat, and a crumbling turret.

"The author dedicated his life to the comfort of others and died a lonely man," she said.

I closed the book, irritated, and set it on the coffee table. As always, the gift came with an agenda. "Some old guy who ran an old castle in the English countryside won't be of much help where I'm going," I said, getting up.

"Going?" Her eyes fluttered up at me. "Where are you going?"

"I accepted the job at the Harbourside."

Her mouth fell open in shock, but she quickly composed herself and forced a smile. "Well! I suppose congratulations are in order, then!" Disappointment tugged at the corners of her lips. "I thought you didn't want that job?"

"I don't exactly have a lot of options, do I?"

"You have lots of options, Trevor. The perfect job will come along. Did you check back with the Four Seasons? Maybe they—"

"Will you please shut up about the Four Seasons?"

Her lips tightened. I regretted my words but they had the desired effect. She sat quietly, eyes fixed on the book, while I resumed packing. Why were family relationships so complex? Seemingly lighthearted conversations with my mother were always laden with words and intonations that poked and prodded, stirring up emotions I preferred to keep buried. I had missed Sunday dinner for three consecutive weeks, dodged her invitations to meet for coffee or go for a walk, blocked her every attempt to cover this last item on her itinerary. Now she had dropped by unannounced, jittery and dangerous, determined to drag me through the full tour whether I wanted it or not.

"I met the author once," she said casually, fetching a pillow from the floor and placing it beneath her.

"Did you," I said, disinterested. I shooed Nuggle out of a box and threw some books in it.

She reached for the book and placed in on her lap, absently smoothing the cover as she talked. "It was the late sixties, and the hospital where I was doing my practicum had invited him to scout a potential visit from the Queen. She was considering coming to Vancouver after opening the World Expo in Montreal, and they hoped she would conduct the ribbon-cutting ceremony for the new pediatrics ward I worked in. He was so tall and charming, we girls were smitten. The next day, he came back for another visit and stopped by my station to ask me out. I was engaged to Charles at the time, but I accepted out of a sense of duty to the hospital. That night, he took me to dinner at the top-floor restaurant in the Hotel Vancouver. I had never been anyplace like it. I was a simple girl engaged to a blue-collar man, and I was dining with a man who spoke to the Queen of England on a regular basis!"

Mom paused, enjoying the memory. "He was much older than me, of course, probably in his mid-forties back then, but even in this photo, twenty years later, he still looks dashing." She handed the book to me, pointing to a photograph on the back cover.

I glanced at the stiff-looking man posing in front of the castle's massive wooden doors in an old-fashioned double-breasted suit and ascot, a black Labrador retriever at his feet. There was something vaguely familiar about him; perhaps I had seen him in a documentary or TV interview. "*The Consummate Host* and his faithful companion Regent," said the caption.

"Handsome devil," I said, handing it back. "The dog, that is. The old guy looks like a pompous windbag."

"Trevor, please." She sat hugging the book with her thin, frail-looking arms, her eyes sentimental. "The Queen didn't visit Vancouver on that trip. She was traveling on the Royal Yacht Britannia. But he was smitten and sent me all sorts of love letters. I never responded; I loved Charles. I never saw him again, but he sent me this book when it first came out in 1988. After all those years, he still hadn't forgotten about me." She flipped a page. "Look, see his dedication."

I gave it a cursory look, not interested in hearing about Mom's old boyfriends, and lifted Nuggle out of another box.

"Trevor, do you remember our conversation in LA last summer, when you were so distraught over Nancy? I told you about the guilt I suffered after your father's death."

"Over being such a bad mother?"

"Dear, be serious. I told you I feared that all my needling had caused his aorta to burst. He had been unemployed for months, and he just sat around and moped. I was terrified we were going to lose the house. When he totaled our only car, I was furious. Then he started complaining about chest pains, and I dismissed them as a cry for sympathy, another excuse to not look for work. I was so distraught, Trevor, I wasn't myself. That morning, when I saw him reading the sports section instead of the classifieds, I flew into a rage. I told him I regretted the day I married him, that my life would have been so much better if I had married the nobleman. With typical arrogance, he told me to leave if I was so unhappy, but the kids were staying with him. I lashed out even more, firing every piece of verbal ammunition I had in my stockpile, and then stormed off. An hour later, your Aunt Germaine found him lying dead on the floor. For twenty years I blamed myself, regretted the terrible things I had said. I finally stopped beating myself up when I was diagnosed with cancer."

"I'm sorry you suffered for so long, Mom, but what do you want me to say? That I wish you had married the nobleman? If you had, Janet and Wendy and I wouldn't be around today, would we?" Somewhere in the rubble around us, my cell phone was ringing. I lowered myself to my knees and dug around for it. "I think you're sitting on my phone."

She stood up. "Listen to me, Trevor. I'm telling you this for a reason."

Reaching under the sofa, I found the phone. "Hold on, this could be the Four Seasons."

"Mr. Lambert," came a distant voice. "It's Lady Elinor Graverly. I've decided to sell you the manor subject to certain conditions. Please come over at once."

★ ★ ★ ★ ★

"You will move into the manor and assume the role of innkeeper for a trial period of one month, during which time I will assess your suitability."

Lady Graverly was standing at the window with her back to me, pulling back the dark velvet curtain and peering out, as though expecting another visitor. Her red wig was piled on her head Marie-Antoinette-style. There were no martinis tonight, no roaring fire, no warm glow of mutual admiration. In the reflection of the window I could see her troubled eyes.

I cleared my throat. "Is a trial period necessary? My experience speaks for itself."

She spun around, letting the curtain fall. "This isn't about experience, young man, this is about your commitment to preserving the legacy of this manor. I shall not allow my home to be turned into an amusement park."

"I've already assured you that is not my intention."

"Think of it as an apprenticeship," she said, her tone brightening. She moved to her chair in front of the fireplace and sat down. "It will be an opportunity for you to acquaint yourself with the manor and for the manor to acquaint itself with you. At the end of the probationary period, should either party wish to part ways, it shall be done without ill will or penalty. For your services, I shall pay you a modest stipend. I trust these conditions meet with your approval?"

I regarded her peculiar little face. Her heavy makeup, intended to make her look younger, had the opposite effect. Her features were slightly lopsided; the left side drooped slightly and looked less guarded than the right. Perhaps she had suffered a stroke. Was it true her husband had run off with the chambermaid, abandoning her with a sickly newborn child? I felt a wave of sorrow and pity.

"During this probationary period," I said to stall her while I mulled over the proposal, "you would like me to run the manor?"

"Precisely. Naturally, you will be expected to abide by manor rules, to conduct yourself as a true gentleman in the spirit of noblesse oblige. Are you familiar with the term?"

"Vaguely," I said, recalling my first-year history class.

"With privilege comes responsibility." She lifted the bell. "Lincoln, Mr. Lambert will be leaving now." She pulled herself to her feet. "Miss Crocker will provide the particulars."

I stood up with her. "Shouldn't we sign a letter of understanding or something?"

Her eyes flashed. "My word does not suffice?"

"Of course it does. It's just that … this arrangement is a bit unorthodox, don't you think?"

"Whatever do you mean?"

Lynne's comment came back to me: *I can't get a straight answer out of the old hag.* "May I ask what changed your mind? Lynne mentioned something about a lost lawsuit."

She fixed her gaze on me, unblinking. After a tense moment, she said, "Young man, my affairs are none of your business. If you must know, I am presently not at liberty to transfer the title of the manor due to a small legal trifle concerning my husband. I expect to have the matter settled in the coming weeks. While I attend to these affairs, I could use a little help around the house. It's that simple."

"And then what? Will you move to England?"

A smile spread over her lips. "Why, I'm abdicating, of course."

I nodded slowly, confused and intrigued. The prospect of moving in with this woman was both attractive and repulsive. Yet she was right, it was an opportunity to get to know the manor, to unearth any unpleasant surprises. If I didn't like what I discovered, I could walk away.

Lady Graverly's expression grew cross. "I see the terms are unsatisfactory to you. Very well, then, I shall inform Miss Crocker to contact other parties. Lincoln, for god's sake, where are you? Mr. Lambert wishes to be seen out!"

She started toward the door.

"When would you like me to move in?" I called after her.

She stopped and turned around, breaking into a resplendent smile. "Sunday would be most suitable."

"In two days?"

"Indeed."

I could bypass moving in with my mother entirely. "Fine, I'll do it."

She came to me and clutched my hands. "Oh, Mr. Lambert, I'm so happy we have come to an agreement."

Her fingers felt like tree bark, but my heart swelled. "As am I," I said, "as am I." I wouldn't have to take the job at the Harbourside. My future was no longer uncertain. I wouldn't die a bachelor in my mother's house. A burst of emotion welled within me, and I suppressed a sob.

Lincoln appeared in the doorway. "You rang, my lady?"

"Mr. Lambert shall be moving into the manor on Sunday to assume responsibility as innkeeper. Kindly remove your belongings from the tower room and occupy the butler's pantry until further notice."

"As you wish, your ladyship."

"Surely that's not necessary," I said, disquieted by the thought of displacing Lincoln. "Why don't I move into one of the guestrooms for the time being?"

"I'm afraid that's out of the question," said Lady Graverly. "The manor will be very busy in the coming weeks. I bid you good night, Mr. Lambert."

I watched her cross the front hall to her apartment and disappear. Weeks ago, I had resolved to be more spontaneous and entrepreneurial, but had I just made a rash decision and a huge mistake? I hadn't even seen her private quarters yet—the place where I would reside after she moved out, possibly for the rest of my life.

"Sir?" Lincoln was holding the door open.

"I really don't need your room," I said. "I'm sure we can come up with some other arrangement."

"Have a pleasant evening, Mr. Lambert."

I stepped onto the verandah and turned to him. "I could stay at my mother's house, and—"

The door closed in my face.

My head swimming, I stumbled down the steps and hurried down the path. When I reached the street, I turned around, hoping my doubts would be allayed by the manor's enchanting facade. A movement drew my attention to the front window of the private quarters. Lady Graverly was peering out. I lifted my hand to wave, but the curtain fell shut, and she vanished.

8

Lord of the Manor

Sunday was a perfect early December day, cold but sunny and bright.

I pulled up to Graverly Manor and shut off the ignition, turning in my seat to admire the house. Its exterior sparkled through the evergreen foliage in the late-morning sun. The windows, curtained and still, invited intrigue. In only one month, this sizable piece of property, in a highly desirable neighborhood in one of the most beautiful cities in the world, would be mine.

My home.

A jolt from behind caused my head to snap back. Spinning around in my seat, I saw Wendy lurch up behind me in her '84 Dodge Caravan. I shot her an angry look, but she was looking over her shoulder, backing up. I saw her nudge the car behind her before settling for a position three feet from the curb. Inside the suburban express, with its laminate paneling and corroded wheel wells, five rambunctious children were pawing at the windows, desperate to escape after the long drive from Surrey. As I climbed out, the door of the van slid open, and the kids charged toward the house. I shot a nervous glance at the front door, praying Lady Graverly was not in residence. Circling to the rear of my car, I squatted before the bumper and ran my finger along a scuff in the paint.

"Sorry," Wendy said. "Quinn bumped me."

Mom's silver Audi pulled up in the space in front of me, and Mom and Janet got out. Donning a cowboy hat, Janet waddled to the rear door and unstrapped Wendy's infant daughter from the car seat. The baby was shrieking.

"Shut up, Kailie," said Janet.

"Janet!" Wendy cried. "Be nice."

"She's been crying since we left the freeway."

"She's not a city girl," Wendy said, taking the baby from Janet and bouncing her in her arms, glancing around warily. "Just like her mother."

Janet turned to regard the house. "It's pink!" she said with a snicker.

"Dusty rose," I corrected her with an exaggerated simper, making a mental note to add a paint job to my plans. Janet and Wendy were observing the house with the same squinty-eyed, dubious expression—a Lambert trademark I had not inherited. It was like I had just introduced them to a new girlfriend they had already decided to dislike. "All right, let's get to work," I said, pulling open the hatch of the van.

"You could have bought five houses in Maple Ridge for that price," said Janet.

"I haven't paid anything yet." I glared at my mother, who must have told them the price. Sliding a box of my belongings out, I handed it to Janet to put her to work, and then grabbed one for myself and followed her to the gate.

Lady Graverly's immaculate yard had been transformed into a playground, with kids chasing one another across the lawn, swinging from the branches of the oak tree out front, and peering into the windows.

"Look, Emily, a monster!" Jordan cried, banging on the curtained window of the private quarters. Emily screeched in terror and fled. Jordan chased after her, arms outstretched like a zombie, making loud moaning sounds.

"Aiden, put that … thing … down!" Janet hollered as we made our way up the path.

Aiden was lugging Sir Fester out of the bushes. The cat's ears were pinned back, his matted tail whipping back and forth. I opened my mouth to caution him when it emitted a yowl and leapt from his arms. Aiden chased him along the verandah railing and into the shrubs. I was glad I had let Nuggle bunk down at Mom's house for the time being; Sir Fester could have taken the chubby little furball out with one swipe.

Setting my box down on the steps, I followed Janet back to the van, observing her clothing with a mixture of shock and resignation. I hadn't expected her to wear a ball gown on moving day, but why did she insist on wearing relics from the eighties? Tight acid-wash jeans and a checkered Mac jacket. Wendy trotted past in green plastic Crocs and a baggy sweatshirt that made her look pregnant, lugging the faux Louis Vuitton bag she had lent me for the move, a souvenir she had picked up on Canal Street in New York. Where they had acquired their fashion sense was beyond me. Certainly not from my mother, who clipped past in a stylish white turtleneck and grey wool slacks. She was humming as if she were having a marvelous time, a public persona she tried to project even when moving.

"JORDAN, where is Emily?" Janet barked. "I told you not to let her out of your sight!"

"I think she went into the house, Jan," Wendy called out.

"Why don't you take the kids down to the park?" I suggested to Janet as we reloaded. "I can finish this up in a few trips. I don't know why Mom insisted on making this a family occasion."

"These days, Mom turns a trip to the 7-Eleven into a family occasion," Janet said. "AIDEN, STOP TORMENTING THAT CAT!"

Her voice bounced off the buildings around us, causing passersby to stare. It was not the first impression I had hoped to make on my new neighbors.

Aiden crawled out of the underbrush, hugging Sir Fester.

"Aiden, careful," I called out. "That cat is—"

Before I could finish my sentence, Sir Fester lunged at Aiden, clawing both sides of his face, and darted into the underbelly of the house. Aiden let out a cry and clutched his face with both hands, falling to his knees.

"Oh, for Christ's sake!" Janet cried, dropping her suitcase and marching over. "I told you to put that cat down!" She knelt in front of him. "Lemme see."

Aiden lowered his hands, revealing a trail of scratches down both cheeks. Seeing smears of blood on his hands, he burst into tears.

"Oh, please," Janet snapped. "It's just a couple scratches. Don't be a baby."

I felt sorry for the kid. The cat's claws could inflict serious pain, and I had the scars to prove it. I'd always figured that Janet's tough-love approach was based on her own discomfort with sentimentality.

Janet wiped down Aiden's face with a tissue and gave him a hug, heaving herself to her feet.

"You gonna be okay, buddy?" I asked.

"He'll live," Janet said, returning to pick up the suitcase.

"That savage beast attacked me a few weeks ago," I told Aiden, showing him my battle wound. "I think it's possessed."

Aiden gave a cursory look at my hand and squinted up at me with a look that said, "Who are you, and why should I care?"

"JORDAN!" Janet growled from the verandah. "If you don't be nice to your sister, I'm going to lock you in the trunk of Grandma's car."

"Tate, honey," came Wendy's pleading voice from the Caravan, "whatever that is in your mouth, please remove it at once."

I climbed into the van and contemplated hiding there. There was only one item left, the copy of *The Consummate Host* Mom had given me, which I intended to stuff in the garbage at the first opportunity. I was carrying it to the house when one of the boys approached me, his hair netted with cobwebs.

"Is this place haunted, Uncle Trevor?"

"No … Tate … it's not haunted."

"I'm Quinn. Tate is my cousin. He's only four. I'm seven."

"Just testing you."

He trailed after me to the gate. "How come you don't want to manage hotels anymore?"

"I'm still going to manage a hotel," I said. "It's just a very small hotel."

"Grandma said an evil old witch lives here."

"Well, it takes one to know one."

"When I'm growed up, I wanna be a hotel manager like you."

"I thought you wanted to be a figure skater."

"That's Tate. Grandma says I should work at the Four Seasons."

"Of course she does. Here, take this book and read it carefully. Do the opposite of everything it says, and you'll be a great hotel manager some day." I ruffled his hair, catching a handful of silky spider web, and watched him run off to put the book in the van. Quinn was now officially my favorite.

In the front yard, all activity had frozen as though a spell had been cast. Elinor Graverly had swanned onto the verandah in one of her period costumes and was eyeing the children around her with a stricken expression, as though she had heard about this barbaric species but had yet to encounter it. Catching sight of me, she gave a cry of delight and hurried down the steps.

"Why, Mr. Lambert, you're here! How perfectly divine!" She turned each cheek for a kiss, and I complied awkwardly, conscious of my sisters' mocking stares. "This must be your charming family!" she said, turning around. "How do you do, everyone! I'm Lady Andrew Graverly." She gestured to Janet, who had removed her cowboy hat and was smirking at her. "This must be your mother. Delighted to meet you!"

Janet's smirk disappeared. "I'm his sister."

"Why, of course you are! Do forgive me, my eyes aren't what they used to be." She turned to Wendy. "And who is this lovely creature?"

"I'm Wendy," she said, giving a mock curtsy. "Pleased to meet you, ma'am."

"And where is your delightful mother?" asked Elinor, spinning in a circle.

I looked around but couldn't see her. "She's around here somewhere."

"I cannot wait to tell her what an absolute prince she has for a son. And look at her daughters, how robust and fertile they are, with all these adorable little offspring." She beamed at Wendy. "And another on the way!"

Wendy let out a gasp.

Lady Graverly looked down at Tate, who was staring at her wide-eyed, a knuckle in his mouth. "And what's your name, little one?"

He burst into tears and hid behind Wendy, who looked like she might do the same.

"I see I haven't lost my magic touch with children," Lady Graverly said. "Now where on earth is Lincoln? We can't possibly have you ladies doing manual labor, particularly in this one's condition."

"I'm not pregnant," Wendy growled.

"Lincoln? Lincoln! Come out here at once! Mr. Lambert, I do apologize, but I cannot stay. I'm late for church. Lincoln will show you to your room. He and the chambermaid, Agnes, have been so looking forward to your arrival. I shall see you at cocktail hour. Au revoir, little ones!" She waltzed down the street, as spry as a woman twenty years younger.

As she rounded the corner, Mom climbed out of the Caravan.

"Were you hiding, Mom?" I asked.

"Hiding? Of course not. I was just checking the vehicles to make sure we didn't miss anything."

I shot her a dubious look and hurried up the steps, where Lincoln was trying to wrestle a suitcase from Janet's hands. She refused, unwilling to give it to someone so old. At last he surrendered and lifted a box from the floor, shuffling into the manor.

"Your new girlfriend's really cute," quipped Janet.

"Thanks, Mom," I shot back.

I caught up with Lincoln on the landing, where he had stopped to catch his breath. "I'll take that," I said.

"First door on the right," he rasped.

On the third floor I passed a sign marked Private: Servants' Quarters and mounted a narrow flight of stairs. At the top, I entered a dimly lit vestibule with three closed doors. Pushing open the first door on the right, I entered a small, circular room. It was sparsely furnished, with a single bed, a nightstand, a bookshelf, and a metal washbasin.

The hardwood floors were worn, the wallpaper yellow and faded. As I crossed over to the closet, my hair grazed the ceiling.

"Fancy," Wendy remarked as she came in, dropping a box on the bed. She walked to the far wall to inspect an oval-framed oil painting. "She looks happy."

Over Wendy's shoulder I observed a long-necked, mournful woman in a milkmaid hat, cradling an alabaster baby in her arms.

Wendy let out a gasp. "Is that baby sleeping or …?"

"It's sleeping," I said quickly, shuddering. "I hope I remembered to pack my Pamela Anderson poster."

Janet barged in and tossed the faux Vuitton on the bed. "Why is there a deadbolt on the outside of this door?"

Mom squeezed around her. "You're staying in the top of the tower. How fun!"

"Yeah, the Tower of London," Janet muttered, walking to the small, rectangular window overlooking the street. "There are bars in this window! This house is creepy."

I went downstairs for another load and looked around for Lincoln.

"JORDAN!" Janet shouted behind me. "Don't climb on Uncle Trevor's fancy car! You know he doesn't like people touching his precious things."

I shot her a look, and she flashed her teeth.

Ten minutes later, we were done. Janet and Wendy went to explore the house while Mom helped me unpack.

"It's stuffy in here," Mom said, rattling the window. "Gosh, I think it's nailed shut."

A thump on the wall made us jump.

"The walls are so thin," Mom whispered. "Who's next door?"

"It must be the housekeeper, Agnes."

Mom cleared the bed and lay down. "Oh my, I could fall asleep right here."

"It's that comfortable?"

"I'm that tired. It feels like a bed of nails." She observed me through the mirror on the wall. "I assume you won't be coming back to the house for dinner tonight? How about next Sunday?"

Our conversation in my apartment the other night had been cut short by Lady Graverly's call. "Depends," I said, placing a stack of the self-help books she had given me over the years on the bookshelf. "You making your rosemary chicken?" Now that I was moving into the manor, I didn't feel the need to avoid her anymore. Whatever she so desperately wanted to tell me, I was ready to listen.

"If that's all it takes to get you to come, then sure," she said, rolling over to gaze up at the shallow ceiling.

Janet and Wendy returned. "The house is beautiful, Trevor," said Wendy.

Janet nodded. "But you'd never catch me alone here at night."

"Where are the kids?" I asked, peering out the window.

"They're hiding in the van," said Janet. "They're afraid the scary lady will come back."

"She's not scary," I said.

"She looks like an evil clown with that red wig and white makeup."

Wendy giggled. "More like a drag queen."

"You're just mad because she thought you were pregnant," I said.

"At least she didn't think you were his mother," Janet said to Wendy, turning to glare at me.

"That woman is remarkable," Mom said from the bed. "She must be in her eighties and still going strong. We should all be so lucky."

"You sure you know what you're getting yourself into?" Janet asked me, looking around. "This place looks like it's going to need a lot of work."

"Maybe you and Wendy could help," Mom suggested, sitting up. "We could turn it into a family business."

"It's not going to be a family business," I said. "Listen, we're done here. You guys are free to go anytime."

"Why don't we all go for a walk down to the lagoon?" Mom suggested. "I have a little story about an Englishman I'd like to tell the kids." She gave a wicked cackle.

I thought about telling Mom that the drowned Englishmen was Elinor Graverly's husband but decided to wait for another time, not wishing to delay their departure. "You guys go ahead," I said. "I need to get settled in."

Downstairs, Wendy asked me if I was free for lunch on Friday. "I could swing by around one o'clock," she offered.

"Sure, anytime. I'm not going anywhere."

Outside, Wendy opened the van door and did a head count. "Where's Quinn?"

I turned to search the yard and spotted Quinn across the street, rounding the corner of an apartment building. He was chasing Fester. "Quinn, careful!" I called out. "A car's coming!"

Not hearing me, he dashed toward the street, heading directly into the path of a speeding Land Rover. Sir Fester reached the curb and stopped, turning his head as though checking to make sure the boy was following, and then scurried across the street. Quinn charged after him.

All four of us shouted for Quinn to stop.

He stumbled onto the street, tripped, and fell headfirst in front of the truck. The driver slammed on his brakes, screeching to a halt only inches from the boy. Quinn let out a yelp and rolled away.

We rushed over and helped him to his feet.

Feeling sick to my stomach, I stepped back to give Wendy some space as she comforted her son. She was trying to show a brave face, but I could see the terror in her eyes. A matter of seconds and things might have turned out tragically. As she walked the boy to the car, the driver, looking traumatized, called out further apologies and then drove off. I stayed behind, surveying the neighborhood with wary eyes. With kids around, danger lurked everywhere.

A few minutes later, the Caravan pulled away. I waved to the kids but they stared straight ahead, rendered mute by the near-fatal incident.

I stood with my back against the front door, listening for signs of life. The house was silent. Having resided in urban environments most of my adult life, I had grown to prefer noise over silence, though not the frenetic sounds of rambunctious children and stressed-out parents. Now, the prospect of being alone in the manor was suddenly unsettling. Not yet the owner, nor a paying guest, nor even a bona fide employee, I felt like an intruder.

I made my way up the winding staircase, running my hand along the well-worn mahogany banister, and tried to imagine whose hands had followed this trajectory in the past hundred years. On the landing between the second and third floors, I stopped to regard a framed black-and-white photograph of four young women in wide-brimmed hats posing in an open-topped Studebaker. Judging by their style of clothing and the old-growth trees in the backdrop, the photo had been taken in the early 1900s in Stanley Park. Three of the women sported similar dour expressions—the Denby sisters, I guessed, the house's original occupants. The fourth woman, who looked partly aboriginal, had broken the photographic conventions of the day by smiling. I tried to picture the sisters in the house. Which bedrooms had they occupied? Why had none of them married? Perhaps their grim expressions had frightened away suitors.

I continued up the stairs, passing more closed doors. Where were all the guests? I decided there must be a lull between weekend travelers, who would have checked out by now, and weekday travelers, who were likely to arrive later in the day. How strange it would be to cohabitate with guests. In hotels I had watched them come and go, and at the end of the day I could retreat to the privacy of my own home. Here I would live among them, obliged to pass through a gauntlet of guestrooms to reach my own room. It would take some getting used to.

On the fourth floor, Agnes's door remained shut. It struck me as odd that she hadn't come out to greet me, yet there would be plenty of time to get acquainted. I entered my room and looked around. How could Lincoln have endured this tiny circular cell for fifty years—assuming this had always been his room? There was no trace of his presence save for a few scuffs on the walls and scratches on the sideboards. Last night the room had been Lincoln's home; tonight it would be mine; in the future it would host different guests every few nights. Hotel rooms had an uncanny way of reinventing themselves with each new guest, making occupants feel at home, if only for one or two nights.

The floorboards squeaked under my feet. Not wishing to disturb Agnes, I sat down on the bed. I wanted to explore the house but thought it appropriate to wait for a chaperone. If Agnes came out, maybe she would be willing to show me around. I got up to listen at the wall. I could hear nothing, yet I sensed she was there, reading or napping, perhaps even pressing her own ear against the wall. I lay down again, my legs dangling over the side of the cot. The pillow felt as flat and heavy as a lead x-ray apron. I closed my eyes, allowing my mind to drift... I was in a sleek, modern hotel room, luxuriating on a king bed, buried in soft linens and down pillows... Agnes struts in, buxom and breathy, with blotches of red on her ivory cheeks... Her sheer nightgown falls to the floor...

A loud cough yanked me from my reverie. It was followed by a phlegm-filled hack that continued for several minutes, dispelling any notion of a wholesome young maiden next door. I stared up at the ceiling. Why wasn't it cone-shaped like the peaked roof that housed it? It must be a false ceiling. If I opened it up, enlarged the window, and replaced the wallpaper and furnishings, the room would be reasonably appealing; small but rentable. Of course, that would require money I didn't have. So much money was needed. I sat up, suddenly claustrophobic. I crept to the door and opened it, craning my neck toward Agnes's door. Still closed. What was behind the other door? I tiptoed over.

Inside was a bathroom—a filthy, disgusting bathroom. Items of women's clothing were strewn across the floor and over every surface, blouses and frocks, stockings and bras. A pile of soiled towels sat in the bathtub, and no-name beauty products crowded the sink and the back of the toilet. I retreated hastily, thinking I had trespassed in Agnes's private bathroom. How could a housekeeper, of all people, keep such an untidy room? Lady Graverly would never tolerate such disorder, to be sure; she must never come up here. Something told me that Agnes was not going to be easy to manage.

Back in my room, I finished unpacking, and then lay down and closed my eyes. My mind was whirling. Janet's voice rang in my ears: *You sure you know what you're getting into?* Followed by Shanna's:

Sometimes we think we want something, and when we get it we realize it's not what we need. The image of Quinn running into the path of the Land Rover flashed and replayed itself over and over.

At last my mind settled, and I sank into a troubled sleep.

9

A Shriek in the Night

A knock at my door jolted me from sleep. I sat up and gazed around in the darkness. Where was I?

A deep, raspy voice called from behind the door. "Master Lambert, are you there?"

"I'm here," I replied, scrambling out of bed. My legs became tangled, and I fell to the floor, striking my shin on the bed's metal leg. With a stifled groan, I pulled myself to my feet, hopping around on one foot and biting my lip to stop from crying out in pain. I flicked on the light and gazed down at the bed. Where had that army blanket come from? I had fallen asleep on top of the thin floral bedspread. Had someone come into the room while I was sleeping?

I shivered.

"Is everything all right in there?" Lincoln called out.

"Yes, fine! Just a minute!"

"Lady Graverly wishes to remind you that you were expected for cocktails at seven."

Uh-oh. "What time is it now?"

"It is 7:03 PM."

No wonder I felt so groggy; I had slept for hours. "Tell her I'll be right down."

"The lady does not take kindly to tardiness, Master Lambert."

I rolled my eyes. Why was he calling me 'master'? "Duly noted, Lincoln. I'd prefer to be called Trevor."

"Duly noted, Master Lambert."

Through the wall I heard a burst of shrill laughter, following by hacking. Agnes. The stairs creaked as Lincoln descended them. Had Agnes covered me with the blanket? Lincoln was likely more inclined to smother me with a pillow after having been displaced from his room. Lady Graverly? Whoever it was, the gesture was appreciated, but from now on I was going to keep the door locked.

I stared into the closet, trying to decide what to wear. I would have loved to pull on a pair of jeans and a sweatshirt, but I had a hunch casual clothing would be greeted with a cry of horror. I selected a collared shirt, navy blazer, and grey slacks, then grabbed my toiletry bag and dashed across the hall to the bathroom.

To my surprise, the bathroom was clean and tidy. Had I dreamed its former state? I went to the sink and splashed water on my face. Several strands of long, grey hair were stuck to the basin. Lifting my head, I saw my reflection blurred by a streak of lipstick. Agnes wasn't thorough, but at least she had made an effort.

When I arrived in the parlor, I found Lady Graverly seated in her usual chair before a roaring fire. "Mr. Lambert, how marvelous to see you!" she cried, rising from her chair to collect her kisses. She was dressed in her finery again, a yellow crinoline dress with a red ribbon tied around her waist.

"I guess we can dispense with the formalities now that I'm a resident," I said as I sat down across from her. "Please, call me Trevor." I waited for her to reciprocate, but she pursed her lips and looked away. "May I call you Elinor?" I asked.

She turned to face me. "I prefer to be addressed by my proper title, but you may call me Lady Graverly if you wish." She gave me a reassuring smile.

"Fair enough," I said, feeling like a cad.

A movement drew my attention to the corner of the room. Lincoln, who had been standing in the shadows, stepped forward with a tray containing a martini. Seeing that Lady Graverly was well into hers, I accepted mine gratefully, hoping it might alleviate the uneasiness I felt in these strange new environs.

"How is everything with your room?" Lady Graverly asked, her dominant eye peering at me over her glass.

"It's perfectly fine, thank you," I replied, sneaking a guilty look at Lincoln, who had his back to me. He reached up to place a martini glass on the shelf of the liquor cabinet, hands trembling, and almost knocked it to the floor.

"Did you meet Agnes?" Lady Graverly inquired.

"She hasn't come out of her room. Is she not well?"

"She keeps to herself mostly. A typical Scot—temperamental, fiercely proud with little reason to be so, and a dreadful housekeeper. We may have to let her go. Pity."

I sneaked another glance at Lincoln, who was now polishing a silver ice pick. Such talk was unwise in front of employees, who tended to gossip. Yet it seemed likely that Lincoln's loyalties lay solely with his mistress.

"I haven't run into any guests," I said. "Are we expecting late arrivals?"

"Tonight we're having a small lull. We have but one guest—a student, a horrid little creature from one of those vulgar southeastern states."

"Kentucky, my lady," Lincoln said, holding a brandy snifter up to the light. There was a chip in the rim, but he placed it on the shelf anyway.

"Lincoln, I feel a draft," said Lady Graverly. "Kindly close the door on your way out."

"Certainly, your ladyship."

I watched Lincoln hobble out, and turned to her. "Is he blind?"

"Blind? I certainly hope not. I've never really paid much attention." Her tone brightened. "Tell me about your charming family."

"What would you like to know?"

She set her drink down and observed me, a bemused expression creeping over her face. "You aren't like them, are you?"

"What do you mean?"

"They are lovely people, of course. But ever so common."

My fingers tightened around my glass. "I'm not sure I understand."

"You, Mr. Lambert, are a true gentleman. You remind me of what my husband once was, what my son might have been. Do you ever feel as though you were born into the wrong family? Once in a while, the good lord makes a mistake. A blueblood is born into a common family, a commoner is born into a noble family."

I was not sure whether to be flattered or offended. "I wouldn't trade my family for the world," I said.

"And why would you?" She gave an expression of distaste. "But those children, oh, how unruly they are!"

"They're actually pretty good kids," I said, chuckling.

"Chaos reigns in the presence of children. Yet they are a necessary evil; without children, there is no one to carry on the family name. For a bloodline to go extinct is truly tragic, don't you think? Do you intend to have offspring of your own?"

"One day. Soon, I hope."

"But you have no wife. Your heart was broken?"

I shifted in my seat. This woman had a way of dropping personal questions like comments about the weather. "We all get our hearts broken at some time."

"Indeed."

I had hoped our conversation might lead to an explanation of the demise of her husband, but her attention remained focused on me. "You are an old soul, Mr. Lambert. And so underappreciated." She leaned toward me, her eyes intense. "Tell me, do you believe in destiny?"

The door to the dining room creaked open. Sir Fester padded in and hopped onto Lady Graverly's lap. I watched her fingers, as thick and gnarled as the roots of bonsai tree, rake over the cat's fur. She seemed unbothered by the cat's scabs and patches of exposed skin. Sir Fester turned his head and gazed at me languidly.

"What exactly do you mean by 'destiny'?" I asked.

"Entitlement. Justice. Being put on this earth for a purpose."

"In a way, I suppose, yes," I replied, deciding it wasn't the right time to share my bleak views that life was random, a solitary journey with no purpose or meaning, a constant struggle to ward off chaos and alienation. "Why do you ask?"

"Because I think destiny brought you and I together."

I thought of the comment I had made to Shanna: *It's fate*. It was true that I felt a connection to the old woman, but we had been brought together to conduct a business transaction and nothing more. Instinct told me to beware, to avoid getting attached. I was growing weary of her cryptic intercourse anyway; I wanted answers to questions that had bothered me since I first toured the manor.

"Lady Graverly," I said, "can you tell me about the rumors about this house?"

"Rumors? What rumors?"

"People say the manor is haunted."

She pressed a hand to her chest. "Haunted? By whom?"

"By your husband."

"How preposterous!"

"That's what I thought. Forgive me, but I needed to ask."

"Ghosts at Graverly Manor, imagine!" She tittered.

I leaned toward her. "May I ask what happened to your husband?"

Sir Fester bolted upright and scurried out of the room.

"Lord Graverly? Why, he vanished into thin air."

"Didn't you say he drowned?"

"That was the popular sentiment at the time, but I never believed it. I suppose it will remain one of life's mysteries."

I braved another question. "I heard another rumor, about a chambermaid who used to work here. They say Lord Graverly ran off with her."

She gave a cry. "How could you say such a thing? Lord Graverly was a good man. He would never ... " She drifted off, lost in thought.

I felt awful for upsetting her, and yet I was surprised to hear her defend him, having assumed she felt nothing but bitterness toward him. "I'm sorry. I shouldn't have asked. It's none of my business."

She did not respond. She sat, quiet and pensive, her fingers pressed to her lips.

I swallowed the contents of my drink.

Lincoln appeared in the doorway. "Dinner is served, my lady."

"Very well." Lady Graverly pulled herself from the chair and headed toward the door. "Good night, Mr. Lambert."

"We won't be dining together?" I said.

"Lady Graverly takes her dinner in her private quarters, sir," Lincoln said, turning to follow her into the apartment.

The door closed behind them. I heard the click of the lock.

I spent the next couple of hours in my room, folding and refolding clothes, arranging my meager belongings. I set a framed family photograph on the bookshelf and paused to observe it. My sisters and I were standing near the foot of the Emerald chairlift on Whistler Mountain. A trompe l'oeil made the chairlift look like it was about to strike us from behind and decapitate us. Placing the photo next to the stack of self-help books, I slid a pile of back issues of *Hotelier* magazine in front of it. My conversation with Lady Graverly was troubling me. I felt bad about asking such personal questions, forcing her to unearth painful memories she had likely buried long ago, but could she be that oblivious to rumors that seemed so prevalent outside of the manor? Either she lived in denial or had been spared the gossip.

As I puttered around my room, I heard the occasional cough through the wall, but otherwise Agnes kept quiet. Only a paper-thin wall and a few feet of wooden floor separated us, yet she hadn't bothered to emerge from her room to greet me. I felt resentful of Agnes for ignoring me, and of Lincoln for being cold and distant, and of Lady Graverly for being secretive and elitist. It was going to be a long month. Yet I had not been the easiest guest. I had caused havoc upon arrival, had displaced Lincoln from his room, had arrived late for cocktails, and had pried into her personal affairs. I resolved to be more respectful in the coming weeks.

Just past ten, forced by hunger to leave my room, I crept downstairs to the kitchen to forage for food. On the stovetop, I found a large pot hissing and sputtering. Lifting the lid, I discovered a thick brown substance that vaguely resembled beef stew. It looked edible enough. As I searched for some bread to accompany it, I stumbled upon Lincoln's makeshift bedroom in a nook off the pantry. A fold-out bed covered with a wool blanket occupied the space, surrounded by shelves stocked with canned goods, condiments, and bulk foods. On the lowest shelf rested a ratty old toothbrush, a disposable razor and shaving brush, and a tattered copy of the Holy Bible. Observing these sad little living quarters, I was glad I hadn't complained about my own accommodation.

Back in the kitchen, I found a stale baguette in the breadbox, loaded a bowl with stew, and carried the items into the dining room. The stew was bland, but I ate voraciously. As I scraped up the last of the gravy, I heard the front door open. My spirits lifted at the prospect of company, anything to bring life to the house, but the footsteps climbed the stairs and faded off, and a hush fell upon the manor once again.

I washed up the dishes and nosed around the kitchen. It needed a good cleaning, but I was too restless to work. I thought of watching TV and realized I hadn't seen a television set in the house. Deciding I could read in the parlor for a while, I headed down the hallway toward the stairs. As I passed the parlor, I saw a movement out of the corner of my eye and halted, peering through the beveled glass in the upper part of the door. To my surprise, a young, dark-haired woman who looked to be in her mid-twenties sat cross-legged in Elinor Graverly's chair, reading. She lifted her head to turn the page, and I saw swollen lips and an upturned nose. Had Lady Graverly neglected to mention she had a hot young daughter? Or could this be the "horrid little crea-ture" she had referred to—the student? Regardless, things were look-ing up at Graverly Manor. I opened the door.

Absorbed by her book, she didn't look up.

I greeted her cheerfully.

Slowly, she lifted her head. How jarring to see this attractive young woman in the chair normally occupied by Lady Graverly, as though I had closed my eyes and made a wish. For a brief moment, I thought she had two black eyes, but then realized they were thick with mascara. Her hair fell in all directions from a plastic clip. She gave me a quick once-over, grunted hi, and returned to her book.

The fire had long since died, and the room was freezing, yet she seemed perfectly comfortable in yoga tights and a T-shirt. A silver skull with red jewel eyes grinned up at me from the T-shirt.

"I'm Trevor," I said, taking a few steps into the room.

She looked up again, as though surprised I was still there. "Yeah, I know. You're the new butler."

I laughed. "Is that what Lady Graverly told you?"

"Lincoln told me you're his replacement."

"Well, I suppose I am, in a way. Are you the student?"

"Uh-huh. Clarissa Larch." She looked back down at her book.

I did not have a book. To run upstairs and return with one might seem contrived, so I crossed the room and pulled down the lone book from the upper shelf. To my surprise, it was *The Consummate Host*. I wondered if my mother had brought it in from the van, not realizing I had leant it to Quinn. But it was caked with dust. Lady Graverly must have a copy of her own. Dusting it off, I carried it to the chair.

"Mind if I join you?" I asked.

"It's a free world."

I sat down. So she was going to be like this. Opening the book, I flipped to the introduction and pretended to be drawn in immediately. "Running an inn is like raising children," the author wrote. "All of your own needs become secondary. Your work will never be fully appreciated. After you have invested your blood, sweat, and toil in the comfort of your guests, they will check out, and you'll be left alone. Yet if you are anything like me, at the end of the day you will do it all over again, without hesitation, because you are a consummate host."

The author's words, however bleak, rang true. Perhaps I had been too quick to dismiss this book. I sneaked a look at Clarissa. She was pretending I wasn't there, so I resumed reading. "The notion of a bed-and-breakfast originated in Britain, when elderly couples earned extra income by renting a room or two in their home to travelers. Today, bed-and-breakfasts come in all sizes and shapes. My inn is housed in a thirty-two-room castle in the outskirts of Greater London. In this book, I will share some of the lessons I have learned over the years, both as head of travel accommodation for the Queen of England for almost three decades and as innkeeper of my family's castle." I flipped a few pages. "Above all, the key to a successful inn is excellent staff. If you rent four or more rooms, I strongly recommend that you live in separate quarters. The smaller the inn, the more guests will expect the owner to interact with them. Having paid to stay at your inn, they should not be denied this privilege. However, it is essential to set parameters; your guests will find strange and unusual ways to occupy your time at all hours of the day. My sister-in-law manages—"

Clarissa cleared her throat.

I looked up and caught her eye briefly, but she jerked her head down again. I smiled inwardly, thinking she wasn't as disinterested as she pretended. After a moment, she set her book down on the floor and stood up to stretch. I followed her with my eyes as she wandered to the bar in lithe, graceful movements.

"You want a drink?" she asked.

I rose quickly, having temporarily forgotten my role. "Allow me," I said.

"No, *god*. Please, just sit down. I can't stand people doing things for me."

I retreated and sat back down. "Are you enjoying the manor?"

She turned to me and rolled her eyes, showing the whites of her eyeballs in a ghoulish display. "I can't stand it."

I was taken aback. "Why?" I asked.

"The house is fine, I guess. It's the old lady who drives me crazy. She's been scheming to get me out since the day I arrived. I don't quite fit in with her target demographic."

That was going to change the moment I took charge, I resolved, sneaking a furtive look at Clarissa's taut figure.

"I could have stayed in a hotel," she said. "My dad's loaded. But hotel staff drive me nuts. All that obsequiousness—spare me. At least they leave me alone here."

It was not the time to divulge my profession. Rubbing my arms, I said, "Aren't you cold?"

"I like it cold. The colder the better." She poured Canadian Club into a glass and lifted the bottle to the light. "If I go as much as a drop over, she bills me for a full ounce. She calls it an honor bar, but I swear she dusts the bottles for fingerprints. The night I arrived, I was so traumatized by the prospect of living in this old ladies' knitting den, I sneaked a few shots of Cuervo. The next day, she slid a bill under my door." She set the bottle down. "Please stop ogling me."

I quickly averted my gaze. How could she know? She had her back to me. I looked back, searching for a mirror or a reflection in the glass.

"I said stop it."

"I wasn't! How do you—?"

"I can feel your eyes on me." She returned to her chair, brandishing a snifter containing several ounces of whisky, and sat cross-legged again. She reached up to spruce her hair, as though the disarray were intentional. "Anyway, this place is ideal for my research, so I'm not going anywhere."

I looked down at the book she had set on the floor, *Legends of Vancouver*. "What are you studying?"

She sipped her drink. "I'm working on my master's thesis at the University of Kentucky. Right now, I'm reading up on Pauline Johnson, the poet. If you're from here, you've probably read her work."

"I'm sure I have," I said, as though I read poetry all the time.

"She was half-Mohawk, half-white. She used to hang out with the first occupants of this house, the Denby sisters. Have you seen that photo on the second-floor landing of four women in a Studebaker? That's Pauline and the sisters. She was buried not far from here, in Stanley Park. I visit her grave sometimes for inspiration."

"Really."

"Totally."

It figured she was crazy. It was a good segue though. "Have you heard rumors that this house is haunted?"

She choked on her drink. "What do you mean by 'haunted'?"

"Seen any ghosts drifting about?"

She shrugged. "I'm an insomniac. I'm up most of the night, and I sleep during the day only when medicated." She lifted the glass to her mouth, sipped, and let out a cry, pressing two fingers to her lip. A droplet of blood trickled down her chin. I sprang from the chair and grabbed a napkin from the bar, bringing it to her. She took the napkin and pressed it to her mouth, soaking the monogrammed initials *LAG* with blood.

"Thanks," she said casually, reaching for the snifter.

"I'll get you another glass."

"Forget it. They're practically all chipped." She rotated the glass and gulped down the whisky.

I stood over her, concerned. A delicious, intoxicating scent wafted toward me from her hair.

She waved me away. "Sit down, you're making me nervous." As I returned to my chair, she said, "Why, have you seen a ghost?"

"Me? No. I don't believe in ghosts."

"We're all haunted in some way."

"I suppose there's still time. I only arrived today."

She inspected the napkin and set it down. The bleeding had stopped. Picking up the glass, she curled it in her hand, tracing its rim with her finger. I watched, mesmerized, fearing she'd cut herself again, but her finger stopped just as it reached the chip and turned in the opposite direction. An eerie wailing sound rose from the glass. She watched me watching her, and a trace of a smile formed on her lips, softening the glint of hostility in her eyes.

"So what makes you want to work at this mausoleum?" she asked.

"I'm buying it."

"You're buying this place?"

"Why so surprised?"

"No reason." She set the glass down and stood up. "I'm going out for a smoke. I'll see you later, maybe."

"Wait," I called as she headed for the door. "You never told me if this house is haunted."

She turned. "There are no haunted places, only haunted people."

"It's not, then?" I said, feeling relieved in spite of my own skepticism.

"Oh, it's haunted all right—haunted by a pathetic old lady in a red wig who's still pining for her husband, as though he's going to walk through the door after fifty years."

★ ★ ★ ★ ★

I woke up with a start, lungs heaving.

The room was black. Reaching for my cell phone, I pressed the light, blinking to clear my vision. 3:20 AM.

Something had awakened me. What? A piercing shriek. It was still ringing in my ears. Had I dreamt it? Pushing the blanket away, I climbed from the bed. The room was icy cold. I went to the window and parted the curtains. The moon glowed behind a veil of dark clouds. Down the street, a hooded figure was pushing a wheelchair toward the lagoon.

I turned from the window. In the light cast by the moon, my eyes caught the portrait of the mournful woman. She stared back at me, and for a chilling moment it struck me that it was she who had screamed.

Impossible.

Shivering, I climbed into bed and folded the blanket in half, hugging it around me. Curling into a fetal position, I willed myself back to sleep.

Another shriek sent me flying out of bed.

Crouching on the floor, I heard the murmur of a woman's voice, then another shriek. Agnes. I flung open my door and pounded on her door.

"Agnes? Are you okay?"

Silence.

I thrust the door open. In the dim light of the tiny room, I could see two figures writhing on the bed. I grappled for the light switch. The ceiling light flickered on, exposing two naked bodies, a black man on top of a grey-haired woman. They were regarding me in shock.

"Lincoln?" I said. "What are you doing to her?"

"He's givin' me pleasure, ya lunatic!" cried the woman in a thick Scottish accent. "Now get the hell out!"

"I'm sorry! I thought—"

"Goo!" cried Agnes.

"Goo?"

"Go!" barked Lincoln.

I pulled the door closed. My heart was pounding. Lincoln and Agnes? Lincoln could barely make it up the stairs. How unexpected—and disturbing. Fearing the image of his ebony limbs tangled among her pale limbs and wild grey hair was forever imprinted on my mind, I pulled on a bathrobe and crept downstairs.

In the parlor, I tried to open the liquor cabinet in the dark, but the door was stuck. Switching on a lamp, I discovered a large padlock fastening the doors closed. Lady Graverly's way of controlling beverage costs? Deciding a glass of milk would be better for me anyway, I headed through the dining room to the kitchen. The refrigerators were padlocked too. I went into the dining room and sat down. My first day at the manor had been a strange one, and there was only one guest in-house. What would it be like when the house was full? Only twenty-nine days to go, I reminded myself.

Cold air was streaming through cracks in the window frame. I stood up, trembling with cold, and made my way to the stairs. On the third floor, I stopped. Light showed beneath the door of the Edward VI room. I considered knocking but decided it would be inappropriate to disturb Clarissa at this hour. Reluctantly, I climbed the stairs.

Back in my room, I placed the lead-like pillow over my head, feeling like a patient getting a brain x-ray. Eventually, I drifted off, only to be jolted awake by a final ear-splitting shriek. At least I had solved the mystery of the haunting sounds of Graverly Manor, I thought dreamily. It wasn't the dead Scottish chambermaid from fifty years past but the very-much-alive Scottish housekeeper in the throes of ecstasy, courtesy of the septuagenarian butler.

10

Splendid Isolation

"We do not stand on ceremony in this household," Lady Graverly announced. "We genuflect before it."

We were standing in the foyer, the only source of light provided by the pale morning sun shining through the stained-glass window to the left of the front door. It was my first day on the job, and I was feeling nervous and excited—and hungry. After a restless night, I had slept through my alarm. I had hoped to duck into the kitchen for a quick bite, but Lady Graverly had been waiting at the foot of the stairs when I came down, a peevish look on her face. She had begun the orientation session immediately, her commanding voice rising above the gurgling of my stomach.

"I hope you do not intend to dress like this every day," she said, scrutinizing my attire. "Perhaps you thought we would be moving furniture?"

I looked down at my black dress pants, cashmere sweater, and patent leather shoes, perfectly clean, pressed, and of excellent quality. "Is something wrong?"

"As an employee of Graverly Manor, you are expected to wear a three-piece suit and tie or classic tuxedo at all times. I find an ascot to be an exquisite complement to the manor's exalted ambience.

Colorful ties are strictly forbidden, naturally, as are ties with nontraditional patterns, cartoon characters, and any material aside from the finest silk."

"Not to worry, I'm not a loud tie-type of guy. As for a three-piece suit, I haven't worn one since I was twelve." It had been for my father's funeral, but I kept that part to myself.

Arching her brow disapprovingly, she resumed her overview. "Each morning breakfast is served at seven, lunch at noon, tea at four, cocktails at seven, dinner at eight. That is the schedule, and you are expected to respect it."

"You provide all that for your guests?"

"Certainly not; this is my schedule. Guests enjoy a lavish English buffet breakfast each morning between the hours of seven and ten, and cocktail hour in the parlor each evening at seven. I attend when possible—it pleases guests so—but my hectic schedule does not always permit. You, however, are obliged to attend without exception. You will note the words 'cocktail' and 'hour' are singular. Should a guest wish to indulge further, a fee is placed on his or her account. Is that clear, Mr. Lambert?"

I nodded slowly, making a mental note to abolish these rules the moment I took over.

"You think me stringent," she said, "but you will feel much the same way in time. If rules are not clearly communicated, guests will take liberties. Because they are staying in a private home, they fancy themselves entitled to the same courtesies as a relative or friend. They expect the intimacy of a private home and the services of a large hotel. Can you imagine a hotel guest wandering into the kitchen at midnight to help herself to a snack—and then becoming indignant when a surcharge appears on her account? It's simply preposterous."

"Sounds like you get some challenging guests at the manor," I remarked.

"I adore my guests and will do anything for them. But yes, they do get on my nerves on occasion. When it all becomes too much, I take a suite at the Four Seasons, if only for a few hours. There I can be myself. I enjoy a glass of wine, afternoon tea or an evening meal, and I return to the manor rejuvenated." A twinkle of humor appeared in her eyes. "Whereas my guests come here to escape hotels, I go to hotels to escape my guests. I do my best to screen out undesirables, but occasionally one slips through."

The patter of footsteps drew our attention to the stairs. A pair of shapely legs nicked with razor cuts appeared, and for a breathtaking moment I thought Clarissa Larch was stark naked. Then the hem of a black silk negligee came into view, followed by her body, its contours visible through the sheer material, and finally a shock of black hair.

"Why, speak of the devil," Lady Graverly said under her breath.

Clarissa reached the bottom of the stairs and lifted her arms in a loud stretch. Her eyes were smudged with last night's mascara.

"Good morning, Clarissa!" I said cheerily. "How's the lip?"

She squinted at me as though she had no idea who I was. "What time is it, like six AM?"

"It's nine thirty, Miss Larch," Lady Graverly said. "I presume you just arrived home?"

"I was sleeping, actually, for the first time in about a week, and I was awakened by a shrill voice. I thought the Queen had dropped by and someone was strangling her." She wandered down the hallway toward the kitchen. "Hope I'm not too late for breakfast."

"Miss Larch," Lady Graverly called after her. "This is not a sorority house. You are expected to use the bathrobe provided in your room."

"That ratty old thing? I thought it was a bathmat."

I grinned, watching Clarissa disappear through the doorway, and then turned to Lady Graverly.

Her eyes were livid. "Mr. Lambert, at Graverly Manor we always address our guests by surname and title. It creates the necessary distance between guest and innkeeper. Do you understand?"

"Sure," I said affably. "As you wish."

"Now where were we? Oh, yes. As innkeeper, you are required to greet guests upon arrival regardless of the time of day. You are to attend to their needs in a gracious and dignified manner. Graverly Manor has achieved its lofty reputation due to my personal touches, and guests will be deeply disappointed if I am not present to welcome them. A generous amount of goodwill and charm will be required on your part to appease them. Over time, perhaps, they will come because of you." She blinked her eyes in rapid succession, a gesture that suggested she considered this unlikely.

It was becoming clear that Lady Andrew Graverly was not a morning person. I missed the warmth and conviviality of cocktail hour, when she had lavished me with praise, got liquored up and flirty, and called me an aristocrat. Now I was being treated like a servant.

"Elinor," I said, deciding to dispense with the silly formality whether she liked it or not, "mind if I duck down to the kitchen to grab a coffee and a quick bite? I didn't have time for breakfast."

"Why, yes, I do mind," she said, looking shocked by my audacity. "I have two hours to spend with you, young man, and it shan't be wasted while you chase after licentious women. The manor will be extremely busy soon, and I will not always be here to provide guidance. Graverly Manor has achieved its renown due to strict adherence to the cherished traditions of British—"

"With all due respect, I understand that tradition is important here—and you'll be happy to know that providing excellent service is one of my strengths. Maybe we could move on to more practical concerns, such as reservations policies and procedures?"

"Policies and procedures? What on earth do you mean? It's frightfully simple. The phone rings. I answer it, if convenient, and qualify the caller. If the caller sounds suitable, I quote rates. Should he wish to reserve, I record his name in the ledger. What more do you need to know?"

I nodded to the monitor on the desk. "The system isn't computerized?"

"For heaven's sake, child, Graverly Manor has only eight rooms. A hospitality student from Mexico brought that vile contraption in last summer and built a website for the manor. In fifty years, I haven't needed a computer, and I can't imagine why I would need one now. Lincoln likes to tap away at it occasionally, but as far as I've seen, he accomplishes nothing."

"Are room rates recorded in the ledger, then?"

"Certainly not. Our rates vary considerably."

"According to season, day of week, room type?"

"Yes, and also the caller."

"You screen callers?" I said, recalling my mystery shopper call. "Children are not welcome at the manor?"

"Children are banned. As are Germans, Spaniards, and Italians, who are informed without exception that the manor is sold out. Germans are rude and aggressive, stuffing blocks of cheese into their suitcases and whatnot. Spaniards are uncivilized, always breaking things and never tipping staff. And Italians will steal anything that isn't nailed down. The French are marginally more tolerable, but they are contemptuous of anything that isn't French, and I accept their reservations judiciously, charging a premium for their arrogance. I used to furnish this house with priceless antiques, but no more. You will learn not to grow attached to anything at Graverly Manor. Everything and everyone leaves, is broken, or disappears." Her eyes grew wistful, and she turned to gaze at a large portrait on the wall of a British cavalryman on a prancing horse.

"Was that Lord Graverly?" I asked gently.

"No, no. I purchased that painting at a flea market years ago for twenty-five dollars."

"Your target market must be the British, then?"

The phone began to ring, but Lady Graverly made no move to answer it. "Not at all," she said. "The English are lovely, naturally, but they consider Canadian heritage mildly amusing and entirely irrelevant, like schoolchildren performing a Shakespearian play. Only Americans properly appreciate Graverly Manor. Here they enjoy the pomp and splendor of a distinguished British estate but with superior food and better plumbing and without having to cross the Atlantic Ocean. Americans will believe anything told to them in a cultured British accent. They leave generous tips to ingratiate themselves to staff, a flagrant extension of their foreign policy of bribery and coercion. I do not discourage the practice, for nothing abates the incessant whingeing of servants better than money."

"Do you want me to answer that?" I asked, nodding to the phone.

She looked down at the phone as though not having heard it. It had stopped ringing. "They will call back if it's important."

"Don't the staff answer the phone?"

"Lincoln tries to answer when he hears it, but by the time he reaches the phone the caller has usually hung up. I do not encourage it, really. He has all the warmth of an executioner and becomes flustered when asked questions. Agnes is forbidden. Last week, she confirmed a number of reservations without first consulting me, and she neglected to record them. I suspect she's illiterate, as many of her countrymen are. We really have no idea who might show up at the door."

The mention of Agnes's name made me wince in recollection of last night's incident. "Is Agnes here today?" I asked.

"Mondays and Tuesdays are her days off. Lincoln is off on Wednesdays and Thursdays. Please follow me."

As we made our way up the stairs, I asked if there was a guestbook I could browse through to get an idea of guest feedback.

"There used to be, but I grew weary of the comments."

"Lots of complaints?"

"It was all praise, naturally. Every guest wrote a variation of the same trite comments. Reading them became a bit tedious."

"I see," I said, thinking back to the TripAdvisor comments, which told a different story. It was typical of travelers not to complain in person, allowing management an opportunity to rectify the problem. It was more punitive to post a nasty, anonymous comment online.

Over the next hour, Lady Graverly guided me through the guestrooms, providing commentaries about the furnishings, décor, and the reigns of the monarchs the rooms were named after. She appeared to take special pleasure in reporting the atrocities and tragic ends of royal figures. "Mary I was called Bloody Mary for having hundreds of religious dissenters burned at the stake," she said brightly as we finished up in the Mary I suite. "I do adore the Tudor monarchs."

The last room was the Edward VI room on the third floor, where Clarissa had gone back to bed. "My least favorite room," Lady Graverly said loudly beside the door. "Edward VI was the son of Henry VIII and his third wife, Jane Seymour, who died due to complications during childbirth. He was crowned in 1547 at the age of nine and died in agony six years later, his body ravaged by measles, smallpox, and tuberculosis. The bed in this room is said to be the very bed in which he expired." She gave a wicked smile.

Downstairs, she showed me where to find cleaning supplies and equipment, although it took her some time to find them and she seemed only dimly aware of their functions. Next we reviewed the contents of the breakfast buffet, which, in spite of my growing hunger, looked sparse and unappealing—and unnecessary, considering there was only one guest. In the kitchen, her vague references to recipe books, ingredients, and utensils made it obvious that she did none of the cooking.

Again I was drawn to the view of the oak tree in the back yard. As I lingered at the kitchen window, I spotted a stout, black-haired woman exiting the private quarters. "Who's that?" I asked.

Lady Graverly came to the window and peered out. "That is the woman who cares for my private apartment." She pulled the drapes shut. "Shall we continue?"

We returned to the foyer. "Lincoln is out shopping for groceries at present, but he has prepared a detailed list of items to review with you in the afternoon." She went to the door of her apartment. "Have a pleasant day, Mr. Lambert."

Once again, she had called an abrupt end to a meeting, without giving me a chance to ask questions. "Lincoln will tour me around the rest of the house, then?" I asked.

She turned around. "You have seen all there is to see."

"Isn't there a basement or cellar?" Lynne Crocker's claim that there wasn't one that she was aware of hadn't been convincing.

"I showed you the laundry room downstairs. There is nothing else."

"What about your apartment? I'd love to have a look, considering I'll be living there soon."

"Mr. Lambert, my private quarters are strictly off-limits. When I am on the other side of this door, I live in splendid isolation. It is the only way to maintain my sanity, given the enormous demands of running this household. You shall see it in due time. In the meantime, should you dare to disturb me there, I shall call our arrangement off at once."

"What if there's a fire?"

"A fire?" A flicker of worry passed over her eyes. She went to the supply closet behind the reception desk and reached inside, pulling a set of keys from a hook. "In the event of an emergency, these keys will allow you access to my apartment. A thorough sweep of my quarters must be conducted prior to evacuation. Otherwise you are forbidden to trespass. Is that clear?"

"With all due respect, as the purchaser of this property, I have the right to see the entire house."

"Until such time as we agree to sign a formal transfer of ownership, I am the owner of this house, and you are my employee. I expect you to govern yourself accordingly."

"Elinor, I have no intention of signing anything before I've seen every inch of this house."

Her eyes flashed. I half-expected her to cry out, "Guards, seize him! Off with his head!" But she broke into a grand smile. "Why, Mr. Lambert, I had no idea you could be so assertive. You will do well as master of this household. Good day, then."

She slipped inside her quarters, pulling the door closed.

★ ★ ★ ★ ★

Upon returning to my room that night, I found a three-piece navy suit and paisley ascot laid out on my bed. Lifting the coat, I ran my fingers along the fine material, admiring the elaborate stitching and gold buttons. A matching silk handkerchief was tucked into the breast pocket. Mystified, I wondered if the suit had belonged to Lord Graverly. Opening the coat, I found a Holt Renfrew tag stitched into the inside pocket and realized it was brand new. A gift?

Unable to resist, I tried on the jacket and stood in front of the mirror. It fit perfectly. Pulling the ascot around my neck, I tried to figure out how to tie it and eventually gave up, letting it drape over my shoulders like a scarf. The clothing was far too old-fashioned and showy for my tastes, and the ascot made me look pompous, but the overall effect was surprisingly pleasing and perfectly suited to the manor. I turned left and right, touching my chin and posing, thrilled by the transcending effect of such fine clothing. "Once in a while the good lord makes a mistake," Lady Graverly had said. "A blueblood is born into a common family…"

A hard lump drew my attention to the vest pocket. Inside I found a small blue box from Tiffany & Co. Opening it, I pulled out a gleaming gold pocket watch on a chain. There was a card inside the box: "To Trevor Lambert, my prince. Welcome to Graverly Manor. With all my love, Lady Andrew Graverly."

A rush of blood rose up my neck, and my ears and face flushed with embarrassment. I hastily replaced the watch and slipped the box into the vest pocket, hanging the suit and ascot in the closet. Tomorrow, I would return them. Not only could I not accept such lavish gifts, but I was quite certain that any feelings of indebtedness to Lady Graverly were to be carefully avoided.

11

Ghost Call

I was up first thing Tuesday morning. No one was around when I went downstairs, so I proceeded to set up the breakfast buffet on my own. It turned out to be an exercise in futility; Clarissa didn't show her face all morning, nor did anyone else, for that matter. I had not seen Lincoln since Sunday night.

As I dismantled the untouched buffet, it occurred to me I was being taken advantage of; the others had left the new recruit to do all the work and had gone out shopping or socializing, perhaps even skiing in the local hills. The image of Lady Graverly on skis made me chuckle, and throughout the day to amuse myself I conjured up other scenarios involving the dignified old woman: snowboarding in a bala-clava, performing waterskiing stunts, propped up at the bar at the Dover Arms Pub doing shots with the locals.

During the course of the day, I heard the occasional opening and closing of doors, the patter of footsteps, a cough, a hack, murmurs of conversation, but I did not see a soul. Left to my own devices, I explored the house. Every room was in need of a thorough scrubbing. I had never minded cleaning, having always admired and somewhat envied the work of the housekeeping department in hotels, the satis-faction they gleaned from seeing the results of their labor. Deciding to start with the kitchen, I filled a bucket with soapy water and rolled up my sleeves.

As I scrubbed the floor, I brooded over the state of the house. Dirt could be removed easily, but what was really needed was paint. The tired furnishings would have to be replaced, and that would require several years' worth of capital reserves. I would have to find additional sources of revenue. Lynne had mentioned the potential of the back yard for weddings and events, but that would require landscaping. If Lady Graverly's quarters proved to be spacious, they could in part be converted into additional guestrooms, possibly even a small restaurant or lounge. However, a food and beverage facility would require a larger kitchen and ample storage space. How could a house of this size have no basement or cellar? At the very least, there had to be a crawl space, but I could find nowhere to access it.

After cleaning the kitchen, I went to the foyer to mop the floor. Eyeing the Gothic door, I wondered why Lady Graverly had so adamantly refused to allow me in. Being a private person myself, I respected her desire for privacy, but her words had been so vehement I suspected there was more to it. Maybe the apartment was rundown and neglected, and she was ashamed. Her fierce pride was obvious, and I suspected it also fueled her refusal to accept that her husband had run off with the chambermaid. She had assured me I would see her quarters in due time, but I needed to start planning now. On a whim, I went to the phone and called the housing inspector Lynne had recommended, Hal Farnsworth, to request an appointment and ask him to track down the manor's blueprints. He promised to check with the city and get back to me.

Next, I called Mr. Chagani at the Harbourside Hotel and told him thanks, but I wouldn't be accepting the job.

"Don't tell me you bought that manor?" he said.

"Yes, as a matter of fact, I did," I said. "So whenever your hotel is sold out"—*or, say, it topples over into the ocean*, I thought—"I'd appreciate it if you could send travelers our way." I thanked him again and quickly hung up, hoping I had made the right decision.

That afternoon, I was in the back yard chopping firewood when the door to the private quarters opened and out walked the stout, black-haired woman I had seen the previous day. My curiosity caused me to miss the block, and the blade grazed my shin. As I lifted my pant leg to inspect the wound, the woman walked by without acknowledging my presence and hurried down the paved path to the back alley. There was something familiar about her purposeful gait and the black leather bag she carried. I had worked with hundreds of housekeepers in my career, and this woman did not fit the profile. Stinging pain redirected my attention to my leg. The wound was superficial, a shaved layer of skin, but it was bleeding. I limped into the kitchen and found a first-aid kit. After bandaging my leg, I returned and gathered an armload of wood.

A few minutes later, while lighting a fire in the parlor, I heard someone clear his throat behind me and turned my head to see Lincoln standing in the corner, perfectly rigid, his white-gloved hands glowing in the shadows.

"There you are!" I said. "I wondered what became of you."

"I've been here, sir."

"Well, I haven't seen you. Elinor said you had a list of things to review with me yesterday."

"Which things, Master Lambert?"

The fire blazed to life, licking at my fingers, and I lunged back, feeling a stab of pain in my injured leg. Concealing my discomfort, I stood up and made my way over to him. "Please, Lincoln, call me Trevor. You'll find I'm a tad less formal than Lady Graverly."

"Of course you are, sir."

"I was hoping you could tell me who does what around here—the breakdown of responsibilities, the schedule? I want to be as helpful as possible, but I don't want to step on any toes."

"It's quite simple, really. We do whatever is necessary to care for the house and its occupants. Have you made up Miss Larch's room?"

"I didn't know I was expected to. Why don't we do it together? You can show me the ropes."

"Given your pedigree, I should expect you know how to clean a room."

I studied his face, unsure how to take the remark. Was he referring to my hotel training or sneering at my modest upbringing? His face was expressionless.

"In hotels, we use checklists to ensure nothing is overlooked," I said amicably.

"I suppose such a system is quite useful in a hotel."

There was no doubt now: beneath the veneer of politesse lurked condescension, even a trace of contempt. Leaving him, I went to the kitchen and ran cold water over my scorched fingers. The burns were superficial, a source of irritation more than anything.

"Master Lambert," Lincoln said, startling me from behind, "I shall be preparing Lady Graverly's dinner in her private quarters now. Perhaps you will be kind enough to tend to Miss Larch's room?"

I shut off the tap. "Sure. Is she out now?"

"I do believe so."

"I'll need a key."

He reached into his pocket and removed a brass ring. His hands shook as he withdrew a large key.

I thanked him and waited for him to leave so I could tend to my burn, but he remained where he was. "Is there anything else?" I asked. His clouded pink eyes, seeing yet unseeing, made me uncomfortable.

"Her ladyship wishes to remind you that Mr. and Mrs. Wainright arrive at eight thirty this evening. She will not be at liberty to greet them."

"We're expecting guests?"

"Perhaps you might consider reviewing the guest register. You will find it quite helpful in keeping current on arrivals and departures."

"Yes, of course," I said, feeling stupid for not having thought of it. "Where can I find the Christmas decorations? This house could use some cheering up."

"Oh no, that won't do at all. The lady no longer permits anything of a festive nature."

Another rule I would change immediately. "Oh, I need to ask you for the user name and password for the computer."

"The computer has not worked for several months, sir."

"Okay, then. I'll see if I can fix it. I'm planning to make a few changes to the manor's website, set up an email account for inquiries, maybe post some testimonials from previous guests. Elinor mentioned you used to have a guestbook. I thought it might be a good source for quotes. Can you dig it up for me?"

Lincoln gave me a faintly perplexed look, the first expression I had seen aside from a blank stare. "I'm afraid that won't be possible, sir. The lady grew weary of—"

"All the praise, I know."

"—the negative comments. She found some of them quite offensive."

"Is that so," I said. A contradiction between Lincoln and Lady Graverly—a fissure in what had appeared to be an unbreakable wall. "You threw away the old guestbook, then?"

"Lady Graverly throws nothing away, as you can clearly see. There's an entire shelf filled with old guestbooks. You won't find much praise in them, however—not in recent years."

"What about all those great comments I saw online?"

"Lady Graverly wrote them, and the summer student posted them."

"You're joking."

"I don't make a habit of joking, Master Lambert."

The door opened and Sir Fester slinked in, taking a swipe at my leg as he passed. "Scram!" I yelled after him.

"Sir Fester becomes quite ornery when hungry," said Lincoln.

"It's my job to feed him?" I asked, glaring down at the cat. Then I recognized an opportunity: maybe I could starve the cat into good behavior. "I'd be happy to," I said, shooting the cat an evil grin. My shin began to throb where his paw had struck, in the very same place as the axe, and I squatted down to check on the wound. Blood had begun to seep though the bandage. Sir Fester approached me, meowing and licking his lips. I quickly pulled down my pant leg and stood up.

Lincoln was gone.

I went looking for him, but he was nowhere to be found. How could a man who moved so slowly disappear so quickly? In the parlor, the fire crackled and hissed. I returned to the kitchen, found a stack of 9Lives with chicken and liver, and fed Sir Fester, deciding to start with a truce. He attacked the food ferociously, and I left him to feast, heading down to the foyer to study the guest registry. Flipping to today's date, I found the words "Wanerite 4 nites" scrawled in a horrendous script. It appeared that Agnes wrote in the same sloppy manner as she tended the house.

As I climbed the stairs to the Edward VI room, I felt a small thrill at the prospect of entering Clarissa's bedroom, but a tasseled Privacy sign hung from the door handle. Could she be there? I was not yet attuned to the comings and goings in the house. I put my ear to the door and listened. Nothing.

In the hotel business, employees often learn about the inviolability of privacy signs from embarrassing encounters. I myself have walked into rooms the front desk insisted were vacant only to find a couple fornicating, an elderly man in high heels and ladies' panties, and two front-desk agents snorting cocaine. Sometimes guests check out without removing the privacy sign or informing the front desk, and if the privacy sign is heeded, the room could remain forever unoccupied, resulting in an irreplaceable loss of revenue. To avoid this, and to avoid blatantly disregarding the privacy sign by knocking, the front-desk agent places a "ghost call" to the room. If the guest answers, the agent hangs up, and the guest assumes it was a random misdialed call. If there is no answer, the agent can safely assume the room is empty and can disregard the privacy sign. Deciding a ghost call was in order, I made my way downstairs and picked up the phone at the reception desk. The shrill ring of Clarissa's phone shattered the silence of the household. After six rings, satisfied, I remounted the stairs.

Giving a quick rap on the door, I let myself in and flicked on the light. A sudden movement made me start. Clarissa shot up in bed, breasts bare, and emitted a piercing scream. I let out a yelp, doubly alarmed by her corpselike appearance: blackened eyes, pale skin, and scraggly hair.

"What the hell are you doing?" she shouted, pulling a sheet around her.

"I'm sorry! I thought you were out." I quickly retreated, pulling the door closed, and then called through the door. "I tried phoning. You didn't answer."

"Pervert!"

Mortified, I climbed the stairs to my room, chastising myself along the way. I had violated a rule I had instilled in hundreds of hotel employees: knock before entering a room, no matter how certain you are that it's vacant, count to five, and, if there is no answer, open the door a crack and identify yourself. If there is no reply, then—and only then—enter. In the two days since had I arrived at the manor, I had seen every occupant naked except Elinor Graverly.

And if God had mercy, *that* would never happen.

Clarissa went out a half-hour later, slamming the door so hard it felt like a smack in the face. I searched the house for Lincoln, eager to share the blame, and found him in the kitchen, sweeping the very floor I had washed that afternoon in short, ineffectual strokes.

"Why did you tell me Clarissa was out?" I demanded.

"One should never open doors without permission."

"I tried calling her room first. She didn't answer. You told me she went out."

"I believe I heard her leave just now, should you wish to try again."

Exasperated, I stormed off.

That night, I prepared a simple pasta dinner, making enough for the others, but none of them came around. I was surprised to discover that, after only forty-eight hours in the manor, the solitude was beginning to bother me. I was looking forward to receiving the Wainrights, who I hoped were reasonably young, pleasant to be around, and not crazy. After dinner I stayed close to the front door, checking the street every few minutes, determined to be present to greet them upon arrival. By ten, they had not arrived. It had been a long day, and I was exhausted, but I could not go to bed before I had settled them in.

At ten thirty, my cell phone rang.

"How's everything at the pink palace?" Janet asked.

"Couldn't be better."

"And the new girlfriend? Do I hear royal wedding bells?"

"Not funny, Janet. What's up?"

"I'm picking up tickets for the carol ships tomorrow. Wendy thought you might want to come."

"Gee, I don't know... It's not really my thing." The prospect of singing Christmas carols with strangers in toques on a firetrap boat was about as appealing as going to the Ice Capades.

"It's not my thing either, Trevor, but the kids love it. You're always away at Christmas. We thought you could join some of the festivities this year. If not the carol ships, then how about a show?"

"Now *that* I can do. What are you thinking?"

"I heard the Ice Capades are coming back to town."

I stifled a groan. "Any other options?" Peering through the front window, I spotted a black sedan rolling down the rain-slicked street.

"The Nutcracker?"

"Why don't I meet you for a drink afterward?"

"We'll have to get the kids home, and they really want to see you."

"Janet, they look at me like they have no clue who I am."

"Maybe if you saw them more than once or twice a year..."

Up the street, I saw the red glow of brake lights. I pulled on my coat, grabbed an umbrella, and hurried out to the street. "Wouldn't your boys rather see a Canucks game or something?"

"That's a fantastic idea." Janet shouted in the background, "BOYS, GET OVER HERE! Uncle Trevor wants to take you to a hockey game!"

The sound of cheering.

Glancing across the street, I envisioned Quinn dashing into the path of the speeding truck. The prospect of being responsible for all those hyperactive kids was suffocating. What if something happened?

"Janet, I didn't say...I meant—"

"You should see these guys, they're so excited!"

"I'm going to be buried in this house for a while. I won't even have time to leave the property. Maybe sometime in January."

"Why don't I come out for a visit with the kids on Saturday, then?"

"Um, jeez, I'm not sure that's a good idea," I said, flagging down the sedan. "Elinor isn't really a kid person."

Silence.

"Janet, I've got to run. My guests are here. Go ahead to the carol ships without me, okay? We'll chat closer to Christmas."

"'Bye, Trevor."

The sedan slowed to a stop in front of me. I opened the rear door, and an elderly woman peered out.

"Mrs. Wainright?" I said, my heart sinking. "Welcome to Graverly Manor."

"Chuck, wake up! We're here!"

I helped Mrs. Wainright out first, holding an umbrella over her head to shelter her from the rain.

Steadying herself on my arm, she turned to regard the manor. "How lovely!" she said in a loud voice. "We've been so looking forward to our visit!"

"And we've been looking forward to having you," I said, ducking into the car to help her husband out. "Where are you from?"

"Raleigh, West Virginia."

I propped Mr. Wainright against the car and went around to the trunk to retrieve his walker and cane. The driver made no move to help, choosing instead to talk on his cell phone in the comfort of his seat. Leaving the luggage for the next trip, I escorted the Wainrights to the house, trailing Mr. Wainright as he took baby steps with his walker. I held the umbrella over Mrs. Wainright's head as the rain drenched me. At the foot of the stairs, Mr. Wainright abandoned the walker and began to climb the steps on his own. Fearing he would topple over, I offered him my arm but he brushed it aside.

"How did you find out about the manor?" I asked Mrs. Wainright.

"Oh, it's a long story. Is your mother up?"

I chuckled. "Lady Graverly isn't my mother. I'm an employee. She's retired for the evening, but I'm sure she'll be around in the morning."

"Well, we'll save the surprise until then!"

I gave her an inquiring look. Something told me Lady Graverly did not like surprises.

Mrs. Wainright's attention was drawn to Sir Fester, who was perched on the verandah railing. "Well, hello there, darling little kitty!" she cried, reaching out.

"Careful," I warned, taking her arm and steering her into the house. "He's got a nasty temperament."

An hour later, the Wainrights were settled in the Elizabeth II suite. Considering Mr. Wainright's frail state, to house them on the third floor was completely impractical, but I was reluctant to meddle with Lady Graverly's room assignment. As I placed the last of the bags on the ottoman at the foot of the bed, I asked Mrs. Wainright if there was anything else. She was exploring the room, uttering cries of delight over various furnishings and knickknacks.

"Chuck likes a spot of sherry before bedtime," she said. The wall next to her shifted and made a loud crack, as though protesting the volume of her voice. She jumped back, pressing her hand against her chest. "Dear, it gave me such a fright!"

"The house shifts sometimes," I said, smiling to reassure her.

She pressed her lips together, consternated. "Oh, and I would love a cup of Earl Grey tea. We're a bit peckish too. Perhaps some cheese and crackers to nibble on?"

"I'll see what I can rustle up," I said, eager to please.

In the kitchen, I searched the refrigerator and cupboards for food that wasn't stale or moldy. I wondered how Lady Graverly would have received such a request. Not enthusiastically, to be sure, but I had resolved to do things differently. Fortunately, I had coaxed a key to the liquor cabinet from Lincoln in anticipation of the Wainrights' visit. They were my first official guests, and I was determined to do whatever it took to make them happy.

12

Private Parts

On Wednesday morning, I came downstairs at six fifteen, expecting to have plenty of time to prepare breakfast, only to find the Wainrights seated at the dining room table.

"Good morning!" Mrs. Wainright hollered, turning to her husband. "Look, Chuck, it's the bellboy who was so kind to us last night!"

Mr. Wainright nodded and half-lifted his hand in a wave.

"Can I get you started on some breakfast?" I offered.

Mrs. Wainright, looking pretty in a buttercup-colored dress and red lipstick, said, "I asked that woman in the kitchen for some tea, but I don't think she speaks English. A bowl of oatmeal with a sprinkle of brown sugar would be just fine for Chuck—his stomach is very sensitive. And a slice of dry white toast and some fresh cut fruit for me. Oh, and a dollop of plain yogurt, if it's not too much trouble."

"I'm sure that can be arranged." I entered the kitchen whistling, expecting to find Lady Graverly, but a ragged-looking woman wearing a checkered yellow-and-white apron over a faded floral dress was bent over the oven.

"Top o' the morning to you," I said, recognizing Agnes's straggly grey hair.

"I'm Scottish, not Irish," she barked.

"Right, sorry. I don't believe we've been formally introduced. I'm Trevor."

She closed the oven door and straightened, turning to me with a severe expression. "Oh, I remember ye, all right." She looked to be in her early sixties, with a hooked nose and wrinkles like penknife stabs around her eyes and mouth.

"Again, I'm sorry about that. I thought you were being assaulted." Feeling my face color, I went to the refrigerator and ducked inside.

"Wot are ye doing?"

"Making breakfast for the Wainrights."

"Breakfast's noot served 'til seven, and we doon't take special orders."

Her accent was so thick, I could barely understand her. "Not to worry," I said. "I don't mind doing it myself." I wandered into the pantry in search of rolled oats. Lincoln's cot was empty and neatly made. Pulling a container of Quaker Oats from the shelf, I returned to the kitchen. "Lincoln's up and about already?"

"He stays at 'is girlfriend's on 'is days off."

"Oh. I see." For an old guy, Lincoln was quite the ladies' man. I sneaked a sidelong glance at Agnes to see if his philandering bothered her. She was making a ruckus, slamming drawers and cupboard doors, yet I suspected this was her natural disposition. The kettle was boiling, and I reached to unplug it.

She slapped my hand. "Oot! *I* make breakfast, *you* clean up. Here, take this." She handed me a plate containing two burnt pieces of toast. "This better keep 'em quiet."

In the dining room, I placed the black toast before the Wainrights with great ceremony, as though delivering a steaming quiche. Grabbing a jar from the buffet table, I liberally spooned jam into a bowl and slid it toward them. Even the smell of burnt toast made my stomach rumble. I would be obliged to wait until the Wainrights were finished before I could eat. Judging by how long it took Mr. Wainright to reach for the toast, my breakfast was a long way off. Taking a seat at the table, I inquired as to how they had slept.

"Chuck slept like a log, as usual," Mrs. Wainright said, her head lolling slightly. "But I tossed and turned for hours. Such strange noises this house makes! I swear it's alive and breathing. It was like listening to Chuck complain about his aches and pains all night."

"I'm sorry you didn't sleep well," I said, watching Mr. Wainright concentrate on getting a piece of toast into his mouth. "We can move you to another room if you'd like."

"Oh no, we're quite content where we are," Mrs. Wainright said. She reached to stuff the toast into her husband's mouth and wiped his face with a napkin. "To think we slept in the same bed as Queen Elizabeth!"

Thinking she must be kidding, I gave a laugh.

"Will she be in residence today?" asked Mrs. Wainright.

"Queen Elizabeth?"

"Lady Elinor."

"Oh, I expect so. You have a surprise for her?"

Agnes stormed in and slammed a plate of shriveled orange slices on the table, then stomped back to the kitchen and returned with a pot of tea. While splashing tea into two cups, she broke into a fit of coughing. Setting the teapot down, she leaned over the buffet table and hacked.

I scanned the food items on the table, making a mental note to throw them away. Still coughing, Agnes returned into the kitchen.

Mrs. Wainright looked disconcerted as she watched the door swing back and forth. She turned back to me. "I suppose I could tell you if you promise not to tell her. Chuck wants it to be a surprise."

I held up my hand. "I promise."

"Well," she said, her head bobbing to Mr. Wainright and back to me, "in the Second World War, Chuck's battalion fought side by side with the Brits in Normandy, and one of the soldiers Chuck got friendly with was Andrew Graverly, Lady Elinor's late husband. For over a decade, he's been looking up old war buddies. Most are dead now, but he likes to meet their families too. For years he tried to track down Andrew Graverly, but with no success. Right, Chuck?"

"I remember him, all right," said Mr. Wainright in a throaty voice. "He was a brave little dickens."

"A few months ago, Chuck read in the veteran's newsletter about the death of Lord Wakefield Graverly," continued Mrs. Wainright. "He recalled that Andrew had a brother who was a year older, and that he claimed to come from a noble family, but at the time Chuck had thought it was all part of his act. Andrew was quite an entertainer, Chuck tells me, and he liked to perform for the troops. Boys will be boys." She pursed her lips and gave Mr. Wainright a reproachful look, from which I surmised that the performances were bawdy. "Well, our grandson George helped us track down Lord Wakefield's widow, an American woman who lives in the family estate just outside of London. We went to visit her, and she was absolutely charming. She told us the brothers had lost contact years ago after a family feud. Lord Andrew had moved to Canada, and she was certain he had long since died. She said his widow still lived in Vancouver. Well, our George managed to track her down here, and Chuck sent several letters, but she didn't reply. When we found out she operates a bed-and-breakfast, we decided it was a perfect excuse to visit the city. George made a reservation, and here we are. Isn't that right, Chuck?"

Mr. Wainright lifted his head, eyes bulging. "Damned Kraut ambushed me while I was reloading my rifle! Didn't see him comin'. I woulda been dead if Andy hadn't shot him clear in the head."

"Andrew saved his life," Mrs. Wainright chimed in. "Chuck has always been grateful."

"Just a little fella," Mr. Wainright rasped. "Not your typical soldier. Real flamboyant. Made us laugh and holler for more."

"Andrew was awarded the Victoria Cross for his bravery. Chuck can't wait to tell his son about his valiant father."

I turned and caught Agnes peeking through the open door. The door swung shut, and she disappeared. Turning back to the Wainrights, I decided I could save them some awkwardness with Lady Graverly. "I'm sorry to say," I said gently, "but the son passed away."

Mr. Wainright lifted his head. "Huh?"

"Dear god, what happened?" asked Mrs. Wainright.

"He was born quite ill, from what I understand."

"How terrible," exclaimed Mrs. Wainright, reaching over to rub her husband's back.

I excused myself and left them to absorb the news.

Agnes was sitting on the back porch, smoking.

"Yer not serposed to be gossipin' with the guests," she said.

"I wasn't gossiping," I said through the screen door. "I was playing host."

She only snorted.

I opened the door and sat down beside her, shivering in the crisp outside air. "So what brought you to Vancouver?"

"Me sister."

"She lives in Vancouver?"

She flicked her ashes onto the cement steps, not answering.

"Do you like working at the manor?" I asked, trying another angle to get her to talk.

Two tunnels of smoke escaped from her nostrils. "I despise it."

Another happy resident. "How long have you been here?"

"A week."

"A week?" I had assumed she had been there for decades.

She nodded, stubbing her cigarette out on the brick wall, and went inside.

I sat still for a moment, enjoying the fresh air, and then got up. Agnes was no longer in the kitchen. A pot of oatmeal bubbled on the stove. Next to it sat a plate of sliced bananas and strawberries. It appeared that Agnes was more accommodating than she liked to let on. Spooning some oatmeal into a bowl, I carried it and the fruit plate into the dining room.

"Young man," said Mrs. Wainright as I set the plates down, "would you be so kind as to help Chuck clean up after breakfast? My son requested a handicapped room, but there are no safety bars in our bathroom. I'm too weak to be much help to him anymore."

"Uh, sure, of course," I said with a note of apprehension.

"Did you hear that, Chuck? This fine young man is going to help you shower!"

Mr. Wainright stared up at the ceiling, eyes unblinking.

I returned to the kitchen, torn between sympathy for the former soldier's frail state and trepidation over having to help him shower. Agnes was back, furiously scrubbing a pot at the sink.

"Does Lady Graverly take breakfast in the dining room?" I asked her.

"She always eats in her quarters."

"Maybe I'll bring her some tea, then," I offered, angling for a way to get into the private quarters.

"You wouldn't!" she said, reaching out to clamp her soapy hand over mine.

"Why?" I asked, unnerved.

She released my hand and turned back to the pot. "A lady comes in to prepare her meals on Lincoln's days off," she said matter-of-factly.

I returned to the dining room and helped Mr. Wainright up the stairs and into the bathroom. Mrs. Wainright and I undressed him. He was unable to step over the rim of tub, so I lifted him over. I turned on the shower and stood back, ready to assist where needed. He swayed precariously under the downpour. Realizing I had no choice, I asked Mrs. Wainright to leave and took off my suit, climbing in with him.

"Is everything all right in there?" Mrs. Wainright called from behind the door.

"Just fine," I said, lifting Mr. Wainright's arm to wash under his armpit.

"Do you need a hand?"

"That won't be necessary," I said. Showering with one senior was enough.

Early that afternoon, I was polishing the dining room table when the telephone rang. I had heard it ringing when I was in the Wainrights' suite but had been unable to leave Mr. Wainright. Now I hurried out to answer it.

Agnes was mopping the floor next to the phone.

I snatched up the receiver. "Good afternoon, Graverly Manor. This is Trevor. How may I help you?"

"Trevor, it's Hal Farnsworth from Historic Home Inspections. I got ahold of those blueprints from the city. Does Monday afternoon work for the inspection, say around three thirty?"

"You can't come sooner?"

"Sorry, I'm booked solid these days."

"Fine," I said, glancing at Agnes, who stood hunched over the mop, one ear cocked in my direction. I turned my back to her and lowered my voice. "What did you find out about the private apartment?"

"According to city records, it was added in 1961, increasing living area by 1,965 square feet."

The news was heartening. It was more living space than I needed, which meant room for expansion. "What about a basement or underground storage area?" I asked. "Did you find anything?"

"Let me have a look." Hal grew quiet as he studied the blueprints. "Looks like there's a cellar of some sort."

"A cellar?" I glanced over at Agnes. She was staring at me, one eye bulging. I shooed her away.

"It might have been filled in when she added the wing," Hal said. "According to these plans, the master bedroom sits on top of it. We can have a look on Monday."

I thanked him and hung up, turning to Agnes. "Next time the phone rings, I'd like you to answer it."

"I'm not serposed to."

"Well, I'm the innkeeper now, and I'm telling you it's okay. We can't afford to miss any reservations calls. Just try to be pleasant on the phone, okay? And write everything down as legibly as possible."

"If ye insist."

"Thank you." Sitting down at the desk, I opened the ledger and turned to today's date, December 6. The page was blank. I flipped ahead. On the next page, I found what appeared to be a doodle in

Lincoln's near-illegible writing. On the following pages, I found no reservations whatsoever. Hadn't Lady Graverly said the manor was always busy? Only when I reached a full week later did I find a reservation. "Heritage Tours, seven rooms, two nights, welcome cocktail, farewell dinner," Lady Graverly had written in her florid script. At least there would be some action next week.

The mail slot on the front door opened and a stack of envelopes spilled to the floor. I got up and went over to gather up the mail.

Agnes hurried over. "All mail goes directly to the lady," she said, trying to snatch the envelopes from my hands.

"Fine, I'll deliver them myself," I said, sorting through the mail as I walked to the door of the private quarters. Elinor Graverly seemed to have an aversion to paying bills; several envelopes were stamped URGENT or FINAL NOTICE. "Why are these bills in the name of Lord Andrew Graverly?" I asked Agnes, puzzled.

"How should I know?"

"Fifty years is a long time to procrastinate over a name change." I lifted my hand to knock.

Behind me, I heard Agnes gasp. "Yer not serposed to bother her."

I turned my head to her. "Dare me?" Lady Graverly's words echoed in my ears. *Should you dare to disturb me here, I shall call this arrangement off at once.* I lowered my hand, suddenly apprehensive.

"She's noot there anyway."

"Then why don't we have a peek inside?" I whispered to her conspiratorially, placing my hand on the doorknob. "I won't tell if you don't tell."

"You wouldn't!" Agnes cried, backing away. The mop clattered to the floor. "No one's allowed to see her private parts but Lincoln."

The terror in her eyes made me lose my nerve. I crouched down to slide the envelopes under the door and stood up. "Why all the secrecy in this house, Agnes? Where are we, Bluebeard's castle?"

She only shook her head and resumed mopping.

There were footsteps on the verandah. The front door opened and Clarissa entered, looking pale and gaunt in a black overcoat. I froze, embarrassed by our last encounter.

"Morning," she said in a hoarse voice. She took off her coat, revealing a clingy black dress, and headed for the staircase. "I won't need service today, Agnes."

"As ye wish, Miss Larch."

On the landing, Clarissa turned suddenly and caught me staring. "Oh, Trevor? Next time you need to get into my room, knock first, okay?"

"Yes, of course. I'm terribly sorry. I didn't—"

"Perv," she said, and disappeared up the stairs.

Agnes turned to me and let out a shrill laugh.

I shrugged as though I had no idea what she was taking about and hurried down the hallway to the kitchen. My face was on fire.

After waiting around for Lady Graverly all morning, the Wainrights departed on a sightseeing tour in the early afternoon.

I tried to get the computer working, with no success, and spent the next hour checking the house for leaks, cracks, structural damage, and any signs of what Mr. Chagani had referred to as a "sick house." The inspector would do this on Monday, I knew, but I wanted to get a feel for the place sooner. To my relief, I found little of concern aside from general aging and wear-and-tear. The house appeared to have good solid bones. As for its soul, I was still undecided. Mrs. Wainright's remark about the house being "alive and breathing" was troubling me. The house did seem alive—and not very happy. Sadness permeated the air like a foul odor, materializing in potent waves and evaporating before I could locate its source. I was certain that when the manor's occupants left they would take all the sorrow with them, and the house's good old soul would prevail.

I asked Agnes to do a thorough cleaning of the parlor, pointing out areas that had been overlooked, and she dedicated the afternoon to the task, uttering long-suffering sighs and curses every time I traversed the room. Around three o'clock I heard a fit of coughing and hurried into the parlor. Spotting me, she stopped hacking and dipped her hands into her bucket of soapy water, ringing the rag and wiping down the mantle.

"Have you seen a doctor about that cold?" I said, concerned.

"What cold?"

"Oh. Nothing. Carry on."

"I'm going out to the back for a smoke."

"Don't be long. We've still got the dining room to clean."

With a grumble, she retrieved her coat and rubber boots and went out the back door. An hour later when she had not returned, I went to look for her; she was nowhere to be found. Deciding she must have gone out for breakfast supplies, I took over the cleaning of the parlor. Her efforts had made the situation worse—the dust and grease that had originally lay unobtrusively on every surface were now mixed with soap and streaked quite visibly over the areas she had worked on.

As I worked, I thought of Lady Graverly. How many hours had she spent in this parlor listening to the tick of the clock, praying for her husband's return? The isolation I had felt in previous days, temporarily softened by the arrival of the Wainrights, descended on me like a wet blanket. How lonely the manor felt; no Internet, no television, an old-fashioned phone that made callers sound worlds away. Yet the manor was in the heart of the city, surrounded by Vancouver life. When the clock struck five, I realized Agnes wasn't returning today. I was alone in the house again.

Cocktail hour arrived and passed. I had hoped Lady Graverly would join me for a drink, but her side of the house remained quiet. With only the ticking clock as company, I scrubbed and polished into the evening.

Around ten, my phone rang.

"You were supposed to call," Derrick said, sounding like a jilted girlfriend.

"Sorry, I forgot. I've been preoccupied with this house."

"Try being cooped up with three-year-old twins and a depressed wife. You free Saturday? I've got tickets to the Canucks game. I thought we could go to the Roxy afterward for a few beers."

"I wish I could, but there's no way. I'll call when things settle down, okay?"

"Sure, Trevor. Whatever." He hung up.

The Wainrights arrived, and I helped them to their room, fetching tea and sherry and a plate of cookies. At midnight, my limbs sore and aching and my spirits low, I went to bed.

I was on my knees, my neck stretched over a wooden block, eyes straining upward at my executioner. Lincoln heaved the axe over his head and held it suspended in the air, turning to Lady Graverly for assent. She was sitting primly in the bleachers, Sir Fester draped around her neck like a fur collar. In the prisoners' dock next to her, Janet and Wendy were begging for mercy. Lady Graverly's eyes flashed. *How dare*

you disturb me! she cried. *Off with his head!* The blade flashed in the morning sun as it came down on my neck.

I bolted upright in bed.

Moaning.

The strange, eerie sound reverberated through the walls. I thought of Agnes, but it was coming from lower down in the house. The foundation shifting? The oak tree bending in the wind? Sir Fester? No. It was a human sound, a guttural, undulating drone. Mr. Wainright? I was certain it was coming from the main floor, perhaps even from beneath the house. Could Lincoln be back, bemoaning his displacement to the pantry? I thought of Mr. Chagani's remark that Lady Graverly had murdered her husband and buried him under the house, and that his rotting corpse had poisoned the foundation.

The moaning ceased.

I lay still and waited. After a few minutes, it resumed. Unable to ignore the sound, I climbed out of bed, pulled on pants and a sweater, and slipped out of the room.

The door to Agnes's room was shut. The stairs squealed as I descended. When I reached the main floor, I stopped to listen.

Nothing.

In the butler's pantry, Lincoln's bed sat undisturbed. I made my way back down the hallway and stopped in the foyer. The moaning was coming from Lady Graverly's private quarters. I stood outside the door, listening, and remembered the online review. *I was awakened in the night by an eerie moaning sound. I was so freaked out I checked out the next day.* I glanced at the front door, feeling the same impulse.

After a few minutes, the moaning stopped. I scampered up the stairs to my room and crawled under the covers. The sound did not resume, but I was kept awake by the beating of my heart and the creaks and groans of the walls. After a while the house settled, and I drifted off to sleep.

13

The Lure of Lost Lagoon

On Thursday morning, the Wainrights slept in. Agnes was her usual sunny self, growling at every opportunity and clamming up when I tried to make friendly conversation. I wanted to ask whether she had heard the moaning, but it was an awkward subject given the noises she had awakened me with earlier that week. We fell into a domestic routine: she prepared breakfast, cleaned guestrooms, did the laundry, and bitched; I washed dishes, took phone calls, bathed Mr. Wainright, and tried to remain optimistic.

I was growing attached to the Wainrights, who were like the grand-parents I had always wished I had, and I felt personally responsible for their disappointment over Lady Graverly's absence. She hadn't even dropped by to say hello. I slipped a note under her door to inform her that the Wainrights were anxious to see her, but late that afternoon the private quarters remained quiet. As I helped the Wainrights into a taxi headed for the Museum of Anthropology, I promised them they would meet Lady Graverly before they left Vancouver.

Back at the house, I encountered Agnes sweeping the front steps.

"Any idea where Lady Graverly is?" I asked. "She'll be terribly disappointed if she misses the Wainrights."

Agnes chuckled. "The lady's been avoiding those two like the plague."

"She knows who they are?"

She nodded. "I almost got the axe when she found out I took their reservation. How was I serposed to know?"

"Why won't she speak to them?"

"You think she wants to hear stories about the bravery of the man who ruined her life?"

"Why doesn't she just tell the Wainrights the truth? They came all the way from West Virginia. They'll understand."

"Doon't ask me." She set down the broom and followed me inside.

Sensing something was on her mind, I stuck around, taking a seat at the reception desk and pretending to review the guest ledger.

She pulled a soiled rag from the pocket of her apron and began to wipe down the phone. "So yer buying the manor, then?" she said.

"That's my intention."

"Have ye seen the papers?"

"The sale papers? Not yet. Why?"

She lifted her shoulder in a shrug. "Maybe the house isn't in her name."

"If it's not in her name, then whose? Surely not Lord Graverly's?"

"How should I know?" She continued to clean the phone, taking greater care than I had seen her take with anything before. After a moment, she said, "Do ye ever leave this house? It's noot good for ye, bein' inside all the time."

"Don't worry about me, Agnes. You might want to wash that rag out though. It's only making the phone dirtier." Her cloying presence was beginning to irritate me. I preferred her distant and aloof.

"All's I'm sayin' is ye look a little flushed. A bit o' fresh air might do ye good."

I reached up to touch my face. It did feel a bit warm. Her concern for my well-being was suspect, yet the prospect of getting out of the house—and away from Agnes—was enticing. There was nothing that couldn't wait a half-hour.

"I think I will," I said. I went to the coat rack to retrieve my coat.

"Suit yerself," she said, back to her apathetic self.

"You'll be around in case the Wainrights come back early?"

"Do I look like I'm goin' anywhere?"

"I won't be long." I slipped out the front door.

"Take yer time."

The instant I reached the street, I felt better. Afternoon had begun its surrender to evening, and a sooty grey mist hovered in the air. I turned to regard the manor, hoping its pleasant exterior would restore my faith, but in the dreary light it looked drab and devoid of life. The curtains in the private quarters were closed, as always, and I fell to musing about what lay behind them. On impulse I strolled around to the back alley. Peeking into the garage window, I saw that the car Lady Graverly drove, a big, black Cadillac Eldorado from the fifties, was gone. I hurried to the rear bay windows of the private quarters and stood on my tiptoes on the sloping ground, searching for a gap in the curtains.

A ripple in the drapes made me start.

I froze, fearing Lady Graverly was there. Deciding it must be Sir Fester, I lifted myself onto the ledge and peered through a tiny opening in the curtains. I spotted the edge of a canopy bed covered in red-and-white striped fabric. Lady Graverly's bedroom. On the far left, I could see the edge of a fireplace. The room looked predictably ostentatious, although more ravaged by age than the main part of the house. Next to a closed door, which I assumed led to a closet, a strip of peeling wallpaper exposed a large crack in the wall. Directly in front of me was an oak roll-top desk. On top of the desk sat a ceramic lamp in the shape of an elegant lady, her parasol acting as the shade.

The light flickered on.

I ducked.

After a minute, I braved another peek. I caught a flash of grey hair. Agnes. She was bent over the desk, rifling through a drawer. The ledge groaned under my weight. Agnes lifted her head, and our eyes met. Her mouth fell open in a silent scream. I dropped to the ground and ran, circling to the front of the house and stopping on the street to catch my breath. Shame washed over me. Caught peeping—again! And then I had run off like a scared little boy. Embarrassment gave way to indignation. Why was Agnes snooping in Lady Graverly's private quarters? In the brief moment our eyes had met, I had seen a different person: she looked frightened and vulnerable. What was she hoping to find?

My heart was pounding. To calm myself down, I decided to go for the walk originally intended. I had planned to take a stroll along Denman Street, where I could be among people without having to interact with them, but my legs pulled me in the opposite direction, down the street toward the steep path leading to Lost Lagoon. By now, darkness had swallowed daylight, and a few streetlights flickered on. On the path the rotting leaves made the slope treacherous, and I had to tread carefully to avoid slipping.

The lagoon was enshrouded in mist. The low cloud suspended over its surface had crept to the water's edge, obscuring the path in places, making a misstep into the murky deepness a profound possibility. An acrid odor that reeked of rotting flesh permeated the damp air. My mother's story echoed in my mind, and I envisioned Lord Graverly rising out of the lagoon, ripping the anchor from his jaw, and using it to pull me into the lagoon. With a shudder, I picked up my pace to escape the stench, veering to the far edge of the path to avoid plunging into the lagoon's cold depths.

A hunched man with a white beard shuffled past; a small misshapen figure toddled after him. In the corner of my eye I detected a glowing white apparition on the water, keeping pace with me, intermittently vanishing in the mist. I thought of the young housemaid, Sarah, and imagined her rising from the lagoon dressed in a white nightgown, her face hideously bloated. Fear rising, I stopped and turned toward the water.

A swan.

I resumed walking, relieved but still shaken, and disconcerted to have allowed my imagination to spook me in this familiar place. The stench was gradually replaced by the earthy scent of decaying vegetation. I had been walking for about twenty minutes when the silhouette of a figure appeared in the path ahead. As I drew close to the figure, it turned toward me.

"Hi, Trevor." Clarissa's tone was matter-of-fact, as though she had been expecting me.

"Clarissa? What are you doing here?" A breeze rife with the odor of carrion ruffled my collar.

"Observing." Peering out of a black hoodie she wore under her coat, she surveyed the lagoon, scanning back and forth over the water, hands thrust deep in the pockets of the coat.

"Hey, I'm sorry about barging in on you like that."

"Let's just pretend it never happened, okay?"

"Fine by me."

I followed her gaze and saw nothing but mist. I stole a sidelong glance, but her face was hidden by the hoodie. "What are you observing?" I asked.

She began to recite:

> It is dusk on the Lost Lagoon,
> And we two dreaming the dusk away,
> Beneath the drift of a twilight grey,
> Beneath the drowse of an ending day,
> And the curve of a golden moon.

"Pauline Johnson wrote that almost a hundred years ago," she said, her voice somnolent. "She used to paddle around here in a canoe before that causeway was built. When the tide went out, she would lose her favorite place, so she named it Lost Lagoon."

I wondered if this was the same poem my mother had alluded to several weeks ago. I imagined my mother as a little girl, skipping along this very path under the watchful eye of her mother and father.

"Um, Clarissa? Why are you down here in the dark?"

"I'm doing research."

"Okay … What kind of research?"

"I want to capture the sights and smells, the feel of this lagoon, in my paper." She was quiet for a long time. I remained silent too, wishing to respect her dedication to her work but a bit disquieted by her strange behavior. The wind came up. It was time to light the parlor fire. I turned to say goodbye.

"They say he roams the lagoon at night, searching for his lover," she said.

I shivered. "Lord Graverly?"

She nodded. "They couldn't be together, and so he drowned her. Then he drowned himself rather than face life without her. Isn't that romantic?"

"Not particularly. Aren't you cold?"

She reached for my hand and lifted it to her neck. The gesture was so unexpected I almost pulled away. Heat radiated from her skin.

"You'd probably see more in the daytime," I said.

"I like the park better at night. The screeches and howls, the cries from creatures you never hear in the day. They found the bodies of two little boys not far from here. They had been bludgeoned to death."

I withdrew my hand. "Really? When?"

"Back in the early fifties. Their little bodies had been there for five or six years. A woman's fur coat covered them, and at their side lay a lady's shoe, a lunch box, and a hatchet. They called them the Babes in the Woods."

"You're kind of freaking me out, Clarissa. Are you implying there's a connection to Lord Graverly?"

She shook her head. "Lord Graverly moved into the manor in 1957, long after the bodies were found. There is so much history in this neighborhood, so much tragedy, so many ghosts. A young Korean student was attacked and nearly beaten to death near here a few years ago." She turned to look at me squarely. "I interviewed one of our neighbors today."

"Who?" I asked, feeling an urge to back away from her.

"Mr. Spencer Stuart Ross. Sweet old guy, and what a flirt. He's lived in the same apartment on Barclay Street for almost seventy years. He remembers Lord Graverly well, and the housemaid Sarah. She was a chestnut-haired beauty, he said, and she quickly fell for Lord Graverly's charms. Their relationship didn't raise eyebrows because nobody knew there was a Lady Graverly until she arrived in town with a baby in her arms. By then, Lord Graverly and Sarah were gone."

She turned again to scan the lagoon. "Mr. Ross's mother, Frances, knew Pauline and the Denby daughters. They used to hide out in the cellar and drink their father's wine, eat dried venison, and write poetry. Mr. Denby was a hunter, and he used the cellar as a butcher room."

"Then there was a cellar," I said.

"There still is, isn't there?"

"The house inspector thinks it was filled in when the private quarters were built."

"Edith was the last sister to survive. She hanged herself in that cellar."

"How tragic." Remembering the photograph in the manor of the sisters with Pauline Johnson, I wondered which of the sisters was Edith. Judging by their dour expressions, any one of them might have been depressed.

"The house sat empty after that until Lord Graverly bought it," said Clarissa. "Some of Pauline's work has never been found. Maybe it's been in the cellar all these years. I'd love to have a look."

"Wouldn't the police have searched the manor after Lord Graverly and Sarah disappeared?"

"Mr. Ross said the police never suspected foul play. They believed from the start that the two were lovers and ran off together."

"So the story about them drowning in the lagoon is a myth?"

"I think Lord Graverly drowned Sarah and then himself." She reached for my hand and placed it on her neck again. "Your teeth are chattering. Are you cold or scared?"

"A bit of both. I better get back to the house. The Wainrights will be back soon."

"I'll come with you."

As we climbed the path, Clarissa trotted beside me, as carefree as a little girl. It was hard to reconcile this innocence with the macabre stories she had been telling. She told me about her roommate in Lexington.

"She wants to come back with me in the summer," she said. "But I have a feeling I won't be back."

"When are you leaving?"

"In a week or so."

This news saddened me. It was a relief to have someone under retirement age around the manor. But I had to get used to guests coming and going.

When the manor came into view, I asked, "Have you ever been in Lady Graverly's private quarters?"

"Not yet. I'd love to get a look, though. I think that's where the entrance to the cellar is. You know about Elinor's son, right?"

I was nodding when I noticed a light coming from my room on the top floor. I had turned off the light when I left. Had Agnes been snooping there too? "I saw Agnes in the window of Lady Graverly's bedroom earlier," I said. "She was searching for something."

"I'm not surprised."

"Why?"

"I came across her passport the other day. Know what her last name is?"

I shook my head, opening the front gate for her.

"Kilpatrick."

The name sounded familiar. "So?" I asked.

"That was Sarah the housemaid's last name."

I stopped and turned to her, my eyes wide. "Agnes is Sarah?"

"Shh!" She gripped my arm. "Look."

I turned toward the house.

Lady Graverly's rigid figure stood in the foyer window.

★ ★ ★ ★ ★

"Where in god's name have you been?" Lady Graverly cried as I entered the house.

"I was out for a walk. I—"

"How dare you abandon the manor!"

Clarissa squeezed around me, making a beeline for the stairs. Lady Graverly's eyes followed her as she disappeared up the stairs. She turned back to me. "You were out with that … that *harlot*?"

"Elinor, for god's sake," I said under my breath, hoping Clarissa hadn't heard. "I told Agnes I was going for a walk. She promised to look after things."

"Agnes is not responsible for receiving guests, *you* are. Did I not inform you to be present at the cocktail hour? Because you were not here, I had to do everything. How dare you make me deal with those horrid people!"

"Who?"

"The Wainrights."

My eyes darted toward the stairs. Surely her voice had carried to the third floor.

"They've gone out to dinner," said Lady Graverly. "I scared them off."

"Do you know that they traveled across the continent to meet you?"

"They're insufferable! Four other guests have checked in as well. Had I not been here, there would have been no one to greet them."

"We had walk-ins?" How long had I been gone? It had seemed like a short time, but time moved quickly in Clarissa's company.

"They had reservations, you fool! Do you not consult the registry? Must I do everything?"

"I did check the registry!" I marched over to the desk and opened the book, flipping to today's date.

Elinor pointed at Lincoln's scrawl. "Can you not read?"

Upon closer inspection, I could make out two names, Phipps and Sherman. "That's a reservation? I thought it was a doodle."

"A *doodle*? Good gracious, child. I mean *really*."

"Are they here now?" I whispered, peering into the parlor.

"Everyone is out. What were you doing with that trollop?"

"Jesus, Elinor, be more respectful. She's a paying guest."

"Why show her respect when she has no respect for my privacy?" She clutched my arm, her nails digging into my skin. "I want her out of here!"

I pulled my hand away. "Elinor, relax, Clarissa is harmless. Why don't we go to the parlor and have a drink and talk this out."

"And you—you were peeking in my windows!" she hissed.

I clenched my fists. Had Agnes ratted me out? She was the one rifling through Lady Graverly's drawers. "If you extended the courtesy of showing me your apartment, I wouldn't have to resort to such measures, would I?"

"You promised to respect my privacy! You promised to conduct yourself in the spirit of noblesse oblige! I trusted you!"

"What are you hiding in there, Elinor?"

"If you ever violate my privacy again, so help me, I will make sure you regret it," she said, grabbing me by the shoulders and shaking me. "Do you hear me?"

I wrestled from her grasp and backed away, alarmed by her vitriol. "I understand," I said quietly. "I apologize."

"Now go to your room and stay there. And tell Agnes I wish to see her at once."

I climbed the stairs, stomping hard on each step like a teenager to voice my displeasure. I did not have to listen to that woman. She was not my mother. I should pack my bags and walk away. On the third floor, I stopped at Clarissa's door. Was she hiding under the bed, terrified, or on top of the bed, laughing hysterically? I felt both impulses. Lady Graverly's outburst had been scary.

As I reached the fourth floor, I heard the sound of weeping. Agnes. I felt an urge to slip into my room and close the door, but knew that her sobs would be amplified through the wall. I was angry at her for tattling like a nosy older sister when she was far more culpable than I. But I had never been able to bear the sound of a female crying, not since the days following my father's death, when I had been kept awake by sobbing from my sisters' and mother's rooms. I had been so paralyzed by my own grief that I had not been able to comfort them. Now, I did not have that excuse.

I tapped on the door. "Agnes? It's Trevor. Are you okay?"

The weeping stopped. "Go away!"

I stood with my hand on the doorknob, trying to decide what to do.

Suddenly the door flung open. Agnes glowered at me, her face wet and blotchy. "Why did you tell her?" she demanded.

"I told her nothing! *You* told her I was peeking in her window."

She placed her knuckles on her hips. "I did no such thing!"

"If you didn't, then who?"

Her eyes searched mine, suddenly fearful. She pulled away, made the sign of the cross, and tried to close the door on me.

I jammed my knee in the door. "Agnes, what the hell is going on in this crazy house?" She was pushing with all her might, crushing my knee. "What are you afraid of? Are you Sarah?"

The door gave way suddenly, and I stumbled into the room. Quickly I pulled the door closed behind me. "You are, aren't you? You're Sarah Kilpatrick."

She crawled backward on the bed, regarding me as though I were the devil. "How do you know about me sister?"

"Sarah was your sister?"

She nodded slowly, her eyes fixed on me. "Come one step closer, and I'll scream bloody murder."

"It's okay," I said, holding up my hands. "I won't hurt you, I promise."

"I know why you're here," she said.

"What do you mean?"

"You're here for the house."

"Of course I'm here for the house. You think I'm here on vacation? What happened to your sister, Agnes?"

Agnes snatched a heart-shaped locket from the nightstand, as though fearing I would steal it. She sat quietly, threading the fine gold chain through her fingers, and then began speaking in a low voice. "When I was a little girl, Sarah had a terrible quarrel with my father, and she ran away to Canada. She was only nineteen. A month later, she sent me a letter to tell me she had found a job in Vancouver, keeping house for a nobleman. She said he was very unattractive, a small man with a big temper, but he was a British war hero and very charming and funny. In the next letter, she said he asked her to marry him. She was very excited—she would become a titled lady—but also frightened, because he was a very strange man."

Agnes lifted her head, her eyes glassy. "I didn't hear from her for several months after that. I was dying to know if she married him. Then one day I received a short note from her, saying she was pregnant. She was terribly distraught and wanted to come home. I wrote back to her, begging her to return, telling her our father was certain to forgive her. But I never heard from her again."

"I'm sorry," I said.

"It was a long time ago," she said. A tear rolled down her cheek, falling on the yellow apron.

I sat down next to her and gave her my handkerchief. "How could Lord Graverly have offered to marry her when he already had a wife?"

"He must have lied to her. He wanted to trick her into lying with him."

"Maybe he intended to divorce Lady Graverly."

Her eyes filled with anger. "If Sarah knew he was married, she never would have stayed. She was proud and headstrong. When I didn't hear from her, I convinced my father to come to Canada and try to find her. He returned a week later a broken man. He had come to this house, and Lady Graverly told him Sarah had stolen her husband. My father never spoke my sister's name again. But I never believed Sarah would do that. I knew something terrible must have happened to her."

"Why are you here now, Agnes, after all these years?"

"I'm here to find out what happened to my sister and to claim what rightfully belonged to her. A few months ago, I read in the papers that Lord Wakefield had passed on and Lady Graverly had come forward to claim the estate. I decided it was time to solve the mystery once and for all, and I traveled to London to meet with Lord Wakefield's widow. Then I came here to meet with Lady Graverly."

Only now did I realize that Agnes's persona had transformed. The uneducated shrew had been replaced by a polite, articulate woman. "Does Lady Graverly know who you are?" I asked.

She lowered her head, turning the locket in her fingers. "I had intended to tell her, but when I came to the manor, Lincoln thought

I was here about the vacant housekeeper position. I know nothing about being a housekeeper—I was a schoolteacher for almost thirty years before I retired—but when Lincoln offered me the job, I decided it would put me in a good position to find out what happened to Sarah."

Now I understood why Agnes was such a lousy housekeeper. I noticed the state of her bedroom for the first time. It was even smaller than mine and more drab, with a grey, water-stained ceiling that sloped almost to the floor. Articles of clothing were strewn everywhere—peasant dresses, old stockings, and slipper shoes. The no-name beauty products I had seen in the bathroom now littered the vanity and floor.

"What do you hope to find here?" I asked.

"Sarah kept a diary." Following my gaze, she added, "She stayed in the tower room."

"In my room? Is that why you were in there tonight?"

She looked away, her face coloring.

"Did you find anything?" I asked.

She shook her head and gave a sigh. Then she held out the locket, urging me to take it. "I found this in Lady Graverly's dresser today."

Taking it from her, I pried it open and saw a tiny black-and-white photo of a pretty blond-haired girl inside. "This is you?"

She nodded, her lower lip trembling as she struggled not to cry.

"Why would Lady Graverly keep Sarah's locket?"

"I don't know."

I handed back the locket. "Do you think your sister is still alive?"

"I think Sarah's been dead for a very long time," she said, holding the locket to her lips.

A noise outside the door made us jump. I crept over and opened the door. The vestibule was empty. Closing the door, I turned to Agnes and whispered, "Lincoln must know what happened to your sister."

She gave a grim smile. "I've tried everything to get him to talk—and I mean everything—but he's either too loyal or he simply has no idea. He came here after Sarah disappeared, but I'm convinced he knows something and is too afraid to speak. In the past few days, I've begun to wonder if his loyalty is faltering."

"What do you think happened to your sister?"

Her expression hardened. "Lord Graverly seduced Sarah with the false promise of marriage, impregnated her, and, upon receiving word his wife was coming from England, murdered her."

Her words were chilling. "Then what happened to Lord Graverly?"

She closed her eyes. "I don't know."

"And Lady Graverly? How does she fit into all this?"

The chain snapped in two in her hands. She gave a small yelp and placed the pieces on the nightstand. "Graverly Castle is worth a vast sum of money. Under peerage rules, if a title holder is convicted of murder, the conviction taints his blood and the blood of all descendants, and the property and title are forfeited to the crown."

"You think she covered up Lord Graverly's crime to protect her inheritance?"

She lowered her voice to a whisper. "Tonight, as I was leaving her bedroom, I left the curtain open. When she came home, I went to the back yard to spy on her. As she was undressing, she noticed the open curtain and came to the window, yanking it shut." Her eyes grew wide. "Trevor, I saw the strangest thing. She—"

"Agnes!" Lady Graverly's voice bellowed from the stairs. "Where are you?"

Agnes let out a cry and covered her mouth. She tiptoed to the door, reverting to her deferential manner. "Yes, m'lady?"

"Why do you insist on keeping me waiting? Come down here this instant!"

She turned to me and whispered, "You better go."

"But—"

"Out! Now!" She held the door open, gesturing frantically.

I stepped out and turned in the hallway, uneasy about leaving her alone. I watched Agnes as she went to the mirror and gazed at her reflection. Picking up a hairbrush, she lifted her grey hair to brush it, exposing her thin, delicate neck.

"Are you in danger, Agnes?" I whispered.

Her head spun around. "Go, I beg you! I'll tell you the rest tomorrow."

Reluctantly, I retreated to my room.

★ ★ ★ ★ ★

Late that night, I was awakened by the sound of a shriek.

I sat up. Agnes. It had come from somewhere deep within the house. The pantry? Lincoln must be back, I thought, a smile spreading over my lips. Agnes was pumping him for information.

I drifted back to sleep.

14

Palace Intrigue

I was roused from sleep by a pounding on my door. I fumbled on the nightstand for my cell phone.

5:23 AM. "Who is it?" I called out.

"Lady Andrew Graverly."

I quickly pulled on a pair of pants and a shirt and opened the door.

Lady Graverly was standing in the shadows of the vestibule in a green velvet robe, only her pale lips visible under the hood. "I require you to prepare breakfast," she said wearily, leaning heavily on a cane. "Agnes has returned to Scotland."

"So suddenly? Why?"

"There's been a family tragedy."

"Oh no. What happened?"

"The poor dear's sister passed on."

"That's terrible."

"A dreadful pity."

"Give me a minute to get dressed, and I'll be right down." I went to close the door, then remembered how many guests we had in-house. "Is Lincoln around?" I asked.

"He stayed at his lady friend's last night, but he promises to come as quickly as possible."

"Good. Elinor, are you okay? You don't look well."

She pulled the robe closer to her neck. "It seems I've come down with a touch of fever."

"Go and rest. Don't worry, I'll take care of everything."

"Thank you, my prince. I am ever so grateful."

I watched the shadow of her profile on the wall as she hobbled down the stairs with the cane, looking like the grim reaper in her hooded robe.

★ ★ ★ ★ ★

I stood before the mirror in the three-piece suit Lady Graverly had given me, the gold watch tucked into the pocket, its chain draped across the vest. I had forgotten to return the items to her, and decided that wearing them for a day would be harmless. She had looked so distraught, so sickly, I hoped that seeing me in the suit might cheer her up. As I struggled to figure out how to tie the ascot, Agnes's shriek replayed in my mind. It now took on new meaning: a cry of anguish upon receiving news of her sister's death. How ironic that she had come here to solve the mystery of one sister's death only to lose another.

My thoughts drifted back to our conversation. Agnes had accused Lord Graverly of seducing Sarah with the promise of marriage, of concealing the fact that he was already married, and of killing her upon receiving news of his wife's pending arrival from England. Her version was consistent with others I had heard, but with one major difference: Sarah had been pregnant when she died. If it was true, the story was doubly tragic. I closed my eyes, imagining Lord Graverly drowning the pregnant Sarah in the lagoon. The image was so lucid that my eyes snapped open. *They say the lagoon is bottomless*, my mother had said. Could their bodies still be roiling within its depths?

The ascot was not cooperating. Every attempt to tie it looked unnatural and affected. My skin was still warm from the shower, and beads of perspiration were forming on my brow. Guests would be rising soon and gathering in the dining room with growling stomachs. Losing patience, I yanked at the ascot with both hands, choking, and then let go, swearing out loud. Taking a deep breath, I started over.

How disappointing that Agnes had left so suddenly, before I had a chance to find out what she had seen through Lady Graverly's window that had troubled her so. Why was she so terrified of Lady Graverly? If Lady Graverly was covering up Lord Graverly's crime to protect her inheritance, then Agnes posed a viable threat, but if Lady Graverly knew Agnes's true identity, surely she would have thrown her out of the house. If Lady Graverly was covering up a murder for her own personal gain, I had little sympathy for her. But hadn't the lawsuit already been settled in court against her favor? Lady Graverly had inferred that she was merely resolving a small legal matter concerning the title of the house. Earlier yesterday, Agnes had questioned whether the manor was in Lady Graverly's name. If it was still in Lord Graverly's name, would the sale be delayed? I wasn't sure how much longer I could bear living with Lady Graverly and Lincoln—not to mention Sir Fester.

I thought back to Lady Graverly's cryptic remarks about privacy and discretion, about loyalty and forgiveness. Lynne Crocker had advised me to treat our meeting like a job interview. Did Lady Graverly consider it inevitable that the new proprietor would learn of the manor's troubled past and so had screened applicants in search of someone who would turn a blind eye? Had I been selected not for my hotel experience but because I was naïve and easily manipulated?

Then what about her prattle about destiny, entitlement, and justice? *Without children, one has no heirs, no one to carry on the family name,* she had said. *For a bloodline to go extinct is truly tragic.* Perhaps the estate was still being contested; it wasn't in her nature to give up easily. She had insisted that titles and money meant nothing to her, but all evidence was to the contrary. Did she want it so badly that she had covered up Sarah's murder for almost fifty years? On the night of the open house, Lincoln had introduced her as the Marchioness of Middlesex, yet I hadn't heard that title used in reference to her since. Had she lost it along with the estate—and if so, why? If Lord Andrew was dead, did she have any claim to his title? She herself had said that titles were passed down through male descendants; if there were none, the title reverted to the crown. Even if she had a claim to the title, with no heirs it would go extinct upon her death, wouldn't it?

Do you intend to have offspring of your own? she had asked me.

At last, the ascot fell into place. I stepped back to admire it, pleased to see how the outfit transformed my appearance, transported me back to a previous century, elevated me to a higher social status.

A thought struck me with such force that I stumbled back. What if Lady Graverly intended to adopt me as her son? Would that make me the Marquess of Middlesex?

By the time I got downstairs, it was after six, and I was forced to set aside all thoughts of titles and castles and concentrate on the less-exalted reality of my multiple roles as cook, server, bellboy, housekeeper, and butler. With so many guests in-house and such little practice, I could have used some help, but I decided it was better to not have the sloppy Agnes or the sluggish Lincoln around. Soon I found myself whistling happily as I shuttled from kitchen to dining room to parlor, organizing the buffet and setting the table.

Next I went to light a fire. Discovering that the supply of kindling was low, I searched for the axe to cut some more, but it was nowhere to be found. I used the last of what kindling remained, and in a few minutes there was a roaring fire. Digging out an old Rachmaninoff record from the cabinet, I placed it on the gramophone and sat down in the parlor with a cup of coffee, enjoying a moment of peace before the guests came down. My thoughts kept returning to Agnes, to her sister Sarah and to the evil Lord Graverly, but I pushed them away. I refused to get further involved in this palace intrigue. In a matter of weeks, all of these characters, dead and alive, would be exorcized from the house, and I would be able to focus my attention on building my new business. Gazing around at the cozy parlor, I realized that for the first time in years, maybe even for the first time ever, I felt a sense of home. These moments of peace and well-being would be fleeting, and I needed to cherish them.

The first stirrings of guests sounded upstairs: a door opening, footsteps, a flushing toilet. If I didn't eat now, it might be hours before I had another opportunity. I rose from the chair and headed toward the kitchen, stopping to inspect the buffet on the way. I decided it looked sparse. In the kitchen, I took a pound of bacon from the refrigerator, arranged the strips on a pan, and slid the pan into the oven. Then I slathered jam on a croissant and wolfed it down standing up. Dusting crumbs off my apron, I tried to imagine what life would be like as a marquess. I envisioned Graverly Castle, set on acres of rolling green hills on the outskirts of Greater London, with manicured gardens, a stable of horses, and a pack of hunting dogs. I would have a circle of fantastically rich, title-bearing friends and acquaintances that included royals, heads of state, and celebrities. I wondered whether the title marquess came with robes and a crown. If so, I would wear them on my wedding day, when I would marry a beautiful, young marchioness. Each night we would dine at opposite ends of a mile-long table, a cast of first-rate servants standing at attention at our side. Soon there would be little marchionettes—or whatever one called them—and I would teach them how to play polo, perhaps take up cricket, and—

The kitchen door swung open, and a short, muscular black man in boxer shorts and a tank top walked in. "How's it going?" he said, giving a stretch and yawn.

"Fine," I said, pulling off the apron and adjusting my ascot. I held out my hand. "I'm Trevor, the"—I almost said "Marquess of Middlesex," if only to hear it out loud, but stopped short—"the innkeeper."

He shook my hand, introducing himself as Aldus from Denver. He observed my outfit, blinked several times, and then went to the refrigerator.

"There's a full buffet in the dining room," I informed him, holding the door for him. "May I pour you a cup of coffee?"

"Totally! Decaf nonfat cappuccino, please."

"I'm sorry, but I don't have a cappuccino machine."

"Oh, okay. Coffee is fine. Decaf, please."

In the dining room, he frowned at the buffet, scratching his stubble.

"Are you looking for something in particular?" I asked. Detecting an alarming note of condescension in my tone, I changed my tune immediately. "I'd be happy to prepare something for you."

"Really? An omelet would be awesome."

"It would be my pleasure."

"Egg whites only—and spinach," he said, following me into the kitchen. "You got any feta and red bell peppers kicking around?"

"I'll see what I can rustle up," I said affably.

"Stephen will be down in a minute. He loves blueberry pancakes."

Suddenly I felt very busy. To get him out of my hair, I escorted him back to the dining room and sat him down at the table, then returned to the kitchen. Rummaging around the freezer, I found an old can of Taster's Choice decaf covered in frost. It looked as old as Lincoln, but it would have to do. Substitutions would be necessary in the omelet, I discovered upon taking stock of the refrigerator. Cooking had never been my strong point; in hotels, meals were provided, and I spent so much time at work I rarely ate at home. It was an opportunity to be creative. Plugging in the kettle, I began chopping a wilted green pepper. The kettle began to boil at the same time the telephone rang in the foyer. Unplugging the kettle, I hurried down the hallway, cursing the absence of a portable phone.

"Good morning, Graverly Manor," I said, lifting the receiver. "This is Trevor. How may I help you?"

"WE NEED OUR BAGS BROUGHT DOWN," shouted Mrs. Wainright into the phone.

I yanked the phone from my ear. "I thought you were departing tomorrow, Mrs. Wainright?"

"ELINOR TOLD US WE HAVE TO LEAVE."

"She what? There must be a mix-up. I'm sure I can—"

"CHUCK WANTS TO LEAVE ANYWAY." Her voice reverberated through the house. "SOMETHING ABOUT THAT WOMAN DISTURBED HIM DEEPLY. HE'S BARELY SAID A WORD SINCE."

I cringed, imagining any number of offensive things Lady Graverly might have said or done. "May I help you with arrangements at another hotel, then?"

"WE'RE BOOKED AT THE FAIRMONT."

"Very well. I'll come up to retrieve your bags now. Is there any-thing—?"

The phone clattered down.

Taking three steps at a time, I climbed to the third floor and knocked on the Elizabeth II suite. Behind me, the door to the Victoria suite opened, and a heavyset woman in a man's T-shirt emerged, trailed by a burly, shirtless man scratching his belly.

"You must be the Phipps from Seattle," I said, pleased to see another youngish couple. "I'm Trevor. The bathroom is just to your right."

"Where's breakfast being served?" asked Mrs. Phipps, running a hand through her hair and squinting.

"Downstairs, in the dining room."

As they headed downstairs, I eyed Mr. Phipps' hairy back, under-standing why Lady Graverly supplied complimentary bathrobes. To have Clarissa wander around in a negligee was tolerable—should even be encouraged—but this was another matter entirely.

Mrs. Wainright opened the door in a floor-length baby blue night-gown. She peered out, taking a moment to recognize me. "Chuck, hurry, it's the bellboy!" she hollered over her shoulder. Turning back to me, she said, "He's going to need some help down the stairs. He's not well at all, I'm afraid. It's just one of those mornings. Oh gosh, our bags aren't ready yet either."

"That's okay. Take your time. I'll come back."

"No, wait here. It'll take but a moment."

Through the open door of the en suite bathroom, I could see Mr. Wainright sitting on the toilet. Mrs. Wainright fussed about the room. On the second floor, I heard the door of the Mary I room open. No question, now I was experiencing a rush. In hotels, there were always other staff members around to pitch in. Here I was alone, and I couldn't help but feel a flutter of panic.

"I'll be right back, Mrs. Wainright," I said.

On the stairs, I encountered a tall, chisel-faced fellow, the first fully dressed guest of the day. "You must be Stephen," I said. "I'm Trevor." *The Marquess of Middlesex,* a little voice whispered in my head, sending a tiny thrill through me. "I hear you like blueberry pancakes."

"Sure do! But I've got a hankering for French toast today."

In the dining room, I introduced Stephen to the Phipps, who were heaping buffet items onto their plates. Dashing into the kitchen, I returned with pots of coffee and tea and a cup of instant decaf for Aldus.

"I'd die for an espresso," I heard Stephen say as I poured the sludge into his cup.

Holding my smile, I pretended not to hear him. Where was Lincoln? He wouldn't have been much help, but a warm body to greet guests and top up beverages would be better than nothing. Back in the kitchen, I cracked eggs, separated whites from yolks, and dug out an eggbeater from the cupboard. The ring of the telephone interrupted me again, and I hurried out to answer it, scolding myself along the way for getting rattled. I should be grateful to be busy; I had always loved being in the thick of things.

A woman with a thick German accent demanded to know if I had rooms available in April. I told her yes, and she drilled me on various aspects of the manor and the neighborhood. I answered courteously, mindful of my guests but excited by the prospect of my first sale. "That would be the Victoria suite, our largest," I informed the woman, hoping I had gotten it right. "The size? ... hm ... approximately 750 square feet, I believe ... yes, it is quite large." Had I overestimated? "The rate? One moment, please." Setting the receiver down, I flipped through the guest registry, searching for rates from previous or future stays with no success. I would have to improvise. I picked the receiver back up. "Here we are. The rack rate for the Victoria suite is $1,200 per night, but I can offer a special—"

"*Ja*, I take it. Five nights, coming April nine."

The ka-ching of a cash register went off in my head. "Terrific! I'll just need your credit card number to hold the reservation." As I rummaged around for a pen, a clatter drew my attention to the staircase. I craned my neck and spotted Mr. Wainright teetering at the top of the steps. Mrs. Wainright was nowhere in sight. Fearing disaster, I asked the caller to hold and charged up the stairs, catching Mr. Wainright just as he was about to fall. Hooking his cane over my arm, I guided him down the stairs one agonizing step at a time.

Halfway down, the doorbell rang.

Christ. Where the hell was Lincoln? And Lady Graverly, for that matter? To not come out to assist during all this commotion, she had better be on her death bed. *I am the Marquess of Middlesex*, my little voice declared. *I am above this kind of work.*

The doorbell rang again.

Losing patience, I picked up Mr. Wainright in both arms and carried him down the stairs, steadied him against the banister, and handed him his cane.

The doorbell rang three more times, followed by several raps on the brass knocker.

"I'll be there in a minute!" I called out. I returned to the phone, deciding that a six-thousand-dollar sale was more important than visitors right now. But a noise on the other side of the door to Lady Graverly's private quarters made me freeze. Moaning. It started low and rose in volume. I felt my skin spasm over my skull. I glanced at

Mr. Wainright, who was clinging to the banister and gaping in the direction of the Gothic door. The moaning stopped.

"Hey Trevor?" Aldus called from the parlor. "Mind if we put on something a little more upbeat?"

"Be my guest," I said. Keeping an eye on the Gothic door, I slowly lifted the receiver. "Hello, ma'am? I'm terribly sorry to keep you waiting … Pardon me? … Oh yes, we do keep a busy little manor here. Now about that credit card … I'm sorry? … Things to do in Vancouver? Well, there are lots of options. I can send you some information with your confirmation, if you like. What kind of credit card—the art gallery? I'm not sure of the hours, but …"

A flicker of shadow drew my attention to the stained-glass window beside the front door. A little girl pressed her hands and nose against the glass. Behind her stood figures in all sorts of shapes and sizes—a small crowd. For a moment I feared that a group of neighbors had gathered, like peasants storming the castle gates. In the parlor, Madonna began singing "Like a Prayer." The volume steadily increased until it was all I could hear. I was partly relieved, having feared that the moaning would resume and frighten the guests.

Mrs. Phipps came running down the hall. "Something's on fire!"

"Oh no, the bacon! Would you mind taking it out of the oven for me?"

She retreated down the hallway.

Mr. Wainright left the banister to gawk at her bare legs. His cane clattered to the floor, and he lost his balance, pitching forward. Dropping the phone, I rushed over to catch him, managing only to soften his fall.

"What have you done to my husband?" Mrs. Wainright cried, hurrying down the stairs.

"I didn't—he fell!" I said, kneeling down before him. He was writhing on the floor, opening and closing his mouth like a fish out of water. "He'll be fine. I think."

"Chuck, can you hear me?" Mrs. Wainright shouted.

"Get that crazy fellow away from me!" he cried, kicking his legs, having fallen into some kind of delirium.

"Is someone going to get that door?" Aldus shouted from the parlor.

I stood up and went to the door, flinging it open. A round-faced man, a round-faced woman, and six grubby children stared back at me.

"Checkin' in!" shouted the man, grinning ear to ear.

"We're the Tattersalls!" the woman chimed in. "Hope we're not too late for breakfast! We drove all night from Red Deer, and we're *starving*!" She peered around me and spotted Mr. Wainright on the floor. Her smile faded.

"Welcome to Graverly Manor," I said, forcing a smile. I stepped aside, gesturing for them to enter. "Excuse me for just a moment."

As I returned to help Mr. Wainright, Sir Fester raced in and pounced into my path, and I stepped on his tail. He let out a blood-curdling yowl and hissed at me, baring his fangs. I hissed back, and he scurried down the hall and out of sight.

Mr. Wainright was back on his feet, but smoke was now billowing from the kitchen. Racing down the hallway, I found the oven door open and a pan of charred bacon on the stovetop. Mrs. Phipps was on the back steps, bent over and coughing. I hurried back down the hall. Lady Graverly's words came back to me: *When it all becomes too much, I take a suite at the Four Seasons, if only for a few hours.* I wondered if it was too early to check in.

In the foyer, Mrs. Tattersall looked at me with an expression that suggested she wished she had booked the Holiday Inn.

"Where's that moanin' sound comin' from?" asked Mr. Tattersall.

One of the kids pointed at the entrance to the private quarters, eyes bulging with fear.

I snatched up the phone. "I'm so sorry to keep you waiting, ma'am. May I call you back in a few minutes?"

But the line was dead.

★ ★ ★ ★ ★

There was no sign of the Tattersall reservation in the guest registry.

"First time I called, some lady who sounded like the Queen said you were sold out," Mrs. Tattersall told me, bouncing a Buddha-like baby in her arms. "My sister's wedding is at the Rainbow Community Church just up the street, so we wanted to stay here. When I called back, a different lady answered and said there were lots of rooms, we didn't even need a reservation, we could just show up whenever."

Agnes. A former schoolteacher, not an illiterate maid. Had this been part of her act, or had she deliberately sabotaged reservations to make Lady Graverly's life miserable? Meanwhile, Lady Graverly was resting in her quarters while I was dealing with the aftermath. My eyes moved to her door. The moaning hadn't sounded in some time. I hoped it would stay that way.

"I booked two rooms," said Mrs. Tattersall. "The kids can double up and sleep on the floor."

Given Lady Graverly's ban on children, I had serious misgivings about registering this boisterous family. But they had been on the road for almost twenty-four hours, and I wasn't about to turn them away. Hoping for the best, I assigned them the Henry VIII and Edward I rooms on the second floor and offered to escort them up.

"Sure would be nice to have some breakfast first," said Mr. Tattersall. "Kids are real hungry."

★ ★ ★ ★ ★

A half-hour later, I carried plates heaping with omelets, banana pancakes, and scrambled eggs into the dining room, where the Tattersall children had gathered around the table, forks poised, eyeing the dishes hungrily. In the corner, Aldus was chatting with Mr. Tattersall, one arm around Stephen. I had been apprehensive about mixing this eclectic group—a gay couple in gym attire, a middle-aged couple in bedclothes, octogenarians dressed for church, and a small-town family in denims and plaids—but they appeared to be getting along marvelously. Even Clarissa had joined the group, having been awakened by the commotion. She was sitting by the window in a sleeveless midriff yoga top, looking sleep-deprived as she listened to Mr. Wainright's war stories. As I set down the plates, I caught a glimpse of a tattoo peeking out of her waistband of a leather-clad woman cracking a whip. I quickly averted my eyes and met Mrs. Wainright's smiling, oblivious gaze.

"Not a man," Mrs. Tattersall was saying to her. "A woman. My sister's marrying a woman."

"Oh, I see," said Mrs. Wainright, still not comprehending.

"Did you hear that scream last night?" Aldus asked Mrs. Phipps.

She nodded, her jaw dropping. "I thought somebody was being murdered. It was so loud I was afraid it had come from inside this house."

"Cats can make the spookiest sounds," I said.

"I'll always be grateful, no matter what he's gone and done," Mr. Wainright was telling Clarissa, rubbing his bruised arm. "He saved my life!"

An hour later, breakfast was over, and all the guests got up to leave at the same time. Clarissa stayed behind to help clean up.

"It's really not necessary," I said, although I wasn't entirely averse to having her around. "This isn't a co-op."

"I don't mind. Where's Agnes, anyway?"

"She had to go back to Scotland. Her sister died."

"What? That's horrible."

"Last night, you were about to tell me Agnes was Sarah Kilpatrick's sister, weren't you?"

She nodded. "Is it true? Did she tell you why she was here?"

"She wants to find out what happened to her sister."

"Did you tell her to go for a swim in the lagoon?" She pressed her hand over her mouth. "Sorry, that wasn't even funny."

As she rounded the table to gather dishes, I sneaked another peak at her tattoo. Something glinted in the morning sun, and I saw a silver amulet next to the tattoo, a tiny shield piercing her bellybutton. My mouth suddenly felt dry, and I reached for a glass, gulping down water.

"Did you hear Agnes cry out last night?" I asked. "It was the eeriest sound."

"She must have been at it again with Lincoln."

"That's what I thought," I said, following her into the kitchen with an armload of dirty dishes, "but Lincoln stayed at his girlfriend's last night."

"I didn't hear anything. I was out until five, and after that I was heavily medicated."

"What do you do when you go out so late at night?"

"Research. I visit Pauline's grave, walk through the lagoon, explore the neighborhood."

"I can't wait to read your thesis. I'm sure it's uplifting." Dance music was still playing in the parlor, and I went to turn it off.

When I returned, Clarissa was feeding Sir Fester.

"When is a good time for me to clean your room today?" I asked, filling the sink with water.

"You're cleaning my room?"

"You don't want me to?"

"It's kind of weird."

"I can ask Lincoln if you prefer, but it might take a week."

"No, it's fine. I'm going back to bed for a while, but I'll be out in the late afternoon. I have a date with my new boy-toy, Spencer Stuart Ross. Knock first, okay?"

"I promise."

I was in the kitchen compiling a grocery list when Mr. Tattersall wandered in.

"Kids are gettin' real hungry," he said, opening and closing cupboard doors.

"I'm sorry, Mr. Tattersall, but lunch isn't part of the package," I said, already a bit resentful that I had been obliged to throw in an extra breakfast for eight.

He went to the refrigerator and pulled out a carton of milk, giving it a sniff. "Not even a few sandwiches?"

"Sorry," I said. Fearing he was about to drink from the carton, I handed him a glass. "There are lots of family-friendly restaurants on Denman Street."

He filled the glass, chugged it down, and filled it again. "We were thinking about packing some lunch and heading down to the park for a winter picnic," he said, eyeing the contents of the fridge.

"I can call a deli for you," I offered.

"Swell!"

Upstairs, I could hear the kids jumping on beds and screech-ing. Surprisingly, Lady Graverly had not emerged from her quarters. Remembering the moaning, I went to her door and knocked. When there was no answer, I tried the door handle. It was locked.

★ ★ ★ ★ ★

An hour later, the last of the children scrambled down the front steps. I slammed the door and fell against it, praying for a period of peace to focus on my housework. I had four rooms to clean, and I suspected the Tattersalls' rooms would require a major cleaning too, even though they had not yet spent a night.

Sure enough, I opened the door of the Henry VIII suite to find the floor and furnishings covered in feathers. A half-hour later, I had just put the vacuum away when the doorbell rang downstairs. Fearing more unexpected arrivals, I made my way downstairs and peeked out the window. A woman in a white wool coat stood on the verandah, her back facing me. It took a moment to recognize my sister. I had been so consumed by the manor, I had forgotten about the outside world. I opened the door and called her name. She turned around, and my spirits soared at the sight of her friendly, familiar face.

"Hiya, Trevor! You ready?" She half-opened her arms, expecting a hug.

I stared at her dumbly. "Ready for what?" A vague recollection of lunch plans fluttered in the back of my mind. Impossible. I had far too much work to do.

Her smile faltered. She looked pretty and unusually stylish in the white coat and a burgundy turtleneck. Her dirty-blond hair was tied up, lips sparkling with purple gloss. Behind her, a little boy climbed up the steps. I recoiled, fearing the Tattersalls were back already.

"Hi, Uncle Trevor," he said.

"Hi there ... Jordan!"

"It's Quinn," Wendy said. "Jordan is Janet's son. I hope it's okay I brought him. He has no school today."

Quinn peered into the house, eyes wide, and boldly stepped forward, holding up the copy of *The Consummate Host* I had lent him.

"You read the whole thing already?" I said, taking it from him.

"I mostly just looked at the pictures."

"Well, I hope it was enough to scare you off from wanting to be a hotel manager," I said, grinning as I tucked the book under my arm.

"Mom was really mad when she found out you gave it away," Wendy said. "She said it's a collector's item or something. Did Lady Graverly's husband write it?"

"Lord Andrew?" I said, puzzled. "No. Why do you ask?"

She gestured to the book. I lifted it and read the author's name for the first time: Lord Wakefield Graverly, the Marquess of Middlesex. "How strange," I said, turning the book over and taking a closer look at the man's photograph. "Lord Wakefield was Lord Andrew's brother," I said. Now I understood why Mom had given the book to me. It was Graverly Castle the author had converted into an inn.

Wendy's eyes perused my attire, and the Lambert expression gripped her facial muscles. "Um, what are you wearing, Trevor?"

I moved my hand to my neck self-consciously. "It's an ascot. Lady Graverly gave it to me." I held up the book to show her the back cover. "Look, he's wearing one too. You don't like it?"

"I guess it kind of suits you—if you're going for that pompous-ass look."

Beside her, Quinn giggled. Then he grew serious, and his eyes darted into the house on a sharp lookout for the scary lady.

"My good woman," I quipped. "Here at Graverly Manor, we dress in accordance with the exquisite traditions of ye olde England."

She flashed a fake smile. "Uh, yeah, so you're not going to wear that to lunch, are you?"

I looked down at her shoes. Purple Crocs, the same hue as her lip gloss, ruining an otherwise acceptable outfit. "Only if you promise not to wear those."

Her jaw hardened. "I like Crocs, Trevor. They're practical."

"Wendy, there's no way I can go for lunch. I'm too busy."

"What? We drove all the way from Port Coquitlam. We got all dressed up."

I noticed the collared shirt under Quinn's ski jacket—and the blue Crocs on his feet. I felt a stab of guilt. "I'm really sorry, but I'm on my own today. I've got a half-dozen rooms to clean, plus laundry, groceries, a million other things."

"I could give you a hand."

"Thanks, but I don't need your help."

Wendy pressed her purple lips together. "Mom thinks you need a *lot* of help."

"Yes, well, she always has, hasn't she?"

"She thinks we should turn this place into a family business. I could cook and clean, Janet could serve breakfast, you could play host. Even Jas and Dave would be handy around the house."

Wendy's husband, Jas, worked at Langley Hospital too, as an orderly; Janet's husband was a mechanic. Mother had never approved of my vocation, yet she had recognized an opportunity to maneuver her way into my life and had invited the family along. I knew she wouldn't be able to resist meddling. The truth was, I could have used

Wendy's help. She was a hard worker and far more efficient than Lincoln or Agnes. But I feared that if I opened the door even a crack, the entire family would charge in, in the same manner the Tattersalls had arrived that morning, and I'd be subject to their judgments, their mockery and ridicule. The Inn at Lost Lagoon would not be serving hospital food or donuts. It would be a luxury five-star inn, a—I stopped my train of thought, alarmed by the similarity to Lady Graverly's words.

"Thanks for the offer, Wendy. You can tell Mom I can handle things on my own just fine. I always have."

She crossed her arms. "Aren't you even going to invite me in?"

Beside her, Quinn crossed his own arms in solidarity.

"I have to get back to work. Can we do lunch another time?"

"Fine," she snapped, grabbing Quinn and pulling him toward the stairs. "I'll see you Sunday."

"Sunday?"

She spun around. "Dinner at Mom's. She said you confirmed."

"Right. Uh, I don't think I can make it."

"Trevor, Mom has been talking about this dinner all week. She wants just the four of us—no husbands, no kids. Just like the good old times."

Our eyes locked briefly in silent acknowledgement that there had never been any "good old times" in our household, at least not after Dad died.

"I'll try," I assured her, knowing it would be impossible now that Agnes was out of the picture.

"For Pete's sake, Trevor, we've barely seen you since you came back. You act like you still live thousands of miles away." Her chin began to tremble—a precursor to tears, something I did not want to see, not ever again.

"Okay, I'll come," I told her quickly.

Her face relaxed, and she forced a smile. "Great. See you Sunday, then."

As the Caravan rolled down the street, I felt a pang of regret. I would have far preferred spending the afternoon with them over being trapped in the manor scrubbing toilets. Why did I find it so hard to demonstrate my affection for my sisters? Life put so many obstacles in the way. As soon as I got the manor under control, I vowed, I would repair and rebuild my relationships with family members and find a way to integrate them into my life.

For now, I had chores to do. Grabbing a mop, I headed upstairs.

Later, while making beds, I searched high and low for extra linens but couldn't find any. I was obliged to strip the beds and launder the linens before remaking them; this was a time-consuming process that occupied most of the afternoon. As I made my fifth trip to the laundry room, a stuffy, decrepit hovel located down a set of rickety steps off the kitchen, I resolved to introduce an environmental program to allow guests to opt out of daily linen service, a tactic employed by hotels to save laundry expenses by playing on traveler guilt.

By five o'clock, I had turned over all guestrooms save for Clarissa's. I knocked on her door several times, counted to twenty, opened it a crack and identified myself, and then entered. The Edward VI room was cramped and starkly furnished, its floor covered with a threadbare, tapestry-like carpet, the walls decorated with miniature oil paintings depicting nineteenth-century battle scenes. The canopy bed was draped in worn green velvet, the sheets and blankets tangled like a wild animal had slept there. I stripped the bed, placed the sheets in the washer, then went back up to dust and wipe down surfaces.

In passing I noticed Clarissa's notebooks, yellow notepads filled with scribbles, and stacks of poetry books, history books, and books about Vancouver—and, curiously, several books about ghosts. I lifted the top one and glanced at its title: *Missing Pieces: How to Investigate Ghosts, UFOs, Psychics & Other Mysteries*. It seemed that her thesis on Pauline Johnson required a broad range of reading. I set it down and resumed cleaning.

In the bathroom, an assortment of glass apothecary bottles lined the counter. Curious, I unscrewed one and sniffed. The scent produced an instantaneous image of Clarissa standing before me stark naked. Alarmed and titillated at the same time, I sniffed it again and quickly set it down.

A couple of hours later, I retrieved the clean sheets from the laundry room and returned to Clarissa's room to make the bed. Folded into one of the sheets I found a pair of cotton panties. I crawled across the mattress to the dresser to put them away and paused, holding them up. They were plain, baby blue in color, and rather large—not exactly the style I would fantasize about her wearing, but sexy nonetheless. Closing my eyes, I envisioned her sliding them down her shapely, razor-cut legs. Why did she have such a hold on me? With her dark mascara, tattoos, and macabre behavior, she was different from any woman I had ever been attracted to. My girlfriends had always been wholesome and sweet, only later turning out to be poisonous inside. Clarissa was bad ass and dangerous on the outside, and, I felt certain, wholesome and sweet inside. My crush was harmless; she would be gone in less than a week. Maybe the manor could become a source of fleeting relationships, providing a constant stream of prospects who checked out before I became too attached. It was an ideal scenario, really, a—

"What the hell are you doing?"

My eyes flew open. The panties fell from my hands. Clarissa was standing at the door, gaping at me. I burst into motion, reaching to tuck in the sheet. "Just, uh, finishing up your bed," I stammered. "Almost done!"

"Uh-huh."

"Can you give me five minutes to finish up?"

"I want you out of here *now*."

"Fine," I said, scrambling off the bed and standing up, straightening my ascot. "I wasn't—I didn't—I—"

"Out!" She pushed me out the door and slammed it behind me.

I stood in the hallway, lungs heaving. Turning back to the door, I opened my mouth to explain myself but closed it, fearing I would only make things worse. I lumbered upstairs to my room and threw myself on my bed, feeling humiliated and despicable. What had come over me? Had sexual frustration turned me into a pervert? Or ... that potion in her bathroom ... had it cast me under a spell? I thought of the ghost books. Was Clarissa a witch, an evil temptress? Or was this house corrupting me, destroying my decency—and my soul?

Yes, I told myself, *blame it on the house.*

When I emerged from my room an hour later, Clarissa was gone. I desperately wanted to apologize, to explain myself, but I was at a loss as to how. What if she told Lady Graverly? I was already treading on thin ice. I would be thrown out and forever known as the perv.

Downstairs, the telephone was ringing.

"I THINK I LEFT MY UNDERGARMENTS ON THE BED," Mrs. Wainright hollered into the phone. "THEY'RE POWDER BLUE AND COTTON."

Feeling the blood drain from my face, I assured her I would have a look.

The phone clattered down in my ear.

The rumble of footsteps on the verandah trumpeted the return of the Tattersall family. I held the door open as they marched in single file, saluting me, and headed up the stairs in their muddy shoes. I sneaked a nervous look at Lady Graverly's door, expecting her to fling it open and give a cry of horror at the sight of children.

Nothing. I was almost disappointed.

Pulling up the rear of the procession was Lincoln.

"There you are," I said. "It's about time."

"Where in god's name did all those children come from?"

Closing the door, I told him about the Tattersall family's unexpected arrival.

"Agnes must have taken the reservation," he said. "Have you asked her?"

"Lady Graverly didn't tell you? Agnes went back to Scotland last night."

"Whyever for?"

"Her sister died."

Lincoln's face looked stricken. "Her sister?"

"Yes, why?"

"She told me she only had one sister. She died five decades ago."

15

To the Manor Born

Saturday morning, I was sifting through the rubble left by the Tattersall family during breakfast when Clarissa wandered in. Shooting me a cold, hard stare, she went to the buffet and picked at the scraps. I offered to make her something, but she shrugged me off, opting to help herself to a bowl of cereal. She ate quietly, staring down at her Cheerios, responding to my nervous banter with one-word answers. I struggled for a way to tell her I had confused Mrs. Wainright's undergarment for hers, thinking we might share a good laugh over it, but I was still too mortified to raise the subject. While she was eating, I crept up to her room to retrieve the panties and found them on top of her dresser. Stuffing them into my pocket, I raced upstairs to my room and placed them in a plastic grocery bag along with a pink hairbrush I had found left in the Wainrights' bathroom.

As I slinked back downstairs, I encountered Clarissa on her way up.

"No service to my room today," she said, keeping her eyes on the floor. "I'm going back to bed."

Fine, be that way, I thought. *One less room to clean.* My new environmental policy was already working.

All morning, Lincoln puttered around the house, looking busy without accomplishing anything, while I ran circles around him to keep up with the needs of our guests. His usual expressionless demeanor had returned, and he was even more taciturn than usual. I wondered if his attraction to Agnes had been more than just physical.

Around noon, he informed me he was going out to pick up some groceries. Grateful to see him be of use, I gave him a list of items and asked him to deliver Mrs. Wainright's belongings to the Fairmont. He opened the bag and peered inside, a barely perceptible flicker of interest passing over his eyes.

Next, I handed him the ascot, suit, and watch. "And please tell Lady Graverly that the gesture is much appreciated, but I cannot accept these."

Lincoln took the items without comment and disappeared into the private quarters.

A half-hour later, I was cleaning up after the Tattersalls in the Henry VIII room when I heard the back door open. I parted the curtain and looked out. The stout, black-haired woman I had seen leaving Lady Graverly's private quarters a few days prior was hastening down the path. Something about her purposeful gait reminded me of my mother—perhaps she was a nurse. She glanced up, as though sensing I was watching her, and our eyes met. I lifted my hand in a wave, but she averted her gaze and continued down the path. Another household mystery. I resumed my work, holding my breath as I transferred a soiled diaper into a plastic bag.

Moaning.

I stopped to listen. The sound repeated itself, and I hurried out of the room to the stairs. All guests save for Clarissa were out. I made my way downstairs and listened outside the door of the private quarters. Had the mysterious woman tied up Lady Graverly and gagged her?

I knocked. "Lady Graverly?"

There was no response.

I tried the door. Locked again. "Hello? Is everything okay in there?"

Silence.

Glancing over my shoulder, I eyed the stationery closet behind the reception desk. Did I dare fetch the key and let myself in? My eyes moved to the Private sign next to the door. Elinor's angry words rang in my ears: *If you ever violate my privacy again, so help me, I will make sure you regret it.*

The moaning sounded again, like a closed-mouth cry for help. The sound was so primeval, so angst-ridden, I couldn't ignore it. The spare key was to be used in an emergency—wasn't this an emergency? For all I knew, someone was dying on the other side of the door.

It took several attempts to find the key that fit. Large and brass, it was tarnished by age. I slid it in the slot and turned. The door would not open. I tried to coax the key out, but it became stuck. In a moment of panic, I envisioned Lady Graverly throwing open the door in a fit of rage. I stepped back.

The door popped open, as though by its own will, emitting a soft sigh.

The moaning ceased.

Heart pounding, I peered inside. I could see a dimly lit corridor with cracked, yellow walls. Stuffing the keys into my pocket, I slipped inside and pulled the door closed behind me. I stopped to listen. There was absolute silence, as though the house were breathlessly waiting to see what happened next.

A stale, faintly caustic odor greeted my nostrils. To the left, a doorway led into a parlor in the front part of the quarters. Unsure where the moaning had come from, I turned right and crept down the hallway. The floorboards squealed with each step. I felt my pulse throbbing in my neck. To the right hung a series of framed black-and-white photographs. In the first, a small, proud-looking man posed in a British army uniform before a pastoral backdrop. Lady Graverly's brother? She had never mentioned her side of the family, but there was a distinct resemblance. In the next photograph, the same man posed in a similar manner next to a taller, handsome man. I recognized Lord Wakefield Graverly, *The Consummate Host*, and decided the other man must be his brother, the infamous Lord Andrew Graverly.

The slam of the front door jolted me into action. I hurried down the hallway, intending to flee out the back exit, but stopped halfway when I heard the patter of little feet climbing the stairs. The Tattersalls were back. I breathed a sigh of relief.

Unsure where to look, I stopped to listen for the moaning sound. All the doors to the rooms off the hallway had been removed, an odd fact in light of Lady Graverly's obsession with privacy. There was a bedroom on my left, spacious and sparsely furnished, with a double bed, an oak dresser, a reading chair, and a night table stacked with comic books and children's storybooks. On the dresser sat a black comb and an electric shaver. I continued down the hall and came to a four-panel Victorian-style door painted a deep red. I peeked down the hallway to the rear exit, scoping my escape route should one be necessary. Pressing my ear against the red door, I listened. Nothing. I pictured Lady Graverly in her boudoir, surrounded by dilapidated furniture and old clothing, gazing in despair at her weathered reflection like Mrs. Haversham in *Great Expectations*. Taking a deep breath, I knocked.

There was no answer.

I tried the door handle. Locked. Pulling the keys from my pocket, I worked quickly, until at last a key fit. As I turned the knob, a noise from behind made me freeze.

Creaking... the movement of floorboards.

Slowly, I turned my head. The hallway was empty. The noise had come from the front parlor. Abandoning the bedroom, I tiptoed down the hall.

The parlor door was missing too. Stepping inside, I gazed around. The only source of light was a small table lamp in the corner. The acrid smell was sharper here. On a bookshelf to my right, an entire shelf was filled with old leather-bound notebooks—the guestbooks Lincoln had referred to? My skin prickled. I sensed a presence in the room. Slowly, my eyes scanned the room, moving over a green-striped sofa covered with a crocheted blanket, a grandfather clock, its pendulum unmoving, a portrait of Henry VIII and Ann Boleyn. My ears detected the sound of labored breathing. Then, a soft moan.

The back door slammed. Footsteps approached in the hallway. In a panic, I searched for somewhere to hide. Only then did I see the presence I had first only sensed. My heart leapt.

In the corner of the room, a man was watching me from a wheelchair.

Lady Graverly burst into the room.

Tearing my eyes from the man, I turned to find myself staring into the barrel of a rifle. Taking a step back, I held up my hands. "Jesus, Elinor, it's me! Put that thing down!"

She lowered the gun. "Mr. Lambert? What in god's name are you doing here?"

"I—I heard moaning. I was afraid someone was hurt." I braced myself for a tirade, but her face remained remarkably calm.

"I see you've met my son," she said.

"Your son?" I turned back to the man. He sat slumped in the wheelchair, his body hunched over, head lolling to the side, one eye staring up at me. A pair of bony, emaciated knees poked out from under a grey wool blanket on his lap.

"His name is Lord Alexander Graverly," Lady Graverly said.

I felt ashamed that I had reacted as if the man was a monster. "Nice to meet you, Lord Alexander," I said, concealing my shock. "I'm Trevor."

"Don't expect him to get up and shake your hand," Lady Graverly said bitterly, leaning the gun against the wall.

"Is he ..."

"A vegetable? More or less."

I winced at the term, recalling Mr. Chagani's interview question. Lowering my voice to a whisper, I said, "I thought you said your son was dead?"

"I beg your pardon? Alexander is very much alive, as you can see."

I tried to recall the words she had used in reference to her son and realized they had been ambiguous. *There was a terrible mishap at birth. The doctors said the poor boy would live for no more than a few months.* Yet he had survived. Had this living, breathing man been in the house all this time without my knowing? I recalled the moaning sounds, the nurse, the hooded figure pushing the wheelchair down the street. Was this the reason for Lady Graverly's jealously guarded privacy? Remembering that I had informed the Wainrights that Lady Graverly's son was dead, I felt my face drain of color.

"Why are you hiding him?" I whispered.

"My son is no one's business but my own."

"Can we discuss this somewhere else?" I said, glancing uneasily at Alexander.

"There is no need to whisper. My son has the mind of a three-year-old."

I looked back at him. Except for the wispy, greying hair, Alexander looked like an overgrown schoolboy in his father's clothes. His skin was almost translucent; his arms, as thin as bones, poked from a checkered, short-sleeved shirt. In his facial features I saw traces of Lady Graverly, and even of Lord Andrew from my brief look at the hallway photos.

"Why do you keep him locked away? Does he ever see daylight?"

"I do not keep him locked away," Lady Graverly snapped, nervously pacing the room. "Lincoln and I take him for regular walks, but only at night. His eyes are too sensitive to be exposed to sunlight. His health is most fragile. The doctors did not expect him to live more than a few months, and here he is, almost fifty years old. Every day is a gift. If I were to lose Alexander, I would walk down to Lions Gate Bridge and throw myself into the sea. Yet my greatest fear is that he will outlive me and will be put into an institution."

Alexander began moaning, the sound rising from deep within.

Lady Graverly crouched before him. "My darling, I've upset you, haven't I?"

"Didn't you say he comprehends nothing?"

She did not respond, absorbed by concern for her son. "Dear Alec, my handsome prince," she said, caressing his cheek with her cobbled fingers. "Don't be afraid. I'm here now."

"Do you leave him alone often?" I asked.

"He's fine for short spells. The nurse checks on him frequently."

Alexander smacked his hands on the arms of the wheelchair and began to rock back and forth.

"Please, Alec, behave," Lady Graverly said, her tone sharpening.

His moans turned into growls.

She stood up. "He needs a shot." Excusing herself, she hastened out of the room.

I watched helplessly as Alexander thrashed about the wheelchair. I wanted to try to comfort him but feared I would only make things worse.

Lady Graverly returned with a small black case. Setting it down, she withdrew a large needle and bottle and filled the needle with serum. The sight of the needle seemed to aggravate Alexander further.

"Stop it, Alec!" she commanded, bending down to apply the needle.

His right hand flew toward her, connecting with her jaw, and she fell backward to the floor, letting out a cry.

I rushed over to help her.

Waving me off, she resumed her task, pressing the needle into Alexander's arm. Almost instantly, his head fell forward, like a robot being powered down. Lady Graverly stroked his hair for a moment and then stood up, turning to me with the needle in her hand. For a moment I feared I was next. But she placed the needle in the bag and zipped it shut. Lowering herself onto the sofa with a great sigh, she touched the red welt on her cheek and winced.

"Look at the poor boy. Who can blame him for these episodes?"

"Can I ask what happened to him?" I said, taking a seat next to her.

Her eyes grew distant. "The boy's brain was deprived of oxygen for a matter of seconds during childbirth, yet the ramifications have lasted a lifetime."

"I'm sorry."

We sat in silence, listening to the man-boy's labored breathing. I felt a surge of anger toward Lord Graverly. Not only had he abandoned his wife, he had left her with a brain-damaged baby. My eyes moved around the room, observing the ashen wallpaper with its faded coat-of-arms pattern, the crumbling crown molding and cracked wainscoting, signs of grandeur long past. The condition of the private quarters was far worse than I had imagined.

I stood up, suddenly anxious to escape the depressing scene, to be alone and collect my thoughts.

Lady Graverly stood up with me and grasped my hands. "Oh, Mr. Lambert, I'm sorry you've seen this shabby side of the manor, this frail side of me. I've tried to keep up appearances, to remain optimistic, but it's all so overwhelming. I'm too old to take care of the boy much longer, yet I can't bear the thought of losing him. Will you ever forgive me?"

"Elinor, it's okay. I understand."

"How kind you are. You will be happy to know I am making good progress with settling my affairs. You may not have to wait as long as I anticipated."

"There's no need to rush," I assured her, squeezing her hand. "Take your time, and do what you need to do. In the meantime, I promise I'll take care of the manor. You won't have to worry about a thing."

She placed a hand on my cheek. "My prince, how shall I ever repay you?"

"You could lower the price again."

A sad smile spread over her lips. She turned back to Alexander, and I left the quarters, leaving her to attend to her son.

16

Graveyard Fairytales

I climbed the stairs with a heavy heart, torn between sympathy for the old woman and her invalid son and disappointment over the state of the private quarters. The knowledge that Lady Graverly had a son, an heir, changed my outlook dramatically. I had been a fool to think she had chosen me as her successor. She must have put forward a claim to the estate on behalf of Alexander, son of Lord and Lady Graverly and rightful heir. As his mother and keeper, she would manage the estate on his behalf. Alexander was the next Marquess of Middlesex, not me. It was silly fantasy anyway. I would be far more content at Graverly Manor.

On the fourth floor, the door to Agnes's room was open.

I peeked in and was surprised to see Lincoln sitting on the bed, his tattered Bible next to him. I cleared my throat. "Lincoln? Is everything okay?"

Lost in thought, he did not respond. A piece of metal glinted in his hands, and I recognized Sarah's locket. The room looked exactly as I had last seen it, as though Agnes had walked away without taking a thing. Had she left in that much of a hurry? There was little of value, mere props and costumes for her role as the impoverished chamber-maid. But surely she wouldn't have left her sister's locket behind?

"Would you like me to pack up this stuff?" I offered to Lincoln.

He didn't answer.

Not wishing to bother him while he seemed so distraught, I turned to leave.

"The lady asked me to forward them to Scotland," he said quietly.

I took a tentative step into the room. "You miss her, don't you?"

Slowly he shook his head. "I don't grow attached to people. No one stays here for long—no one but me."

I moved the Bible to the nightstand and took a seat next to him. He had treated me with little but insolence and condescension since I arrived, but I understood why. Hotels were full of staff members like Lincoln, career employees mistreated by guests and employers for so long that they have little left to offer but feigned concern, indifference, or contempt. For five decades, Lincoln had served under Elinor Graverly's oppressive reign, deferring his own needs and desires to those of his mistress, hiding beneath a veneer of good manners and dutifulness. He yearned for Agnes yet was so inured to the emotionally repressed environment of the manor that he was unable to express his feelings. I stared into his eyes, moist like two pink rainclouds and fixed on the sloped ceiling, and saw a glimmer of my own reflection. How much did he know about the manor's dark history? Was his near-blindness willful, his near-deafness self-chosen—signs of loyalty to his mistress and willingness to turn a blind eye and deaf ear to the strange and unusual things he had witnessed? Or, as Agnes had speculated, did he simply not know? She had also speculated that his loyalty might be beginning to waver, and I had the same impression now. He seemed vulnerable and afraid. But why?

With trembling fingers, he pried open the locket and gazed at the photo of Agnes inside. He placed the locket on top of the Bible and heaved himself to his feet, bending over to lug a suitcase from underneath the bed. He turned and surveyed the room, and then stooped down to pick up one of Agnes's peasant dresses. He lifted it to his face, closing his eyes for a moment, and then folded it carefully and placed it inside the suitcase.

"Lincoln," I said, watching his listless movements, "why did Agnes leave in such a hurry?"

My words startled him. He seemed to have forgotten I was there. "Her ladyship said you two had a terrible argument."

"That's not true. We talked, but it was mostly amicable. Did you know her sister, Lincoln? The maid, Sarah?"

"Miss Kilpatrick departed before I arrived at the manor."

"What happened to her?"

"Why, she vanished."

"Did she run off with Lord Graverly?"

It took him a while to answer. "So they say."

"But you don't believe it," I said.

"It is not my position to question such things."

"Did you know Lord Andrew?"

He gathered clothes in silence. At last, he spoke. "Lord Andrew's father, the marquess, hired me as a stableman at Graverly Castle. There I met the woman I married, a handmaiden to the marchioness. The marquess was a very religious and intolerant man, but he took liberties with some of the female servants, including my wife. My wife gave birth to a son who was not mine, and she died shortly after. The marquess sent the child away, and I fell to drinking and gambling. One day, I arrived at work five minutes late, and he fired me. Lord Andrew, who had always been kind to me, rehired me as his personal valet. But then he had a terrible falling out with his father, and he left for Canada. I was left jobless and homeless, and I lost the will to live. I wrote to Lord Andrew, begging him to help me, and he sent me money to come to Canada. I have served this household ever since."

"But Lord Andrew was gone when you arrived?"

"Only the lady was here."

"And her son?"

He nodded. "And Alexander."

"Lincoln, why has Lady Graverly been hiding her son from me?"

He did not reply. He lifted a pair of old stockings from the floor and regarded them, shook his head sadly, and placed them in the suitcase. He retrieved the locket from the nightstand and dropped it into an envelope, then tucked the envelope into the pocket of the suitcase.

Something Agnes had said was troubling me. *I'm here to find out what happened to my sister, and to claim what rightfully belonged to her.* I had assumed that Sarah had been pregnant when she disappeared—but was it possible she had already given birth? Agnes had seen something through the window of the private quarters that deeply disturbed her—Alexander in his wheelchair?

I rose from the bed. "Lincoln, is Alexander Lady Graverly's son?"

He turned to me. "I learned long ago to not ask questions in this household, Master Lambert. I suggest you do the same."

"I have too much tied up in this house to not ask questions." I grasped his shoulders. "Alexander isn't Elinor's son, is he? He's Sarah's son."

He gaped at me. His eyes were so pink they looked like they were marinating in blood. "Lord Alexander is Lady Graverly's son, but she is not his mother."

I loosened my grip. "What? You're speaking in riddles."

His face darkened. "Hush! The lady is coming."

"I don't hear anything."

A look of terror passed over his eyes. "The house is awake now."

In the distance I heard a muffled squeak, like a door opening or a branch scraping against a window. "Why are you afraid of her, Lincoln?" I whispered.

He bent over to zip the suitcase shut and lugged it off the bed. It struck the floor with a loud thud, and he began dragging it toward the door. I tried to help him, but he brushed me off. He went to the nightstand to retrieve the Bible and turned to me, clutching it against his chest.

"I advise you to leave this house at once," he rasped.

"If you're trying to scare me off, it won't work."

He reached out and clamped his hand on my shoulder. His entire body was shaking. "I implore you, for your own sake, leave and never come back!"

"But why?"

"There is evil in this household."

I sat ruminating in the parlor. I felt certain Lincoln was trying to intimidate me into leaving, yet there was truth in his words. I did sense evil in the house; like the sadness I had sensed all along, evil floated around like an evasive odor. I was convinced that its source was Lord Andrew Graverly, yet it was growing likely that Lady Graverly was not just an innocent victim. *Lord Alexander is Lady Graverly's son, but she is not his mother,* Lincoln had said. Sarah Kilpatrick must have been Alexander's birth mother, and Lady Graverly had adopted him, which meant he was illegitimate and had no entitlement to the Graverly estate. Why was Lady Graverly hiding him, then? When Agnes said she was here to claim what rightfully belonged to her sister, was she referring to Alexander or the estate—or both? Had Lady Graverly discovered her secret identity and sent her away? Or had something more sinister taken place?

I shuddered, pushing away these thoughts. It was Saturday night, and I was tired of being trapped in the manor. I craved the company of normal people. I had hoped the residents would join me at cocktail hour, but the Tattersalls had left for the wedding hours ago, and the others were upstairs getting ready to go out. Closing my eyes, I listened to the distant thunder of a running bath, the high-pitched drone of a blow dryer, snippets of chatter about outfits and hair. Never had I lived among so many people, yet felt so alone.

Footsteps descended the stairs. I got up and went into the foyer. Aldus and Stephen were there, dressed in form-fitting T-shirts and jeans.

"We're going dancing at Celebrities," said Aldus. "You want to come?"

"Thanks, but not tonight. Can I call you a cab?"

"No, thanks. We'll walk."

As I opened the door for them, Stephen regarded me curiously. "Do you live in this house or is this just your job?" he asked.

"Both, actually."

"Oh. I see."

They disappeared into the night.

Next came the Phippses, so dressed up they were almost unrecognizable. I called a taxi and waited with them in the front hall, feeling Mrs. Phipps' eyes on me as I thumbed through the reservations book.

"That elderly woman with the red hair—is she your mother?"

"Lady Graverly? Oh, no—she owns the house. I'm in the process of purchasing it from her."

A barrage of questions followed, concluded by the arrival of the taxi. I walked them to the street, enjoying the scent of Mrs. Phipps' sweet perfume.

As I returned to the house, I fretted over the awkward encounters. I had been asked more personal questions from guests in one week than in my entire career in hotels. However innocent the intentions, the questions felt intrusive. In this hotel masquerading as a home—this home masquerading as a hotel—I was stripped of the barriers I had hidden behind in the past—the front desk, my uniform and nametag, superficial pleasantries, and business protocol. I felt naked here, my life exposed to scrutiny, my solitude something to pity. No wonder Lincoln maintained his aloof manner and Lady Graverly's privacy was inviolable. I had hoped to operate the manor differently—to bring more warmth, attention to detail, flexibility—but I was uncertain about the social dynamics. How to strike the perfect balance—to be friendly without being cloying, to be professional without being too formal, to be attentive without being solicitous? I would need to intuit the expectations of each guest and adjust my approach accordingly. My role in the manor felt tenuous and undefined. I assured myself that the feeling was only transitory; once I assumed ownership and moved into my private apartment, I would have more of the privacy I yearned for, and I would feel as if I belonged.

I entered the house and closed the door, stopping to listen. An hour earlier, Lincoln had slipped into Lady Graverly's quarters to prepare dinner and had not yet emerged. Clarissa had been locked in her room for hours. I returned to the parlor and sat down, staring into the dying embers of the fire. It was too late to visit my mother or sisters. Derrick had invited me to the hockey game tonight—why hadn't I taken him up on the offer? Why was I so closed off to others? Why did I prefer to be alone?

The door to the dining room opened, and I felt Sir Fester's lithe body rub against my feet, his loud purr vibrating against my legs. Had he called a truce? Grateful for any company, I lifted him to my lap.

His claws stabbed into my arm.

"Fester! Christ."

He scurried away. I rubbed my arm. The attack felt premeditated; was Sir Fester retaliating for my not feeding him regularly and for inadvertently stepping on his tail?

I decided to go to bed. I would get up early to prepare breakfast; by then the gloom would have lifted. After breakfast, I would confront Lady Graverly and demand to know the real reason Agnes had left. Closing the fireplace grate, I headed for the stairs.

On the third floor, I saw a light under Clarissa's door. The murmur of her voice made me stop. There was a lyrical note to her words, and for a chilling moment I thought she was speaking in tongues. I pressed my ear against the door.

> O! lure of the Lost Lagoon,—
> I dream to-night that my paddle blurs...

The Pauline Johnson poem. I lifted my hand to knock but saw the Privacy sign hanging from the doorknob. Even Clarissa had shut me out. I debated whether I should knock anyway, feeling drawn to this strange girl and the beautiful poem.

The door flew open.

Clarissa stood before me, glowering. "Are you eavesdropping?"

"No! I—"

"Your behavior is highly inappropriate. I'm going to report you to management." A hint of a smile passed over her lips. She was wearing a black concert T-shirt imprinted with the words DEAD AGAIN over the silhouette of a rocker chick. Over her shoulder, I could see papers and books scattered across the bed.

"I was going to knock," I said. "But I saw the privacy sign."

Her eyes searched mine, as though she were trying to decide whether to believe me. She folded her arms and leaned on the door. "You here to give turndown service or something?"

My natural compulsion was to flee in the face of flirtatious banter but the desire to grab her and pull her lips against mine was stronger. I stood rooted to the floor, unable to act on either impulse. "I just thought I'd check in on you," I said.

"Why were you sniffing Elinor's underwear on my bed? You got some weird fetish or something?"

I choked. "Elinor's underwear? It was Mrs. Wainright's!"

She raised an eyebrow. "That's supposed to make me feel better?"

"I'm not a perv, I promise," I said. "I was—"

"Don't," she said, lifting her hand to press her fingers on my lips. "I'd rather not know."

I pulled her fingers away, holding on to her hand. "I was wondering…" I hesitated, searching for appropriate words to ask her out without offending her further, and finally gave up. "Hey, want to steal a bottle of Elinor's cheap wine and go grave hopping?"

Her eyes lit up. "Are you serious? Totally."

"It's always struck me as funny that graveyards are named like hotels," I said to Clarissa as we dodged gravestones in the frozen grounds of Mountainview Cemetery. "As if dead people care about the view."

"Cemeteries are like funerals. They're for the living, not the dead."

"And yet I'm about to buy an inn whose name sounds like a cemetery."

"I like the name Graverly Manor. It's got character. But then I've always been drawn to graveyards. The Cherry Grove Cemetery in Kentucky was my childhood playground."

The revelation explained a lot about Clarissa. I had been kidding about grave hopping, but she hadn't let me back out.

"How about here?" she said, gesturing to a tombstone engraved JACOB ELLIS 1933–1971. OUR HERO. "Jacob could probably use some company after all these years." She spread a blanket over the marble slab and sat down, patting the place beside her and smiling, as if we were at the beach on a sunny afternoon.

I looked down, apprehensive. The dull glow of the moon made her skin look phosphorescent. Her eyes looked like two dark abysses behind the thick mascara. Frightened and exhilarated at the same time, I lowered myself to the blanket and uncorked the wine.

She took the bottle from me, guzzling from it like soda. "Tastes like rancid grape juice," she said, making a face and handing it back.

"Only the best at Graverly Manor," I said. As I drank, I watched her out of the corner of my eye, intrigued by her weirdness. The wine had left a smear around her mouth in the same place she had cut her lip. She wiped away the smear and tilted her head back, closing her eyes.

"I smell dead people," she said, letting out a giggle.

"You're not going to talk to them, are you?"

"Only if they talk to me first." She sat up and looked around, surveying the tombstones like the crowd at a party. "Know anyone here?"

"Nope. My dad's at Forest Lawn."

"Now that's a great name for a hotel." She fixed her gaze on me. "Do you miss your dad?"

I shrugged. "I guess. I felt abandoned when he died. But I'm not sure we would be close if he had lived. He was more like my sisters. How about you—know anyone here?"

She shook her head. "It's not really my crowd. My grandma's at Cherry Grove. I used to sit on her grave and chat with her for hours. I didn't have any brothers or sisters to talk to."

"Graveyards freak me out," I said, looking around at the dark tombstones surrounding us like a crowd of observers.

She laughed, scraping at the wine label with a chipped fingernail. "I like getting scared. It's the only time I really feel alive."

"I prefer to feel numb."

"Are you afraid of death?"

I regarded her in the darkness, unable to read her expression. "When I was a teenager, I used to look forward to it like summer vacation," I said, half-joking. "When my mom got cancer, it scared the hell out of me." I shivered, shifting on the hard, cold surface of the marble slab beneath the blanket. Clarissa, in a light coat and thin V-neck sweater, seemed perfectly comfortable. "How about you, are you afraid of death?"

Without replying, she handed me the label intact and turned her back to me, lowering her head onto my chest. I rested my chin on her head and closed my eyes, breathing the intoxicating scent from the apothecary bottle in her room.

"How does Cinderella like working for the wicked stepmother?" she asked, burrowing into my arms. "Is she making you sleep in the cinders in the fireplace?"

"I'm sure it's only a matter of time. Does that make you Prince Charming?"

"Oh no, you're the prince in her eyes. I see how she looks at you. She wants you big time."

"Clarissa, she's old enough to be my grandmother."

"She's more like a wolf dressed up like your grandmother. You better just hope someone's around with an axe when she tries to eat you."

We laughed, comparing various aspects of the manor to other fairytales as we passed the wine back and forth.

Clarissa's fingers trailed the seam of my jeans. "I was looking forward to seeing you out of a suit."

"I'd say the same about you, but you haven't left much to my imagination."

She turned her head to look at me. "Are you one of those creepy innkeepers who spy on their guests? Maybe you should rename the manor the Bates Motel."

"And keep my mother around long after she's dead? Don't worry, I might have an old ladies' underwear fetish, but I'm not a psycho."

In the distance, a dog howled. The haunting sound reminded me of Alexander. What compelled him to moan like that—physical pain, loneliness, fear? His lifelong sentence to a wheelchair?

"I met Lady Graverly's son today," I said.

"Alec?"

"You know about Alexander?"

"Sure. I've gone on a couple walks with him and Lincoln."

"Why am I the last to know these things?"

"She's quite protective of him. His health is fragile."

"Lincoln said something strange today. He said Alexander is Lady Graverly's son, but she is not his mother. Does that make sense to you?"

"It makes total sense now." She got up to pull a second bottle of wine from her gym bag. "Remember that old neighbor I told you about, Spencer Stuart Ross? I went to visit him again yesterday."

She sat on her knees, facing me, peeled the aluminum foil from the bottle's neck, and handed the bottle to me to uncork it. "He told me Lord Graverly and Sarah were fairly well known in town. They used to get all dressed up, and he would parade her around. Lord Graverly was a small man, unattractive and a bit theatrical, whereas Sarah was statuesque and demure. It became obvious she was more than just the housekeeper. Then all of a sudden he stopped taking her out. Rumors circulated that he was holding her prisoner in the house and abusing her. Spencer sometimes saw her staring out the window of the tower room. Just like Rapunzel. Remember that fairytale?"

"Refresh my memory," I said, enjoying watching her in the moonlight.

"Let me see … a childless couple longs for a baby, and the wife finally becomes pregnant. She craves a vegetable in the garden next door owned by a wicked enchantress. The enchantress catches the husband stealing it and agrees to have mercy on him if he promises to give her the child when it's born."

"Sounds equitable."

"The man agrees, and the witch names the girl Rapunzel and imprisons her in a tower with no stairs or door. One day, a prince is walking in the woods, and he hears her singing. He begs her to throw down her hair so he can scale the tower."

"'Rapunzel, Rapunzel, let down your hair.'"

"Exactly." Clarissa pulled a cigarette from her bag and lit it. "The prince knocks up Rapunzel, and the witch is furious. She cuts Rapunzel's hair off and casts her into the woods. Devastated, the prince leaps from the tower and is blinded by the thorns below. Rapunzel gives birth, and the prince wanders the country in despair, until one day he hears her singing. They reunite, and her tears of joy restore his eyesight."

"And they live happily ever after."

"In the fairytale, anyway."

I pondered the story. "Okay, I think I get it. Sarah is Rapunzel. Lord Graverly is the prince. And Lady Graverly is the witch, naturally."

Clarissa's face glowed orange as she smoked. "The analogy kind of falls apart from there. But listen to this: one day Spencer was walking down the back alley behind the manor when he saw Lord Graverly's car pull in. As he passed the garage, he saw Lord Graverly helping Sarah out of the car. He was shocked to see that she was very pregnant."

"So she was pregnant," I said.

She gave me a look of surprise. "You knew she was pregnant?"

"Agnes told me."

She continued. "A few days later, the neighbors learned of the existence of Lady Graverly for the first time when she called the police to report that her husband was missing. She had just arrived from England with her newborn son."

"So Spencer thinks Lord Graverly and Sarah abandoned their son, and Lady Graverly pretended he belonged to her?"

"Spencer said he's not one to gossip, he was only telling me what he saw."

"Then what happened to Lady Graverly's baby? Did it die or was she never pregnant?"

"If you ask me, she was never pregnant. She made up the story as a cover. I think she killed them both and stole their baby."

I sat up, alarmed. "Then what did she do with the bodies? Dump them in the lagoon?"

Clarissa dropped her cigarette butt into the empty wine bottle. I watched it fill with smoke. "Get this," she said. "You know the rumor that Lord Graverly and Sarah were spotted rowing in the lagoon around the time they disappeared? Guess where it originated?"

"Where?"

"From Lady Graverly."

"But why?"

"To divert attention away from the manor." In the darkness, I could feel her eyes staring at me intently. "Trevor, we need to find that cellar."

I thought of the rumor Lynne Crocker had told me about Lady Graverly hacking her husband to pieces and burying him in the cellar and of Mr. Chagani's theory that Lord Graverly's remains had poisoned the house's foundation. Was this why Lady Graverly had the cellar covered over years ago—because her husband and his lover were buried there? Suddenly, I felt extremely cold.

"Clarissa, didn't you say Lady Graverly acts as though she's expecting Lord Graverly to come home any minute? If she murdered him, that doesn't make sense."

"I think she's created a fictional reality that he's still alive. That's often at the root of a haunting: the survivor keeps the dead person alive in his or her mind."

"You sound like an authority."

"Elinor Graverly has gone insane, Trevor."

"No. I don't believe it. She's not capable of murder. She's a victim. She's been caring for an invalid who's probably not even hers for fifty years."

"She's a wolf dressed in sheep's clothing, Trevor. Tomorrow morning, while she's at church, let's break into her apartment."

"No way."

"Scaredy cat."

"Who are you anyway, Clarissa? Are you really writing a thesis on Pauline Johnson, or are you an investigator with the missing person's bureau? Or maybe you're a ghostbuster—the big, bad wolf determined to blow my house down."

"I'm a student."

"I refuse to do it," I said resolutely. "I promised to respect her privacy, to take care of the manor while she attends to her affairs. If she catches me snooping again, she *will* eat me. I'm too close to closing this deal to jeopardize it now."

"How badly do you want the house if it comes with bodies in the cellar?"

I stood up. "Let's get out of here. This place creeps me out."

She looked up at me. "If you won't come, I'll go on my own."

"Be my guest."

"I am your guest."

I looked down at her and smiled. "You're beautiful, Clarissa." I knelt down before her. "I want to kiss you, but I'm afraid your mascara will smudge and I'll come away looking like I have two black eyes."

"They wouldn't be from the mascara."

"Sorry," I said, embarrassed. "I thought . . ."

She pushed me back and climbed on top of me, pressing her mouth over mine. We wrestled on the marble slab, rolling onto the frozen grass. The headstone loomed over us, lit up by the moonlight. OUR HERO. Jacob was my age when he died. I pushed Clarissa away.

"What is it?" she said, running a hand over her swollen lips.

"Not here."

"Why not? This is hot."

"I can't have sex surrounded by corpses. Besides, if I don't get home soon, my car will turn into a pumpkin."

★ ★ ★ ★ ★

We stopped to kiss on the verandah as I fumbled for my keys and unlocked the door. Parting reluctantly, we tiptoed in. As I turned to close the door, my foot struck the copper umbrella stand, sending it tumbling over.

"Shh!" Clarissa said, giggling. "You'll wake the old witch up!"

In my haste to replace the umbrellas, I knocked the stand over again.

Clarissa burst into laughter, setting me off too. She knelt down beside me, and her black hair lashed my lips as she reached for an umbrella. I inhaled her lovely scent and took her head in my hands, lowering myself to the floor and pulling her on top of me. The floorboards screeched beneath us.

Suddenly, the chandelier above flared to life, flooding the room with light. Lady Graverly's voice pierced the darkness. "What on earth is going on here?"

We froze. Slowly, I lifted my head. At the entrance to the private quarters, Lady Graverly was peering at us from beneath her hooded robe, her mouth open, hands squeezing her neck.

Lifting Clarissa off of me, I scrambled to my feet, knocking the stand over again. "Elinor, hi! Sorry to wake you. I, uh, knocked over the umbrella stand. We were just—." I righted the urn again.

Lady Graverly gasped. "How dare you! Engaging in a vulgar act in my own front hall! With this ... this *hussy*!"

"Elinor, for god's sake, that's totally uncalled for." I placed a protective arm around Clarissa. Feeling her body tremble with mirth, I let my arm fall.

"Did you not promise to conduct yourself with propriety in this household? Since the day you arrived, you have acted like a spoiled child. Poking your nose where it does not belong, fraternizing with guests, calling me 'Elinor' as though I am your equal—I'm speechless. Is this your idea of tending to Graverly Manor?"

"I apologize, Lady Graverly," I said, lowering my head in shame. "I'm out of line."

"We shall discuss this in the morning." She cast a withering look at Clarissa, emitted a huff of indignation, and disappeared into her quarters, slamming the door. Behind me, the copper urn toppled over again.

"Witch," Clarissa muttered under her breath.

"I heard that!" Lady Graverly shouted from behind the door.

Clarissa made a lewd gesture.

As we climbed the stairs, Clarissa leaned on me, laughing, but I was too distraught to join her. After a glimpse into the depressing life Lady Graverly led behind that door, I had promised to help her. I had let her down, and the consequences would be severe. In the morning, she would send me away.

Outside Clarissa's door, I pecked her on the cheek. "Well, good night."

"That's it?"

"I'm sorry, I can't."

"It's none of her business what you do outside of work."

"That's the problem. I'm not outside of work." I started up the stairs.

"So this is what you meant by turndown service?" she called after me.

I smiled. "I like to respect privacy signs."

Safely in my room, I flopped onto the bed. How could I have turned down an opportunity to be with that smart, sexy girl? Sure, she was crazy, but who wasn't? I tried to tell myself I had done the right thing. My future wasn't worth jeopardizing for a quick, meaningless romp. Placing my watch and cell phone on the nightstand, I stripped down to my boxers. The oil painting caught my eye, and I wandered over to regard the milkmaid's sorrowful eyes. There was no doubt in my mind anymore; her child was dead.

I opened the door and headed for the bathroom.

Clarissa was standing outside the door, her naked body glowing in the pale light. "I forgot to answer your question," she breathed. Her lips were trembling.

"What question?"

"I'm terrified of death."

I pulled her into my room, closing the door.

17

The Tower Room

When I woke up the next morning, my head was throbbing.

Wine … graveyard … Clarissa.

I rolled over and reached for her, feeling dead air. She had slipped away in the night. My thoughts returned to our time together. Clarissa had teased me, taunted me, enticed me into doing things I had never imagined. Part of the allure had been the sense of danger, the fear of getting caught, and an unexpectedly sublime feeling of rebellion. Yet the warm afterglow I had felt after my first night with Nancy, the feeling that something intense and forever had taken place, wasn't there. It was sex—uninhibited, incredible sex—and nothing more. No emotions, no insecurities, no strings. In the coming days, like a faithful husband I would make her bed, scrub her bathroom, and prepare her breakfast. And then she would leave, and our encounter would be a titillating memory, free of yearning and heartbreak.

I stretched in bed, letting out a loud, purgative yawn, and rolled back over, closing my eyes. I tried to conjure up the image of Clarissa writhing in my arms like an untamed animal, but less desirable images interfered. Alexander hunched over in his wheelchair, one eye fixed on me accusingly. Lady Graverly's crestfallen look under the hooded robe. Lincoln's cloudy eyes and nebulous words. Clarissa kneeling by the tombstone, trying to convince me to look for the cellar.

I sat up, suddenly remembering Clarissa's threat to break into the private quarters on her own. A beam of light filtered through a gap in the curtain. The sun was unusually high. What time was it? I reached for my watch—10:43 AM.

Breakfast. I had told Lincoln I would prepare it. There were thirteen guests in-house! Stumbling to the closet, I caught my haggard reflection in the mirror. I couldn't go downstairs looking like this, not without a shower and shave. Grabbing my toiletry kit, I headed for the door, but a wave of dizziness stopped me. My forehead was burning. Could I be this hung over? Was I too old for Clarissa's wild ways? Or … had I been drugged? I thought of her intoxicating potions … Alexander's medication and its instantly tranquilizing effect. In a moment, the spinning subsided, and I groped for the door. It wouldn't open. I tugged at the handle, twisted it, jiggled it, gave the door a kick, but it refused to budge. Remembering the lock on the outside of the door, I wondered if it had somehow fallen into place when Clarissa left. But no, a key was required.

I banged on the door. "Hello? Is anybody there?"

The house was silent.

Could all the guests have departed already? It was possible, particularly if no one had been there to serve breakfast. Why hadn't Lincoln or Lady Graverly come looking for me? I went to the window and peered out. It was a clear, sunny morning. An elderly woman in a leisure suit power-walked by, followed by a man in a long leather coat, smoking, a cell phone pressed to his ear. Where was my cell phone? I was certain I had placed it on the nightstand. I searched under the bed, inside the bed, my pockets, every inch of the room. Had Clarissa confused her metallic red Motorola Razr for my clunky old Nokia? Not likely.

I pounded on the door again, shouting Lincoln's name, Clarissa's name, the name of every occupant of the household. I stamped my feet and hollered.

Nothing.

Why couldn't they hear me? From four floors up, I had heard Alexander moaning. It was Sunday; Lady Graverly should be at church. Clarissa would be fast asleep—unless she was acting on her plan to explore Lady Graverly's apartment. That thought sent me into renewed paroxysms of pounding and stamping. Eventually I wore myself out, my stamina somewhat compromised by the hangover. I sat on the bed. Elinor would be furious that I had missed breakfast, particularly after last night's incident. The Tattersalls would have helped themselves, leaving a huge mess. I had five rooms to clean, laundry to do, loads of chores. No arrivals were expected, but for all I knew, another family of eight was on its way.

I told myself to relax. Lincoln would come looking for me soon enough. He was too lazy to do all the work himself. If not Lincoln, then Lady Graverly—if only to tell me to pack my bags and go.

I had to pee. An incident at the Universe Hotel came to mind. A convention of disabled people had checked in, and staff had undergone training to handle their special needs. One night, an elevator broke down, trapping several delegates inside, including a blind couple, a deaf woman, a woman in a wheelchair, and two mentally disabled men. The repair company was called, and I tried to keep the group calm via the elevator phone. After about three hours, the guests began panicking. One of the mentally disabled men couldn't hold it any longer and peed on the floor. The group was stuck for another hour, their feet steeped in a puddle of urine. By the time the elevator doors finally glided open, the occupants were apoplectic. Offering profuse apologies, I comped their rooms and later sent up handwritten apologies. I got a nasty call. "You sent a handwritten note to a blind person!" That was one of the most blistering rebukes of my career. Now, trapped in the tower room, I fully understood the trauma they had experienced.

I eyed the sink, then got up and turned on the tap.

After finishing my business, I ran the tap for a few minutes and then lay back down on the bed. It was a good excuse to sleep off my hangover. The housework could wait. I was expected at my mother's house at six for dinner, but by then I could gnaw my way out if I had to. The circular room began to spin like an amusement park ride. I closed my eyes, willing it to stop, and my mind began to whirl. Had Clarissa locked me in deliberately to make sure I didn't interfere while she searched for the cellar? If she was down there now, was she in danger? My suspicions moved to Lady Graverly, furious with me last night. Was she punishing me? Or was this part of Lincoln's campaign to frighten me into leaving? Or had Sir Fester locked me in to exact his revenge?

I was being paranoid. I needed fresh air. Pulling myself to my feet, I went to the window and tried to open it, pushing and tugging and banging until the glass cracked. I stared out, hands pressed against the fractured glass, and thought of my mother, of my sisters, and their children, and how I had sent them away. The idea of going to the park with them now held enormous appeal. A man walked by with a dog, a rottweiler, and I recognized them from the night of the showing. I pounded on the window frame. The dog gave a cursory look in my direction, and he and his master disappeared down the street. Had I triumphed over the other buyers that night, or had I been selected for some kind of curse? What should have been a simple real estate transaction had turned into a complex, emotionally draining nightmare. If the manor caught fire, I could die here, all for nothing. Clarissa's Rapunzel story came back to me. The notion of young Sarah imprisoned here suddenly felt very real. Was that why there was a lock on the outside of the door? Had Lord Graverly locked her here after impregnating her, fattening her up like a Christmas pheasant?

No. There was no forced pregnancy, no imprisonment, no murder. Bodies didn't just vanish. Lord Graverly had fallen in love with Sarah, and they had walked into the sunset, raising their child together and living happily ever after, like Rapunzel and the prince.

I lay down and closed my eyes.

Hours passed. I fell in and out of sleep. At various times, I got up to call for help, shouting foul words and insults to provoke any reaction, banging on the window, stomping on the floor, lunging at the door until my shoulders were bruised. Downstairs, I heard the occasional ring of the telephone, but otherwise there was no sign of life. To quench my thirst, I drank metallic-tasting water from the tap. Every thought led to food. A cheeseburger … a slice of pizza … the rosemary chicken Mom would be placing in the oven about now. Even one of her vile organic concoctions sounded appealing. I pulled the copy of *Our Food Is Killing Us* from the shelf and flipped through it, licking my lips over photos of diseased chickens, malformed vegetables, and genetically mutated fruit.

Darkness fell. My sisters would be making casual observations about my tardiness. Seven o'clock arrived. Their remarks would carry an air of indignation. Seven thirty. Janet would be mad, Mom stoically optimistic, Wendy worried. I heard the phone ring again, and anxiety gripped me. If I died here, would anyone miss me? I had broken off ties with all friends but Derrick. Shanna would miss me, but she had concerns of her own. Did I deserve to be missed? Wendy was right. I had been acting like I lived thousands of miles away.

I began to feel feverish. My body was bleeding sweat. I thought of Alexander, confined to his wheelchair … Sarah, imprisoned in the tower … Lady Jane Grey, locked in the Tower of London awaiting execution … Lady Graverly, creeping up the stairs with an axe.

I leapt from the bed. If I got out now, I could still make dessert at Mom's house. I searched the room for something, anything, to pry open the door. Moving the chair to the closet, I inspected the shelf. A thick layer of dust. The chair tipped, and as I struggled to regain my balance, I spotted an uneven patch of drywall in the corner above the shelf. Steadying myself on the chair, I reached out and felt around it. After some coaxing, a square of drywall came loose. Pushing my hand into the hole, I nudged something. It took a few minutes to extract it, but soon I had an old notebook in my hands. Stepping down from the chair, I blew the dust away and inspected it. It was an old leather-bound journal with gold trim. Carrying it to the sink, I wiped it down with a hand towel and held it to the light. It looked identical to the guest books I had seen in the private quarters. Fascinated, I sat down on the bed and opened it. On the inside cover, the name "Sarah Kilpatrick, 1957" was written in flowery script. Sarah's diary.

My heart pounding, I carefully turned the brittle pages. In some areas, the ink was so faded the writing was illegible. I flipped back to the first entry, dated November 11, 1957.

> *The house is lovely but rather large, and minding it is a great*
> *deal of work. Lord Graverly is very kind to me, but he is a*
> *strange man. I miss Agnes very much.*

I turned the pages, scanning the mundane thoughts and girlish musings. Near the middle of the book I came upon a red smudge on the side of the page—a bloody thumbprint. I stared at it, this little smear of Sarah Kilpatrick's DNA, a drop of blood she had shed like a tear almost fifty years ago. Near the back of the book, I found the final entry, dated November 6, 1958, a full year after the first entry.

> *I feel like a big wet balloon that will burst any minute! Lord*
> *Graverly is a sick man. I shall not rear my child in this house.*
> *As soon I am well enough, I shall escape. I truly hope my father*
> *will forgive me. He is my family, and I miss him so.*

The sound of creaking steps alerted me to the door. Someone was coming up the stairs.

"Hello?" I called out, hurrying to the door and pounding on it.

No answer.

"It's me, Trevor. I'm locked in! Who's there?"

When the voice came, it was so close I yanked my head back: "Are you feeling better now, my dear?"

"Elinor? Let me out of here!"

The door rattled. "You'll have to unlock the door for me."

"If I could do that, I wouldn't have spent the entire fucking day here! Get the goddamn key, for god's sake!"

"Goodness! There's no need for such language. Wait there, and I'll see if I can find the key."

"Hurry! I'm dying in here."

While I waited, I wiped down the diary and placed it under my mattress, and then sat down, mulling over Sarah's words. Sarah had not been in love with Lord Graverly like I assumed; rather, she seemed to loathe him, or at least had learned to distrust him over time, and had been plotting to leave. What happened after she wrote her last entry? Had she given birth only to have Lord Graverly kill her? Or had Lady Graverly killed them both in a jealous rage?

I heard a key in the lock. "This cursed lock is jammed again," Lady Graverly muttered through the door.

"This has happened before?"

"Not in quite some time."

"Then I suggest you call a bloody locksmith and get it fixed."

"My, my! So ornery." I heard her struggling with the handle.

"Why has no one checked in on me?"

"Miss Larch said you were ill and didn't wish to be disturbed."

"She said what?"

"We had no reason to doubt her, given where she spent the evening."

At last, the door sprang open.

I leapt out. Despite my anger, I was so happy to see her I threw my arms around her, feeling a sob of relief burble within me.

"You poor boy, you must be famished!" she said, running her clawed hands down my back. "Come along, I'll serve you some dinner."

Sitting me at the dining room table, Lady Graverly said she would be back in a moment and hurried out. I heard the door to her private quarters open and close. A moment later, she returned with a bottle of fine French wine. I watched impatiently as her gnarled fingers attempted to unpeel the foil, then snatched the bottle from her hands and uncorked it. She retrieved two crystal goblets from the cabinet and set them down.

"I'll get you something to eat," she said as I poured the wine.

I watched her disappear through the swinging door, surprised she knew where the kitchen was. She was wearing a black silk dress with billowy sleeves, and her hair was fastened at the top with a wiry contraption that looked like a big spider.

While I waited I gulped down wine, tasting blackberry and oak and something faintly bitter. Soon a sense of well-being washed over me. I wouldn't die in the tower room. Food was on its way. As my head cleared, I felt embarrassed by my delusional thoughts, by my panicked, crazed behavior. I had been locked up for a single day, yet I had acted as though I had been imprisoned for a lifetime.

Needless to say, Lady Graverly had some explaining to do. I now had a written testimonial of Sarah's pregnancy, and I was certain that Alexander was not Elinor's son. If Elinor had stolen the baby, I intended to report her and hand over the diary to the police, leaving them to figure out the rest. Then I would pack my belongings and leave. Compared to this house of horrors, the Harbourside Hotel didn't sound like such a bad place to work after all.

Lady Graverly returned with a plate heaping with roast chicken, potatoes, and vegetables. I eyed it ravenously as she placed it before me, the scent of rosemary wafting to my nose.

"How did you know this is my favorite?" I asked, slicing into the chicken breast.

"Is it really? How wonderful."

"Where is everybody?" I asked, realizing I hadn't seen anyone.

"All the guests have checked out, of course. Lincoln and I managed to feed them all, and they were gone by eleven. I made sure of that."

She watched me closely as I ate, smiling and nodding in encouragement, as though watching me take my medication, all the while muttering sympathetic words about my plight.

"I truly can't imagine what it must have been like, locked up like that all day," she said. "Though I suppose it must have given you time to think about what is important to you."

I glanced up. I had not ruled her out as a suspect in my imprisonment. Was she asking if I had learned my lesson?

She gave a tender smile and patted my hand. "There, there. Eat, my child." She lifted her wine and sipped, leaving a smear of crimson lipstick on the rim of the glass. "Oh, I almost forgot. Your sister called."

My eyes moved to the clock on the wall. It was after midnight, too late to call her back now. "Have you seen my cell phone?" I asked.

"Why, yes, I believe it's on the desk in the front hall. Lincoln found it in Miss Larch's room."

So Clarissa had taken it. "Where is Clarissa now?"

"Why, she checked out this morning."

"Checked out? Why?"

"Miss Larch was always due to check out today."

"She told me she was here for another week."

"Why, that's impossible. We have a tour group taking all our rooms on Wednesday. They've been booked for several months." She poured more wine into my glass. "I can't say I'm sorry to see her go. Why a man of your pedigree would associate with a person of such inferior breeding is beyond me."

"Did she leave a note?" I asked, choosing to disregard the comment. "A forwarding number?"

"No, nothing. Would you like another helping?"

"No." I pushed the plate away, now a pile of bones. Had Clarissa drugged me, locked me in the tower room, and lied about my state of health? Was it all part of her crazy-girl allure, a sick joke—a dominatrix game? What else could explain why she had left so abruptly? Yet, in spite of my misgivings, I felt hurt that she hadn't bothered to say goodbye. This perfect scenario, this casual, no-strings-attached encounter, suddenly felt very complicated. I didn't want to believe she had betrayed me. But if not her, then who?

"Where's Lincoln?" I asked.

"Oh, dear Lincoln," she said with a sigh. "After five decades as my loyal servant, he has retired. I shall miss him ever so much."

I was dumbfounded. "He resigned *today*? Wasn't that a little abrupt?"

"He has been contemplating retirement for years. His eyesight is failing, his bones stiff and sore, but he has been too loyal to leave. Selfishly, I let him stay. When you arrived, he knew his time was up. Rather than wait for the axe to fall, he took it upon himself to go with dignity."

I felt a pang of guilt. It was true I had no intention of retaining him, but had I made it that obvious? If he had planned to leave, why had he tried to scare me off? *There is evil in this household.* Occupants were abandoning the manor like rats from a sinking ship. Did they know something I didn't?

"It's just me now, one person to do all the work," I said bitterly. "This must be saving you loads of money."

"Mr. Lambert, please. I had no idea this would happen."

I threw my napkin down. "Elinor, is Alexander your son?"

"I beg your pardon? Of course he's my son."

I fixed my gaze on her. "Did you give birth to him?"

She flinched, but her eyes were defiant. "What unsavory thoughts have been planted in your head? Did Agnes share one of her desperate fabrications? Or Miss Larch—was she once again sticking her nose where it doesn't belong?"

I continued to regard her without replying.

"Lincoln, then?" she said. "What has Lincoln told you?"

I blinked, surprised she would consider Lincoln a potential traitor. Still, I remained silent, waiting to see what kind of lies would come out of her mouth next. Minutes passed. She fidgeted with her wine glass. Her eyes darted around the room as though searching for an escape route. Outside, the wind rattled at the window.

At last, she relented. "I suppose it is time you knew the truth, Mr. Lambert. No, I am not Lord Alexander's mother. But I have played that role since the day he was born. I have earned that title."

"Sarah Kilpatrick is his mother, then?"

She looked away.

"Elinor, did you steal Sarah's baby?"

Her head snapped back in my direction. "Certainly not! I saved that baby."

"What? How?"

"The poor girl died in childbirth."

"Sarah?" I thought of Sarah's girlish script in the diary: *I feel like a big wet balloon that will burst any minute.* My mother had described my father's death in a similar way: *His aorta burst like a balloon.* "Here, in this house?"

"In the very room where you're residing."

"And what about your baby? Were you ever pregnant?"

She took a sharp intake of breath. I braced myself for an outburst, but she lowered her head and said quietly, "I cannot bear children."

"Tell me what happened, Elinor."

A clump of red hair fell from the spider-like fastener, and she reached up to tuck it back in, revealing a flash of white hair under the wig. Arranging her arms neatly on the table, she began. "When I arrived from England, I knew at once something was the matter. Lord Graverly was not himself. He took me on a tour of the manor, which I found agreeable, if modest, and our last stop was the tower room. There he introduced me to the housemaid, a lovely young lass with hair the color of dark honey. She was very pregnant and looked unwell. In an instant, I knew what had taken place. I would have left that very moment had I anywhere to go. Instead, I retired to what is now the Henry VIII suite to collect my thoughts. Lord Graverly came to beg for my forgiveness, assuring me that Sarah would return to Scotland after she gave birth. I was heartbroken, naturally. I loved Lord Graverly with all my heart and was crushed by his betrayal. I resolved to return to England the next morning.

"Later that evening, Lord Graverly went out for a walk by the lagoon. Soon after he departed, I heard Sarah cry out in the tower room. I rushed upstairs and found her lying on the floor, writhing in pain. She told me she had fallen while climbing onto a chair to reach the closet shelf."

I nodded slowly and remembered my own near fall. Had Sarah been putting away her diary at the time?

"The girl had gone into labor," Lady Graverly continued. "I was frantic. Lord Graverly had forbidden me to call a doctor; he did not want to cause a scandal. I fetched some towels and a basin of water. When I returned, she was sitting in a pool of blood. Kneeling before her, I lifted her dress and pressed a towel between her legs. It came back soaked with blood. I told her to push with all her might. I saw the crown of the baby's head appear. Afraid she would die before she gave birth, I urged her to push and push, until at last the baby came out. Then all at once Sarah grew absolutely still. The poor boy wasn't breathing. Fearing I had lost them both, I held him against me and sobbed. Then, miraculously, he began to cry. I cut the umbilical cord and started to clean things up, but there was so much blood I must have fainted. The next thing I remember is waking up in bed with the baby in a bassinette and a bottle of formula beside me."

"And Lord Graverly?"

"I never saw him again."

I was stunned. "He abandoned you with Sarah's baby?"

"He loved Sarah, not me. He couldn't bear to be without her. I had always yearned for a son, and now I had one. He knew I would care for him as if he were my own, and so he left me the house and a small sum of money for its upkeep. It was the best arrangement for all, under the circumstances."

"For all? What about Sarah's sister, her parents? All these years they hoped she might still be alive, and you deprived them of her son. How could that possibly be the best solution for all?"

"Isn't a glimmer of false hope better than no hope at all?"

I grew silent. Was this how Lady Graverly had coped with the loss of Lord Graverly, by maintaining a glimmer of false hope that he would come back to her after all these years? Clarissa had implied as much.

"I did them a favor!" Lady Graverly said haughtily. Then her tone softened. "Caring for the boy is a joy, but it is also a terrible burden. For forty-eight years, Alexander has ruled my life. I fell in love with him the moment I set eyes on him. The boy was so helpless, so indefensible, and I felt responsible for his condition. Sarah Kilpatrick's family was poor. They would have had him institutionalized, and I couldn't bear the thought. To support him, I had to take boarders. I built my private quarters to ensure he had a proper home. But the older I've become, the more difficult it's been to do it all. I've been forced to take on fewer guests, and yet I need the income to operate the house, to pay my staff. When Lord Wakefield died, a solution presented itself. The Graverly estate would provide the wherewithal to ensure Alexander received the best of care for the remainder of his life, whether I was alive or dead. I put forward a claim on behalf of Lord Alexander, but it was contested by Lord Wakefield's widow, a vile American woman whose greed knows no bounds. She lives in Graverly Castle and continues to fashion herself as the Marchioness of Middlesex, even though her husband is dead. The courts ruled against us."

"You got nothing?"

"Not a farthing. An illegitimate son has no entitlement."

I nodded, slowly piecing things together. "Why did you tell me Agnes's sister died? She doesn't have a sister."

"She had a sister—Sarah."

"Why did she leave so abruptly?"

"She deceived me! She entered this house under false pretenses! The night she left, she accused Lord Graverly of murdering her sister and me of colluding with him. Well, I told her exactly what happened to her sister, and I introduced her to Alexander. But she had no interest in her nephew. She only cares about money. She has no claim to anything! I ordered her to leave at once, and she returned to Scotland."

"Then why did she scream, Elinor?"

"She screamed in shock upon seeing Alexander. He reminded her so much of her sister."

"So what happens now?" I asked quietly.

"Oh, Mr. Lambert," she said, clutching my arm with both hands, "if anything should happen to me, promise me you'll ensure Alexander is taken care of?"

"Of course," I said. Seeing fear in her eyes, I said, "Why, are you in danger?"

"It's more complicated than you can imagine. But don't fret, dear boy. On Friday I must go away, and before I leave I intend to have everything in place. Graverly Manor will be yours, and you will be able to forget that Lady Andrew Graverly ever existed."

★ ★ ★ ★ ★

I sat with Lady Graverly for a long time, listening to her reminisce about her early years in the manor. She told me how she had loved to welcome guests, adored entertaining, was an attentive and fun-loving host who was beloved by her guests. Every week, she had held a salon in the parlor, welcoming distinguished guests, wealthy travelers, performers, and local artists.

"This was long before I started despising my guests," she said with a cackle. "They called me the Grande Dame of Graverly Manor. My parties were legendary. You shan't believe it, but I was quite beautiful back then. Many men courted me."

"You're beautiful now, Elinor," I said, gazing at her fondly. I wished I had known her in her prime. She was formidable now; imagine her back then.

She gave a sad smile and reached over to caress my cheek. "You are so very kind, Mr. Lambert."

"Did you ever consider remarrying?"

She shook her head. "My heart will always belong to Lord Graverly."

"You don't think he's still alive?" I asked gently. "That he'll come back?"

"I do not know." A girlish smile spread across her lips, and her eyes became glassy and distant, as though she were keeping a secret she was desperate to tell.

I realized she was still waiting for Lord Graverly to sweep her off her feet. My heart ached for her. Here was the real story of the haunting of Graverly Manor: Lord Graverly existed, but only in Lady Graverly's head. Clarissa was right: she had gone insane.

"Goodness, how late it is," she said. "Will you help me to my quarters?"

She rested her head on my shoulder as we walked, seeming older and frailer than I had seen her before. I ushered her down the creaky hallway, past the images of her husband in happier days, and laid her on the bed. I pulled off her shoes and stockings, glancing briefly at her gnarled feet, and began to undress her.

"No," she whispered, reaching for my hands to pull me to her. "Just lie with me, please. If only for a moment."

I climbed onto the bed and settled next to her, listening to her breathe. Betrayed by the man she loved. Witness to the tragic death of his lover. Left to raise the brain-damaged boy on her own, a burden for fifty years.

Emitting a soft sigh, she turned on her side and nuzzled against me. I stared up at the canopy, its striped pattern and peaked roof like the inside of a circus tent, and felt her breath on my neck. I was in her bedroom at last, yet I hadn't even looked around. I searched the room with my eyes. A red, old-fashioned telephone sat on the bedside table next to a pair of eyeglasses and a glass of water. The walls were grey and peeling, decorated with portraits, their faces dark. The furnishings leaned to one side or sat hunched over in defeat.

"Elinor, are you awake?" I whispered.

She lifted her head. "Yes, my darling?"

"What do you want from me?"

She was silent for a moment. "Nothing. I simply want you to have the manor."

"Nothing else?"

"Let us talk another time. I'm ever so tired."

I rolled over to face her. "I need to know your intentions."

She smiled and reached out to caress my jaw. "My darling, if I were to find a way to take my rightful place as head of Graverly Castle, would you come with me?"

"In what role? As your butler? The innkeeper?"

Her eyes glittered. "As so much more."

"Such as?"

She pressed her fingers against my lips. "It's time to rest." Moving closer, she rested her head on my chest.

I lay still, waiting for her to fall asleep so I could slip away.

"Oh, Trevor," she breathed. "I'm so lonely."

I stiffened. She had called me Trevor for the first time. I felt her leg move over my thigh. The hard bone of her knee pressed against me. She placed an arm over my shoulder, clinging to me. Reaching down, I extracted her leg and pushed it away. My fingers felt something silky and coarse on her thigh. Sitting up, I looked down. Her gown was riding up her legs, exposing a large, unsightly mole on her inner thigh. I sat up and put my feet on the floor.

How could I have been so naïve? She wasn't interested in me as an adopted son or as an innkeeper. Her feelings were deeper than that: she wanted me to be her lover and husband. Disquieted by the notion, I stood up and began making my way to the door. Halfway there, I stopped. I heard the sound of labored breathing and smelled a faintly acrid odor. Slowly, I turned around.

Alexander sat slumped in his wheelchair in the far corner of the room. A part in the curtains cut a slash of light across his neck and face. He was staring at me.

"Hello, Alec," I said softly. I made my way over, trying to steady my breathing, telling myself there was no reason to fear him. A mother's fall, a few minutes of oxygen deprivation, and he had suffered for life.

My eyes moved back to Lady Graverly, who lay asleep, her grandeur reduced to a tiny figure, a pile of bones on the bed.

I squatted down before Alexander and smiled to put him at ease. How long since he had been outside, since he had breathed fresh air? "Would you like to go for a walk?" I whispered, taking his clammy hand in mine. Feeling a slight squeeze, I took it as consent and steered the wheelchair toward the door.

"Oh, Trevor," Lady Graverly breathed somnolently. "My prince … my handsome prince."

Outside, the night was perfectly calm. The wheelchair veered in my hands, as though having a mind of its own, and we turned down the street. "O! lure of the Lost Lagoon," I said aloud, remembering the poem. I chattered to Alexander as we made our way toward the lagoon. The grade dipped, and the wheelchair felt heavy in my hands. Fearing I would lose my grip and the wheelchair would hurl down the street and into the lagoon, I turned it in the other direction and pushed it up Chilco Street and away from the lagoon.

After a few minutes, I sensed Alexander's spirits lift. Like me, he had been trapped in that suffocating house all day, perhaps longer. How could one not feel a sense of elation to breathe the city's fresh winter air?

An hour later, I wheeled him back to the house. Lady Graverly had changed into her nightclothes and was snoring loudly under the blankets. The hair fastener sat on the nightstand next to her like a giant spider. Pushing the wheelchair into Alexander's bedroom, I found a pair of pajamas in his dresser drawer and readied him for bed.

"Good night, Alec," I whispered, standing over him. "Sweet dreams."

His eyes fluttered open, and I thought I detected a glimmer of gratitude. I flicked off the light and made my way down the hallway.

As I entered the foyer, I was startled to hear footsteps on the verandah. It was past three AM. Clarissa? I went to the door and peered out the window. A heavyset woman in a dated pink-and-blue ski jacket was pacing the verandah. I flung open the door.

"Wendy?"

"Oh my god, you're alive!" Her look of relief quickly changed to anger. "Where the hell have you been? We thought you got into an accident!"

"I was locked in my room all day."

"What? The crazy lady said you were out with some girl."

"Lady Graverly said that?"

"If you forgot about dinner, at least have the decency to tell the truth."

"I am telling the truth! The lock on my door got jammed. I was trapped all day."

She let out a huff, not buying it, and resumed pacing. "Mom and I were so sure you'd show up. I kept telling Janet to be patient, you promised, but she knew better."

"I intended to come, Wendy. Believe me, there's nothing I would have wanted more."

She stopped pacing and turned to me. I noticed her eyes were red and puffy. "Didn't you get my messages? Why didn't you call?"

"I lost my cell phone. It was too late by the time I got out."

She was trying not to cry. "I was so worried about you."

"I'm sorry, I've been preoccupied by this house, by Lady Graverly."

Anger flashed in her eyes. "What about your own mother? Did you forget about her?"

"Of course not. I'll call and apologize. I'll make it up to you, I promise."

"It's too late!" The words came out as a shriek. "You missed more than dinner, Trevor. A lot has happened since you opted out of the family, but you don't seem to have any desire to catch up. Remember that game we used to play when we were kids, when you were a king and Janet and I were peasants? You still treat us that way, like we're begging at your door."

"I do not! That's not fair. You're overreacting."

"It was an important dinner, Trevor."

Wendy's knees gave out suddenly, and she fell to the floor.

I rushed to her. "What is it, Wendy? What's wrong?"

"It's Mom. The cancer is back. She has less than three months."

18

Dark in the Lost Lagoon

My night was filled with feverish dreams. I was locked in the tower room, listening to my mother's horrified screams reverberate through the walls as Lady Graverly tortured her in the cellar. At last I broke the door down and raced down the stairs. In the foyer, I encountered Sarah Kilpatrick, hanging from the chandelier by her hair, pleading for help. I tried to cut her down but was thrown to the ground as Lady Graverly burst through the door, swinging an axe. She cut Sarah down like a side of beef and pulled a hideously shrunken, shrieking Alexander from her womb. In the private quarters, I searched in vain for the cellar entrance, only to realize my mother's cries had died off.

I woke up with a start. Reaching for the phone, I called Mom and asked if I could drive out to the house to see her. I had expected her to be angry about my no-show at dinner or emotional about her health, but her tone was casual.

"I'd love to visit, dear, but you know I go to Pilates every Monday. I'll be downtown later this afternoon to get my hair done. I could swing by the manor beforehand?"

I loitered in my room for hours, feeling both trapped and insulated in the tiny, circular space. If I didn't leave, I wouldn't have to deal with my mother's illness, nor would I have to face Lady Graverly after last night's disturbing incident. Yet at the same time I was a prisoner of my thoughts. I channeled grief for my mother toward resentment for Lady Graverly. For weeks, Mom had been vying for my attention, struggling to find a way to tell me about her illness, yet I had been dismissive and evasive, allowing Lady Graverly to dominate my time.

By late afternoon, I was unable to stand another minute in the room. I crept downstairs. In the foyer, I was surprised to find Lady Graverly at the reception desk, humming cheerfully as she sorted through mail.

"Darling, there you are!" she said, rising from the chair. "I was worried about you!" She came to me and clutched my hands, turning each cheek for a kiss. "Thank you ever so much for your company last night. You truly are a prince. I am feeling so much more optimistic about the future today."

I forced a smile. At least one of us felt better. She looked radiant, years younger than she had seemed last night. Glancing down, I saw her bony knee poking against the fabric of her tartan skirt. I shuddered as I remembered the grotesque mole, the layer of fine hair covering the crusty exterior, like a tiny parasitic rodent burrowing on her leg. Pushing the image away, I hastened down the hallway toward the kitchen. I could feel her eyes on me and sensed that somehow she knew about the drama that had unfolded last night. Either she had overheard my conversation with Wendy or she had heard my stifled sobs after Wendy left. I couldn't help but wonder if she felt a certain glee over my mother's misfortune, the imminent removal of a major obstacle to my affections. As the kitchen door closed behind me, I felt a stab of guilt. For all Lady Graverly's faults, she couldn't possibly be that wicked.

Now I was trapped in the kitchen, unable to exit out the back without my coat and shoes, which were in the foyer. I did not want Lady

Graverly to see how distraught I was, fearing she would probe. In the pantry, Lincoln's cot had been stripped, his Bible and scant personal belongings removed. I folded the cot and leaned it against the wall. Agnes, Clarissa, Lincoln—all three had vanished within days. Was I crazy to stay?

I went to the window. It was barely three o'clock, yet the sky was growing dark. A tin soldier sat on the windowsill, looking into the back yard, and I moved it aside and leaned there, watching the grey mist drift by like smoke from a nearby house fire. I observed the decrepit oak tree, clusters of dead leaves clinging to its branches, the grown-over lawn with patches of brown, the dilapidated garage, its roof sagging. How had I envisioned quaint wedding receptions in this dreary setting? My mother's illness changed everything. To squander my own money would be foolish; to squander her money would be unforgivable. The thrill of entrepreneurship was gone; the prospect of failure seemed certain. To go forward with this enormous endeavor at a time when my family needed me, when only a few months remained of my mother's life, would be lunacy. But if I gave up now, what would happen after she was gone? I would be motherless—but also homeless and jobless. And I would have sacrificed my dream.

My cell phone rang. Mother was parking down the street.

"I'll be out for a few hours," I told Lady Graverly as I rushed into the foyer and pulled on my shoes.

"Are you not expecting the housing inspector?"

Damn, I had forgotten. "Would you mind showing him around?" I asked her, disregarding the alarm bell that sounded in my head. Nothing was more important than my mother right now.

"I'd be delighted to. I thought you and I might enjoy a drink together this evening. It might be our last respite before the tour group arrives."

"Sorry, I can't." I went to the door and opened it.

"As you wish. Alexander has an appointment with the doctor tomorrow at one. I thought you might like to come with us. You seem so fond of one another."

She was manipulating me, using Alexander to guilt me. "I'm sorry, but I can't. I need to focus on my family right now, okay?"

"Very well, then."

As I stepped onto the verandah and pulled the door closed, I heard her call out, "Shan't you be needing a coat?" Pretending I hadn't heard, I hurried down the steps, expelling the manor's stale air from my lungs and replacing it with fresh air. I tried to open the gate, but the latch was jammed. What was it with doors and windows at this cursed manor? Giving up, I leapt over the gate, catching my sweater and tearing it. On the street, I searched for my mother but couldn't see her. I waited, keeping my back to the manor, certain that Lady Graverly was watching. It was a typical December day in Vancouver, cool but not freezing, and cold wind nipped at my skin. I knew I should return for a coat, but I couldn't bear the thought of Elinor's scrutiny again.

A girl in a red windbreaker was making her way up the street, hopping around puddles. As she drew closer she pulled off her hood, and I recognized my mother. I rushed to her, my frosty mood melting, and put my arms around her.

"I'm so sorry I missed dinner, Mom."

"It's okay, dear," she said, wriggling from my grasp. "Wendy told me you were tied up."

We walked toward the lagoon, knowing our destination without discussing it. I searched for words to say, but everything sounded melodramatic or trite or insensitive. My throat felt constricted. Determined not to become emotional, I opted to remain silent. The wind picked up as we reached the lagoon, sending a spray of rain into our faces.

Replacing her hood, Mom turned to me. "Aren't you cold? Your sweater will be ruined."

"It already is," I said, showing her the tear. "I've never liked it, anyway."

"Isn't that the one Janet gave you for your birthday?"

"Um ... I don't think so."

"Here, take my umbrella."

"I don't want it," I said, pushing it away.

A quartet of ducks glided along the water to our right, keeping pace with us. I sneaked a sideways glance at my mother. Was it my imagination or did her face look thinner? Yet her blue eyes were shining.

She stopped and turned to face the water. "Even on a gloomy day, the lagoon looks beautiful. Look, they've decorated the fountain like a Christmas tree."

I lowered my eyes, not wishing to acknowledge beauty in the face of sorrow. "How long have you known?" I asked her.

"A few weeks."

"A few weeks? Why didn't you say anything?"

"I've sensed the changes in my body for some time, but I got the results back just a few days ago. I needed to be certain first, and then to come to terms with it myself before I could talk to you and the girls."

We walked in silence.

"I've drawn up a will," she said. "I named your uncle Thomas executor."

"Do we have to talk about this now?"

"Yes, we do. We don't have a lot of time, Trevor. I'm leaving the house to you and your sisters. Do what you wish with it, but I won't pretend I don't care whether or not you keep it in the family. Nearly forty years of family memories live in those walls."

Lady Graverly had similar wishes for the manor. These two matriarchs shared an attachment to their homes I didn't fully comprehend, perhaps because I had never lived anywhere long enough.

"I'm hoping one of your sisters will move in," Mom said.

"Not me?"

"Of course I'd love you to, but it doesn't quite fit with your plans, does it?"

"I've decided not to buy the manor, Mom."

"What? Why?"

"You were right. If I buy that house, I'll be a slave to it. I'll never lead a normal life."

"What's a normal life? The important thing is to follow your heart. What does your heart say?"

"It says I need to spend as much time as possible with you."

"You'll still have plenty of time for me, dear. But what will happen after I'm gone? If you truly believe the manor will make you happy, I want you to buy it. That money is yours now."

"I don't want your money."

"Well, I can't take it with me."

I grew quiet, not wanting to argue. "Is there any chance you'll …?"

"Go into remission? No. The cells have spread to my lymph nodes, my liver, my pancreas. Six months ago they were undetectable, now they're everywhere."

A sob welled within me. I bit hard on my lip to keep it down and tasted blood.

She hooked her elbow around mine. "Don't feel bad, Trevor. I consider myself blessed. I was given a five-year wakeup call, and I chose to listen." She looked up at me and smiled. She looked beatific in the dying light of the sky. "I've told you before, cancer saved my life. It pulled me out of my self-imposed exile. Since that first diagnosis, I've been living life to the max, savoring every moment. When Charles died, I lost my joie de vivre. Cancer helped me get it back."

I waited for her to apply this rationale to my own life, to lecture me about being stuck in my own self-imposed exile, about my lack of joie de vivre, but she said nothing more. I felt relieved, and then disappointed, and then frantic. Who would diagnose my afflictions after she was gone? I contemplated her behavior in the past weeks. The arguing and judging had ebbed almost to a stop; at last, she had simply accepted me. It was what I had always wanted, I thought, but now I realized I needed the fight. No one was more interested in me, more willing to expend time and energy to analyze my past, to fret over my future, to uncover my neurotic disorders. Without her, there would be an irreplaceable void. I would be completely alone—something I had thought I wanted but now feared more than anything.

The rain was gaining momentum, soaking my sweater and seeping into my skin. "I'm glad for you, Mom. But forgive me if I'm not ready to see the bright side of things."

She took my hand, lightheartedly swinging it. "Remember New York, how much fun we had? That crazy time in LA during the opening? Thanks to you, I've stayed in some fantastic hotels. I've been treated like royalty."

I recalled being busy and distracted during those visits, exhausted by her need to make every moment meaningful. Why hadn't I been able to get over myself and be there for her, for us? "Those visits were amazing, Mom," I said, squeezing her hand.

She stopped walking and turned to me. "Promise me you'll take care of your sisters. You may think you don't need them, but the three of you will need each other more than ever."

Lady Graverly's words replayed in my head. *Promise me you'll ensure Alexander is taken care of.* My chin trembled. After evading familial responsibility all my life, I now had two families who needed me.

"I promise."

"I have so many things to tell you, Trevor, but now is not the time. I have to get to my appointment."

"A doctor's appointment?"

"No, I'm getting my hair done."

"Can we sit down for a few minutes, Mom? I have something for you." I walked her to a bench facing the lagoon, and we sat down. Reaching into my pocket, I unfolded a piece of paper and read:

> It is dark in the Lost Lagoon,
> And gone are the depths of haunting blue,
> The grouping gulls, and the old canoe,
> The singing firs, and the dusk and—you,
> And gone is the golden moon...

"That's it!" Mom exclaimed. "That's the poem my mother used to recite. How did you find it?"

"A friend. It was written by Pauline Johnson."

"Yes, of course. Read it again for me, please?"

Droplets of rain splattered on the paper as I read, blurring the ink. When I finished, I folded up the sheet and gave it to her. She tucked it in her pocket, smiling through her tears. We sat in silence. The rain ceased, and a red, post-apocalyptic-like sun emerged to take its final bow. I held my mother, not wanting to let go of this once-invincible woman. Looking down, I saw wispy silver roots sprouting from her white-blond hair. I felt the warmth of her skin, the hum of her body, and thought about the cells invading it, turning off lights and shutting down organs along the way. In the aftermath of my father's death, I had abdicated my role in the family. It was time to step up again.

Lifting my head, I allowed myself to look at the lagoon. The sun had disappeared, and the surface looked as dark and thick as blood.

19

A Slippery Slope

Tuesday morning, I woke up to see snow falling on the oak tree in the front yard, a layer like white moss having accumulated on the branches. With no guests expected at the manor until tomorrow, I called Mom and asked if I could come out for a visit, but she said she was driving out to Abbotsford with Uncle Thomas to see some old friends. I tried Wendy next, but she was at work. The phone at Janet's house rang and rang, and her cell phone went straight to voice mail. I spent the morning leafing through old copies of *Hotelier* magazines, restless and depressed.

In the early afternoon, I considered paying a visit to Lady Graverly and Alexander in the private quarters but realized they would be leaving for the doctor's office shortly. Now I wished I had agreed to accompany them.

I reached Shanna in her office.

"Darling, I can't talk right now, I'm swamped," she said, her abrasive tone reminiscent of the early days we had worked together. "I'll call you back."

"Sure."

"Is everything okay?"

"Fine."

I called Derrick next. When the phone picked up, I listened to a bawling baby, and then his wife came on, sounding harried. "Hello? Hello?"

"Hi, it's Trevor. Is Derrick around?"

There was a pause. "He's ... not home. Bethany, shush!"

"Do you expect him back soon?"

The crying ceased, and for a moment I thought she had hung up. "Derrick won't be back," she said.

The baby resumed crying, and she hung up.

I stared at the phone. Had Derrick left his wife, or had she thrown him out? I tried his cell phone, but there was no answer. I left a message and went downstairs to make some lunch.

In the kitchen, the slam of the back door of the private quarters drew me to the window. A HandyDART van was parked in the back alley, and the driver was lowering the lift for Alexander. Lady Graverly was dressed for a Moscow winter in a Russian-style fur hat and full-length sable coat. She climbed into the front seat, and the van pulled away.

The house was freezing cold. I went into the parlor to light a fire and remembered I had used up all the kindling. The axe was still missing; I cursed myself for not having tracked it down. I went out to the back yard and searched for small logs, but only a stack of oversized logs remained. I settled on turning up the heat.

Shanna didn't call back. Janet phoned in the late afternoon, and I agreed to meet her and Wendy that evening. Around six thirty, I left for Coquitlam, driving through the gathering snow to the Cozy Corner Café, a trashy little joint off Lougheed Highway that seemed to mock the gravity of the occasion. As I passed the counter, I gave a cursory glance at the stale-looking confections on display and made my way into the crowded dining room. Wendy and Janet were waiting in a booth, their faces glum. We exchanged hugs, and I sat down to debrief them on yesterday's visit with Mom.

"I can't believe how strong she's being," Wendy said, dabbing her eyes. "She's just going about her business like usual."

"She might seem fine now," said Janet, "but the doctor says her condition will deteriorate rapidly."

"She refuses to check into a hospital no matter how bad it gets," Wendy said, and gave a sad laugh. "She says she's worked in hospitals all her life, she's not going to die in one."

"Care won't be a problem," I said. "I'll move into her house and be there twenty-four hours."

They turned to me in surprise.

"What about the manor?" Wendy asked.

"I've decided not to buy it."

"What?" the two cried in unison.

"For my entire adult life, all I've done is work," I explained. "I've completely screwed up my priorities. Mom says her first cancer diagnosis was a wakeup call for her. Well, this one is a wakeup call for me."

"There's no need to do anything that drastic, Trevor," said Janet, regarding me with the Lambert expression. "Don't worry, Wendy and I worked out a care schedule. We've got it covered."

The waitress arrived, and Janet and Wendy ordered Diet Cokes and slices of Boston cream pie. "The pies are really good here," Wendy said.

I frowned at the menu. Nothing sounded palatable. "I'll have a San Pellegrino with lime, no ice," I said. "And … do you have any crème brûlée? I'm craving—." I stopped, realizing she was looking at me like I was speaking a foreign language.

Janet and Wendy squirmed in their seats.

"I'll have the pie and a Diet Coke too," I said.

After the waitress left, I said, "I want to take responsibility for her care. It's the least I can do."

"You don't have to, Trevor," Janet said, a trace of irritation creeping into her voice. "Wendy and I will alternate. I plan to cut down my hours at work."

"I'm going to take a leave," said Wendy. "Jas will look after the kids."

"You can't afford to make those sacrifices," I said, looking first to Wendy, then to Janet.

"I want to," said Wendy.

"So do I," said Janet. "We want you to buy the manor, Trevor. It's a great investment, even if it's a bit creepy, and it'll keep you in Vancouver, where we want you."

I decided to defer the discussion. There were more important matters at hand. "We need to talk about, you know, funeral arrangements," I said gently. "I can call her and ask her what she wants. And we'll need to figure out what we're going to do with the house."

"We already discussed all that stuff," said Janet, glancing at Wendy. "We really have no choice but to sell the house, but we'll wait until, well, after. Why don't you just focus on the manor? You have enough on your mind. Let us take care of everything."

I felt confused, almost subverted. I had come expecting my sisters to step aside to allow me to resume my responsibilities as eldest in the family, and they were resisting, but not in their typical sarcastic, mocking way. They were being respectful and gentle. Who were these two pleasant woman, and what had they done with my sisters?

Seeing my distress, Janet said, "We'll still need your help. I'll need you to come to Maple Ridge for a few hours a week to babysit the kids."

"And twice a week in Port Coquitlam with my kids," Wendy added.

I tried to conceal my alarm. "Sure. Anything I can do to help."

They burst out laughing.

"I wouldn't trust you with my kids," said Janet as our Diet Cokes arrived. "They'd be demanding crème brûlées all the time."

Wendy tittered. "And wearing ascots."

I glowered but couldn't help but break into a smile, relieved. My bitchy sisters were back.

"Speaking of which," Janet said, reaching into her purse and sliding over a thin wrapped gift. "Here's an early Christmas present from Wendy and me."

"It's a tie," Wendy burst out, unable to contain her excitement.

I unwrapped the box with trepidation, anticipating a Santa tie, a skinny red leather tie, a tie patterned with images of Lady Graverly. To my surprise, I found a Gucci box, and inside a very tasteful black tie.

"It's beautiful," I said in shock. "But how could you afford …?"

"Don't worry, we didn't steal it." Janet turned to Wendy. "You didn't, right?"

Wendy giggled and shook her head. "Trevor, promise us you'll lose that ascot."

I nodded, grinning. "I already did."

For the next hour we reminisced, dredging up memories of our mother both happy and sad, occasionally tearing up but more often breaking into hysterics.

Just like the good old times.

Outside in the parking lot, I hugged my sisters good night and walked them to their cars. The snow had stopped, but the temperature had dropped, and little crystals of ice had formed on my windshield. I scraped them off and drove away.

As I steered onto the freeway, I received a call from Hal Farnsworth. I had completely forgotten about yesterday's inspection.

"The old lady said you're eager to close the sale," he said. "So I thought I'd give you a quick call before submitting my report."

I was about to tell him not to bother, that I was calling the deal off, but held off, curious about the assessment. "How did it go?" I asked.

"I checked everything: heating and electrical, plumbing, foundation, septic system, roof, paint, insulation—the works. Everything looks to be in remarkably good shape for its age. They don't build houses like that anymore. A few little things need attention, but nothing major. Overall, I give it top marks."

"Really?" I said. Part of me had hoped he would say the manor was sick, a money pit, that I should run in the opposite direction.

"You got a real gem there, Trevor. And the price—what a steal. If you don't buy it, I will."

"No chance of that, Hal," I said, feeling suddenly possessive.

"By the way, I found the entrance to the cellar but couldn't get inside to have a look. She said you have the key."

"Me? I've never even seen the cellar."

"That's strange. She said you were down there the other day."

"In the cellar?" I laughed. "Maybe she meant the laundry room."

"Yeah, well, she's a pretty old dame, probably losing her mind. Sounds like it's working to your advantage, though—that price!"

I thanked Hal and hung up.

A while later, as I was driving up First Avenue, my phone rang again.

"Is this Trevor Lambert?" said a sharply accented voice.

"Yes. Who's this?"

"Brandon. I'm Agnes Kilpatrick's son. I'm calling from Edinburgh."

"Hi, Brandon! How's Agnes?"

"That's why I'm calling, actually. I called the manor looking for her, and the woman who answered told me you would know where I could find her. I haven't been able to reach her for several days, and to be frank, I'm a little worried. A suitcase full of her belongings just arrived at our door."

I felt a niggling of dread in the pit of my stomach. "Agnes left the city four days ago, Brandon. You haven't heard from her at all?"

"No."

I didn't know what to say. Why had Lady Graverly referred him to me?

"Well, now that I know she left Vancouver, I'm not as worried," said Brandon. "She must have stopped in London. She had some business there."

"That must be it," I said, relieved.

"I'm terribly sorry to have bothered you."

"Not at all. Brandon, when you see her, will you ask her to call me? I have something I want to send her, an old diary. And if you don't hear from her soon, will you let me know?"

"Will do."

Late that night, as I lay on my cot, staring up at the false ceiling, my cell phone rang.

"Oh, darling. I just talked to your mother. I'm so sorry."

"Please, Shanna, no sympathy. No tears or eulogizing. I can't deal with it right now."

"Evelyn Lambert is one of the most remarkable women I know," she said, ignoring my request. "This world will be a lesser place without her. You poor boy. What are you going to do?"

"I'm going to spend as much time as possible with her, if she'll let me."

"And the manor?"

I stood up and went to the window, gazing out onto the dark street. A hooded figure was pushing a wheelchair down the road. Lady Graverly and Alexander. "I've decided to go through with the sale."

"You have? But isn't this a bad time for such an undertaking?"

"Yes, but it's the only time I have. Mom and my sisters have given me their blessing, the inspector gave the house two thumbs up, and Lady Graverly says she'll be ready to sign off by Friday. Everything is falling into place."

"Darling, wouldn't you prefer to focus on your family at a time like this?"

"Of course I would, Shanna, and I will. But my sisters have their families to comfort them; I don't. The manor will be my anchor. Without it, I fear I'll drift out to sea and be swallowed by grief."

"I understand, but …" I heard her light a cigarette and take a long drag. "What if the burden is so heavy you capsize?"

"I'm a strong swimmer."

"I don't know, Trevor. I have a bad feeling about this. I'm not convinced you're thinking straight. You're unduly influenced by that woman."

"Shanna, this is all I need right now."

"I'm sorry. Will you be taking some time off, at least?"

Down the street, the wheelchair had stopped. Concerned about Lady Graverly and Alexander on the icy road, I hurried downstairs and put on my coat and shoes as I continued talking to Shanna.

"I can't. I have a group arriving tomorrow, and they're taking every room in the house. Their package includes a cocktail reception, breakfast each morning, and a farewell dinner. I'm going to be crazy busy."

"Surely the other staff can cover for you?"

"What other staff?" I said. "The chambermaid's gone, the butler's gone. I'm the only one left."

As I reached the sidewalk, I saw Lady Graverly struggling to keep the wheelchair from sliding down the road.

"Shanna, I have to run," I yelled into the phone, hanging up and bolting down the street. Up ahead, Lady Graverly had fallen down, and the wheelchair was spinning in circles down the road. Racing past Lady Graverly, I caught the handle and halted the wheelchair just as it was about to strike the curb and tumble down the slope toward the lagoon.

All was still.

I stood on the cold pavement, panting, as Lady Graverly hobbled toward me.

20

Smart Alec

On Wednesday morning, I was racing around, getting the manor ready for the arrival of the tour group, when I heard the distant tinkling of a bell. Curious, I followed the sound, which led me to the door of the private quarters. It was unlocked, and I made my way down the hallway to Lady Graverly's bedroom, rapping on the door. It stood partly ajar, and I pushed it open.

"There you are! It's about time." Lady Graverly cried, setting the bell down. She was propped up in bed in a pink cotton robe with a white fur collar.

"You were summoning me with a bell?" I asked, incredulous.

"I am not well," she said, pressing her hand against her forehead. "It must be the stress of last night's terrifying incident. Be a dear and bring me a spot of tea, will you?"

"Elinor, I'm really busy. I could use your help out there."

"You needn't worry, my dear. I expect to be back on my feet by the time the group arrives. They will be terribly disappointed if I'm not there to greet them. Be a darling and check on Lord Alexander, will you? The poor boy probably had nightmares all night."

"When is the nurse coming?"

"She shan't be coming. I had to let her go."

"What?"

"She was far too unreliable. Portuguese, naturally. I do detest unreliability." She crossed her arms and looked off to the side, as though pondering this thought for the first time. Then she looked back at me. "Did I ask for toast? My mind is such a muddle these days."

"Elinor, I refuse to play butler, chambermaid, *and* nurse. I hope you're planning to call in another nurse."

"I'm afraid that's not possible. We'll have to make do for now." She gave me a reassuring smile. "Not to worry. In two days, I shall be out of your hair."

"Where are you going?"

"Away."

"Where to?"

"You needn't concern yourself with my affairs, Mr. Lambert."

On my way out, I stopped. "Elinor, have you heard from Agnes?"

"Not a word."

"I received a call from her son last night. She hasn't turned up in Edinburgh."

"How peculiar. I wonder what's become of her."

"I'm a little concerned. Did she tell you where she was going?"

"I don't believe so. She's probably gone to visit Lord Wakefield's widow at Graverly Castle. I understand they've gotten quite chummy. Now, about that tea …"

On my way down the hallway, I ducked into Alexander's bedroom. He was exactly as I had left him the previous night, curled onto his side in a fetal position, a sleeping man-child with greying hair. What was it about this man and his mother, both strangers until recently, that touched a nerve in me? My own mother was dying, and yet their needs felt more urgent and acute. It was a matter of helplessness, I decided, and attitude. Mom still had her faculties intact; she was fiercely independent and not about to waste time feeling sorry for herself or eliciting sympathy from others. The future of these two, on the other hand, seemed hopeless. Lady Graverly had said she would be leaving on Friday. Where would they go?

I thought of the bills she received daily, stamped PAST DUE and FINAL NOTICE. It suddenly struck me that the departures of Agnes and Lincoln, and now the nurse, were due not to coincidence but to desperation; Lady Graverly could no longer afford to pay them but was too proud to admit it. Now, her greatest fear seemed imminent: Alexander would be taken from her and put into an institution. I recalled asking her what she would do after she sold the manor. *Why, I'm abdicating, of course,* she had replied. Indeed, she was stepping down as the Grande Dame of Graverly Manor and would inevitably be entering a senior's home. Meanwhile, she was pretending to be in full control, acting like the Graverly estate was still within her grasp and any day now she would have a joyful reunion with her husband. She was in denial, at best, but more likely, my earlier bleak conclusion was true: she had gone insane.

No wonder I felt sorry for these two.

Deciding to let Alexander sleep, I went to the kitchen to prepare breakfast.

When I returned with the breakfast tray, Lady Graverly was dozing, her head tilted back, mouth open. I set the tray on the nightstand and returned to the kitchen to retrieve a second tray for Alexander. When I entered his bedroom, his eyes were open. I sat him up and tried to feed him some tea and porridge, but he refused to open his mouth. It became evident he needed a shower, and I carried him into the bathroom, undressed him, and sat him on the stool inside the shower, turning the water on. Stepping back, I observed him hunched over under the downpour like a little boy left out in the rain. With a sigh, I stripped down to my boxers and stepped in, telling myself that if things didn't work out as an innkeeper, I could always apply to be a hospital orderly.

After the shower, Alexander was more receptive to food. Seated on the edge of the bed, I spoon-fed porridge to him, wiping his face after each swallow. He followed me with his eyes, occasionally lifting a limp hand to signal me to stop or continue. His eyes seemed alert this morning, almost intelligent, and I wondered how much cognitive capacity he possessed. Had there been attempts to rehabilitate him, to train him to speak and use his limbs, or had he been considered a hopeless case from the beginning? When Lady Graverly said that Alexander had lived much longer than the doctors had expected, I had detected a note of resignation in her voice. I thought of my own mother and wondered how she would have reacted if I had been born this way. A nurse by profession, a life coach by nature, she would undoubtedly have dedicated her life to me in the same way Lady Graverly had dedicated her life to Alexander. At least there would never be a threat of me moving away, I thought wryly. Lord Graverly had abandoned Lady Graverly, but he had left behind a constant companion.

As I fed Alexander, I told him about my sisters, about my mother and her illness, and pretended he responded in kind. "Yes, Alec, my mother and I are very close, thanks for asking. Just like you and your mother. What's that? ... No, I've decided to pretend she's not sick. It's easier to believe our mothers will live forever, don't you think? If it doesn't happen, we'll deal with reality when the time comes. No use grieving in anticipation—right? I knew you would agree. Smart Alec. You and I think so much alike. We're just like brothers, aren't we?"

He closed his mouth, refusing the spoon, and squeezed his eyes shut. A high-pitched hum like a mosquito rose from his throat. His eyes snapped open, and a tear rolled down his cheek. His body began to tremble.

"I'm sorry," I said, alarmed. "Did I upset you?" Fearing he was about to have one of his episodes, I gently took his hands and tried to calm him. "It's okay, Alec," I said, looking into his eyes. "I understand. I'm here for you."

The hum turned to moaning.

Fighting the urge to run to Lady Graverly for his medication, I attempted to calm him down naturally. The moaning was so intense, so visceral, I felt he was giving voice not only to his own sadness but to my sadness, to the sadness in the house, and to all the sadness in the world. I closed my eyes and listened to his beautiful, eerie aria, this dying man's lament.

The moaning stopped.

I opened my eyes and smiled at him. He stared back, a glint of curiosity in his eyes. A shadow passed over us, and his eyes widened in fear.

Looking over my shoulder, I saw Lady Graverly standing in the doorway, a needle in her hand. "Does he need a shot?" she asked.

"No. He's fine. Go back to bed. I'll bring him to you."

She left, and as I lifted Alexander from the bed to place him into his wheelchair, I felt his hands on my back, gripping me as though hugging me.

Or holding on for dear life.

★ ★ ★ ★ ★

Around one o'clock, I drove to Costco to buy appetizer platters for the reception; I intended to replate them and try to pass them off as homemade. Upon my return, I detected an unpleasant odor in the foyer like stale garbage. I couldn't find the source, and the odor soon dissipated, only to materialize in occasional flashes throughout the day. I sprayed Febreze all over, even on Sir Fester, who hissed and swiped at me.

"You better be nice to our guests!" I shouted as he scampered off. "No clawing or scratching! No locking them in their rooms!"

The group was expected at four. By three thirty, I had fallen hopelessly behind, and panic welled inside me. I still had to prepare for the reception, sweep the verandah and sidewalk, finish the laundry, assign rooms, and prepare keys. The tour and travel market would be an integral part of my business, and I wanted everything perfect for my first group. Racing from room to room, I began to spin out of control. In the kitchen, hurriedly arranging canapés on a pan, I lifted my arm and decided that, above all, I needed a shower.

As I passed through the foyer, I was surprised to see Lady Graverly perched at the reception desk, fully dressed and resplendent in a pouffy red dress and a flowered hat.

"The tour leader called," she said brightly. "The group will arrive momentarily."

"Oh, Christ."

"No need to blame him."

"Will you assign rooms and prepare keys while I take a quick shower?"

"That is precisely what I'm doing, my dear."

I approached the desk and saw that she had written the names of each guest on envelopes and was now coordinating the keys. "Where's the eighth?" I asked, counting.

"Only seven rooms are reserved," she said breezily. The keys clinked like gold coins as she stacked them.

"You mean to tell me Clarissa could have stayed?"

"Perhaps the group had a last-minute cancellation."

I glowered at her. "Did Clarissa say where she was going?"

"I recall she said something about her favorite place."

"The cemetery?"

She blinked. "I assumed she meant Kentucky."

I was in my room toweling off when I heard the tour van pull up out front. I dressed quickly and hurried out.

Lady Graverly had swanned onto the sidewalk and was greeting guests as they climbed from the van. "Welcome to Graverly Manor! Welcome!" she sang out. "I'm Lady Andrew Graverly. I've been so looking forward to your arrival. My, my, what a gorgeous little dress! You must be Miss Woo, the tour leader."

"Nice to meet you!" Amy Woo said.

The Grande Dame of Graverly Manor was back and in fine form, and her audience was lapping it up. They stopped to admire her period costume, assuming it was part of some kind of performance, and turned to gaze at the house, which sparkled magnificently in the afternoon sun. At the gate, I paused to observe the guests, trying to guess what might be in store for me over the next two nights. They ranged in age from early fifties to mid seventies, and, to my relief, all looked agile and fully capable of bathing themselves.

"Please, my dear, put that bag down, I beg of you!" Lady Graverly called out to a tall woman with straight grey bangs. "The bellboy will be out in a moment to gather everything." Spotting me, she gave two quick claps of her hands. "Make haste, dear boy! These world-weary travelers must be exhausted."

The tall woman introduced herself as Barbara James from Bakersfield, California. "This is my companion, Donna Edwards," she said, gesturing to a stout woman with jade earrings who was staring bug-eyed at Lady Graverly.

"And who is this handsome woman?" Lady Graverly asked, as the last guest stepped down from the bus.

"I'm Mrs. Fishburne. How do you do?"

To my surprise, it was the elegant woman from New England who had been at the open house. What was she doing here? As I opened the hatch of the van, I tried to catch her eye, but the steely-eyed gaze I recalled from the showing was fixed on the manor's façade.

"Trevor, please stop dillydallying!" cried Lady Graverly. "Come along, everyone! I shall take you on a brief tour."

The guests followed her in, chattering excitedly.

I unloaded the suitcases, over twenty in all, and stacked them on the sidewalk. As I arrived in the foyer with the first load, I found the group gathered around the portrait of the soldier on a prancing horse that Lady Graverly had picked up at the flea market.

"…was my dear grandfather," she was saying. "A war hero and great cavalryman, he was knighted by Queen Victoria in the First Boer War."

I turned to her, eyebrows raised, but she refused to meet my eye.

Her audience was enthralled; their eyes moved in awe from Lady Graverly to the portrait and back again.

Lady Graverly continued, "Her Majesty was so impressed by his gallantry she sent him numerous invitations to join her state affairs. But the duke was dedicated to his wife, a homely German princess whose father owned most of Bavaria, and he remained faithful to the very end." A devilish smile crept over her lips. "Or so goes the official story. Trevor, please! Chop-chop!"

Clenching my teeth, I began stacking the bags at the foot of the stairs.

"What about this vase?" asked Mr. Potts from Savannah, Georgia, an elderly man with a thin moustache. He pointed to the copper umbrella stand I had kicked over after my night out with Clarissa. It was now perched on the desk and stuffed with paper flowers.

"Why, that is a priceless relic dug up from the sands of the Sahara Desert," said Lady Graverly. "I purchased it years ago, while traveling by elephant caravan with my good friend, Sheik Hassam El-Sayid."

Dropping the suitcases with a thud, I went out for my next load, shaking my head. When I returned, Amy Woo was reading names from a roster while Lady Graverly handed out keys, dispensing commentaries about the monarchs after which the guest rooms were named.

"Gertrude Fishburne?" Amy called out.

Lady Graverly searched the roster. "I don't have a Fishburne on my list."

"Oh right, I forgot to tell you," said Amy. "Mrs. Fishburne was a last-minute sub for Erma Clayton, who got hit by a car."

"How tragic." Lady Graverly's eyes scrutinized Mrs. Fishburne as she handed her a key. "Have we met before?"

"I don't believe so," Mrs. Fishburne replied, to my surprise.

"We have you in the Elizabeth I suite, named after my favorite monarch of all time," said Lady Graverly, her mouth contorting into an expression that suggested she regretted having assigned the room to this insipid woman. "Elizabeth became queen at twenty-five years of age, after being imprisoned in the Tower of London by her half-sister, Mary I, and only narrowly avoiding execution. She began her reign during a time of great strife in England—poverty, battles for the throne, religious turmoil, and a multitude of executions—yet when she died almost forty-five years later, England was one of the richest and most powerful countries in the world."

As I shuttled up and down the stairs to deliver luggage, sweat pouring down my forehead and soaking my suit, I heard cries of delight as guests entered their rooms. I felt relieved, having feared cries of horror over the gaudy décor, cheap trinkets, and weathered furnishings. Lady Graverly retired to her apartment, clocking in her workday at just under an hour and leaving me to scramble to keep up with requests for extra towels, blankets, foam pillows, maps, snacks, and talc powder. Again I recalled her cure for stress and wondered if the Four Seasons had a room available. Or better, a dose of Alexander's medication, with its instantaneous tranquilizing effect.

At five o'clock, I was in the Henry VIII room playing maintenance man, assisting Barbara James and Donna Edwards with a jammed window, when I heard the doorbell ring. *Go away,* I thought, resenting any further demands on my time. I heaved at the window. It wouldn't budge.

"It's just so stuffy in here," Miss Edwards said.

"Maybe it's nailed shut," Miss James suggested.

"I don't think so," I said, wishing the women wouldn't gawk while I worked. Downstairs, the doorbell rang again. I yanked at the window with all my might. It shot upward and slammed into the frame at the top, shattering.

Miss Edwards let out a cry and leapt away as glass showered over us.

"Oh my gosh!" cried Miss James. "Are you okay?"

"I got it open," I said with a sheepish smile. Ducking my head through the opening, I peered below, praying no one was there.

Miss Edwards screamed. "Watch out!"

I yanked my head out just as a shard of glass fell from the top of the frame, narrowly missing my neck. It landed on the floor, breaking into pieces. Miss Edwards and Miss James gaped at me, hands pressed against their faces.

Downstairs, the doorbell was still ringing. Brushing glass from my shoulders, I advised the ladies to steer clear of the window and assured them I would call a repairman and return with a broom. As I hurried out, I felt them staring after me, traumatized by what might have happened.

As I headed for the stairs, my cell phone rang.

"Trevor! It's Derrick. How you doin'?"

"This is a *really* bad time, Derrick."

Lady Graverly was standing at the top of the stairs, arms crossed, a haughty expression on her face. "What on earth happened in there?" she demanded.

"I won't keep you," Derrick said into the phone. "I just wanted to say how sorry I am about your mom. I always wished my mom was more like her."

"Thanks, Derrick. I appreciate it. Hey, is everything okay? Are you back at home yet?"

"No."

"Oh, no. Jeez, I'm sorry. Listen, I'll call you back, okay?"

"Sure, whenever. And let me know if you need anything."

I stuffed the phone into my pocket. "I broke the window," I told Elinor. "It was stuck. Don't worry, no one was hurt."

"Someone is here to see you," she said with a sniff.

"Who?"

"A drag queen of some sort. He says he's a friend."

Curious, I pried past her and made my way downstairs. The door was open, and a pale shaft of late-afternoon light illuminated the frame of a petite woman with big hair in a designer suit and oversized sunglasses.

Shanna Virani.

21

Swan Song

"I'm here to help in any way I can," Shanna announced upon arrival, "provided it doesn't involve cooking, cleaning, or anything domestic."

Nevertheless, she immediately took charge of preparations for the reception. She took stock of the bar, kitchen supplies, and food items, turned up her nose at my Costco platters, and compiled a list of ingredients for homemade canapés, dispatching me to the local market. By the time I returned, she had reorganized the parlor, overseen replacement of the broken window, charmed the guests with anecdotes about her career in hotels, and taken two reservations calls.

"I upsold a caller from San Francisco to the most expensive suite," she informed me, rolling pastry dough into a circle as I unpacked groceries. "They'll be staying for six nights in January. I quoted a special rate of $825 per night. I hope you have a Marie Antoinette suite."

"At that rate, I'll rename one of them."

A group of guests had gone out for a stroll, and the others were resting. This gave Shanna and me time to catch up. After the reception, the tour van would take the group to dinner at Greencroft, a heritage house in Shaughnessy, and would bring them back to the manor afterward. While they were out, I planned to turn down their rooms and place fresh-baked cookies on their nightstands.

Now, as I watched the worldly and sophisticated Shanna Virani, who had always claimed to be domestically disabled, bustle around the kitchen in a frilly apron, I experienced a rush of gratitude.

"I can't believe you quit your job to come up and help me," I said. "You're a true friend."

"Don't flatter yourself, darling. I couldn't stand another minute at Chateau Beverly Hills. Of all the blowhard general managers I've had to endure over the years—present party excluded, *bien sûr*—Montgomery Neville was the worst. When he finally deigned to show up this morning, I announced that I had taken a job at the Peninsula. The poor sod almost choked on his crumpet. Only yesterday, he told me I had a bad attitude. Can you imagine?"

Having managed Shanna before—or, more accurately, having been managed by Shanna—I could well imagine. The smirk on her face now, her lip curling upward to reveal a flash of white teeth against bright red lipstick, hinted that she well knew the allegation wasn't entirely preposterous. There were good reasons why staff in New York had called her Queen of the Fucking Universe.

"Clearly he's the one with the attitude problem," I said.

"Naturally." She began to cut half-moons into the pastry dough and place them on a pan. "In the first month alone, I brought in more than a million dollars in room revenue. When King Abdullah found out I was there, he called me up and bought out three floors for a week."

Listening to her talk, it occurred to me that she and Lady Graverly would get along famously, but Lady Graverly had disappeared into her quarters shortly after Shanna's arrival.

Shanna set down the cutter. "I've never had to prove myself before. Hotel managers always just know I'm fabulous. On Friday, he threatened to suspend me for making the revenue manager cry."

"Why did you make her cry?"

"I didn't! She cried out of her own free will after I explained to her how utterly incompetent she was. If I were that daft, I would cry too. Mr. Neville runs the hotel like an absolute monarchy—with the budget of a state prison. I really loved that hotel, Trevor—the guests, the staff, the prestige—but I simply could not work under such feudal conditions." Reaching under the sink for a rag, she kneeled down to scrub pastry dough off the floor.

Grinning at the sight of this washerwoman in Chanel, I resumed the task she had assigned me: cutting truffles into paper-thin slices and placing them on crostinis with Fontina cheese. "Are you really going to the Peninsula?"

"Of course not. I knew he would walk me right out the door, which he did. *Et voilà!* At your service." She lifted herself to her feet and curtsied. "I'm here to free you up to spend time with your family, and to see your mother myself, of course."

My mother and Shanna had made a connection when Mom was visiting Los Angeles for the opening of Hotel Cinema. Now they enjoyed a close relationship. I found it a bit unsettling, my mother hanging out with my close friend. Shanna, however, now well into her fifties, was closer in age to my mother than to me.

"So," I said, "what do you think of the manor?"

Wringing out the rag in the sink, she made a face. "Hmm."

"You don't like it."

"You know how I feel about bed-and-breakfasts and old things in general. The house is lovely, I suppose—if you're into the shabby florals look. Your mother and I were talking, and we've both always imagined you running a Four Seasons." She walked to the window and peered at the oak tree outside. Its branches seemed closer to the house than I remembered, as though the tree were bending over to listen. She lifted the replica of a Tower of London guard from the windowsill and held it up. "My god, this place is like some tacky souvenir shop on Buckingham Palace Road." The guard fell from her hands and hit the floor, its head snapping off. "Oops," she said, stooping to retrieve it. "I hope this isn't an heirloom."

"I'm sure she'll claim it is," I said, taking the pieces from her and dropping them in the garbage. "Don't worry, the kitsch will go the moment I take possession."

"Speaking of kitsch, you never told me Lady Graverly was a man. And where did he get that outfit, Scarlett O'Hara?"

I covered my mouth to suppress my laughter. "You're just mad because she thought you were a drag queen."

"She's not the first. I consider it a compliment. The woman is mad about you, darling, it's painfully obvious. And I thought I was the oldest cougar alive."

"Are you here to help me or to torment me?"

"Both, naturally." She sniffed the air and made a face. "What's that smell?"

"What smell?"

"That fetid odor." She opened the cupboard and bent down to sniff at the garbage. She opened the fridge next, then ducked her head out the back door. "Strange, it's gone now." With a shrug, she took the knife from my hands. "I said paper-thin slices, not slabs. Why don't you go light a fire?"

A few minutes later, I was stuffing old newspapers into the fireplace, hoping they would substitute for kindling, when Shanna sauntered in, making a beeline for the bar. "We have just enough time for a martini before the seniors brigade storms in. If I'm going to play housemaid tonight, I'm going to need to dull my senses."

"I'm not sure that's a good idea. We're staff, after all."

"Darling, relax! This isn't a hotel. There's no danger of setting a bad example for employees—you've scared them all off." She stood on her toes to retrieve a bottle of Bombay Sapphire from the shelf.

"Careful of the glasses," I said. "Most are chipped." While Shanna made drinks, I went out to the back for firewood, choosing the smallest log in the pile.

Shanna looked askance as I lugged it passed her. "Planning to set the house on fire?"

"I can't find the axe, and there's no kindling."

"Maybe your mistress is hiding it under her pillow to use on us tonight."

"Not funny," I said, remembering my nightmare. I stuffed the log into the firepit and tried to close the doors. "So do you plan to stay in LA?"

"Who knows? With Bantu and Eliza leaving for Princeton, there's really no point in suffering that city any longer."

"Where will you go?"

"Honestly, I have no clue. I've felt homeless for so many years, it doesn't seem to matter where I live anymore. My career will be downhill from here, directly on the heels of the utter collapse of my looks. I'm destined to be one of those sun-baked, aging party-girl sales managers at the Journey's Inn with leopard-print shoes and a smoker's voice."

"Sounds like my realtor. With your credentials, you could work anywhere, Shanna."

"The good hotels in LA want anorexic supermodels to run the sales department, and there's no shortage in that city. Frankly, I'm suspicious of any hotel interested in hiring me. Who wants a washed-up has-been representing a luxury hotel? I'm thinking of applying at the Ben & Jerry's store near my home. No stress, all the ice cream I can eat, and everyone will understand why I'm fat." She handed me a martini glass filled to the brim. "These old-fashioned glasses are so impractical—you can barely get two ounces in. To your health."

"To your health." Gin slopped on my hand as we clinked glasses. I took a sip. "A definite improvement over the butler's caustic concoctions," I said.

"My martinis used to be legendary. A chilled glass, two queen olives, a breath of vermouth, flecks of ice floating on the surface. Ramin and I used to entertain often, and I always played bartender. The secret to a successful party is to over-pour in the first hour, keep food to a minimum, and close the bar an hour before you want everyone to leave."

"Perhaps we can test that theory tomorrow night at the farewell dinner."

"I intend to."

At that moment, Harry and Sal Weiss from Willamette, Oregon, wandered in. Shanna welcomed them warmly and handed them two martinis, which they accepted somewhat reluctantly. She did the same with every guest, and soon the parlor was buzzing with spirited chatter. Shanna, accustomed to holding court in a room, slipped into a deferential role, circling the room with trays of hors d'oeuvres and topping up martini glasses, while I, the shy one, played host.

"Our biggest seller is a coffee mug shaped like a woman's breast," Mrs. Weiss was telling me about her ceramics shop. "You drink out of the nipple."

"How clever," I said, distracted by the tinkling of a bell. I excused myself.

Lady Graverly was standing in the hallway, looking like a Bombay bride in an elaborate lace veil and a white gown sewn with hundreds of pearls.

"If you could be so kind as to introduce me," she said, her eyes fluttering under the veil.

"You want me to announce you?"

"Why, yes, that would be lovely!"

I sighed and folded my arms. "What's your official title again?"

"Lady Andrew Graverly, the Marchioness of Middlesex."

"But—"

"Just do it, my child. It shall be only a matter of time before it's true. And do bring me one of those martinis. I'm ever so parched."

"As you wish, Your Majesty," I said with a bow.

"Lincoln used to play music to signal my entrance."

"Elinor, I'm not putting on 'God Save the Queen.'"

She pursed her lips. "As you wish."

I brought her a drink and returned to the reception, allowing a few minutes for her to get liquored up before calling for the group's attention.

"Ladies and gentleman," I announced, "tonight we have a special treat. The manor's proprietress is here to grace us with a few words about the manor's illustrious history." Once again, I detected an air of affectation in my voice. Lady Graverly's snobbery was rubbing off on me. "Here she is," I said, now sounding like a game-show host, "Lady Andrew Graverly, the Marchioness of Middlesex!"

The crowd broke into applause, and Lady Graverly swooped in, beaming and nodding and making gestures of feigned modesty. Swallowing the rest of her martini, she handed off the glass to me and began her spiel. "My husband, the esteemed Lord Andrew Graverly, of Uxbridge, in the county of Middlesex, was born in 1924, the youngest son of the seventh Marquess of Middlesex and a direct relation of the Windsor family. At the time of his birth, he was forty-second in line to the throne…"

My jaw dropped. I was now accustomed to the little white lies, told, I suspected, as much for her own amusement as to impress, but this one was a whopper. It occurred to me this was her swan song, her final performance, and she was making the most of it. The revelation caused a stir of excitement in the group. Only Mrs. Fishburne looked unconvinced. She stood in the back of the room, her elegant figure towering above the others, and regarded Lady Graverly with half-closed eyes and a thin, tolerant smile. Who was she, and what had brought her back to the manor? She looked out of place in a tour group with her expensively coiffed hair and regal comportment.

Lady Graverly was still speaking. "Though of noble blood, Lord Andrew was a humble man. Over time, he grew disenchanted with the excesses of his wealthy family and opted to sever ties with them, moving to Canada to begin a modest life among common people." She went on to tell the story she had told at the open house, although the facts and figures were recklessly skewed; she had either confused them or was pulling them randomly from the air.

Ten minutes later, she concluded: "And thus you see the manor today, a taste of merry old England in the heart of Canada." She surveyed the group, hands clasped at her chest, allowing the drama of her story to sink in. "Well, then! If there are no questions, I shall bid you good night." She turned to leave.

"I beg your pardon," Gertrude Fishburne called out. "If you don't mind my asking, how exactly are you related to the Windsor family?"

Lady Graverly turned around. "Pardon me?" Her face puckered as she searched the room for the author of the question. Spotting Mrs. Fishburne, she forced a smile, grew serious, then forced another smile. "Why, there are a number of familial connections between the Graverlys and the Windsors," she said.

Gertrude Fishburne nudged her way toward the front of the room. "How very intriguing. I am quite familiar with British history, having married into a noble family myself, and this is certainly not my understanding. I'm also a bit confused about how you came upon the title Marchioness of Middlesex."

Lady Graverly's lips trembled. She smiled at the others in the room; all were watching the exchange with open mouths. "You really must brush up on your history, my dear," she said, her tone cordial but defiant. "Middlesex was incorporated into Greater London in the 1950s, but the Graverly peerage is very much extant. When my husband's father, the seventh Marquess of Middlesex, passed away in the 1980s, his elder son, Lord Wakefield Graverly, became the eighth Marquess of Middlesex. Upon Lord Wakefield's death several months ago, my husband inherited the title, which makes me the Marchioness of Middlesex."

"Did you know Lord Wakefield Graverly?"

"Sadly, no. My husband was estranged from his family, as I do believe I mentioned. From all accounts, Lord Wakefield was a miserable man stuck in a dreadful marriage. He was a close confidant of the Queen for several decades before he left Her Majesty's service to convert the family castle into an inn."

"And what became of his wife?" Mrs. Fishburne persisted. "It is my understanding that *she* holds the title Marchioness of Middlesex."

"Oh dear, no, no, no. That woman resides at Graverly Castle, it is true, and continues to fashion herself as nobility, but she has no right to the title or the estate."

"And why is that?"

"Because they rightfully belong to my husband. And in turn, to my son," she added, shooting a troubled glance in my direction.

All heads turned to me, the audience making the assumption that I was her son. Alarmed, I held up both hands to indicate I was not.

Lady Graverly continued, "That dreadful woman took advantage of my son's compromised health to cheat him out of his inheritance. But she will get her just desserts."

"I hardly think your bastard son is entitled to any inheritance," said Mrs. Fishburne.

There was a chorus of gasps. Eyes darted from Gertrude Fishburne to Lady Graverly and back again. At the entrance to the dining room, Shanna almost dropped her tray.

"How dare you!" cried Lady Graverly, lifting her veil. "Who do you think you are?"

"Me? Why, I am Lady Wakefield Graverly, the Marchioness of Middlesex."

★ ★ ★ ★ ★

It was almost midnight.

I was seated at the reception desk, flipping through the blank pages of the reservations book and waiting for the tour group to return. Shanna had insisted on staying behind to help clean up, and I could hear her humming in the kitchen as she put the last of the dishes away.

My thoughts were on my mother. I had fought for her attention as a teenager during her walking coma, and resentment had been branded into me like a permanent scar. My father had been distant, sometimes oblivious to my presence, other times baffled by it, displaying rare bursts of playfulness that rang forced and insincere. For my mother to fall into a similar role after my father's death was tantamount to abandonment. My sisters had turned to me for comfort, but I withdrew, emotionally at first, and then physically, moving out of the house and then out of the country. By the time Mom experienced her awakening, an impenetrable barrier had fallen between us, a wall of beveled glass that distorted our perceptions and kept us from getting close. Now I felt this barrier was lifting, but I was afraid it was too late.

The sound of footsteps on the verandah interrupted my thoughts. I sprang from my chair and pulled on my suit jacket, shaking off my thoughts as I stood at attention by the door.

Outside, I heard a burst of laughter.

"Shhh!" someone said. "The Munsters might be up."

The door opened, and Sir Fester skittered in. Was this how outsiders perceived the manor—a haunted house occupied by monsters?

"Good evening, everyone," I said to the group, beaming and trying not to look creepy.

Miss Edwards was the first to enter. "Howdy, Trevor!" she said, slapping me on the arm and heading for the stairs.

A gust of wind sent a flurry of leaves fluttering in with the other guests. Sir Fester chased after the leaves, growling, while the guests greeted me and followed Miss Edwards up the stairs. The last to enter was Mrs. Fishburne. I had hoped to pull her aside, but she gave me a frosty glare and followed the others.

"How was dinner?" I asked after her.

"Long."

"Mrs. Fishburne, I was wondering if I might—"

"Good night, Mr. Lambert."

I stood at the foot of the stairs and listened to the sounds of doors opening and closing, muted conversations, shrieks and giggles. I felt gratitude for the guests and hope for the future of the manor. Spotting a folded sheet of paper on the steps, I picked it up and gave it a cursory look, then looked closer. It was a flyer for Heritage Tours, advertising a tour called "Haunted Houses of Vancouver and Victoria." "Days 3 & 4," read the itinerary, "Stay at Graverly Manor, the city's most infamous haunted house, where you'll meet the eccentric noblewoman whose late husband is believed to haunt the manor, searching for the chambermaid he murdered five decades ago."

I stared at the flyer, aghast. Lady Graverly would be humiliated if she knew the manor was being sensationalized in this way, her tragic past turned into an amusement park show. I thought of how she had sprung to life upon the arrival of the tour group, basking in the center of attention as the Grande Dame of Graverly Manor with her extravagant outfit and affected manners, spinning outrageous tales about her royal bloodlines. Meanwhile, her audience considered her merely an attraction, a stop on the horror tour, and hoped to get a glimpse of the ghost of her husband.

"What's that?" Shanna asked as I entered the kitchen.

"Nothing," I said, stuffing the flyer into the garbage.

"In the mood for some tea?"

"Sure am."

As she filled the kettle, I went into the parlor and sat down, still disturbed by the flyer. In the fireplace, the big log was burning bright. Shanna carried in a tray and poured steaming tea into two cups. We settled into our chairs, the pleasant aroma of Earl Grey leaves wafting from our cups. Back to her glamorous self, Shanna had removed the apron and untied her hair. In the light of the fire, her expression looked serene, projecting an aura of contentment I had never seen before.

"You never told me you were in line to the British throne," she said.

"It must have slipped my mind."

"Too bad you're a bastard. You could be king someday. I always thought you had the air of an aristocrat."

"You should have seen me in my ascot the other day."

She sipped her tea, her pinky pointing out. "We couldn't have staged a more dramatic performance tonight, could we? When Elinor slammed her door, I feared the house would collapse on us."

"Pure theatre," I said, thinking of the flyer. Perhaps the guests thought the performance had been staged for them, that Mrs. Fishburne was an actress planted in the audience. If only it were that simple. "I wonder what she's doing here," I said.

"Gertrude Fishburne? Sizing up the competition, I would think."

"But Elinor said the courts had already ruled in favor of the marchioness. Why would she consider Elinor a threat?"

"Maybe she considers the son a threat."

"Somehow I find that unlikely," I said, thinking of Alexander slumped in his wheelchair. Staring into the leaves in my teacup, I wondered if this could be why Lady Graverly was being so protective of her son. Was he in danger?

"Whatever became of that student you told me about?" Shanna asked. "The one who liked cemeteries. She sounded like a good catch."

"She went back to Kentucky," I said. "You know, I actually quite liked her."

"Why not look her up, then?"

"What's the point? She's not my type." The fire flared suddenly, sending flames licking at my feet. I jerked them away.

"Listen to that wind," Shanna said. "A storm is expected tomorrow night." She observed me for a moment. "You know, darling, a girl like that might be exactly what you need. Someone to pull you out of your comfort zone."

"And into graveyards?"

"Precisely."

Not wanting to think about Clarissa, I told Shanna about my plans for the manor. "Flat-screen TVs in every room, a DVD player and stereo, mini-bar, nightly turndown service, daily newspaper, wireless Internet access, and—"

"Trevor," she interrupted, "why convert this house into a hotel? Guests don't expect those amenities. They come to a B&B because it is like a home. Your heart is still in hotels, admit it. Why don't you abandon this crazy scheme?"

"No," I said resolutely. "This is what I want."

She gave me a skeptical look. I glared back at her.

The chimney's damper slammed shut, making us jump. Smoke began pouring into the room. I grabbed the stoking iron and rammed it up the chimney until the damper reopened. Wind whistled angrily inside the flue. Covering her eyes and coughing, Shanna fled the room. I tried to open the front window, but it was sealed shut. I opened the front door, using it as a fan to clear the smoke.

Shanna reappeared, her purse slung over her shoulder. "I'd better be getting back to my hotel," she said.

"You're welcome to stay. Agnes's room is empty. We could tell ghost stories through the wall."

"I think I've heard enough ghost stories for one night. Besides, I told you how I feel about B&Bs. I'm happy to go back to my modern suite at the Opus."

I walked her out to her rental car. "It's good to have you here."

"It's been a pleasure," she said, standing on her toes to peck my cheek. "I'm driving out to see your mother in the morning. Do you want me to come by beforehand and help with breakfast?"

"I'll be fine."

"I'll come over in the afternoon, then."

After she drove away, I turned to face the manor. Once again, it had taken on a different countenance, like a face with many expressions. The lights were out, curtains drawn, front door ajar like an open mouth—it looked frightened. Shanna's words came back to me: *Why don't you abandon this crazy scheme?* Was I projecting my own fear onto the house?

As I climbed the stairs to my room, it occurred to me the manor guests were on high alert for ghosts. I hummed a tune to reassure them it was only me.

22

Persona Non Grata

The group was up early Thursday morning to eat breakfast before embarking on a historic tour of Vancouver. The term "historic" was amusing to me, given that the city was little more than a hundred years old; it was incorporated in 1886 and destroyed by fire two months later. Nevertheless, the participants were excited, and conversation at the breakfast table was lively. As I refilled their coffee cups and cleared their plates, I thought this must be what innkeepers live for: a house full of appreciative guests and strangers who become friends.

The exception was Mrs. Fishburne, who sat quietly in the corner sipping tea, ignoring everyone while she perused a city guidebook. Even when the bus arrived and the others gathered up cameras, purses, and maps and hurried out, she resumed reading.

I lingered in the dining room, hoping for a chance to talk. "Finished with that?" I asked, reaching for her teacup. She had consumed six cups of scalding black tea, refusing all offers of food.

"Hm?" she said, looking up. "Oh, yes. Thank you ever so much."

"You're not joining the tour?"

"The tour?" She looked around, only then noticing the room was empty. "Yes, of course," she said, rising to stuff the guidebook into her purse. She was dressed in a simple and elegant aubergine-colored dress, a thin white belt tied around her tiny waist.

"Mrs. Fishburne," I ventured. "Or should I address you as Lady Graverly? Perhaps simply as Marchioness?"

"Fishburne is my maiden name, but you may call me Gertrude," she said curtly, heading for the door.

"I remember you from the open house."

She stopped and turned, her expression perplexed and vaguely irritated, as though she couldn't imagine why the hired help was addressing her directly. "Open house?"

"Here, at the manor. I was here too."

"Why, yes, of course. You're the Lambert boy, aren't you?"

"Yes. Are you really Lord Wakefield's widow?"

She sighed and dug into her purse, withdrawing a British passport.

I took it from her and turned to the identification page, reading her name: "Lady Wakefield Graverly, the Marchioness of Middlesex." With a nod, I handed the passport back. "I have a copy of your husband's book. He sounds like he was an impressive man."

"My husband was hopeless. He was brilliant at making strangers feel at home, yet he was a complete failure in his own home. After twenty-five years of marriage, I still felt like an intruder in his house. He left his fortune to his dog, Regent, not to spite family and friends, as people have speculated, but because he had no close friends or family. All he did was work."

"An occupational hazard," I muttered, stacking dirty dishes. Her diatribe had been unexpected; she had been so tightlipped until now. "May I ask why you came to Graverly Manor?"

"Why, to meet the Grande Dame, of course. I had hoped to meet her son as well, but she tells me he's locked away in an institution. I was also curious about you, I must admit."

"About me? Why?"

She arched her eyebrows. "I am told you're an ambitious young man."

Outside, the tour van honked.

"Not really," I said. "But if you're still interested in the manor, you should know it's no longer on the market."

A flicker of amusement passed over her eyes. "Then I suppose congratulations are in order." She reached into her purse and pulled on a pair of long silk gloves. "Though you might wish to confirm whether Elinor has the right to sell this house."

"What do you mean?"

"When Lord Andrew was disowned, his father gave him a sum of money, which he used to purchase this house."

"Lord Graverly wasn't disowned. He disowned his family."

"I suppose Elinor told you this?"

I nodded slowly.

"Lord Andrew brought great shame to his family for his ways," she said. "He was sent away. I never knew the man. I met my husband after Lord Andrew left for Canada. About ten years after Lord Andrew vanished, my husband came to Vancouver on official business for the Queen. He visited this house and attempted to make peace with Elinor Graverly, but she slammed the door in his face. He was so distraught by the experience he never uttered his brother's name again—not until he was on his deathbed, when he told me the most peculiar thing."

"What did he tell you?" I asked.

Outside, the tour bus honked again.

"Well, I must be going," Mrs. Fishburne said, hooking her purse over her shoulder. "It's been lovely chatting with you, Mr. Lambert."

"Wait," I said, following her to the door. "Do you mean to tell me the manor is still in Lord Graverly's name? Wouldn't it be passed down to Lady Graverly as his widow?"

She stopped at the door and turned to me with a thin smile. "His widow?"

"She isn't his widow?"

"Has she not told you? Lord Andrew is alive."

★ ★ ★ ★ ★

I marched over to Lady Graverly's quarters and pounded on the door, then tried the handle. Locked. Deciding she had gone out, I returned to the kitchen to finish cleaning up, resolving to confront her upon her return.

Lord Andrew is alive. The news was staggering if it was true. If he was alive and, as Mrs. Fishburne had implied, the manor was still in his name, then my stay here—the abuse I had endured, my hard work—had been futile. *Has she not told you?* To make matters worse, Lady Graverly knew he was alive. She had lied to me and manipulated me, had used and verbally abused me, and had been stringing me along under false pretences. I felt foolish and betrayed.

If Lord Graverly had chosen to surface now, after all these years, the reason was obvious: his brother was dead, and he was coming forward to claim the family fortune. But if Lady Graverly's account of Sarah's death was true, why had he been in hiding in the first place? I reminded myself I could not trust anything she had said. It enraged me that I had been so quick to believe her. Upon reflection, Agnes's theory made far more sense: Lord Graverly had murdered Sarah, and Lady Graverly had been covering up for him for her own personal gain—or, if she were as charitable as she made herself out to be, to use the fortune to ensure Alexander's needs were taken care of. I recalled

Lady Graverly's remark that Agnes and Lord Wakefield's widow had become "chummy" and cursed myself for not asking Mrs. Fishburne about Agnes. They would have been in London together only days ago.

My thoughts were interrupted by the distant tinkling of a bell. Thinking I must be hearing things, I resumed my work. A moment later, I heard it again. This time it was unmistakable; Lady Graverly was summoning me from her quarters. I was desperate to speak with her but refused to allow her to treat me like a servant from a different century. I began to set the table for dinner, slamming down plates, cutlery, and glassware as I brooded over Lady Graverly's duplicity. A wine glass shattered in my hand, sending a gush of blood onto the white tablecloth. Cursing, I grabbed a serviette and tied it around my hand. While I was searching for the first-aid kit, my cell phone rang.

"Can you not hear my bell?" boomed Lady Graverly's voice.

"I'm sorry, were you ringing for me?"

"Who do you think I was ringing for, Sir Fester?"

"What do you want, Elinor? I'm kind of busy."

Her tone softened. "I was hoping you might serve me some breakfast. I'm feeling quite unwell."

"Sorry, you'll have to serve yourself today."

She sighed. "Very well. But I'm worried about Alexander. The poor boy seems quite out of sorts."

I gritted my teeth. "Fine," I said. "I'll check on him."

"You are ever so kind."

I disconnected. It would be an opportunity to ask her a few pointed questions.

When I arrived in her bedroom, I found it in chaos, the floor and surfaces littered with clothes, used tissues, old newspapers, and dirty dishes. Lady Graverly was propped up in bed, surrounded by pillows and cushions, too weak to feed her son or to tidy up but not to do her makeup and hair.

"There you are!" she squawked. "I thought you mustn't be coming."

Alexander sat slouched by the window.

Balancing the tray on one hand, I wheeled him to Elinor's side and set the tray down on the nightstand.

"I do hope the tea is better today," Elinor said. "Yesterday's pot was ghastly."

"I did my best, your worship. Would you like me to pour it?"

"It'll do no good sitting in the pot."

That she was in such a crabby mood, undoubtedly courtesy of Mrs. Fishburne, cheered me. As I poured the tea, I hummed happily, ignoring her penetrating glare.

"Where is that insufferable tour group?" she asked.

"They're out on a heritage tour of the city."

"With that Chinese tour leader?" she spat. "How could the Chinese know anything about this city's heritage?"

"The Chinese have a long history in Vancouver, Elinor."

"It was the British who colonized this province. It's British Columbia, not Chinese Columbia."

I opted not to dignify the remark with a reply. As I poured milk into her cup, my nostrils quivered, detecting an unpleasant odor. I sniffed the milk. My eyes moved to Alexander. Setting the teapot down, I followed the smell to the closed closet door. I turned in a circle.

"What are you doing, strange boy?" asked Lady Graverly.

"Can't you smell that?"

"What?"

"That stench. It smells like … something died."

"I don't smell a thing. Lord Alexander, do you? Nor does he."

Alexander hadn't so much as blinked. I took a deep breath, and the odor hit me like a baseball bat, almost knocking me to the floor.

"Where's Sir Fester?"

"Why, he's right here."

Only then did I notice the demon-cat perched like a sultan on a silk pillow at the corner of the bed. I braved another breath. The odor was gone, replaced by the usual smell of moldy wood, mothballs, and stale perfume. I went to the window and began drawing the curtains.

"What do you think you're doing?" barked Lady Graverly.

"Opening the window."

"Stop it at once! Alexander will catch a cold and die. And close those curtains. His eyes are extremely sensitive."

I looked at Alexander, whose translucent skin could have used a dose of sunshine, but relented nonetheless and resumed serving breakfast. Cognizant of the seven guestrooms that needed cleaning, I moved quickly, handing Lady Graverly a plate containing two wedges of white toast. She put it aside and pushed back the covers to attend to Alexander.

On the other side of the bed, leaning against the wall, I spotted the rifle she had pointed at me the other day. "I hope that gun isn't loaded," I said.

She didn't reply. She was peering down at my hand. Blood had seeped through my makeshift bandage. "What happened there?" she inquired.

"I broke a wineglass."

"A pity," she said, leaving doubt as to whether her concern was for me or the wineglass.

"I'll live."

"That brown woman," she said, pursing her lips, "is she the new chambermaid?"

"Shanna? Hardly. She's a former colleague—a friend. She'll be helping around the house for a few days."

"Hm," she said in a disapproving tone.

"My mother is quite ill. I'm going to have to spend some time with her."

"She's dying, isn't she?"

My hand jerked, slopping tea onto the tray. "How did you know?"

"I know grief well enough to recognize it, dear boy. You and your mother never saw eye-to-eye, did you? She made you feel like a constant disappointment, refused to acknowledge your true calling."

"My mother has always been supportive," I said defensively. I got up and began tidying the room, gathering up a handful of garments and heading toward the closet.

"Stop!" she cried.

"Why?"

"A lady's wardrobe is no place for a man. You may leave those items on the chair."

"Fine," I said, setting them down.

She nibbled on her toast and made a face, setting it down and dabbing her lips with a serviette. "As the only son, you will inherit the family estate?"

"It's hardly an estate. I'd rather not talk about it, okay?"

"She made her choices in life and obstinately stuck with them. She was a fine woman."

"She still is. How would you know, anyway?"

"I've met your mother. Once, almost forty years ago, and again last week."

"Last week? Why didn't you tell me she was here?"

"She came to see me, not you. She had business to attend to."

I clenched my teeth. "My mother is a silent partner, Elinor. Any 'business' is to be handled by me." Lifting Alexander's arms, I unfolded the tray attached to the wheelchair and tied on his bib. "You must have been shocked when Mrs. Fishburne revealed her identity last night."

"Whoever that vulgar woman purports to be, she is persona non grata in this household," she said calmly. Dipping a spoon into the tea-cup, she waved it in the air to cool the tea, then held it before Alexander's lips. His eyes observed her, faintly hostile. His mouth remained firmly closed. "Alec, please! Open your mouth."

"I had a chat with her this morning. She was actually quite pleasant."

"She is not pleasant!" Lady Graverly roared.

Alexander's mouth fell open in a silent cry. Elinor slipped in the spoon.

A scratching sound drew my attention to the closet door. Sir Fester had left his pillow and was pawing at the door. Letting out a yowl, he turned in a circle and scratched again.

"She told me Lord Andrew was disinherited," I said.

Lady Graverly's back arched, yet her voice was controlled. "An heir to a title cannot be disinherited. It is against peerage rules. The marquess was at liberty to leave his fortune to whomever he wished, but the succession to Graverly Castle is clearly laid out in the Letters Patent. Nothing and no one can change that."

"She said Lord Andrew brought great shame to his family," I persisted.

The spoon clattered to the floor. Lady Graverly's head spun in my direction. "The marquess was a brute! Lord Andrew was a fine man, a war hero. He was mistreated, ostracized for simply being himself. For decades I've waited to right those wrongs, and that evil woman cheated me out of vindication, or so she thinks. She will get her dues. I am not finished. Am I, Lord Alexander?"

Alexander let out a soft moan.

I reached down to pick up the spoon and placed it on the tray. "Why is Mrs. Fishburne here? Does she think she has a claim to this house?"

"That woman has no claim to anything!"

"Who exactly holds the title to the manor?"

"I do, naturally."

I took a deep breath and said, "She said Lord Andrew is alive." I braced myself for her reaction.

Yet her voice remained perfectly calm. "So I've heard," she said dryly, not at all sounding like a woman who had been pining for her husband's return for fifty years.

"Have you seen him?"

"No."

"May I ask—?"

"No, you may not."

"But—"

"That will be all," she said.

Clearly I wasn't going to get any more information from her while she was in such a foul mood. I stood up and took my leave.

"Mr. Lambert," Lady Graverly called after me. "Have you given any thought to my invitation?"

"Invitation?"

"To move to Graverly Castle with me."

I hesitated, disturbed by her continued delusions. I sensed a great deal of emotion behind her casual tone. "I don't know, Elinor. I don't think it's a good idea. I'm—I'm not comfortable with … It's just weird. I'm sorry. This manor is enough, it's all I want. I need to stay in Vancouver. My family …" I stopped, hoping she would quickly agree, but she sat perfectly rigid, listening intently. Over her shoulder I could see Alexander staring at me, opening and closing his mouth as though trying to say something. His hands flitted in the air.

"Stop it, Alec," Lady Graverly commanded. "For god's sake, behave."

He began thrashing about in the wheelchair.

I hurried over to help. "I hope I didn't upset him."

"He hasn't been himself lately. He keeps babbling about something he saw the other day."

"He speaks to you?"

"In his own way, yes. I've been amazed by his ability to communicate these days, especially when he becomes emotional."

"What did he see?" I asked, wrestling with his flailing arms.

"Alec, please! Get hold of yourself!" Lady Graverly cried. "He saw Agnes here in my bedroom with a man."

Alexander's hands slipped out of my grasp. His arm struck the teapot, sending it flying to the floor, spraying hot tea over us. Lady Elinor shrieked. I grabbed a napkin and tried to sponge her off, but she pushed me away. I used it to spot Alexander, but he too shoved me away. I stumbled back.

"I had no idea he was that strong."

"He needs a shot. Hold him, please." She hurried over to the bureau and retrieved the black bag, withdrawing a needle and a bottle of medication. Filling the needle, she flicked it and hurried back to Alexander, sliding the needle into his arm. In an instant, his body went limp.

"We shouldn't talk like that in front of him," I said, kneeling down to gather up fragments of china and placing them on the tray. "I think he understands more than we think."

When I finished cleaning up, I excused myself and went to the door, turning to observe them. Lady Graverly was holding Alexander's hand against her cheek and staring lovingly into his drooping eyes.

"Elinor," I said in a hushed voice, "after we close the sale, you and Alexander are welcome to stay. I can't afford to do anything with this part of the house for a while anyway. I can help you take care of him."

She lifted her head. Her eyes were moist. "My prince, you are so kind. But it shan't be necessary."

As I went down the hallway, I stopped to observe the photograph of the Graverly brothers again. Both men carried an air of privilege in the photo, even of entitlement. In the backdrop I recognized Graverly Castle from the pages of *The Consummate Host*. Peering closer, I saw that Lord Wakefield was far more handsome than his brother, with the sculptured features of a 1950s movie star. My gaze moved to Lord Andrew, and I searched for signs of evil in his eyes. He looked harmless enough, almost effeminate, with one foot thrust forward, hands resting on his hips. I continued down the hall, glancing into the drab parlor, and caught sight of the old guestbooks on the shelf. Remarking again how similar they looked to Sarah's diary, I realized she must have taken her book from the same collection. On impulse, I plucked one from the shelf but replaced it when I found the pages empty. Selecting another, I found the withered pages full of commentaries from former guests. *July 19, 1965. What a party! Lady Graverly, you're a wild cat, the hostess with the mostest!* Grinning, I tucked the book under my arm and slipped out of the quarters.

As I climbed the stairs to my room, another explanation for Lady Graverly's protectiveness over Alexander occurred to me. Maybe she wasn't hiding him from Agnes Kilpatrick or Gertrude Fishburne. Maybe Lord Graverly had resurfaced to claim his title and estate—and his son.

★ ★ ★ ★ ★

"Clarissa's not here," said her college roommate. "Who's calling?"

"Trevor Lambert. I'm a friend. Do you know where I can find her?"

"She's in Vancouver."

"She came back to Vancouver?"

"Back? She never left."

I felt a tremor of concern. "Do you know where I can find her?"

"The Grave Inn or something. What's this all about, anyway?"

"Uh ... I'm helping her with her research. I have some information for her."

"Don't tell me you chase ghosts too?"

"Ghosts?" I said. "I'm talking about her Pauline Johnson paper."

"Who? Clarissa's writing a paper on haunted houses."

It all came rushing back to me: the lagoon, the cellar, the 'lost poems'—Clarissa had been lying to me all along.

"If you track her down, tell her she better call her dad," said the girl. "She hasn't answered her cell phone in days, and he's kind of freaking out."

I thanked her and hung up.

So Clarissa had never left town. Then why had she left the manor in such a hurry?

I called Derrick next. "Sorry it took so long to get back to you."

"No worries, man. How's your mom?"

"Not bad, under the circumstances. Did you leave your wife?"

"Nope. She threw me out."

"Jeez, I'm sorry. How are you holding up?"

"I miss my girls. You know, I even miss my mother-in-law. Hey, what are you up to? Want to go for a drink?"

Downstairs, the doorbell was ringing.

"I can't today, Derrick. Sorry. But hey, my group checks out tomorrow. How about tomorrow night? I'm going to take my mom to dinner, but we could meet afterward."

"Sounds great."

"I'll call you after dinner."

I went downstairs to answer the door.

Lynne Crocker was standing on the verandah in a zebra-patterned top and black leather skirt. "Look what I've got!" she sang, waving a handful of documents in the air. "The signed contract and the inspector's report!" She barged past me, heading into the parlor.

"I'll get Lady Graverly," I said.

"God, please don't," she said, plunking herself onto the sofa and looking around. "This place is depressing." She reached behind her and yanked open the curtain. "There, at least we can see now. You have no idea how glad I am that this deal is finally going through."

"Why?" I asked, pulling the parlor door closed.

"Crazy Graverly is a nightmare—I don't have to tell you that," Lynne said, smacking her gum. "But it was the dispute over the title deed that almost drove me insane." Seeing my face fall, she lifted her hand. "Don't worry, hon, it's all settled."

"Settled? How?"

"Trust me, you don't want to know." She handed me the document and dug into her purse, withdrawing a pen. "I've highlighted the places you need to sign."

"I'll need some time to look it over."

"There's not a lot of time, Trevor. She's going away tomorrow and wants everything tied up before she leaves."

"All the same, I'll get it back to you tomorrow."

"Suit yourself." She stood up. "But I wouldn't delay long. I mean, the price, it's crazy! You don't want to risk her coming to her senses. I'm just glad the old hag agreed to pay my commission on the market value."

I walked Lynne to the door.

After she left, I sat down in the parlor to review the contract, but I couldn't concentrate. My thoughts kept returning to Clarissa. If she was still in town, why hadn't she called? Had she locked me up and taken my cell phone? If so, why? And what had prompted her abrupt departure? She was the third occupant of the house to leave in the same manner—and she was not a paid employee, but a paying guest. Didn't Lady Graverly need the money? I realized I hadn't heard back from Agnes's son. Was the manor swallowing people whole? Were bodies piling up somewhere? I thought about Elinor's remark that Alexander had seen a man with Agnes in Elinor's bedroom. If Lord Graverly was alive, had he sneaked into the manor and confronted Agnes? Was he eliminating threats one by one? If so, who was next? Lady Graverly? Me?

I was being paranoid again. Lord Graverly wasn't alive, and his ghost wasn't haunting the manor. The lunacy of this household had seeped into my brain. Lynne was right, I needed to close the sale before it was too late. I looked down at the contract. It was signed in several places, but not with Lady Graverly's florid handwriting. The signature was a masculine scribble. I walked to the window and held the contract up to the light. The name was unmistakable.

Lord Andrew Graverly, the Marquess of Middlesex.

23

Lord Graverly Checks In

Hearing the back door of the private quarters slam, I went to the kitchen and spotted Lady Graverly through the window, walking briskly down the path in a mink coat and matching hat. She was carrying a light garment bag and pulling a small suitcase. Where was she going? I opened the door and called out to her, but she rounded the corner of the garage without looking back. Unwilling to allow her to get away before she had explained how Lord Graverly's name got on the contract, I pulled on my shoes and coat and hastened after her.

As I reached the back alley, I was almost run down by the black Cadillac as it backed out of the garage. "Elinor!" I called out, waving my arms. The car lurched forward and charged up the alley, its tires spraying me with mud.

I ran to where my car was parked on Haro Street and sped after her.

I caught up with the Cadillac at the intersection of Denman and Haro streets, where it had stopped for a red light. Lady Graverly's diminutive frame barely cleared the dashboard of the big car; she looked like a little girl who had commandeered her mother's clothing and vehicle. Fearing she would spot me in the rearview mirror, I slid down in the seat. The light turned green, and she turned left.

I followed her down Denman Street to Robson and left on Hornby Street. I was surprised to see Christmas lights and decorations along the way; in the manor, I had forgotten it was a festive time of year. She drove slowly, and I had to brake frequently to keep a safe distance. As she reached Pender Street she accelerated, swerving right onto Howe Street and cutting off a cluster of pedestrians as they started to cross the intersection. I slammed on my brakes to avoid them, tapping at my steering wheel impatiently as they detoured my car. A young woman pushing a baby carriage cast a hostile look in my direction. The moment the way was clear, I gunned it.

The Cadillac had disappeared up the street. Lady Graverly had gone almost full circle—was she trying to lose me? When I reached Dunsmuir Street, I spotted the Cadillac up ahead turning left into a driveway.

The Four Seasons Hotel.

As I steered up the ramp, I saw Lady Graverly climbing out of her car. She handed her keys to the doorman, along with what appeared to be a small coin for a tip, and disappeared through the front door while the doorman retrieved her bags.

I idled out front, debating whether to follow. *When it all becomes too much I take a suite at the Four Seasons, if only for a few hours. There I can be myself.* Considering all the recent turmoil in the manor, I couldn't blame her for needing a break. To follow her would be to invade the privacy she held so dear. Yet by lying to me and misleading me, she had lost the right to privacy. I couldn't afford to wait for an explanation, not when she intended to leave town tomorrow. Besides, I was certain she was up to something, and I was curious to know what.

A car honked behind me. I pulled over and climbed out, handing my keys to the doorman, along with a five-dollar tip to compensate for hers.

When I entered the lower lobby of the hotel, Lady Graverly was nowhere to be seen. I rode the escalator to the upper lobby and there she was at the front desk, speaking to a tall male employee. In the luxurious surroundings of the hotel, she looked very much at home. I circled the escalator and loitered near the Park Ballroom, where I could observe her in private. The lobby was busy with meeting attendees in business attire, elegantly dressed foreign guests, and a group of holiday revelers enjoying a late Christmas lunch. I realized how much I missed this environment—what an exhilarating contrast to the hushed environment of the manor.

"May I help you, sir?"

An employee in a banquet uniform smiled at me, hands clasped at his chest as though in prayer.

"No, thank you," I said. "I'm waiting for someone."

His eyes flashed with recognition. "Don't I know you?"

There is no such thing as anonymity in the hotel business. I glanced at him and recalled his perspiring upper lip from the Park Harbour years ago, when he was a banquet houseperson and I was director of rooms.

"I don't believe so," I replied politely, turning away. This was not the time for catching up with an old colleague. As he walked off, I searched the lobby for Lady Graverly, catching sight of her as she disappeared inside an elevator. Damn.

I hurried over to the front desk. The tall gentleman had been replaced by a pretty young girl with a mane of thick, dark hair tied in a ponytail.

"Excuse me, Megan, hi," I said, reading her nametag and smiling ingratiatingly. "My aunt just checked in, and I need her room number, please."

"Certainly, sir. May I have her name?"

"Yes, it's Elinor Graverly." While she tapped at the keyboard, I admired her dewy complexion and thought of Nancy Swinton as a duty manager at the Universe, so sweet and good-natured on the outside yet possessing such inner strength and determination. Clarissa couldn't look more different with her blackened eyes and mussed hair. Why had she lied to me and deserted me? I thought we had made a connection.

"I have a Mr. Andrew Graverly registered," said Megan, lifting her eyes. "Lord Andrew Graverly, I should say. Could that be it?"

I was thunderstruck. Lord Graverly was here, in the flesh? Had Lady Graverly's blind faith paid off at last? Then it occurred to me that it might not be a joyous reunion. Lord Andrew could be dangerous, a murderer, and might to do anything to protect his inheritance. Could Lady Graverly be in danger?

"Sir?"

"Yes, that's it. The room number, please?"

"Unfortunately, I can't disclose the room number, but I can dial the room for you, if you wish. Or you can use the house phone."

"Gee, I was hoping to surprise her. Can't you just give me her room number?"

Megan furrowed her brow, reluctant to break the rules. "May I ask your name?"

"Yes, of course. It's Alexander Graverly. Lord Alexander Graverly."

"Oh, you have the same last name. I'm sure we can make an exception, then. I'll just need some identification."

I padded my coat. "Darn, I left my wallet in the car."

She gave a slight grimace. "Not to worry. Let me check with the manager to see if there's anything we can do."

Damn her for being well trained. "No! I'm in a real hurry," I said, raising my voice. "Can't you just give me a key? I'm her nephew, for goodness sake! I don't understand why you're making this so difficult." I was being the aggressive, unreasonable hotel guest employees loathed, pushing her to break the rules by threatening to create a scene. I was going to hell.

Megan surveyed me, looking unsure about what to do. Something drew her attention to my lapel. Looking down, I saw a spray of mud, courtesy of the Cadillac's tires. My hand moved to my face, and I felt a layer of grime.

A door opened behind her and out walked a tall, blond-haired gentleman—Frank Parsons, the hotel's general manager. I quickly turned away.

Too late. "Trevor Lambert!" his voice boomed, coming around the desk and breaking into a toothy grin. "What brings you here?"

Feeling the heat of Megan's stare, I placed my hand on Frank's shoulder and steered him into the lobby. "I'm visiting a friend," I told him. As a fellow hotelier, I knew he would trust me and probably give me the room number, even the key, if I had a good reason. But what excuse could I give him? My mind raced.

"I was just thinking about you, in fact," Frank said, glancing around and then lowering his voice. "It hasn't been announced yet, but I'm being transferred to our property in Taipei. I'd like to put your name forward for my position."

"Really?" I said excitedly. "That would be incredible."

"I think you'd be perfect for the job."

My spirits sank as I remembered the manor. "Unfortunately, I'm already committed."

"Don't tell me you took that job at the Harbourside?"

I shook my head. "I'm buying a bed-and-breakfast."

"Really? Where?"

"Have you heard of Graverly Manor?"

"That haunted place?"

My jaw hardened. "It's not haunted, Frank," I said, forcing a laugh. "It's got a bit of a troubled past, but nothing a little TLC won't fix. The potential is enormous."

He smoothed his jaw, looking apprehensive. "I don't know, Trevor. B&Bs are twice the work with none of the perks. Do you want to be schlepping bags and making toast the rest of your life? A former colleague opened a guesthouse in Cape Cod a few years back and died of a heart attack a year later." He leaned closer. "The crazy old bird who owns that manor takes a room here from time to time. She arrives dressed to the nines, like she's going to a ball or something, and is charming and gracious with staff, then turns into a completely different person. She—my god, she's right there." He nodded discreetly toward the elevator.

I lowered my head. "I can't let her see me."

He chuckled. "You playing hooky or something?"

"No, I … um … I'm here to surprise her. It's her birthday. What's she doing?"

"She's looking for someone. Oh, looks like she found him. They're heading into the restaurant."

It took all my self-control not to look. "An old guy?"

"No, probably in his early thirties. He's in a suit, carrying a briefcase. Looks like a lawyer to me. The hostess is taking them to a table. Looks like an older guy is joining them now. Okay, coast is clear."

I slowly turned around. She was out of eyesight. "Can I ask you a favor, Frank? I have something I'd like to put in her room, a little birthday surprise. Could I get a key?"

He frowned, glancing down at my soiled jacket. "Well, it's not really allowed …" He broke into a grin. "But it's not like I can't trust a fellow hotelier, right?"

I grinned back. "You bet."

"Wait here, I'll be right back."

I cringed as I watched him head directly to Megan at the front desk. How would I explain that I had lied about my name? I considered hurrying off to avoid an uncomfortable confrontation.

But he was already back. "You should have told me she was your aunt," he said, looking sheepish. "I'm sure you'll make the house a huge success." He slipped the key into my hand and whispered the suite number. "Don't tell anyone I gave it to you, promise?"

"I promise."

I headed over to the restrooms to clean up, and then hastened to the elevators.

On the twenty-sixth floor, I knocked on the door of the suite and waited. If Lord Graverly answered, I would introduce myself as the hotel manager and inform him there was a leak on the floor above. As soon as he let me in, I would tell him who I was and threaten to call the police unless he told me the true story behind his disappearance. But there was no answer. Deciding he was downstairs in the restaurant with Lady Graverly and the lawyer, probably reviewing their strategy for claiming the estate, I counted to ten, checked over both shoulders, and slipped inside.

The suite was spacious and beautifully furnished, reminiscent of Graverly Manor in its traditional décor, although in far better condition. To the immediate right was a bathroom, and directly ahead a living room, with French doors leading to a bedroom and en suite bathroom. Lady Graverly's suitcase was sitting on a luggage rack next to the bed. I had no idea what I hoped to find, but I decided the suitcase was a good place to start.

As I crossed the living room, the sound of a key in the door made me freeze. In a panic, I opened the door of a large armoire to my right. It was divided into two compartments, one occupied by shelving containing a mini-bar and safe and the other by an empty clothing rack. I squeezed under the clothing rack and pulled the door closed behind me just as the front door opened.

My heart pounded. I heard footsteps on the carpet. Was it Lord Graverly or Lady Graverly—or a maid? Remembering the mini-bar in the next compartment, I prayed whoever it was wasn't thirsty. Someone picked up a telephone on the desk next the armoire. I heard dialing.

"Nigel, it's Lord Andrew Graverly calling."

Lord Graverly—only inches away! I held my breath. His voice sounded gruff like a smoker's, and he had a regal British accent almost identical to Lady Graverly's. It was all I could do to not open the door and gawk at him.

"I just met with your associate," said Lord Graverly. "The papers are signed. Everything appears to be in good order ... Right, I'll see you at the inquiry on Saturday, then. Very good. Cheerio."

I heard him set the receiver in its cradle. My left foot was cramping. I was afraid to budge, fearing the armoire would shift or creak. I prayed he would leave the suite so I could make my escape. What would I say if he opened the door and discovered me? If he called the manager, I would have some serious explaining to do. In the distance, I heard the sound of a bath running. Which bathroom was he in? I couldn't recall seeing a bathtub in the main bathroom. If he was in the en suite bathroom, I could probably escape without being spotted. It was now or never. I gently pushed the door, cringing as it squeaked, and peered out.

There was a knock at the front door.

I quickly retreated.

I heard the sound of footsteps, followed by a door opening.

A male voice with a heavy Filipino accent said, "Good afternoon, ma'am."

Ma'am? Was Lady Graverly here too?

"What is it?" came Lady Graverly's voice. "You've disturbed me."

The bathtub was still running. I started to panic. How would I escape with both of them in the suite?

"I here to check mini-bar."

The mini-bar! My heart raced. I shrank further into the armoire, willing myself to disappear. Lady Graverly would be apoplectic if she caught me here.

"I've barely had time to remove my coat, much less drain the mini-bar," said Lady Graverly with a chortle. "Though I dare say it's on my list of priorities."

"I make sure everything in stock for you. Take one minute only."

My mind raced. Would it be better to leap out and make a run for the door or subject myself to the humiliation of being discovered? Should I walk out with my head high? After all, if it hadn't been for Lady Graverly's deceit, I wouldn't have been obliged to enter under false pretenses.

"I'd really rather you came at another time," said Lady Graverly. "I'm about to take a nap."

"Okay, no problem, I come back."

The front door closed. I breathed a sigh of relief. If Lady Graverly lay down for a nap while Lord Graverly took a bath, I might be able to escape the suite undetected.

I waited.

Pushing the door open an inch at a time, I dared to stick my head out. The living room was empty. I pushed further and stepped out. Glancing toward the bedroom, I saw Lady Graverly's red silk dress and mink coat in a pile on the floor. The little tart.

I fled across the room and out the door.

When I arrived at the manor, I found Shanna vacuuming the Henry VIII suite. When she saw me, she shut off the vacuum and parked it against the wall.

"How's my mother?" I asked.

"Quite remarkable under the circumstances. Is something wrong? You look like you've seen a ghost."

"I'll fill you in later. Why don't you let me finish up here? Go back to the hotel and relax for a while."

"I prefer to keep busy," she said, picking up a duster and applying it to a porcelain figurine. Looking down, I was surprised to see her wearing flat slippers instead of the usual high heels. "Why don't you drive out to visit your mother?" she suggested. "There's plenty of time before dinner."

"I can't. I have to wait for Lady Graverly to return. We're going to have a little talk."

"Oh?" She stopped dusting and turned to me. "Tell me you've finally come to your senses, and you're going to tell the old harridan where to go."

"I haven't changed my mind, Shanna. I just need some answers."

She frowned and handed me the duster. "Fine, then. I'll be back at five to start dinner." She pecked me on the cheek and left.

By late afternoon, Lady Graverly had not yet returned. I grew worried about Alexander. The door to the quarters was unlocked, and I found him dozing in bed, seemingly content. Opting to let him sleep, I returned to the parlor to wait for Lady Graverly. I was now certain she was colluding with her husband to claim the family estate. How long since they had reestablished contact—had today been the first time, or had they been in contact for months—or years? Perhaps they had always kept in touch. In the suite, they had behaved like an old married couple, sharing the bathroom and barely speaking to one another.

The back door slammed, making me jump. I waited for the sound of Lady Graverly's footsteps but heard nothing. Who else would enter the quarters through the back entrance? The nurse had been fired. Lincoln was gone.

Lord Graverly?

I heard the door to the quarters creak open. I envisioned Lord Graverly creeping across the foyer, the rusty anchor lodged in his jaw, the missing axe in his hands. My eyes darted to the stoking iron next to the fireplace.

Silence.

A noise in the foyer made me turn. Through the glass, I could see a figure on the other side of the parlor door. The door handle began to turn. I reached for the stoking iron.

The door burst open. "Why, Mr. Lambert, you *are* here! How wonderful!"

Lady Graverly bustled in, still wearing the red silk dress, and reached down to pat my cheek. "I was thinking about an early martini. It's been such a stressful day. How splendid that you're here to join me." She lowered herself into the chair across from me, giving me an expectant look.

"Help yourself," I said. "I won't be partaking."

Her eyes fluttered. "Why, I believe I will," she said, rising from the chair and going to the bar, a trace of irritation in her face.

I watched her gazing at the contents of the bar, looking lost. After a moment she reached for a bottle of gin, grappled on the shelf for a rock glass, and slopped gin into the glass. She carried it back to her chair and sat down.

"You won't join me? I do hate to drink alone."

"Nope."

She sipped her drink. "Lovely! How pleasant this is, just the two of us. I'm so happy you're here." Her time with Lord Graverly had worked wonders for her mood. "A fire would be cozy, don't you think? Be a dear and fetch some wood."

"There's no axe, Elinor. It vanished. Just like Lord Graverly and Sarah Kilpatrick."

She blinked, and her smile faded. "How very peculiar."

"What?"

"You'll recall Alexander was babbling about seeing a man in my bedroom with Agnes. He kept saying the word 'ack.' Only now do I realize he must have been saying 'axe.'"

A chill ran through me. "Sounds like Alexander has an active imagination."

"Quite." She gulped her drink and set it down. "Is something the matter, dear boy? You don't seem yourself. Did Miss Crocker come by with the contract?"

"She did." I pulled the contract from my pocket and tossed it at her. "Maybe you can explain why Lord Graverly's signature is on it."

She held her gaze. "Why, the title of the manor is in Lord Graverly's name, of course."

"Oh, really? Why, Elinor? If you haven't seen him in fifty years, why haven't you declared him dead and transferred the title to your name?"

Her lips tightened. "The contract is valid. That's all you need to know."

"Did you forge his signature?"

"Mr. Lambert, please. There's no need for such a belligerent tone."

Sir Fester padded in and nestled at her feet. "Scram, vile rodent!" she cried, sending him flying across the room with a swift kick.

Shocked, I watched Sir Fester scamper out of the room and almost felt sorry for him. I turned back to Lady Graverly. She was fluttering her eyes, deep in thought. "Elinor, I have no intention of signing this contract before you've explained how Lord Graverly's signature got on it."

"Have you not seen the price?" she cried, rising to thrust the contract into my hands.

I looked down and scanned it. My head shot up. "One dollar?"

"*Now* do you understand?"

"What—why?"

"It is time you knew the truth. Lord Graverly and I were never married."

"Never married? How could that be?"

"We had planned to marry in England, but when my mother fell ill we decided to put it off until I could join him in Canada. By the time I arrived, well, you know the story—Sarah was pregnant with Lord Graverly's child. When he left me, he left everything: his son, the house, and all its contents. But none of it is in my name. Had I claimed him as dead, I would have lost everything. It's been in my interest all these years to keep up appearances that he might still be alive. I have no entitlement to Graverly Manor, no claim to the title Lady Andrew Graverly, and no legal guardianship to Alexander. I am a mere caretaker in this house, of no more importance than a house-maid or nurse. For five decades, I have been an imposter."

"Wouldn't you and Lord Graverly be considered common-law spouses in the eyes of the law? That would give you the same rights as a married couple."

She closed her eyes. "I never lived with Lord Graverly."

Astonished, I considered her affected air, her lady-of-the-manor deportment, her prattle about noblesse oblige, destiny, and entitle-ment. It was all a charade. At the core, she was as common as me. It was laughable and heartbreaking at the same time.

"Gertrude Fishburne was right, then," I said, glancing down at the contract I was clutching in my hand. "Graverly Manor isn't yours to sell."

She scowled. "You mustn't believe everything that woman says. It wasn't enough to steal Graverly Castle from my grasp—now she is trying to take away Alexander's only home. She may try to tell you I do not exist at all."

"Why did you visit Lord Graverly at the Four Seasons today?"

"So that *was* you in my suite. I thought as much. I heard someone run out and called the manager immediately. He said my nephew had asked for a key. Tell me, what did you hope to learn by breaking into my hotel room?"

"Have you reunited with Lord Graverly?" I asked, refusing to allow her to evade my questions.

"Certainly not."

"What were you doing with him, then?"

"Did you see him?"

"No."

"Precisely. I told you I like to take a suite there on occasion. I could not bear to be under the same roof as that Fishburne woman." She gulped at her drink with trembling hands and clutched it against her chest.

"You're lying, Elinor. He was there. I heard his voice. The room was registered under his name."

"Are you not listening? *Everything* is under his name. The credit cards, the bank accounts, the bills—the manor. I have nothing."

"The man Alexander saw in your bedroom. It was Lord Graverly, wasn't it? Did he do something to Agnes?"

"It was not Lord Graverly."

"Who was it, then?"

She regarded me squarely. "Alexander said it was you."

"Me? That's impossible. I didn't set foot in your bedroom until after Agnes left. Elinor, what happened to Agnes?"

"Perhaps you should tell me."

"How should I know?"

She pursed her lips but said nothing.

"You're colluding with Lord Graverly to claim the estate, aren't you?" I said, rising from my chair.

She shrank back. "No!"

"Admit it!"

"No! He doesn't want me!" Her glass tipped, spilling gin onto her dress. Her expression grew wretched, and she looked like she might cry.

I softened my voice. "Is he after Alexander?"

"He has no interest in the boy, either. He simply wants his rightful title and estate."

I was quiet for a moment, processing the information. "I don't know how I fit into this mess, Elinor. At first you make it seem like you've chosen me for some higher purpose—to be your heir. Then I discover you already have a son. I began to wonder if you thought of me as a potential husband, someone who could keep the Graverly peerage alive, and then I find out Lord Graverly is alive. What do you want from me?"

"What do you mean, a potential husband?" she exclaimed. "You thought *you* could become the Marquess of Middlesex?"

"Well, I wondered. I—"

"How on earth could you think that?"

"What about your talk of destiny and entitlement?"

"You fool! I was talking about *my* destiny, *my* entitlement! I considered you someone I could trust, someone who could manage this manor while I settled my affairs and would protect its legacy after I departed. Perhaps for a brief time I wondered if you might be suitable to manage Graverly Castle. And yes, I grew very fond of you. But now I understand what you've been up to. Your behavior has been audacious. You are as greedy and self-serving as Agnes Kilpatrick and Gertrude Fishburne. You have no entitlement to the estate!"

"Nor do you," I said quietly.

She jerked her head to the side as though I had slapped her, but quickly recovered. "For heaven's sake, child. How far will you go to reach your lofty ambitions?"

"All I want is this manor, Elinor."

"Well, you have it now."

I waved the contract in her face. "You're trying to buy my silence!"

"No."

"Then why sell it for a dollar when you claim to be broke?"

"Because … because I hope you will take care of Alexander after I'm gone."

"Why were you hiding him from me, then?"

"I didn't want to frighten you away, and I wanted to be certain you were the one."

"Me? Why me?"

"There is no one else. You're so tender and compassionate with him, and yet firm. He adores you. Only you have the youth and experience and fortitude to look after the manor and Alexander. If you will not care for him, he will be institutionalized. I have lived in this house without cost for fifty years as his caretaker. Now it is your turn. It is your duty."

"I owe you nothing, and him even less!"

"But you've already said he could stay."

"How could you ask such a thing?" I said. "I couldn't—I'm not qualified. I—." I stopped. She was distracting me again. "What happened to Clarissa? Her roommate said she didn't go back to Kentucky."

"I haven't the faintest idea."

"And Agnes? Lord Graverly did something to her, didn't he?"

"Why would he hurt Agnes?"

"How come Sarah Kilpatrick's locket was in your bureau?"

"I kept it for Alexander, for something to know his mother by."

I stood over her, gripping the armrests of her chair and searching her eyes. "Sarah didn't die in childbirth, did she? Lord Graverly murdered her. And you're covering up for him. Admit it!"

"No!"

"Tell me the truth, Elinor!"

"Stupid boy, how could you know anything about events that took place fifty years ago?"

"I found Sarah's diary."

She gasped. "Her diary? Where?"

Agnes's words came back to me: *He wanted to lie with her. He promised to marry her and make her a titled lady.* If Lord Graverly wasn't married to Elinor, he could have married Sarah. Suddenly, it all made sense.

"Lord Graverly seduced Sarah with the promise of marriage and the title marchioness. He got her pregnant, but she learned to despise him and refused to marry him, threatening to leave with the baby. He killed her to stop her and stole the baby, didn't he?"

Lady Graverly leapt to her feet. "I want that diary!" she bellowed. "Where is it? Give it to me now!"

"I'm calling the police," I said, marching to the door.

"Don't you dare!" she cried, chasing after me and grabbing my arms, pulling me back. "Please, I beg of you!" She fell to her knees and collapsed over, convulsing with sobs. "I wanted a child so very much."

I looked down at her, stunned. "He killed her so *you* could have her baby?"

"No!" she cried, lifting her head. "Lord Graverly is innocent! It was me, all me! *I* murdered Sarah Kilpatrick and stole her baby!"

24

Vanishing Act

"You must call the police at once," Shanna said over the phone. "I'm coming over."

"No," I whispered, glancing warily out the door of the tower room. Lady Graverly had retreated to her quarters after our confrontation, but now I was paranoid she would regret having confessed and come looking for me. If she had killed once, she could kill again. "She said she's going to turn herself in."

"You believe her? A woman who murdered a young woman, stole her baby, and covered it up for fifty years? What if she goes on the lam?"

"Shanna, she's eighty-two years old. She's not going to screech off in a getaway car. Besides, she would never abandon Alexander."

Shanna sighed heavily. "I wish you hadn't told me. I feel like an accomplice."

"How do you think I feel?"

"What did she say exactly?"

I related the story to her. It was the same one Lady Graverly had told me Sunday night in the dining room, except with one major difference. Sarah didn't die in childbirth, although she lost a great deal of blood, and Alexander wasn't breathing at first. When Lady Graverly tried to revive the boy, Sarah grew hysterical, accusing her of trying to steal the baby and threatening to leave the house and take the baby. A horrible argument ensued, and in a fit of jealousy and rage, Lady Graverly attacked Sarah with an axe.

"My god," Shanna breathed. "How gruesome."

"When Lord Graverly returned from the lagoon and saw what happened, he fled, never to return," I said. "Lady Graverly spent all night cleaning up, and the next day she called the police and told them she had arrived from London with her newborn son to discover her husband had run off with the housemaid. Police investigated and found no reason to doubt her. Lord Graverly was not a popular man, and the neighbors already suspected he and Sarah were lovers. There was an outpouring of support for her, but she kept to herself after that, focusing on building her business. Her aloofness did little to quell the rumors that surfaced, but nothing was ever proven."

Hearing a noise on the stairs, I crept to the door. The stairwell was empty. I left the door open, not wanting to risk getting locked in again, and paced the room, lowering my voice further. "It was only after Lord Wakefield died and Elinor attempted to claim the estate on behalf of her son that Agnes and Gertrude Fishburne started questioning things. Now, Lord Graverly has sent word to the executors of the estate that he is alive and well and intends to claim his rightful inheritance. He's scheduled to appear at an inquiry in London the day after tomorrow."

"And he's in town now—at the Four Seasons?" Shanna asked.

"After confessing to killing Sarah, Lady Graverly admitted to me that she had been in contact with Lord Graverly recently and met with him today. All these years he's been in hiding, fearing he'll be wrongfully convicted of Sarah's death. He made her promise to confess to her crime in return for agreeing to sell the manor to me for one dollar.

He has renounced any claim to guardianship of Alexander. Today she met with a lawyer and signed her confession. Then she returned to the manor and tried to convince me to allow Alexander to live here for the remainder of his life."

"Trevor, why would you assume responsibility for an invalid man to whom you have no relation? I trust you're going to walk away from this outrageous arrangement."

"Shanna, I'm getting a beautiful old house in the heart of Vancouver for *one dollar*. I don't mind if it comes with Alexander. I feel a connection to him. He might not be around much longer, but with proper rehabilitation, I think he could survive a few more years at least and become more mobile and self-sufficient. It must be my mother's nursing instincts coming out in me. It gives me a sense of greater purpose."

"You *have* a greater purpose!" Shanna cried. "To take care of your own family. That woman has brainwashed you. Do you realize that 'bargain price' is blood money to buy your silence? Where did she say she put Sarah's body?"

"She dumped it in Lost Lagoon."

"A little old lady?"

"It was fifty years ago. She wasn't an old lady then."

"And they never found it?"

"They say the lagoon is bottomless."

"That's a myth, Trevor. Nothing is bottomless. Where is Lord Graverly now? Should we be expecting him at dinner? It wouldn't surprise me, given all this craziness."

"He flew back to London this afternoon."

"What about Sarah's diary? Have you read it? Maybe there's a piece of this puzzle we haven't seen yet."

"I haven't had the chance, but I will tomorrow after the group checks out. Then I plan to send it to Agnes. Part of me wants to burn it, it's so depressing. Some secrets are better left in the past."

"Whatever you do, don't let it get into the wrong hands. I better get going. I need to pack my things before I come over. I'm flying home tomorrow."

"So soon?"

"I have an interview with the Viceroy."

"Oh, I see."

"Trevor, I think you should go to the police at once and report that woman, and then walk away from that house. I have a very bad feeling about all this."

"I have a house full of guests, Shanna. I don't want an eighty-two-year-old woman dragged away in handcuffs during dinner. If Lady Graverly doesn't turn herself in tomorrow, I'll turn her in myself. All I ask is that you help me get through dinner tonight. Then I'll focus on my family."

"Let's hope it's that simple," said Shanna.

After I hung up, I reached for the crumpled contract on the night-stand and unfurled it. One dollar, and Graverly Manor would be mine. Climbing off the bed, I sat down on the hardwood floor and ran my fingers along the stained, timeworn wood. I thought of Sarah Kilpatrick, nineteen years of age and far from home, starting a new life as a housekeeper for a nobleman in this stately old Victorian house. Seduced with the promise of marriage and betrayed. A year later, nine months pregnant, unmarried and afraid, plotting to escape, only to be brutally murdered in this very spot. *There was so much blood,* Lady Graverly had lamented. Had Sarah's blood seeped into the manor's foundation, poisoning the house, making it "sick"? My eyes moved to the grieving woman hugging her dead baby in the oil painting on the wall. There was so much sorrow in this household, it was almost palpable. Blood money, Shanna had called it.

In a burst of rage I tore the contract in half, and then into smaller pieces, and then into even smaller pieces, until hundreds of white flakes littered the floor like confetti.

★ ★ ★ ★ ★

"What a gorgeous tie," Shanna said as I hung up her coat.

"My sisters gave it to me."

"They have exquisite taste."

She marched past me and down the hallway. By her expression, I knew she was still angry with me. I followed her into the kitchen, where she put me to work at once. We settled into a domestic routine with remarkable ease, like an old married couple, saying little to one another as we worked. Entrusting me with only the most basic of duties, she handed me a salad spinner and several bags of spinach. She grumbled about the sorry state of the kitchen equipment and the lack of supplies, but soon she was cracking self-deprecating jokes, and our lighthearted banter returned. I watched her slather salmon filets with butter, dill, and lemon. Her efficacy in the kitchen continued to astonish, like a friend claiming to be tone-deaf and one day belting out an aria in perfect pitch.

To keep out of her way, I went to the dining room and set the table, taking great pains to ensure it was immaculate. When she came to inspect it, she shook her head and insisted I dismantle it, marching to the cabinet and pulling out the good china, the silverware, and the damask linens.

She retrieved the silver candelabra from the parlor and set it down. "This is a royal banquet, darling. We mustn't cut any corners. Why don't you make yourself useful and start a fire?"

"I told you, all the logs are too big, and I can't find the axe."

"Then go buy some fake logs, stupid," she said, flashing her lop-sided grin. "We can't *not* have a fire tonight."

When I returned from Canadian Tire, I started a fire, then knocked on Lady Graverly's door to check on her and Alexander. There was no answer. She was expected for dinner, but I was doubtful she would show up under the circumstances.

At seven, our guests began to gather in the parlor. Shanna shooed me out to entertain them, opting to remain in the kitchen to work. By eight, all guests had arrived save for Lady Graverly and Gertrude Fishburne. Deciding to dispel any anticipation that the Grande Dame would make an appearance, I announced that she had fallen ill. There was a collective sigh of disappointment. Just then, Gertrude Fishburne waltzed in, clutching her white gloves and smiling thinly.

At eight fifteen, Shanna announced that dinner was ready. We filed into the dining room and settled into our chairs.

Outside, the wind had picked up, rattling the window.

"There's gonna be a nasty storm tonight," said Donna Edwards, her eyes darting around the table. "Sure glad we're staying in."

Shanna served the first course—hearts of romaine with goat cheese, candied pecans, and truffle oil—while I circled the room, filling glasses with the expensive Italian wine she had insisted I buy.

"Dee-lish!" exclaimed Miss Edwards.

Over the next three hours, as the storm grew in momentum outside, Shanna shuttled courses in and I carried dirty dishes out while the guests gushed over her culinary talents. I had asked Shanna to join us, but she refused. She was dressed for dinner in a white designer suit and heels but insisted on keeping the frilly apron on. When she wasn't working in the kitchen, she stood at attention behind my chair. I was amused and somewhat puzzled by her behavior, which was a sharp contrast to her usual persona, but she seemed content, and a slowly diminishing bottle of wine on the kitchen counter told me she wasn't abstaining entirely.

The storm was expected to gain full force sometime after midnight, by which time I hoped we would all be asleep. But just after ten, I heard a crash out front. I hurried outside, shielding my face in the pelting rain, and circled the oak tree, trying to locate the source. The tree was straining in the wind, its branches leaning heavily toward the exterior of the manor. At the side of the house, I discovered that a branch had punched through the window of Alexander's room. I pulled myself up on the ledge and peered through. To my relief, his bed was empty. Next, I went to the garage. Lady Graverly's Cadillac was parked there, which meant she was home or had taken a taxi or had gone out in a HandyDART van with Alexander.

As I circled back to the front of the building, a bolt of lightning illuminated the house like an x-ray. I envisioned Lady Graverly and Alexander hunkered down in the parlor of the private quarters. I hurried inside to retrieve the emergency key, but the key was gone. I pounded on the front and back doors and banged on windows. No reply. Lady Graverly wouldn't have left Alexander all alone in the storm without asking me to check on him. I decided they were both out. Perhaps she had returned to the Four Seasons and taken him with her. I rejoined the group.

Soon I began to worry about my mother, alone in that big house in Surrey. She wasn't the type to be bothered by a storm, but the past weeks had been an emotional rollercoaster ride for her. She, like me, might be feeling more vulnerable than usual. Excusing myself again, I went to the parlor and called.

"Trevor, what a nice surprise," she said.

"How's the house? The storm isn't damaging it, is it?"

"This sturdy old thing? Not a chance. Is everything okay, dear?"

I felt a lump forming in my throat. "Sure. I was just … concerned about you … and the house."

"No need to worry about us. We couldn't be better."

"Hey Mom, I thought we could have dinner tomorrow night, just the two of us. I want to take you to the Four Seasons."

"That sounds great. We still have so much to talk about, dear."

Back in the dining room, Shanna was serving individual portions of crème brûlée while Miss Edwards was telling a ghost story.

"The next day," she whispered, her bulging eyes flickering in the candlelight, "a policeman found his bloodied sheepskin coat in the shed, only twenty feet from my bedroom window. They called him the Ghost of Bakersfield."

There were gasps.

Miss Edwards sat back, pleased to have scared the wits out of everyone.

Amy, the tour leader, turned to me. "Since the other Lady Graverly's not here tonight," she said, shooting a look at Mrs. Fishburne, "we thought we'd ask you." She lowered her voice. "Is it true this house is haunted?"

I gave a laugh. "I'm sorry to disappoint, but no—not as far as I've seen, anyway."

"I heard the strangest noise last night," said Miss Edwards, cutting into her crème brûlée. "Like someone was moaning. It sounded so sad."

"I heard it too," said Mrs. Weiss.

"The cat makes the strangest noises," I said.

"What's that smell?" said Mr. Weiss, sniffing the air. "I keep catching a whiff of a nasty odor."

"Sorry, that was me," said Miss Edwards, prompting bursts of laughter.

"They say Lost Lagoon is haunted," Mrs. Weiss said in a hushed voice, leaning over the table conspiratorially. "That's where Lord Graverly drowned the maid."

Mrs. Fishburne, who had been sitting quietly most of the evening with a tolerant smile on her face, perked up. "Is that really what people say?"

"It's just a silly rumor," I said quickly. "Lord Graverly didn't kill anyone."

"Then what happened to the maid?" asked Miss James.

"And her baby?" breathed Mrs. Weiss.

"They say she wanders the hallways here," Miss Edwards whispered, her eyes darting toward the door, "weeping for her lost baby."

Mrs. Weiss's eyes grew wide. "Maybe that was her moaning."

"I'm sure it was," said Miss Edwards, pursing her lips and nodding.

A hush fell on the group. Outside, the wind howled.

Shanna was standing at the kitchen door, a stricken expression on her face. "Maybe the maid is buried under this house," she said.

All heads turned to her.

"Shanna!" I said, exasperated.

Miss Edwards turned to Mrs. Fishburne. "What do you think happened to Lord Graverly?"

Gertrude blinked. "I'm told he's very much alive, but I don't know what to believe anymore. I'll know soon enough. I'm attending an inquiry in London on Saturday afternoon, and I was told to expect him there."

The others fell silent, looking disappointed to hear that one of the people whose ghost they had hoped to see might still be alive.

I stood up and cleared my throat. "Ladies and gentlemen, on behalf of Lady Andrew Graverly and the staff of Graverly Manor"—I nodded to Shanna—"I would like to say it has been a pleasure having you as our guests. I am sorry you'll be leaving us tomorrow, but I do hope you will return…"

For the next ten minutes, with all eyes riveted on me, I assumed the role normally played by Lady Graverly, summing up the history of the manor and the Graverly family, providing an overview of the neighborhood, and dredging up what information I could recall, filling in the rest with my closest guesses. I found a poise and eloquence I had never known before.

As I concluded, the group broke into applause.

Miss Edwards held up her glass. "To Trevor Lambert, the Lord of Graverly Manor."

There were cries of "hear, hear!"

I smiled, embarrassed yet elated. Tonight I had experienced a glimpse into what Graverly Manor could be, and it felt like my coronation. Yet tomorrow I would rise early to see the group off, drive Shanna to the airport, and then return to pack my belongings. I would tell Lady Graverly to find another buyer and to advise Lord Graverly to sell the manor for its full market value and use the money to pay for Alexander's care. Although I intended to spend time with Alexander in the future, I could not take full responsibility for his care. Then I would drive out to the suburbs and pick up my mother, take her to dinner, and meet Derrick afterward for drinks. In the coming weeks, I would spend every moment with my mother she would allow. I would resume my job search, and I wouldn't give up until I found the perfect position in the right hotel, here in Vancouver.

I sat down, feeling an enormous sense of relief.

A gust of wind struck the dining room window suddenly, shattering it and sending glass flying in all directions. The guests screamed and leapt out of the way.

The lights flickered out, and we were immersed in darkness.

★ ★ ★ ★ ★

The guests dispersed as soon as the power went out, chattering and giggling nervously as Shanna and I guided them to their rooms by candlelight. Once again, I had the impression they thought things had been staged for their amusement as part of the tour. They certainly were getting their money's worth.

The last to leave the table was Gertrude Fishburne.

"I would like Trevor to escort me," she said when Shanna offered to take her to her room.

When we reached the Elizabeth I room, she turned to me, a grim smile on her face. "Did you know that your mistress's favorite monarch, Elizabeth I, imprisoned Mary Queen of Scots for twenty years before ordering her executed for treason? After she was beheaded, the executioner picked up her head by the hair to show it to witnesses, and the Queen's head fell to the floor, leaving him holding a wig, revealing that Mary wore a wig to cover her graying hair."

"How fascinating," I said. "On that note, I'll wish you pleasant dreams." I started down the stairs.

"I know who you are."

I stopped and turned. "Oh?"

"You think you can appear out of nowhere and claim the estate. It's preposterous. Rest assured, young man, I will ensure you do not get a penny, just as I ensured Elinor Graverly and her bastard son got nothing. I would rather see my husband's estate forfeited to the crown than go to someone unentitled."

"Go right ahead," I said. "You won't encounter any opposition from me."

"We shall see."

"Do you know Agnes Kilpatrick?"

She nodded. "She visited me at Graverly Castle several weeks ago. I had expected to find her here, but I understand she returned to Scotland."

"She hasn't shown up in Scotland. I really need to reach her. I have her sister Sarah's diary. Lady Graverly says Agnes wants nothing to do with Sarah's son, Alexander, but I don't believe it."

"Pardon me? Alexander is not Sarah Kilpatrick's son. He belongs to Elinor Graverly."

"No," I said, "Lady Graverly has cared for him all these years, but Sarah is his birth mother."

"My dear boy, you're confused. Alexander is Elinor's son. It was proved in court."

"What? Elinor said she lost the claim because Alexander is illegitimate."

"Illegitimate, yes, because Elinor and Lord Andrew were not married when the child was born. The DNA samples she provided proved without a doubt that he is her son."

"Why would she say she isn't his mother, then?"

"Don't ask me to explain that strange woman's ways. She did not appear in court once during the entire case—her lawyers did all the work. I became increasingly curious about this woman they called the Grande Dame of Graverly Manor, who claims to be the widow of my brother-in-law and the mother of his son. My lawyers could find no record of her existence. I came here to meet her and to see the house, which is the first time you and I met, at the showing. I left satisfied that, however peculiar she seemed, she was who she claimed to be. Shortly after the claim was settled, however, Agnes Kilpatrick visited me and told me her own suspicions. When I received word that Lord Graverly himself had stepped forward, I decided to do a little investigating myself and signed up for this tour. In my opinion, Elinor Graverly is a fraud. I intend to report her to the executors of the estate upon my return to London, and I expect them to start proceedings at once to reclaim this house."

"You're prepared to throw an elderly woman and her invalid son out on the street?"

"That will be up to the courts to decide. Should Lord Graverly be alive, the peerage and this manor will rightfully be awarded to him. If not, the castle will revert to the crown, as the courts have already ruled. I myself have no interest in the castle nor in this house. I come from a very wealthy family. I am required to vacate the castle at the end of December and am looking forward to doing so. It's far too old and drafty."

"You said your husband told you something peculiar about his brother on his deathbed," I said. "What did he say?"

"He said that his brother has been alive and well all these years, living here in Graverly Manor."

She arched her eyebrows, as though expecting me to respond, but I was speechless.

"Well, then, good night, Mr. Lambert." She slipped into her room and closed the door.

I stared at the door, my head spinning. Yet another version of events—who was I to believe? Guiding myself by candlelight, I climbed the stairs to my room to search for another flashlight to use to clean up after dinner. On the bookshelf, I noticed a gap next to my copy of *The Consummate Host*.

The leather-bound notebook was gone.

I went downstairs to cover the dining room window with plastic.

"Lady Graverly?" I called out. Concerned about Elinor and Alexander, I had found a crowbar and broken into the private quarters.

All was quiet.

"Alexander?"

I ducked into the parlor first, then hurried down to Lady Graverly's bedroom. The first thing that hit me was the familiar anonymous stench. Her bed was empty and neatly made. In the corner of the room, Alexander sat slumped over in his wheelchair.

I set the candle down and rushed to him. "Alec?" His head was hanging forward, eyes closed. I squatted before him and lifted his chin. A large pool of drool had formed on his shirt. Pulling out my handkerchief, I wiped his mouth and shirt. "Where's your mother? She left you all alone?"

He remained perfectly still.

In a moment of panic, I checked for his vital signs. I held my hand under his nose, closing my eyes and praying for the warmth of his breath. At last I felt it, weak and humid on my fingers.

Outside, the wind was battering the house, sending rain at the window in sheets.

"Let's get you to bed," I said, wheeling him around. Half-buried in the folds of the blanket on his lap sat a white envelope. *For Trevor* was neatly printed on the front in Lady Graverly's florid script. I carried it closer to the candlelight and tore open the envelope, pulling out a sheet of perfumed stationery. A metal key was folded inside.

My prince,

By the time you read this, I will have leapt from the bridge to my death. I can no longer bear the guilt of what I did to Sarah. Please understand that you have no entitlement to the estate, and that Alexander is not a threat. I forgive you for what you did to Agnes and have left you the key should you wish to dispose of the evidence.

With all my love, Elinor

I looked up, baffled. *If I were to lose Alexander,* Lady Graverly had told me once, *I would walk down to Lions Gate Bridge and throw myself into the sea.* My first impulse was to run after her to the bridge, but judging from Alexander's state she might have left hours ago. I closed my eyes and envisioned her hobbling over the bridge to its crest, the fierce winds tugging at her red wig and period clothing, halting to say a prayer, and then letting herself fall forward, her body cartwheeling in the air, the raging waters sweeping her away, taking with her all the guilt and remorse, until finally she was at peace.

Alexander moaned.

I look over at him. He was staring up at me.

I went to him and kneeled before him, gripping his frail shoulders. "She's gone," I said softly. "She won't be back. Don't worry, I'll take care of you."

He blinked his eyes in a nod, and I detected a glimmer in his gaze, not of sorrow but of relief. Outside, the winds were making the house creak and shift and scraping branches against the window. The safest place for Alexander was here in Lady Graverly's bedroom. Retrieving a pair of pajamas from his room, I undressed him and tucked him into her bed. His eyes rolled shut, and soon he was fast asleep.

I went back to the letter and reread it, mystified by Lady Graverly's words. Why did both she and Mrs. Fishburne think that I thought I had entitlement to the Graverly estate? I thought of my silly behavior, the ascot, and my emulation of Lady Graverly's pompous airs—maybe they had been given the impression I considered myself to be an aristocrat in training, that I was after Lady Graverly's money—money she didn't have. *I forgive you for what you did to Agnes*—what had I done to Agnes?—*should you wish to dispose of the evidence.* What evidence? I looked down at the key.

The cellar.

"What is that horrid smell?" Shanna was standing in the doorway in her white suite, holding a candelabra in one hand.

I handed her the letter.

She read it and looked up in disbelief. "She killed herself?"

"It appears so."

She noticed Alexander on the bed. "Look at the poor man," she said softly. "He looks so peaceful. What's that gun doing there?"

"Lady Graverly likes to keep it by her bed."

She wrinkled her eyes in concern and looked back at the letter. "What did you do to Agnes?"

"I have no idea."

She handed the letter back to me. "Where's Sarah's diary?"

Absorbed in the letter, I didn't answer.

"Don't tell me you sent it to Agnes?" she said.

I looked up and blinked. "To Agnes? No."

"I warned you not to let it get in the wrong hands."

"It's upstairs in my room. I think Lady Graverly tried to steal it, but I had it well hidden, and she took an old guestbook instead. It's on the bookshelf, hidden inside *The Consummate Host*."

As Shanna hurried off, Alexander stirred and let out a soft moan.

My cell phone buzzed. Who would ring at this hour?

"Is that you, Trevor?" said a familiar voice.

"Clarissa?" I felt a rush of relief. "Are you okay? Where are you?"

"I'm still in Vancouver, staying at the Sylvia Hotel. I heard you were looking for me." There was an edge to her voice.

"Why did you leave without saying goodbye?"

"You didn't get my note? I left it on your night table. I wondered why you hadn't called."

My hands tightened around the phone. "Did you take my cell phone and lock me in my room, Clarissa?"

"What? Are you serious? Of course not. I left my note right beside your cell phone."

Shanna came back into the room and sat next to the candelabra to peruse the diary.

"Why did you tell me your thesis was on Pauline Johnson?" I asked Clarissa.

"I didn't, Trevor. You made that assumption. I'm a psych major, not a lit major. When you told me you were buying the manor, I didn't want to upset you."

"What's your thesis on, Clarissa?"

"The psychology behind haunted houses. Graverly Manor is one of my case studies."

I lowered myself onto a chair and rubbed my forehead, suddenly exhausted. "Why did you leave so suddenly?"

"Elinor caught me in her private quarters and went ballistic. I found the cellar, Trevor. It's off the closet. But it was locked. I tried to … but she … and threw me out."

"Clarissa? Clarissa, are you there? You're breaking up."

The line went dead. The storm. So it was Lady Graverly who had locked me up, I realized. She took my cell phone and Clarissa's note and lied to me about them. Did she drug me too? My eyes moved to the little black medical bag on the desk.

"Trevor," Shanna said, looking up from the diary, "Lord Graverly was a cross-dresser. Sarah says it right here. He used to dress up and put on some kind of performance." She looked down and continued reading, and then let out a small cry. "He raped her! He desperately wanted an heir to reclaim the peerage and avenge his father, but she refused to marry him."

On the bed, Alexander's eyes fluttered open.

"Shanna, we need to find Agnes."

Shanna stood up and handed me the diary, looking dazed by her discovery. "Agnes? Where is she?"

I placed the diary on the nightstand with the letter and my cell phone, and picked up the key.

Alexander was squirming on the bed now.

"Are you okay, Alec?" I asked, touching his forehead. It was cool and damp. I leaned over him. "What did you see here in the bedroom, Alexander? Did you see Agnes?"

Alexander opened his mouth. "A—a—ack."

"Axe? What about an axe?"

"Ack ... A—Ag. Nes."

"Agnes?"

He worked his mouth. "Mudder."

"Murder? Someone murdered Agnes with an axe? Who?"

"Mudder."

"Mother? Your mother murdered her?"

"Fud ... der."

"Your father murdered her? Which one, Alec, your mother or father? Who murdered Agnes?"

Alexander threw his head back and slammed it against the head-board. He began kicking his feet and arms and making gagging sounds. I tried to calm him, but he started screaming like a man possessed.

"Shanna, grab that medical kit on the desk!" I shouted, struggling to control him. "He needs a shot. There should be a needle and a bottle of medication in there. Hurry!"

Shanna quickly pulled out a needle and a small bottle, tearing the packaging open. She stuck the needle into the bottle and filled it with serum, handing it to me. One of Alexander's hands broke free and connected with my temple, sending me reeling backward, temporarily blinding me.

Shanna helped me to my feet.

Together, we held Alexander down as I slid the needle into his arm.

He made a choking sound. His struggling ceased, and his eyes drooped closed.

"That was quick," said Shanna, catching her breath. "I could use some of that stuff myself."

I watched Alexander's limbs twitch and settle. Placing the needle in the bag, I zipped it up. "Shanna, we're going in."

"In where?" she asked, her hand moving to her throat.

I nodded toward the closet. "The cellar."

25

The Resurrection

At the top of the staircase, a dark figure peered into the opening. The door slammed shut. I heard the clang of the metal latch.

"Who was that?" Shanna whispered, clutching my arm in the darkness. "Was it Elinor—did she come back for the diary?"

The silhouette of the diminutive, bald-headed figure still burned in my vision. "Lord Graverly," I said. "He's back."

"Lord Graverly?"

I began to climb the stairs.

"Where are you going?" she called out.

"To get that axe."

"It's not there. I put it in the closet."

I stopped. "You didn't."

"I'm sorry. Had I known…"

Not wishing to believe her, I continued up the stairs. Halfway up, I lost my equilibrium and placed a hand on the steps to steady myself. Blood. I yanked my hand away, smearing the sticky substance on my pants. A vision of Lord Graverly came to me, luring Agnes into the cellar, perhaps with the promise of seeing her sister's remains, and then chopping her down like a tree. Or had Lady Graverly done the deed? I was still confused about her role in this nightmare.

At the top of the stairs, I grappled around for the axe, hoping it had somehow fallen into the cellar. My hands felt something hard and rectangular. I lifted it and carried it down with me.

"I brought you some reading material," I said, handing the book to Shanna as I sat down next to her, our backs against the staircase wall.

"What is it? I can't see a thing."

"*The Consummate Host.*"

"A load of good that's going to do us here," she muttered. "I can't believe I left my cell phone in my purse. I live in LA. It should be surgically attached to my ear." She moved closer to me. "It's cold."

I put my arm around her. "I doubt it would have worked down here anyway."

We sat in silence.

"What do you think he plans to do with us?"

"I don't know. Maybe he's already gone," I said hopefully. But I was starting to piece things together, and I feared I now knew too much to be let out alive.

"Someone will come for us, won't they?" she said.

"Yes."

I managed to get the flashlight working. Shanna and I explored the cellar, searching for a means of escape—a secret door or passage, a device to pry the door open, anything to use as a weapon—but the room was empty save for the icebox and butcher table. The trap door leading to the closet was impenetrable.

Next, full of trepidation, we approached Agnes's body. She lay near the center of the cellar, sprawled in a pool of congealed blood. As I shone the flashlight on her face, a rat scurried out from under her wild grey hair. The axe had struck her body in several places. Her head was severed at the neck. She was still wearing the yellow apron.

Shanna let out a cry. Her knees buckled, and she fell to the floor.

I helped her to her feet and led her away. We sat against the staircase wall, holding one another, and wept.

After a while, she said, "We need to look in that box."

"Are you sure?"

She took the flashlight from my hands and made her way across the cellar, steering a wide arc around Agnes's body. I followed her. The light flickered as she pointed the flashlight on the lid with her trembling hand. Shooting a nervous glance at the tuft of hair sticking out from the lid, I wrenched on the rusty padlock. After several attempts, the padlock broke.

I looked up to give Shanna a chance to reconsider, but she nodded, a look of determination on her face. I lifted the lid, and she shone the flashlight in.

A skeleton lay on its side in the box, curled into a fetal position, strands of long blond hair sprouting from the skull.

"So this is where Sarah's been all these years," I said.

Shanna gasped. "Her skull—it's detached."

With a shudder, I lowered the lid.

We made our way back to our encampment.

"Now I understand why Lady Graverly didn't want the house torn down," I said.

"Even at a dollar, I think you paid too much."

"I didn't pay a thing. I tore up the contract."

Hours passed.

I drifted in and out of sleep, jerked into consciousness by catastrophic thoughts and grisly images.

Shanna was restless too. She turned on the flashlight and began leafing through the pages of *The Consummate Host*. "This man is even more of a blowhard than Montgomery Neville," she grumbled. "He recommends writing personal notes to guests at bedtime to wish them pleasant dreams. When was the book written—the eighteenth century?" She flipped to the front of the book. "1988. Oh look, he's signed it here."

"My mom went on a date with him forty years ago, and she's still talking about it."

Shanna read, "'For my darling Evelyn and son Trevor—with all my love, Lord Wakefield Graverly.' It almost sounds like he's calling you his son."

The flashlight sputtered out.

My mind raced. I examined every word of recent conversations with my mother, every inflection and nuance. *Your father was not the man you think he was,* she had said during our first walk in the lagoon. Later, in regard to Charles's death: *For twenty years I blamed myself, regretted the terrible things I said.* What had been so hurtful she feared it had burst his heart open? Why had she been so insistent on telling me about her fling with Lord Wakefield—and why had I been so averse to hearing about it?

That last item on her agenda—I had assumed it was her illness, but was there something more? On impulse, I reached for the book and shone the flashlight on the back cover. Studying Lord Wakefield's face, I recognized a weathered, imperious version of myself. My heart jolted.

"Shanna, are you awake?"

"Unfortunately."

"I think Lord Wakefield was my father."

★ ★ ★ ★ ★

Footsteps sounded in the main part of the house.

We scrambled up the stairs.

"It must be departure time," said Shanna.

"Six AM already?"

"Already? It feels like we've been here for days."

There was a distant flurry of activity in the house: doors opening and closing, water running through pipes, the roll of suitcase wheels on the floor. We banged on the door and hollered for help until our voices grew hoarse.

"Won't they find it strange that no one's there to see them off?" Shanna said, panting. "They'll come looking for us."

"Maybe," I said, not wishing to dash her hopes. No breakfast had been scheduled; the group was heading straight for the airport. They would think I had slept in and would depart without a second thought.

The front door slammed. The house fell silent.

"Oh god, Trevor," Shanna breathed. "What if we die in here?"

"We won't, I promise."

She made her way down the stairs. I remained at the door, fiddling with the flashlight and thinking hard. There had to be a way out. The flashlight flickered to life, and then died.

I heard the sound of floorboards creaking. Someone entered the closet.

I hammered on the door with the flashlight. "Who's there? We're trapped in here! Let us out!"

Silence.

A deafening clang sent me reeling backward. I doubled over in agony on the landing, covering my ears in an effort to drown out the screeching sound.

Shanna came to me and led me down the stairs. She sat me down and cradled my head in her arms. By the vibration of her chest I could tell she was talking, but I could hear nothing but the piercing ring.

After a few minutes, the sound began to subside.

"What happened?" I yelled.

Shanna led me up the stairs and pointed to a tiny circle of light in the trap door—a bullet hole. "I think Lord Graverly found the rifle."

Shanna's voice broke the silence. "How long do you think it's been?"

"Sixteen hours, maybe more." I thought of Alexander, paralyzed on the bed, abandoned, his panicked eyes darting around the room. If Lord Graverly didn't feed him, how long could he last without food or water? How long could Shanna and I last?

"I missed my flight," Shanna said.

"If we don't get out of here soon, I'm going miss dinner with my mother."

"I can't stop shaking. Hold me closer."

"I can't hold you any closer, Shanna. Here, put your face in my neck." I felt her face nestle into me. I reached up to stroke her hair.

"Don't get any ideas," she said, her lips moving at my neck.

"You're burning up," I said.

"I feel feverish. I can't stop thinking about those poor women over there."

"Me neither."

My mind was whirling. Lady Graverly's words repeated in my ears: *I take a suite at the Four Seasons, if only for a few hours. There I can be myself.* And: *My heart will always belong to Lord Graverly.* I had taken her remarks at face value, but was there more meaning to them? Had she been speaking in riddles, amusing herself by dropping hints with double entendres? What had disturbed Mr. Wainright about her? My thoughts returned to Agnes. What had she seen through the window that had ended in her murder? I remembered Shanna's initial impression of Lady Graverly—Shanna, who was always so astute. And Lincoln's cryptic words: *Alexander is her son, but she is not his mother.* According to Mrs. Fishburne, a DNA test had proved that Alexander was Lady Graverly's son.

But not that she was his *mother*.

How could I have been so naïve?

★ ★ ★ ★ ★

I woke up to Shanna weeping.

"Don't worry," I said, comforting her. Her body was trembling violently. "We'll get out of here."

"How? It's hopeless. I don't know how much longer I can bear being trapped in this mausoleum."

"When I don't show up at my mother's house, she'll worry and . . ." I stopped. She would dismiss my no-show as more self-centered behavior. Derrick would draw the same conclusion when I didn't call. "Someone will come looking for us, I know it."

I got up and began searching the room again.

A while later, I sat down beside her, defeated. "Shanna, why is it so difficult to get close to people you love?"

She was quiet for a moment. "Because the closer you get, the more they can hurt you."

"Then it's better not to get close."

"No, Trevor. It's a trade-off. The more pain you're willing to risk, the greater the reward. My children have caused me more pain than I could imagine, but they've brought me great happiness too."

"I like it better when I feel numb."

"No, you don't."

"How come you never told me you were Susie Homemaker?"

"Ramin has fed my kids so much propaganda about my shortfalls as a mother that I've started to believe it." She bolted upright. "What's that sound?"

A rumble of wheels on the floor above. Alexander's wheelchair? I got up and crouched at the foot of the stairs.

The door creaked open. Lord Graverly's bald head peered into the opening. I took a deep breath and prepared to charge up the stairs and tackle him.

In a burst of movement, the wheelchair clattered down the stairs.

Alexander landed at our feet with a thud.

The door slammed shut.

"Is he conscious?" Shanna asked, crouching beside me.

"I can't tell. He's breathing, but barely."

"The poor, sweet man. His body is trembling."

I stroked his hair, as soft as a baby's, until he settled. Then I carried him to our encampment and lay him across my lap, holding him in my arms to keep him warm. His forehead was drenched in sweat.

"What's wrong with him?" Shanna asked.

"He must be in shock."

Something was bothering me.

"What's this?" she said, grappling on the floor. There was a rustle of pages. "Sarah's diary! Why would Lord Graverly put such damning evidence into our hands? Unless..." She gasped. "Trevor, he doesn't think we're a threat anymore."

I was only half-listening. I thought of the choking sound Alexander had made after I administered the medication. And Lady Graverly's cryptic words in her letter: *Please understand that you have no entitlement to the estate, and that Alexander is not a threat.* Now that I was certain I was Lord Wakefield's son, her words made more sense. Did she think I had delusions of being entitled to the estate? Is that what Mrs. Fishburne had meant when she said my ambitions were preposterous? My thoughts jumped to Agnes. Why had Lady Graverly told the housing inspector I had been in the cellar? Later, she had told me that Alexander had said he saw me in her bedroom with Agnes—and an axe. *I forgive you for what you did to Agnes.*

"Shanna, did you read the prescription on that medicine bottle?"

"No. Why?"

"I think I poisoned Alexander. And I've been framed for Agnes's murder."

A loud bang startled us.

"What was that?" Shanna whispered.

Gently I lifted Alexander off of my lap. I moved to the foot of the stairs. The door opened a crack and a sliver of light appeared, slowly widening. I opened my mouth to shout but stopped, recognizing Lord Graverly's profile.

Liquid began flowing down the stairs.

Shanna gave a cry. "Is he urinating?"

As the liquid reached the floor, we backed away.

The smell of gasoline wafted to my nose.

"Stop!" I shouted, charging up the stairs.

Lord Graverly was crouching in the doorway with a candelabra, preparing to throw it into the cellar. The distant ring of the doorbell made him stop.

He slammed the door shut and closed the latch.

★ ★ ★ ★ ★

"I've figured it all out," I whispered to Shanna.

We were positioned at the top of the stairs, waiting for Lord Graverly to return. The moment he opened the door, Shanna would whack him in the face with *The Consummate Host* and I would throw the wheelchair at him, then jump on him and hold him down while Shanna ran for help.

"One person is responsible for these murders," I said.

"Lord Graverly or Lady Graverly?"

"Both."

"That doesn't make sense, Trevor."

"Lord Graverly raped and impregnated Sarah to produce an heir, murdered her when she refused to marry him, and then stole her baby. Then he came up with a scheme to evade arrest and legitimize the baby. He became—"

"Quiet! Listen."

I heard the muffled sound of a woman's voice in the hallway. "Trevor, are you there?"

"Wendy!" I pounded on the door. "I'm in here! In the closet!" My mouth was so dry I could barely get the words out. Pulling Shanna out of the way, I lifted the wheelchair and slammed it against the door.

There was a scream, followed by a gunshot.

Silence.

"Oh god, Wendy!" I cried. "No!" I collapsed on the stairs, sobbing.

Shanna knelt beside me, rubbing my back. "She's okay, Trevor. She's going to be okay."

There was a patter of feet in the hall.

We sat up, alert. I heard a frightened whimper in the closet. A little voice called out, "Uncle Trevor?"

"Quinn?" Tears stung my eyes. "Open the door, quick! Lift the latch!"

I heard his little hands grappling at the door. In a moment, the door opened. Quinn's small frame appeared.

Footsteps approached.

"Wait here," I said to Shanna, scrambling out. Shutting the cellar door behind me, I pulled Quinn behind the clothing rack on the right.

The power was still out. The closet was lit by a three-pronged candelabra on the floor. Near the entrance to the cellar, a gasoline container lay on its side in a pool of gas. The candlewicks flickered precariously.

A shadow fell on the floor. Peeking through the clothing, I spotted the bald-headed, wiry figure of Lord Andrew Graverly. He was lugging something into the closet, struggling with its weight.

Wendy's yellow Crocs slid by, trailing blood.

I placed my hand over Quinn's eyes. My body shook with rage.

Wendy's right foot grazed the candle, almost knocking it over. Lord Graverly opened the cellar door and began pushing her in. Straightening suddenly, he turned toward me and peered into the clothing. I froze. His hand reached out, and his gnarled fingers pulled the army uniform from the rack. He removed the plastic covering and held it up, fingers caressing the medal.

Across the closet, I could see the axe leaning against the wall. My eyes moved to the candelabra. How could I take down Lord Graverly without knocking it over?

Lord Graverly's trousers fell to the floor. He was trying on the uniform.

Quinn let out a sob.

Lord Graverly turned. He reached into the clothing and clutched the boy's neck.

Quinn yelped.

I grabbed Lord Graverly's arm and flung it aside, then dove to the floor and snuffed out the candelabra. Lord Graverly lunged for the rifle, spinning around and pointing it in my face. I knocked it from his hands and snatched it up.

"Quinn, get out of here, now!" I shouted. "Call 911!"

Quinn bolted from the room.

Kneeling on the floor, I pointed the gun up at Lord Graverly. Our eyes locked, and I recognized the twinkle in his green eyes. He lunged at me with both hands. I pulled the trigger.

Nothing.

Sliding back on the floor, I re-cocked and pulled the trigger again.

The chamber was empty.

Behind Lord Graverly, Shanna was crouched over my sister. Wendy's white coat was soaked with blood. Lord Graverly grabbed his trousers and reached into the pocket, withdrawing a pack of matches. His hands shook as he tried to strike one.

Dropping the rifle, I lunged for the axe and jumped to my feet, heaving it over him. "Drop it now!" I warned.

A match flared to life. "No, *you* drop the axe!" he hissed, waving the match in the air.

Leaping forward, I extinguished the match in my fist, then knocked the pack from Lord Graverly's hand. He fell to his knees and scrambled for it. Pulling another match out, he lit it.

I let the axe fall.

The blade struck his neck, sending a splash of blood over the clothing rack. He fell and rolled over onto his back, emitting a gasp. I stood over him, scanning his tiny frame, the cobbled hands and feet, the open mouth and familiar teeth. A pair of pale, skinny legs protruded from his undershorts. On his thigh was a silky growth like a tiny rodent burrowing into his skin.

Lady Graverly's mole.

26

The Consummate Host

I parted the yellow curtains in my mother's kitchen and slid open the window, leaning out to observe the expansive front yard. It was an early spring afternoon, sunny and warm, the air fragrant with budding flowers. The Sanghera girls were sitting on the hood of my car, playing race car again. This time they were joined by my nieces and nephews, seven children in all, looking innocent and cute as they scratched the paint and dented the hood.

Janet set a box on the kitchen counter. "I think that's the last of it. Next time, you're hiring a moving company."

"I don't plan on moving for a long time."

She came to me and rested her hand on my shoulder. "You okay?"

"I miss her."

"Me too."

The bullet had cut through Wendy's left chest, on the same side Mom had lost her breast to cancer, only narrowly missing her heart. Her heart stopped on the way to the hospital. I was tailing the ambulance in my car, careening around debris left by the storm, with Quinn in the passenger's seat holding on for dear life. As the ambulance swerved into the emergency unit at St. Paul's Hospital, the paramedics got Wendy's heart going again. She was resurrected, just like Lord Andrew Graverly.

She wandered into the kitchen now, a copy of *The Consummate Host* tucked under her arm. It had been over three months since the incident, but she was still recovering. I took the book from her and sat her down in a chair.

Janet was peering through the curtains. "Those little brats are on your car," she said, opening the window to yell at them.

"It's okay," I said, stopping her. "They're just having fun."

She shot me a Lambert look. "If you get any more easygoing, I'm calling the hotel police."

"Wait 'til you see what we got you," Wendy said, tittering. "Go get it, Janet."

While Janet went out to her car, Wendy and I unpacked kitchen supplies. Her time in the hospital had been a rehearsal for Mom's final days. While she was in surgery, Mom, Janet, and I had camped out in the waiting room and made a lot of life-affirming statements. Janet vowed to stop yelling at her kids, and I made her promise never to wear acid-wash jeans again. I vowed to dedicate at least one day a week to family, and she made me promise never to ask for crème brûlée in a roadside café again. Mom vowed not to interfere with our lives anymore. Only Mom kept her promise, although it didn't stop her from meddling in the lives of others; she spent a good part of her visits counseling patients in other rooms.

In the waiting room, Mom told me everything she knew about my real father, Lord Wakefield Graverly. He had swept her off her feet that night at the Hotel Vancouver, and she had spent the night in his room. The next day, he took her with him to visit his brother's widow, Lady Elinor Graverly, but the woman slammed the door in his face. For the rest of the day he was brooding and quiet, and only now, almost forty years later, did Mom realize he had recognized his brother in the woman's heavily made-up face.

Full of remorse for being unfaithful to Charles, Mom refused any further contact with Lord Wakefield. When she found out she was pregnant, she resolved to marry Charles, the man she truly loved, and kept my father's identity a secret. Twelve years later, overcome by outrage and despair over the state of her life, she used the secret as a weapon to hurt Charles. An hour later, he keeled over and died. Fearing she was responsible, and that if she told me the revelation might kill me too, she vowed never to tell another soul.

When Lord Wakefield died, he left me one thousand pounds in his will, a pittance compared to the millions his dog Regent inherited, but it was his way of telling me the truth that my mother had refused to divulge. His lawyers were instructed to contact my mother to advise her of the bequest and allow her the opportunity to tell me herself. She took me down to the lagoon but lost her nerve when I started talking about my feelings of displacement and how different I felt from my sisters. She walked me past Graverly Manor, intending to use the manor's connection to my real father as a segue, but was so taken aback when I expressed interest in purchasing it that she lost her nerve again.

Around the same time, Mom had begun to feel ill, and even before the tests came back she knew the cancer had returned. After I moved into the manor, she went to see Lady Graverly to beg her not to tell me about my father until she had spoken to me. Lady Graverly agreed, somewhat reluctantly; she had learned of my existence from Lord Wakefield's will, and when I introduced myself at the open house, she knew in an instant who I was. Because of Mom's procrastination and my evasiveness, I figured out who my real father was before Mom got a chance to tell me. Yet rather than drive me further away, as my mother had feared, the revelation helped me understand why I was different from my sisters, why I felt restless and displaced, and it ultimately brought us closer.

Janet carried in a large wrapped gift and set it on the table.

The two girls suppressed giggles as I opened the box and withdrew a thick velvet robe, a matching cap, and a scroll tied with silk ribbon.

"Here, let me help you," said Wendy, draping the cloak over my shoulders and placing the cap on my head.

Janet unraveled the scroll. "We hereby bestow upon you the title Lord Trevor of Lambert Manor, of Surrey, in the Province of British Columbia."

"It's an authentic title," Wendy said. "We bought it on the Internet."

"I'm deeply moved," I said.

"Just remember," said Janet, "we too are ladies of this manor, so you can't banish us like peasants. Abuse your authority, and we'll send you to the guillotine."

"You have my promise," I said, bowing to each of them.

They curtsied back.

We ordered takeout and called the kids inside, eating pizza and drinking canned sodas while sitting on boxes, crates, and the cushionless sofa. Quinn and Aiden had gathered up cushions, pillows, and blankets to make a fort, and we took turns crawling through it, admiring their work.

"I better get these monsters home," Janet said, picking at a remnant of melted cheese in the empty pizza box. "Kids, you better dismantle that fort or your Uncle Trevor is going to freak."

"It's okay," I said. "I'll do it myself later."

"Suit yourself," Janet said. "You coming, Wen?"

Wendy checked her watch. "Oh jeez, I'm going to be late for my shift." She came over and gave me a hug. "Don't forget the hockey game on Monday. You sure you can handle all the boys on your own?"

"No problem."

Janet came up behind her, frowning. "Are you going to be okay here all by yourself?"

"If I said no, would you stay?"

"No, but I'd leave my kids here and pick them up next week."

"I'll be fine. Derrick's going to swing by later."

At the front door, I handed Wendy the stack of empty pizza boxes. "Drop these in the garbage on your way out, will you? And don't back into my car this time."

"You really are the consummate host," she said wryly, trotting off in her Crocs.

I waved goodbye as the panel van lurched off, trailed by Janet driving Mom's Audi. I was standing in the exact place my parents had waved to us each morning as we drove off to school. I saluted the Sanghera girls playing in the front yard and went back into the house.

Nuggle was stalking the hallway. Scooping him up, I carried him into the living room and sat on the floor in front of the fort. *Are you going to be okay here all by yourself?* Part of me wanted to crawl into the fort and stay there, like I had done as a kid. I began tearing it down, replacing the cushions on the sofa and folding the blankets. Carrying a stack of pillows into my old room, I imagined that my mother was there, sitting on the bed, sorting through old photos, with Nancy beside her, giggling at pictures of me as a kid.

Since Mom died, I have felt her presence everywhere. It's not an eerie feeling, it's a comforting one. My sisters and I were with her during her last moments, and when she finally let go I felt all the energy in the room dissipate, like a beloved tour leader had checked off the last item on her agenda and left, leaving participants wanting more. Last week, as I left the Four Seasons with an employment contract in hand, I sensed she was with me, and Nancy too, both of them cheering me on.

Like Clarissa, I believe that there are no haunted places, only haunted people. Ghosts are memories, reminders of our past. If we have guilt or remorse, they haunt us, lingering in the air like a bad smell, piercing our ears like a shriek in the night. If we learn to accept our past and follow our hearts, they become our guardian angels.

Enough. I'm starting to sound like my mother.

The manor sits empty today, ravaged by the now-legendary storm that destroyed over a thousand trees in Stanley Park. Soon bulldozers will arrive, and the home that my uncle, Lord Andrew Graverly—or Lord-Lady Graverly, as Wendy calls him—had reigned over for almost fifty years will be replaced with a luxury condo tower. As detestable as his actions were, I better understand his motives now. Born into privilege, he was different from his brother—effeminate and probably gay, with a penchant for women's clothing, a valiant soldier who entertained the troops with performances as the fictional Lady Andrew Graverly, a snobbish, blue-blooded aristocrat. Disowned by his father for his flamboyant ways, he was sent away to Canada.

Spurned, he resolved to seek vengeance by regaining his rightful place in the family. When it became evident that his brother would not have children, Lord Andrew conspired to impregnate the housekeeper, Sarah. When she refused him, he raped her. She became pregnant but refused to marry him, threatening to leave him and take her baby. In a fit of rage, he murdered her and stole the baby. To avoid prosecution, he reinvented himself as his alter ego, Lady Elinor Graverly, fresh from

London with her newborn child, and in one bold stroke he created a wife, a legitimate child, and an alibi.

I still have a difficult time thinking of Lady Graverly and Lord Graverly as the same person, so I refer to them in whichever persona they occupied at the time. When Lady Graverly's claim to the estate on behalf of her son was overruled, she realized her only hope was to resurrect Lord Graverly and sent word through a lawyer that he was alive and ready to come forward to claim his rightful title and inheritance. To secure Lord Graverly's innocence, Lady Graverly confessed to Sarah's murder and then staged her own death. Positioning me in the minds of others as having ambitions to the Graverly estate, she framed me for killing two potential obstacles in the path to my ambitions: Agnes and Alexander, whose medication had been replaced with poison. Lady Graverly had turned on her own son. He was no longer of use to her after the courts had established that he was illegitimate, and she grew to resent and despise him. He knew all her secrets and had grown to fear her, and his ability to communicate, despite her efforts to keep him docile through medication, had improved far too much for her comfort. Fortunately, the poison I had administered was a low-enough dosage that he survived. He lives with Lincoln now, and proceeds from the sale of the manor have ensured him the best of care from a team of doctors and nurses. I visit him regularly, and his mobility and speech are remarkably improved.

Lady Graverly might have gotten away with everything had she not taken the wrong notebook. At the airport, having reverted to Lord Graverly's persona, as he prepared to board a flight to London to attend the inquiry, he realized his mistake and came back to the manor to find the evidence and destroy it. There, he discovered Shanna and me in the cellar, Alexander drugged and barely alive, and the diary on the nightstand. He pushed Alexander into the cellar with the diary, intending to incinerate all of us, and then Wendy and Quinn showed up looking for me.

During the subsequent investigation, authorities found prescriptions for the female hormones Lord Graverly had been taking for decades to soften his skin, to grow breasts, and to reduce body hair, as well as evidence of electrolysis treatments and facial feminization procedures. Lincoln was tracked down at his girlfriend's, and after some cajoling he confirmed that Lord Graverly had lived as Lady Graverly for almost five decades, only occasionally appearing as his former self, usually in the anonymous environs of the Four Seasons Hotel. Lincoln had turned a blind eye, but after Lady Graverly announced her intention to resurrect Lord Graverly and then Agnes disappeared, he began to fear for his own safety and fled.

I had planned to send my father's bequest to Agnes's son, Brandon, until I heard his family was expected to be awarded damages from the Graverly estate for the wrongful deaths of his mother and her sister. So I sent the money to the Stanley Park restoration fund. Lost Lagoon was mostly spared in the storm, but across the park great swaths of old-growth trees had been leveled, some of them irreplaceable.

Clarissa helped me to face my inner demons and exorcise them, and I'll always be grateful, but I don't think she's the girl for me. Hopefully she'll be able to do the same for Sir Fester, who arrived at her door at the Sylvia Hotel much like he had arrived at Graverly Manor—in the middle of the night, during a storm, demanding to be taken in.

After her time at the manor, Shanna put her Santa Monica condo up for sale and started looking into bed-and-breakfasts to purchase. She tried to convince me to partner with her, but I had already come to the realization that I'm a hotelier, not an innkeeper. No longer do I feel like a restless traveler, like a hotelier without a home. I have accepted that the hotel business is in my blood, much like it was in my father's blood. In time, Shanna realized it wasn't the life of an inn-keeper she was enamored with, but the rediscovery of her love of caring for others. Like me, she had abdicated her role in her family years ago, and now both of us are determined to reestablish our roles, to become consummate hosts to the people who mean the most to us.

Lately, Shanna has been lobbying me on various schemes: to open a resort in Tofino, on the west coast of Vancouver Island; to manage a five-star hotel in Manhattan; to run the Millionaire Hotel & Casino in Las Vegas. Her latest scheme is to start a hotel inspection company. "We could be mystery shoppers," she said, flashing her lopsided grin. Yesterday, the director of sales at the Four Seasons Vancouver resigned. I might just ask Shanna if she's interested.

Whether I will live the rest of my life in this suburban neighbor-hood, in this house steeped in memories of my childhood, I cannot say. For now, I'm content to stay in Vancouver. I've learned that home is as much a state of mind as a place. If I have inner peace, I can find contentment wherever I live. My home doesn't come with a lofty title or a sprawling estate, but right now it's perfect for me.

For, as they say, a man's home is his castle.

★ ★ ★ ★ ★

THE END

Acknowledgments

A huge thanks to my readers, Linda Craig, Carrie Elrick, Suzanne Walters, and Chelsea Reimer, for your feedback and advice. Special thanks to my mother, Marcia Craig, for your unflinching editorial eye, and to Ursula Siegler for inspiring me in many ways at a young age. My sincere gratitude also goes to Becky Zins, Brian Farrey, Barbara Moore, Steven Pomije, and all the other staff at Midnight Ink Books who have contributed to the success of the Five-Star Mystery Series. Thank you also to Evan Penner of the West End Guest House in Vancouver and to David Marshall and Michael Dwyer of Perth Manor in Ontario for your perspectives on running a bed-and-breakfast (I mean manor). And finally, thank you to my friends and colleagues, both past and present, at Opus Hotels.

About the Author

Daniel Edward Craig began his career in the hotel industry in 1987 and has since worked for luxury hotels across Canada. Most recently, he was vice president of Opus Hotels and general manager of Opus Vancouver, world renowned for exemplary service, cutting-edge marketing, and celebrity sightings.

Originally intending to pursue diplomatic service, he holds a bachelor's degree in international relations and has studied modern languages, new media, film, screenwriting, and acting. Today, he works as a writer and consultant in Vancouver.

In his leisure time, Craig likes to travel, practice yoga, and enjoy a healthy lifestyle. He is particularly passionate about hotels, having stayed at—and managed—some of the best in the world. Visit him at www.danieledwardcraig.com, where his popular blog provides a frank, entertaining look at issues in the hotel industry.

WWW.MIDNIGHTINKBOOKS.COM

From the gritty streets of New York City to sacred tombs in the Middle East, it's always midnight somewhere. Join us online at any hour for fresh new voices in mystery fiction.

At midnightinkbooks.com you'll also find our author blog, new and upcoming books, events, book club questions, excerpts, mystery resources, and more.

MIDNIGHT INK ORDERING INFORMATION

Order Online:

• Visit our website www.midnightinkbooks.com, select your books, and order them on our secure server.

Order by Phone:

• Call toll-free within the U.S. and Canada at
1-888-NITE-INK (1-888-648-3465)
• We accept VISA, MasterCard, and American Express

Order by Mail:

Send the full price of your order (MN residents add 6.5% sales tax) in U.S. funds, plus postage & handling to:

> Midnight Ink
> 2143 Wooddale Drive, Dept. 978-0-7387-1473-8
> Woodbury, MN 55125-2989

Postage & Handling:

Standard (U.S., Mexico & Canada). If your order is:
$24.99 and under, add $3.00
$25.00 and over, FREE STANDARD SHIPPING

AK, HI, PR: $15.00 for one book plus $1.00 for each additional book.

International Orders (airmail only):
$16.00 for one book plus $3.00 for each additional book.

Orders are processed within 2 business days. Please allow for normal shipping time.
Postage and handling rates subject to change.

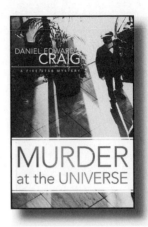

Murder at the Universe

A Five-Star Mystery

Daniel Edward Craig

For thirty-six-year-old Trevor Lambert, life revolves around work. As director of rooms at the luxurious and ultra-modern Universe Hotel in New York, he radiates dignified professionalism and high-end hospitality. But when Trevor inadvertently escorts VIP guest Brenda Rathberger—the cantankerous executive director of the Victims of Impaired Drivers conference—past the dead body of the hotel's owner, Trevor's perfect world implodes. Police believe a hotel executive may be responsible, and their suggestion that alcohol may have been involved encourages Brenda to use the controversy to grandstand her cause. She joins forces with celebrated TV anchor Honica Winters, who exposes the sordid details on national television.

With his dear coworkers under suspicion and his treasured guests turning on him, it's all Trevor can do to protect everyone, particularly his sweet and lovely duty manager, Nancy. In the resulting clash among pampered guests, harried employees, and militant protesters, Trevor struggles to find the killer and to preserve the dignity of the Universe.

978-0-7387-1118-8 • 5³⁄₁₆ x 8 • 480 pp. • $14.95

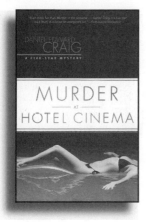

Murder at Hotel Cinema

A Five-Star Mystery

Daniel Edward Craig

In this star-studded sequel to *Murder at the Universe*, Daniel Edward Craig pokes good-humored fun at the celebrity-crazed Los Angeles culture. Dedicated hotelier Trevor Lambert takes a job at Hotel Cinema, a million-dollar rejuvenation of an Old Hollywood motor inn. It's a fabulous opening party until Tinseltown's hottest star, Chelsea Fricks, takes a fatal dive from her penthouse balcony. Was it a reckless publicity stunt or did fame drive her to suicide?

Chelsea's stab wounds tell another story. Suddenly Hotel Cinema is the setting of a hilarious Hollywood murder mystery, starring Chelsea's former pit-bull publicist; a hairy, star-struck detective; tasteless tabloid reporters; and Trevor's incompetent boss, who breaks every rule in the hotel handbook. Cristal champagne is flowing. Business is booming. But when the hotel staff are targeted as murder suspects, the party turns into a publicity nightmare.

978-0-7387-1119-5 • 5 ³⁄₁₆ x 8 • 432 pp. • $15.95